PROTECT ME

The Donovan Family Series (#6)

MARGARET WATSON

ISBN-13: 978-1-944422-03-5

TITLES BY MARGARET WATSON

CHAPTER ONE

Finn shoved his hand through his hair as he paced in front of the window, both appreciative of his godfather's concern and irritated by his interference. "Doug, it's great that you want to protect me. I appreciate it. Really. But I don't need a cop hanging around for the next three weeks. I'll hire private security if the situation escalates."

Finn's hand tightened on his phone as he imagined the field day the paparazzi would have with a cop following him around. 'Cops called on Pretty Boy O'Roarke!' 'O'Roarke a danger to Chicagoans?' 'O'Roake arrested!'

Yeah, he didn't want anything to do with the cops.

"You hire all the private security you want, Finn." His godfather's voice boomed over the phone, as rough as the waves crashing onto Oak Street Beach below Finn's window. "But I'm the goddamned police superintendent in Chicago, and I want a cop in there. This stalker is escalating. First that note, then a wedding ring? This is serious."

"No cops. Okay?"

"No one will know she's a cop. She'll be posing as your girlfriend," his godfather retorted.

5

"That's even worse," he groaned. "I don't want a pretend girlfriend. If the stalker is a woman obsessed with me, the situation could escalate. I'm not going to do this, Doug."

He hadn't dated anyone since the fiasco with Gemma a year and a half ago. Hadn't had the stomach for it. Pretending would be awkward and uncomfortable and unnecessary. And he'd be trapped, since Doug's cop would be staying in his suite if he went along with this crazy scheme.

"Really?" Doug's voice took on the steely tone Finn had dreaded when he'd played with Doug's sons twenty years ago. "You don't want a cop protecting you? You want me to have to look your father in the eye and tell him I let some psycho nut job kill his son on my watch? Huh? Is that what you want, Finian?"

Finn closed his eyes and banged his head lightly on the window. Doug was bringing out the big guns. Finian. If his full name didn't work, the next step would be calling Finn's mother. They both knew what would happen then, and it wouldn't be pretty.

"Damn it, Doug!" Finn knew the hell that would rain down on him if his mother got involved. "Fine. But don't expect me to hold her hand in public. Or kiss her. I'm not giving the vultures any money shots."

"That's fine, Finny. Wouldn't expect you to. Wouldn't expect her to, either." Doug's voice was smooth and happy, now that he'd gotten his way. "She'll be on the job. All business. But she's going to be with you, wherever you go."

And wouldn't that be fun. "Yeah. Fine. Send her over."

"First thing in the morning, son."

Finn could hear the self-satisfied smile in his godfather's voice. "Doug, I know you mean well, but you're a pain in my ass."

"And your ass will still be alive when you leave Chicago," Doug retorted. "Now go be evil and nasty in that movie of yours."

"Give my love to Marie," Finn said, hanging up the phone a little harder than necessary.

**

"Seriously?" Mia shook her head to clear her ears, positive she hadn't heard correctly. "You're kidding, right?" Mia felt her mouth gaping open and snapped it shut as she stared at her captain. "You want me to do *what*?"

Captain Talbott pressed his thumb and index finger into the bridge of his nose. "He needs protection, Donovan. And you're a cop. That's your job, right? Serve and protect?"

"Of course he needs protection. He's 'The Most Hated Man in America'," she said, swiping vicious quotes through the stale station air. "I'm guessing the bastard can't take a step outside his door without being mobbed by a swarm of angry Gemma Radley fans."

"Exactly. Which is why I'm assigning you to protect him."

Mia scowled at her captain. "He's a movie star. He's rich. Why doesn't he just hire private security?"

"Because he's Superintendant Walsh's godson." Talbott pressed his fingers to his nose again, as if he had a massive headache. Which he probably did if the Superintendant was involved.

"Wait," Mia said, grabbing at straws. "This can't be right. How can the Chicago PD pay me to protect a private citizen? The press will go nuts if they find out."

"That's been taken care of. The movie studio is paying your salary, plus a nice contribution to the Police Benevolent Association. So everyone's covered."

Except her, apparently. "Great. Just great. Not only is he a jerk, but he's the super's godson. How can I resist a job like that?"

"Donovan." Talbott sat up straight behind his desk. "You put in for the detective's exam, didn't you?"

"Yes," she said cautiously. She was pretty sure she wasn't going to like where this was going.

"As I'm sure you know, after you take the written exam, there's an oral review board. The Chief of Detectives is head of it. What you probably don't know is that he's a close friend of Superintendant Walsh." Talbott tossed his glasses on his desk and massaged his left temple. "Follow the dots, Mia. You do a good job on this detail, you keep O'Roarke safe, and it will look real good on your record."

Mia narrowed her gaze. "You think I have to suck up to some arrogant Hollywood asshole if I want to pass the exam?"

"No. Absolutely not. I think you're very well-qualified to take it and I'm confident you'll pass. I wouldn't have recommended you otherwise. But having an edge never hurts. Especially for someone so young." He tilted his head as he studied her. "You're only twenty-seven years old, Donovan. That's young to make detective."

"All my brothers made it before they were twenty-seven," she shot back.

"And God help you if you don't." Talbott's mouth turned up slightly. "Nothing like sibling rivalry."

"Exactly." Sibling rivalry was part of it – she'd get endless amounts of grief from her four brothers if she didn't make detective the first time she took the exam. But it was a lot more than that.

She wanted to be a detective so bad she dreamt about it at night. She liked being a patrol cop, but she wanted to be more than that. More than the grunt who arrested drunk and disorderlies and domestics. More than the cop who broke up fights at bars.

She wanted to solve crimes. To collect the clues, put the pieces of the puzzle together and figure out who did it.

"You want to be a detective, Donovan? Then agree to take this job and protect O'Roarke. Catching his stalker would be even better. They evaluate your record when you apply to be a detective, you know. This would make you stand out. Give you a leg up."

"'Agree'?" She narrowed her eyes and watched her boss carefully. "Why are you *asking*? You usually just issue orders." What was Talbott neglecting to tell her?

"Because it's close quarters for three weeks. The Superintendant thinks the best way to protect O'Roarke is to pose as his girlfriend, and I agree with him. But you'll have to stay in his suite at the hotel. Go everywhere with him. I'm not going to put someone on this job who can't handle that."

"I'd have to be with him twenty-four/seven for three weeks?" She stared at Talbott, not sure she heard correctly.

"Less if you catch the stalker right away." His desk phone rang, and he waved her away as he picked up the handset. "I need to know by tomorrow, Donovan. Think about it."

Mia stepped out of the captain's office and slid into the chair of the desk she normally used. Was she willing to protect Finn O'Roarke for three weeks to have a better shot at making detective?

Or would she rather be all righteous and insist on getting the promotion based on her own merits?

She sighed, knowing she'd already made her decision. She wanted that detective's star badly enough to take this job. She could spend three weeks with the devil himself if it gave her an edge.

Finn O'Roarke was the most hated man in America for the cruel way he'd dumped his ex, rocker Gemma Radley. According to Gemma, she'd come home early from a recording session and found him in bed with another woman.

Cheaters were a sore spot for Mia, but since she'd only be pretending to be his girlfriend, she could deal with it. She'd put in her time, do her best to catch his stalker, then take her detective's exam.

He'd go back to Hollywood and she'd start her career as a detective. Win-win for everyone.

***

Twelve hours later, at the ungodly hour of five AM, Mia stepped off the elevator at the Drake and glanced around. The walls were creamy beige with white trim, and the carpet was deep blue. The Drake was a beautiful hotel, and it was a smart choice for O'Roarke. They had good security and plenty of experience with high-profile guests - even Princess Di had stayed here when she visited Chicago years ago.

She took a deep breath and knocked on the door of O'Roarke's suite. *Here we go.*

The door opened almost immediately, as if he'd been standing right behind it. Waiting for her. Finn O'Roarke stared at her for an uncomfortably long moment, and Mia lifted her chin. "If you're done checking me out, I'm Mia Donovan," she finally said.

His ears turned red. "Sorry. I'm Finn O'Roarke."

"I know." He looked a lot better in person than he did in the tabloids, and he looked pretty damn good in those rags. Even in the crappy pictures. Wavy, honey-gold hair that was a little long. Soft, grass-green eyes and a mouth made for sin.

He towered over her – a couple of inches over six feet. His shoulders were broad, but he looked lean and wiry rather than bulky.

He held out his hand, and she shook it. His fingers were warm and strong, and he drew his hand away a little too slowly. Callouses on his palms rasped against her skin, making sparks jump deep in her belly. She closed her eyes. She'd thought she was better than women who swooned over celebrities.

Apparently she was as stupid as everyone else.

"I doubt you have to introduce yourself to many people," she said, snarky because she'd been staring and his twinkling eyes told her he'd noticed.

"You're right." His mouth curved into a self-mocking

smile. "Everyone's seen me in the checkout line at the grocery store. Is that going to be a problem for you?"

Mia stood straighter. "Of course it's going to be a problem. You don't exactly blend in. Hard to protect you when you draw a crowd."

He scowled. "Believe me, a crowd is the last thing I want." He stepped aside and waved her in.

She watched as he closed the door, and the glint of light reflecting off the tiny window reminded her of what he'd neglected to do. "You opened your door without looking in the peep hole." She tapped on the solid wood next to the small circle. "Don't do that again. Ever. You're being stalked. Not checking before you open your door makes you too stupid to live."

He drew his eyebrows together in a frown. "You're right. I can't believe I didn't check. I was expecting you, but that's no excuse."

"No. It's not," Mia managed to say, shocked by his answer. She'd expected him to be defensive. To justify himself. But he'd merely admitted he was wrong.

"We have fifteen minutes before we leave. Would you like a cup of coffee?"

"I'd love one," Mia said fervently. She'd rushed out of the house early, determined to be on time. "I didn't have time to stop this morning."

He gestured her over to the room service cart standing next to a table in front of the window. It held a pot of coffee, a giant bowl of fruit and a plate stacked with croissants. "Help yourself. They brought enough food to feed all ten of my fans."

"I think you're exaggerating," she shot back. "No way do you have ten fans." *Shit.* Did she really just say that?

"Yeah, you're right. I was rounding up."

She glanced at him and caught him smiling. If he was the arrogant jerk she'd been expecting, he was hiding it well.

She let herself smile back as she poured a cup of coffee and added cream. She plucked a fat, juicy strawberry from the bowl and bit into it. It was perfectly ripe. Exactly what she'd expect from the Drake Hotel.

So was the rest of the suite. Beautiful, comfortable furniture. Deep, navy blue plush carpet. Landscape paintings hanging on the wall. And a huge bouquet of red and yellow roses, trailing ivy, orange lilies, tiny blue forget-me-nots, and sprays of purple flowers rose from a vase on the table beside the door.

"Beautiful flowers," she said, nodding at the bouquet.

"A bellboy delivered it yesterday. Said it was from the hotel," he said, glancing at it.

The flowers warmed the room, made it seem less like a hotel room. Mia took another berry as she waited for the coffee to cool a bit, but before she could eat it, she noticed that O'Roarke was staring at her.

Oh, God. Had she dribbled juice down her chin? She picked up the napkin sitting beside her coffee cup and swiped at her mouth, then tossed it back onto the table. "Since we have a few minutes, why don't we talk about how this is going to work?"

"I'd rather watch you eat those strawberries," he said, his eyes gleaming.

Just the slap of reality she needed. She pointed the strawberry at him, irritated that she'd allowed herself to be distracted by his self-deprecating humor. "You *are* too stupid to live, Mr. O'Roarke. You're not taking this threat seriously." She kept her voice even. Calm. "It's really hard to protect an idiot who who'd rather flirt than discuss how to save his life."

He threw himself onto the blue satin loveseat facing the table. "That's twice you've called me stupid. That doesn't bode well for a good working relationship."

"Are you telling me I'm wrong? That it wasn't stupid to forget to check the peephole before opening the door? Or that only an idiot flirts with the person sent to protect him instead of discussing the situation seriously?"

He sighed. "I don't want you here. I agreed to this to

humor my godfather, but I don't think police protection is necessary. I think it's a waste of your time and an expense the city of Chicago shouldn't have to bear."

"I'm not crazy about living with you for the next three weeks, either, but I'm going to do my job and make sure your stalker doesn't get a chance at you." Mia took a sip of coffee and clutched the cup more tightly. "And your studio is paying for this. We're stuck with each other, so I suggest we make the best of it."

"If you don't want to do this, why did you agree to it?" he asked.

Mia loosened her grip on the coffee cup. "My reasons don't matter. My captain offered me the job, and I agreed."

"He didn't just order you to do it? I thought the police were all about giving orders. And obeying them."

He made it sound as if she were a mindless drone. "No," she said, her voice short. "Given the circumstances, knowing I'd have to stay in this suite with you for three weeks, he wanted to give me a chance to say no. I didn't."

She gulped the rest of the coffee, glanced at the stainless steel carafe on the table, then set the cup on the table. She'd kill for another cup, but they needed to talk before they left. "Why don't you tell me about this stalker? What has he or she done? Have you gotten any notes?"

He nodded at the carafe. "Help yourself to another cup." He shifted on the loveseat, and she realized he didn't want to talk about the situation. Intrigued, she poured herself another cup of coffee and sat in one of the chairs at the small table.

Then she waited.

Finally he sighed. "You do that really well."

"What's that?" Mia took another gulp of coffee and tilted her head. She knew what he meant, but she wanted him to say it.

"The cop thing. Staring without saying a word. Does it make everyone blurt out their deepest, darkest secrets?"

"Sooner or later. So why don't you fill me in?"

He leaned against the back of the loveseat and stared at the ceiling for a moment. Finally he leaned forward. "I got a note the day after I checked into the Drake. I was free the day I arrived, so I walked around the area. Went up the Hancock building, got a drink at the Signature Lounge on the 95th. Ate dinner at a pizza place. Pizzeria Uno, I think. Typical tourist stuff."

"Okay." Mia pulled a notebook out of the inner pocket of her jacket and jotted down notes. "Anything seem off? Did you see the same person more than once? Anyone approach you and try to talk to you?"

"Nope. I wore a baseball cap and glasses. Baggy old clothes. I don't think anyone recognized me."

"Now that's just false modesty, Mr. O'Roarke. Of course some people recognized you. They were just too polite to approach you."

"Is that what Chicagoans are? Polite?"

"Most of us," she replied evenly. "There are always a few exceptions."

"Well, the note wasn't very polite," he said.

"When did you find it?"

"The next morning when I walked out of the bedroom. There was an envelope near the door. I figured it was from someone on the production, with an agenda about the meeting or some other information."

"So you opened it, right?"

"Of course."

"And what did it say?"

"It said, 'I'm so glad you came for me. I've been waiting for you. I know that's why you're in Chicago. You're here for me.'"

"What did you do with the note?"

"I called my godfather and he sent someone to pick it up."

"That would be Superintendant Walsh?"

"Yes. He had it checked and there were no fingerprints. Nothing else that could identify the sender. Except for one thing."

Mia glanced up from her note-taking as Finn jumped up and began to pace the room. "And that would be…?"

"There was perfume on the note." He swallowed. "An expensive, almost impossible to find perfume. The one Gemma uses."

CHAPTER TWO

Finn watched the rising sun surround Mia Donovan with a golden glow as she sat in front of the window, scribbling in her notebook. Without looking, she reached into the fruit bowl and curled delicate fingers around a strawberry. White teeth flashed as she bit the berry from its stem and dropped the green leaves onto the plate.

The dark mass of her hair waved around her shoulders and half-obscured her face as she wrote. Finally, she looked up, shoved her hair behind one ear and fixed her gaze on him. Just like when he'd opened the door, he couldn't help staring at her.

Unsmiling, she sat straight in the chair. Her expression was carefully neutral, a complete waste of those full lips. He found himself staring at her eyes again. Surrounded by thick, sooty lashes, they were the brightest blue he'd ever seen.

He wondered if everyone else she met stared at her, too.

"Do you think Ms. Radley sent the note?" she asked.

"Gemma?" He frowned as he stared at the cop. "Why would she do that? What does pretending to be a stalker do for her? What would she gain?" Especially since she'd milked their break-up to shoot her career into the stratosphere.

"Maybe she wants you back," Mia said carefully. "Maybe this is her way of getting your attention."

"No." Donovan's suggestion was almost funny, in a sick, ironic way. He looked away from the woman watching him so carefully. "Trust me, she doesn't want me back."

"Do you know that for certain? Have you talked to her recently?"

"I haven't talked to her since the day I...we broke up. And I'm certain she has no interest in rekindling any flames." He relaxed back into the loveseat, smoothing out the loathing he was afraid his expression displayed. "Even if she did, she knows it would never happen."

Mia studied his face. "It wouldn't be the first time a woman who's been...dropped by her boyfriend stalked him. Tried to get him back."

"Trust me, Ms. Donovan, whoever this stalker is, it's not Gemma." He took a deep breath, trying to ignore the resentment bubbling up from where he'd buried it. "You can rule her out."

He'd thought he'd successfully exorcized his bitterness at Gemma. That he'd put the whole ugly mess behind him and moved on. Apparently, he was wrong.

"I'll check on her whereabouts." She scribbled something in her notebook.

"Not necessary," he retorted.

"Yes, it is," she said without looking up. She finished writing, then faced him again. "You need to lose the 'Ms. Donovan'. That's not what a guy calls his girlfriend. My name is Mia. Make sure you use it."

Mia was a soft name. A girly name. So far, he hadn't seen anything soft or girly about Ms. Donovan.

But she was right. "Mia it is. And you need to call me Finn."

"Right." She took a breath, as if forcing herself to use his first name. "So, Finn, you said it was her perfume. Are you certain of that?" Mia asked.

"Positive." He'd smelled Chypre in his nightmares for a long time.

"You also said it was," she glanced at her notebook, "expensive and almost impossible to get. Who else knew about it?"

He shrugged. "Gemma Radley fan pages have all kinds of details about her life. The name of her perfume is probably out there somewhere."

"And it's hard to find because...?"

He swallowed, hating the memories her questions were stirring. "It's French. Discontinued. They made Chypre just for her. A thousand bucks an ounce." He'd bought her a bottle every time he was in France.

"You can get anything you want if you want it badly enough," she shot back. "If he or she knew it was this Chypre, a stalker could figure out a way to buy it."

"How many people could afford a thousand bucks for a tiny bottle of perfume?"

"An obsessed person could." Mia closed the notebook with a tiny clap, picked up her coffee cup and drained it. "Isn't it time to go?"

"The driver will come up and get me…us," he said.

"What do you know about your driver?" she asked, setting the cup back in the saucer too hard. "Did the studio hire him? Did they use a local service?"

"Pete's driven me for several years. He comes with me to all my location shoots and rents a car. So, no. It's not Pete."

"Are you certain?"

"Yes. I am. Pete's a friend. A good one."

"I'm going to run a background check on him anyway," Mia said, opening the notebook again. "What's his full name?"

"Peter White. California driver's license. You want his address?"

"Please." She didn't even look up, just scribbled the

address he recited.

A few moments later, Finn heard a quiet rap on the door. Recognizing Pete's signal, Finn stood up and opened the door. "Hey, Pete. Come on in." He waved his friend inside. "Have some breakfast and meet my, um, friend Mia Donovan."

The middle-aged man gave him a sharp look as he chewed hard on his ever-present nicotine gum, but stepped into the suite. "Morning, Ms. Donovan," he said.

Mia uncurled herself from the chair and walked over to shake Pete's hand. Finn's gaze followed her tall, slender figure, lingering too long on her ass. Maybe it wouldn't be so tough to play house with Mia Donovan. "Nice to meet you, Mr. White."

"It's Pete," he said.

Mia's mouth relaxed. Finn wouldn't call it a smile, but it was the closest she'd come since she'd walked into the suite. "I'm Mia."

Then she looked at Finn and her mouth hardened again. "You didn't use the peephole," she said, narrowing her gaze at him.

"Chill out. I know Pete's knock," Finn said easily.

"I don't care if you think it's your mother," Mia shot back. "You check before you open that door."

Finn saw Pete's head ping-ponging back and forth like he was at a tennis match. A tiny smile curled the older man's mouth. "You ready to roll, boss?" Pete asked, the smile becoming a smirk. "Or do you want to practice checking the peephole?"

Finn glared at his friend. "I can fire your ass, you know."

"Go ahead," Pete shot back. "There are plenty of people who'll pay me big bucks to drive them. They're all waiting for you to piss me off once too often."

Finn shook his head. "Tell me why I hired you again?"

Pete held up one finger. "Because I'm the best-trained driver in California." He added a second finger. "Aced all the evasive and defensive driving classes. Which you need, since everyone but me and your mother hates you." He added a third finger. "And you'd fire anyone else in about two hours."

"Guess I'll let it go, then," Finn answered, suppressing his grin. Thank God he had Pete on this job. "You want some coffee before we head out?"

"Already had some. Love the room service when we're on the road. I could seriously get used to this lifestyle." A shadow crossed his face. "Not as good as Judy's coffee was, though."

"Yeah. Loved her coffee." Finn bumped Pete's shoulder. "Loved Judy, too." He stepped away from his friend and cleared his throat. "You ready, Mia?"

She nodded. "I am." She slid the notebook into the inside pocket of her gray flannel jacket, and her white shirt highlighted the outline of a dark shape at her right hip.

Her gun.

The sight was a sharp jolt of reality. She was taking this stalker very seriously.

He'd better start doing that, too.

She was right. He was an idiot for not checking the peephole. Chastened, he headed for the door. But she put her hand on his arm, stopping him. "I go first," she said. She squeezed past Pete, who watched her now with a tiny frown.

After taking a long moment to check the peephole, she opened the door and stepped into the empty hall. Turning to Finn, she nodded him out. Pete walked out last and pulled the door closed.

Mia pushed the elevator button. When the ding sounded, announcing its arrival, she stood straighter. Widened her stance. Stood motionless as the doors slid open.

The elevator was empty, and she held the door for him and Pete. They rode to the basement, the air quivering with Pete's unasked questions. Once there, they stepped into a narrow alley where a black Cadillac stood waiting. The windows in the back seat were darkly tinted, and the car looked solid. Imposing. Which it should be, because it was bullet-proof. The studio had insisted.

They'd clearly drunk their own Kool-Aid. They'd hired the most hated man in America to play the villain in their noir thriller. They needed to protect that investment.

Finn played along, because he desperately wanted this role. Pretty Boy Finn O'Roake, star of romantic comedies and bro movies, needed a change. And playing the bad guy in a dark, edgy thriller fit the bill to a tee.

Pete opened the back door, and Finn stepped aside for Mia to climb in first. She shook her head slightly at him and jerked her chin toward the car. She wanted him inside first.

All this caution was making him jittery. Glancing around the deserted loading area, he slid into the car. Mia followed him and pulled the door closed.

A moment later, Pete got into the front seat and glanced over his shoulder. "You want the glass up?" he asked.

"Please, Pete," he sighed. Mia had more questions, and he wasn't sure how much Pete was supposed to know.

The glass rose silently, separating the front from the rear, sealing him and Mia in a silent cocoon. Then the car pulled away from the curb, drove down the alley and slid into the still-light morning traffic.

***

"What else did your stalker send you besides the note?" Mia asked.

He shifted on the seat. *His stalker.* She made it sound so personal. As if the unknown person was part of his life, like Pete.

"He or she isn't *mine*," he said, his voice tight.

"Yes, she is." Mia glanced at him, but he didn't look at her. "I'm guessing your stalker is a woman. Far more likely in your situation. And she *is* yours, because she thinks she is. Your problem, anyway. So what else did she send you?"

He sighed. "A wedding ring. In a fancy ring box. Wrapped up with a bow. Another note."

Mia pulled out her notebook and began scribbling again. Finn leaned over to see what she was writing, but he couldn't decipher her scribbles.

She lifted her head, caught his eye and almost smiled. "Secret code. They teach us at the police academy. Protection against nosy suspects."

"Now I'm a suspect?"

"Hmm." She shifted in the seat to study him. "I hadn't considered that. But I suppose that an aging Hollywood star, bypassed for his usual roles because of a scandal, might try to grab attention by pretending he had a stalker." She tilted her head as she studied him. "Does that sound about right, Finn?"

"Hell, no." He rolled his eyes and shifted to face her. "More attention? I can't even take a piss in a public washroom without some jackass pulling out his phone and recording the event for posterity." He scowled at her. "And what the hell do you mean by 'aging'?"

Mia laughed and tapped the notebook back into the inside pocket of her jacket. "Thank you," she said. "I didn't think you were faking your stalker, but I had to check."

"What are you talking about? You were *testing* me?"

"Yes, I was, and you passed. The first thing you mentioned was attention. That you didn't want it. I would have expected you to object to the lack of good roles first. Then the aging star crack. And I thought all big stars craved attention."

"Not all of them," he muttered as he studied her. Mia Donovan was more than a pair of stunning eyes, a striking face and a killer body.

But then, Doug wouldn't have sent her if she wasn't up to the job. He narrowed his eyes at her. "How do you know my godfather?"

She frowned. "I don't know the superintendent. Why would you assume I do?"

He wasn't going to tell her the truth – that Doug had sent exactly the type of woman he was attracted to – smart, clever, funny. Being easy on the eyes was a bonus. Instead, he shrugged. "I can't imagine my controlling godfather sending someone he doesn't know personally to protect me."

"Well, he did. Because I've never met him."

"Interesting." He'd pursue this with Doug. Because no way was sending Mia Donovan to guard him completely serendipitous.

"Finish telling me about the ring. And the note."

Finn sighed and closed his eyes for a moment. "A shoebox was sitting at the door yesterday morning. The note was attached. It said ' You didn't answer me. But I know this is what you want. Why you dropped that slut Gemma. I have a ring, too. I'll bring it when we meet. Then we can make our dreams come true.' Inside the package was a wedding ring."

"And I'm guessing your godfather had someone pick it up."

"Yeah. No fingerprints. An expensive ring, though. A lot of gold. Heavy. The shoebox was from a pair of running shoes available everywhere." He shook his head. "Doug would have gone over every inch of that box, the note, the ring. So whoever it is, she's being careful."

"We can't rule out a guy," Mia said, continuing to write. "Now that same sex marriage is legal."

"Great. We've just doubled our suspect population."

She looked up at that. "Odds are that it's a woman. The notes have a female feel to them. Waiting for you to come to Chicago. Seeing it as a sign." She tapped the notebook back into her pocket. "She's obsessive. Convinced herself it's going to happen. Convinced that you want it, too. She's built a whole fantasy world around you. And when you don't respond, she'll get upset."

A muscle in her jaw twitched. "That's when it's dangerous. When you've disappointed her. Proved you're not the man she thought you were. The next step is deciding that if she can't have you, no one else can."

He raised his eyebrows. "You have a pretty vivid imagination."

"Runs in the family, I guess."

"Yeah? How so?"

Her hesitation was a couple of seconds too long. "My brother's a writer."

"Really?" He twisted to get a better look at her, but her hair was suddenly obscuring her face. "What does he write?"

"Stuff." She tapped her pen on the notebook. Delicate pink crept up her neck. "So, about that shoebox," she said after an awkward pause. "Man's shoes or woman's?"

Why didn't she want to talk about her brother the writer? He studied the curtain of hair that fell over the side of her face. A mystery to solve later. "Man's, I think." He tried to visualize the box, but saw only the logo. "I'll ask Doug."

"Good." Her knuckles whitened on the notebook and pen. "I'll check the hotel staff for any recent hires. Your stalker could be someone who works there. She knew when you were checking in. Had easy access to your floor, which needs a special key in the elevator. Hotel staff is a good place to start."

The car was slowing, and Finn gazed out the window. "Looks like we're here."

"Quick. Tell me about this meeting," Mia ordered.

He lifted one shoulder. "Nothing unusual about it. Shooting schedule, locations we're using, when everyone will be needed on set. It'll all get thrown out after the first day of shooting."

"Who's going to be there?" Her pen was poised over her notebook.

"You're serious? You think one of the nerdy screenwriters or my co-stars or the director is my stalker?"

"Can't ignore anyone," she said, finally turning to look at him. "One note and a ring in a box are pretty vague clues.

Maybe, when things progress with your stalker, we'll be able to narrow it down. But for now, everyone's on the table."

"Even Pete?" he asked as his driver opened Mia's door.

"I'll do a background check on him, too," she said as she stepped out of the car.

"You hear that, Pete?" he said as he followed her onto the sidewalk. "She thinks you're stalking me."

"Why the hell would I do that? I see too much of your ugly mug as it is."

Mia bit her lip, but he could see the smile itching to break free. "Duly noted, Pete," she said.

Then the smile disappeared as she looked around. She'd replaced the notebook and pen again. So she'd have her hands free, he realized uneasily. This area of Chicago was a ghost town at six AM. The only things moving were the paper wrapper from a fast food burger and a crushed cigarette package, skipping down the gutter, propelled by Chicago's famous wind. Old factories lined the street, cheek to jowl with new, trendy-looking loft buildings. The only other vehicle on the street was a lumbering box truck advertising a seafood company.

Hard to believe they were only a mile or two west of Chicago's Loop.

Mia shooed him toward the door and followed him inside. "This is the studio where we'll be shooting the interior scenes," he said, glancing at her. "Your new home away from home. We'll spend a lot of time here."

They took an old freight elevator to the second floor, then he headed for the office. But when she tried to go in ahead of him, he grabbed her elbow.

"You're not going to be in that meeting."

"Of course I am," she said immediately. "Attached at the hip, remember? For the next three weeks."

"Not in this meeting," he said. "Not going to happen."

"Why not?"

"Because I don't need the gossip that would be stirred up if I brought my 'girlfriend' into a meeting. I want this part. A lot. For a bunch of reasons. So you're waiting out here." The last thing Finn needed was the director thinking he'd hired a diva for the Johnny Santorini role. Bringing his 'girlfriend' into a business meeting screamed 'entitled asshole'.

Finn wanted this role. Needed it. The disaster with Gemma had forced him to take a different direction with his career, and this was the first, critical step.

He wasn't going to screw it up.

"Any other access to this room?" Mia asked.

"Not that I know of."

She stared at him, and he was sure she would insist on being in the meeting. That would completely piss off the producer and the director. He wouldn't allow that. He'd worked hard to land this part.

"Fine," she finally said. "But if you walk in there and see another door, you come out and tell me. And I'll need a list of everyone in that meeting. Even the grunt who brings the coffee." She stared at him, her blue eyes dark with irritation. "And this doesn't happen again. I'm with you *all the time*."

Irritated that she was pushing him, unhappy he wouldn't be alone for the next three weeks, he crowded her. Close enough to feel the heat from her body. Close enough to smell the orangey-tart scent of her hair, the faint sweetness of her skin.

She stilled. Turned her head to frown at him. But her pupils were a little too large. A flush of red bloomed on her cheeks.

An answering arousal stirred in him, spurring his irritation. "So you're gonna be there when I'm pissing? You want a look at the goods?"

She stared straight at him. "'A look at the goods', Mr. Hollywood Star? Really?" She cocked an eyebrow at him. "If you've seen one, you've seen them all. And you know what they say about the size of the package."

Even knowing it was a mistake, he couldn't stop himself from taking her bait. "I'm all ears, Mia."

"If you have to brag, there's not much to see."

CHAPTER THREE

Mia stared at Finn, shocked at what had just come out of her mouth. She couldn't believe she'd said that to him, a guy she was supposed to be protecting.

He held her gaze as red crept up his neck and his pupils dilated. He shifted his feet, as if his jeans had suddenly become too tight.

She swallowed and kept her eyes above his neck. She would not look below his waist.

She didn't have to. The slash of color along his cheekbones, the tiny rim of green around the black of his pupil, the pulse beating too fast in his neck were all too clear. She'd stepped over the line, and she'd wound him up.

She was wound up, too.

Closing her eyes, she swallowed once and reached desperately for control. She was supposed to be a professional. Level-headed. Cool. Always paying attention to the environment. Snarky comebacks were not part of her job description.

Especially *sexually charged* snarky comments.

She was supposed to keep her head even if Finn made a tasteless, suggestive remark. She was supposed to be smarter than that. Smart enough to ignore his crack about watching him take a leak.

"I apologize," she said stiffly. "That was inappropriate and wrong."

"That's too bad," he said, watching her out of half-closed eyes. "I found it very…informative. Very…stimulating." His gaze dropped to her chest, then back to her face. "I'm guessing that put-down came out of Mia's mouth. Not Officer Donovan's."

"Doesn't matter," she said, holding his gaze, even though she wanted to disappear into a hole in the floor. "I *am* Officer Donovan."

"Not now, you're not. You're Mia, and I bet she wouldn't let a guy get away with a dig like that. I think Mia would probably say something even worse."

Finn was right. If one of her brothers said that to her, Mia's comeback would slice and dice until the stupid ass was filleted, gasping, on the floor.

And if it was a guy she was dating, she would have parried with a much more suggestive answer. The kind that would make the guy want to drag her home immediately.

Then she'd make him wait for hours.

"Let's just say we were both wrong and let it drop," she finally said.

Finn smiled. "So I was right." He leaned a hair closer. "Tell me what you would have said to a guy you were really dating."

"I don't think so."

"Why not?"

"Because *we're not* dating." The devil on her shoulder made her add, "That's a need to know basis."

"And I don't need to know?"

"No, O'Roarke. You don't."

He shifted a fraction of a step, but suddenly he was much closer. Close enough to feel the heat pouring off her body. "What if I want to know?"

Before Mia could answer, a door opened behind her.

She spun around, tensing, to find a frazzled-looking guy with wild, curly hair in the doorway.

"Get in here, O'Roarke." He narrowed his gaze at Mia. "Who's she, and what's she doing here?"

"This is Mia," Finn said, wrapping an arm around her shoulders. He tugged her close, and she tried not to notice how the hard planes of his body fit her softer ones perfectly. "She just arrived this morning."

Curly-haired guy studied her for a long moment, and speculation sharpened his gaze. "Why is she here? We have a lot to do today."

"She's here because she wanted to be with me. And because I missed her, too." Finn squeezed her shoulder before letting go. He glanced at Mia over his shoulder as he moved toward the door, and she simpered at him, aware of curly-hair watching them closely. The twinkle in Finn's eyes screamed 'I'm a really good actor, aren't I'?

She wanted to do something childish, like stick her tongue out at him. Instead, she cooed, "See you soon, honey."

"You know it, babe."

Finn followed the curly-haired guy into the room, looking back at her and mouthing a kiss as he closed the door.

Idiot.

But at least he'd been distracted from their conversation. And now everyone in the room would know Finn had a girlfriend. The sooner her presence was accepted by his co-workers, the sooner she could blend into the woodwork and keep an eye on all of them.

Mia sank into a chair against the wall a few feet down from the door and tried to pull herself together. Why had she let that completely inappropriate exchange take place? Why hadn't she simply ignored Finn's crack and moved on?

Because she wasn't good at letting go and moving on. Not good at turning the other cheek. Growing up with four older brothers meant she'd had to fight and claw for every inch of respect. As a kid, she'd been the annoying little sister who wanted to tag along with her big brothers. Brendan had tolerated her, but Quinn, Connor and Mac had teased her mercilessly. The only way to avoid getting squashed like a bug was to have the thick skin of a rhinoceros and a quicker, sharper tongue than her brothers.

Not exactly the best attributes for protecting an egotistical Hollywood guy. Although he hadn't seemed particularly egotistical yet.

Let it go, Mia.

He'd probably forgotten about their little exchange already.

Determined to do the same, she pulled out her phone. Tapped her email icon and sighed.

Way too many emails had accumulated overnight. This was the perfect opportunity to go through them. Erase the lingering hum of arousal from her exchange with Finn.

Fifteen minutes later, as she was typing a reply to Brendan's request that she come to dinner with him and Cilla – she hated to say no, since Brendan was her favorite brother and she was crazy about his fiancée – she heard the sound of the elevator arriving. Hitting send on her email, she pretended to be scrolling through her phone as the elevator doors opened.

A woman stepped out. She looked to be in her late thirties or early forties, with brown hair and a round, pleasant face. She wore running shoes, jeans and a bright pink tee shirt, along with a fleece jacket. She stopped short when she spotted Mia.

Her expression was no longer pleasant. "Who are you?"

"I'm Mia." She smiled in a way she hoped was irritatingly vapid. "And you are…?"

"Ginny," the woman finally said after a too long hesitation. "What are you doing here?"

Mia slipped the phone into her pocket and rested her right hand on her thigh. Close to her gun. "I was looking through my phone."

Ginny's eyebrows squinched together in a scowl. "I mean in this building. It's not public. This is a private business."

"I know." Mia smiled again. "Do you work here?"

"Of course I do," Ginny sputtered.

"Really? What do you do? The movie business is so fascinating." Mia knew she sounded like an airhead. Exactly what she was going for.

Ginny hesitated a beat too long. "I'm in production," she finally said. "Set decoration."

"I bet that's fun," Mia said. "Getting to play with the scenery." She leaned forward in the chair. "Do you get to shop for all the stuff you use? It would be so cool to be paid to shop." A reputation as an airhead could be very useful.

Ginny snorted. "Not exactly how it works. And you didn't tell me why you're here."

"I'm waiting for a friend," Mia said, as if it should have been glaringly obvious.

"Who would that be?"

"Why does it matter?"

"Because no one's supposed to be here," Ginny said through gritted teeth.

"It's okay." Mia leaned back in the chair. "My friend knows I'm here. We came together."

Ginny stared at her, apparently assuming that Mia would crack. Mia stared back. She could do this all day long.

Ginny couldn't. After about a minute, she looked away. "I'm going to discuss this with Mr. Higgins," she said.

From her research, Mia knew that Sean Higgins was the director. "Whatever. Nice to meet you, Ginny."

Mia pulled out her phone with her left hand, leaving her right in her lap. As she navigated through her screens with one hand, she watched Ginny out of the corner of her eye.

When Ginny headed for the door to the meeting room, Mia tensed. As Ginny eased the door open, Mia slipped her hand beneath her jacket and curled it around the grip of her

Glock.

"What do you want?" barked a voice from inside the room.

"Oh! Sorry," Ginny said, backing out the door. "I didn't know this room was occupied."

"Get out!" the voice roared.

Ginny jumped and closed the door. Mia let go of her gun.

Glancing at Mia, Ginny hurried back to the elevator. As she pressed the call button, she glanced over her shoulder at Mia. Mia smiled. Ginny turned away.

A few moments later, the elevator arrived and Ginny stepped inside. She stared at Mia as the doors closed.

Mia let out a long breath and wiped her sweaty palm on her thigh. Then she slid the phone into her pocket.

Could Ginny be Finn's stalker?

It seemed too neat. Too pat, that his stalker would show up the first morning. But maybe Mia was just that lucky.

She'd ask him about the woman after he was out of his meeting. She should have gotten Pete's phone number. Then she could have called him and asked if Ginny exited the building.

There was a window at the end of the hallway, and Mia hurried over to it. There were a few people on the sidewalk now, and several cars moving on the street. She watched for five minutes, but Ginny didn't appear. So either the woman had gone the other way, or she really worked at the studio.

Adrenaline still pumping, Mia prowled the long hallway, examining the doors, opening them after she knocked and got no reply. They were mostly offices, with a few larger meeting rooms mixed in.

Nowhere on the floor was there an office for set decoration.

Ginny could have been looking for anyone.

But she'd gone right to the occupied meeting room and opened the door. Why had she come to this floor and walked into a meeting? Was it possible she'd been looking for Finn?

Mia wasn't about to assume Ginny was the stalker. But she would definitely check the woman out. Make sure she worked in set decoration.

She hadn't asked Finn if he'd gotten any notes or packages in California, or if they'd only started since he arrived in Chicago. Rookie mistake not to ask.

After memorizing the names and titles on all of the doors in the corridor, Mia returned to her chair and pulled out her phone again. But she was too on-edge to focus on it. Too wired up from her encounter with Ginny.

So she paced the hallway. She knew exactly how long the corridor was. Every uneven spot on the dingy gray carpet.

She studied the diagram of the building that hung on the wall, until she was sure she could find her way through the studio blindfolded.

Looked at the photos of past movies in production hanging on the walls, feeling like a giddy fangirl when the titles caused a flutter in her belly. Some of her favorite films had been shot here.

She spun around when she heard the door open forty-five minutes after her encounter with Ginny, and watched the people trickling out. Finn was one of the last few, deep in discussion with the curly-haired guy.

Curly guy finally slapped Finn on the back. "See you at the butt crack of dawn tomorrow, O'Roarke. I'm looking forward to working with you."

"Feeling's mutual, Sean." Finn shook hands, then turned toward Mia.

"Good meeting?" she murmured as he got close.

"Good enough. Not as long as usual, which is a plus. Have to be on the set at five tomorrow morning."

"Oh, God," she said before she could stop herself.

Finn raised an eyebrow. "Not a morning person?"

She wasn't, but he didn't need to know that. "I've been

working the night shift," she said. "Still on that rhythm."

"That going to be a problem?" Finn frowned.

"Not at all." She felt herself bristling at his assumption that she couldn't handle the change. She took a deep breath, let it out slowly before she answered. "Cops move from days to nights all the time. I know how to adjust."

"Not what I meant," Finn said. "I don't want to disrupt your schedule."

Mia shook her head. "You're disrupting nothing, O'Roarke. I volunteered for this detail."

"What happened to Finn?" He leaned closer. "That's more intimate. More girlfriend-y." His breath tickled her ear, but she refused to back away.

"There's no one else to hear me," she retorted. "So there's no reason to call you Finn."

"Yeah, there is. Habit. Familiarity. Body language." He smiled, and his famous toothy grin reminded her of a shark. "Sell the premise, sell the bit. That's what they teach us in acting school. Calling me Finn is selling the premise."

"Fine," she huffed, but she knew he was right. "*Finn.*"

"You ready to go?" he asked.

"You're the one who had the meeting. What's next?"

"I need to talk to the wardrobe people and meet with the screenwriters. Going to be boring for you."

Mia resisted rolling her eyes. "Gee, not sure I can handle that. My job is usually a thrill a minute. Constant action. Gun battles on every other street corner."

"You always such a smart ass?" he asked as he headed for the elevator.

"Sorry," she apologized, not sorry at all. "I'll try to rein it in."

He glanced over his shoulder, and his eyes twinkled. "Not on my account," he said. "But Pete's a delicate flower. Easily offended. You'll have to watch yourself around him."

Her mouth twitched, but she refused to let the smile loose. "So noted. I'll do my best not to hurt his feelings."

He laughed as the elevator dinged, announcing its

arrival. "I'd pay good money to watch you and Pete go at each other."

"Pete and I are fine as long as he does what I tell him to do."

The muffled noise he made sounded like a snort. "This is going to be an interesting three weeks," Finn said as the doors slid open.

Ginny faced them from inside the elevator.

CHAPTER FOUR

Finn eased a little closer to Mia as the elevator doors began to open. Teasing her earlier had been a lot more fun than his meeting with Sean's team, and he wondered if he could get her going again.

As the doors opened fully, Mia tensed beside him. Then she stepped in front of him, crowding him into the wall next to the elevator. "Hey, Ginny." She greeted the woman in a voice he barely recognized as Mia's. Higher pitched than her low, sexy tones, irritatingly breathless, it was somewhere between Valley girl and space cadet. She didn't take her eyes off Ginny. "This is my friend from earlier, Finny," she said. "The woman I was telling you about. From set décor."

Finny? Damn, she was good. He wanted to laugh out loud, but bit his lip instead.

Ginny's eyes shifted from Mia to Finn and back again. "It's set *decoration*." A muscle jumped in Ginny's jaw as she studied Finn. "*Finn O'Roarke* is your friend?"

"Yes," Mia said happily. "Isn't he yummy?"

She used her left hand to keep him behind her, as if making a path for Ginny to get off the elevator. Finn realized she was really putting herself between him and the other woman. Her right hand was at her side. She appeared relaxed and at ease. But he felt the tension pouring from Mia's body, and instinctively moved closer.

The fingers of her left hand curled around his wrist. She pushed him backward, he stumbled into the wall and she pinned him against it.

Message received. She didn't need protecting. *He* did.

Ginny stepped out of the elevator, and Mia went still. The other woman glanced at him one last time, then turned and walked down the hall. Ginny glanced into the now-empty meeting room, then opened a door farther down the hall, stepped inside and closed it softly.

Finn began to step out from behind Mia, but she held out her arm to stop him. Mia stared at the door Ginny had opened, as if she had x-ray vision and could watch what was going on in the room. Finally, after what seemed like an eternity but was probably only a few seconds, she pulled him into the elevator and jabbed the 'close door' button. Twice.

Mia took a deep breath as the slow freight elevator began to descend. Her fingers were still clamped around his wrist, as tight as a handcuff. She shifted her grip on his hand until it was more like a caress than a shackle, keeping her fingers over the pulse point. The feel of her soft but strong fingers made his heart rev, and he edged a little closer to her.

She glanced at him, then down at her fingers circling his arm. She stepped away and let him go as if he were made of burning coals.

"So." He moved to face her. Her pulse was booming in her throat and she was breathing too quickly. Was she worried about the woman who'd gotten off the elevator? Or was she thinking about the way she'd practically been holding his hand?

He cleared his throat, banishing the images hand-holding had conjured. "Yummy?" he asked, lifting one eyebrow. Maybe he could unsettle her a little. Seemed fair, with the way she'd unsettled him.

A faint smile flickered over Mia's mouth. Her breathing

slowed, and in the blink of an eye, she'd regained her composure. Which was too bad. He'd been enjoying flustered Mia.

"Part of the persona," she said easily. "I'm selling myself as a lightweight. An airhead. People don't take you seriously when they think you're a few colors short of a full crayon box."

"Great acting," he said. "You almost fooled me." He nudged her with his elbow. "You want to be an extra in the movie?"

"If I have to be," she said, her voice cool. "I'll be in any crowd scenes with a lot of people milling around if I think it's the best way to protect you. Personal protection is tricky when there are so many unknowns."

"Wow." He studied her, fascinated by the intricacies of her mind. "I didn't even think about that."

"Good thing I did, then. Nothing like using a chaotic scene in a movie to create even more chaos."

The elevator groaned to a halt, and the doors slowly creaked open. "How did you jump from a note and a ring to someone going berserk during a mob scene?" he asked.

She shrugged. "It's my job to consider all possibilities. That one was pretty obvious."

He waited for her to exit the elevator, and got an approving nod in return. He smiled to himself as he followed her out. He'd waited for her to go first for politeness' sake. But he'd let her think he'd been paying attention.

He followed her onto the main floor, moving slightly ahead of her. He stopped abruptly when she stepped in front of him, put her palm on his chest and held him in place. After a long moment, she let her hand drop and stepped to the side.

"Never get ahead of me," she said, her eyes flat and her mouth tense.

"Jeez," he said, rubbing the place on his chest that had collided with her hand. "You look like a good wind could knock you over. But you're damn strong."

One side of her mouth curled up. "Part of my real persona."

"Speaking of your fake identity, are you going to tell me what that scene with the set decoration woman was all about?"

Mia glanced around, then led him to a bench against the wall. "Sit down for a moment," she said quietly.

When he'd seated himself, she eased onto the bench beside him. There was no one in sight, and she finally relaxed against the wall. "Her name is Ginny. She came up on the elevator while your meeting was going on. Acted shocked to see me. Wanted to know what I was doing there. Questioned me aggressively. She's the one who opened the door during your meeting."

She shifted to face him. "The room she went into just now is empty."

"How do you know?"

"Because after Ginny left, I checked all the doors in the corridor. She said she worked in set decoration, so I wanted to see if they had an office on that floor. They don't."

"Don't you mean set décor?" he asked. Yanking her chain was surprisingly fun.

"Oops." She grinned, her eyes twinkling, and need stirred inside him. "Yeah. Set décor."

"Easy enough to find out if she's part of the production. What's her last name?"

The grin disappeared. "I don't know. Couldn't really ask her, since I didn't want to give her my last name."

"There can't be that many people in that department. Let's go check it out."

"Right now?"

"Sure." He held her elbow as she stood up. "You can do your Valley girl impression again. I like that one. It's hot."

She'd started walking, but at that, she stopped dead in her tracks. Swung around to face him. "You're not taking this seriously, are you?"

He shrugged. "My opinion? Doug is over-reacting. Some random crazy doesn't like me, but so what? They need to get in line behind everyone else in the country. So, no. I'm not losing sleep over this stalker thing."

She jerked him around to face her. Got too close to him. As he inhaled her scent, she narrowed her eyes. "Too bad, because I am, Finn. Maybe *you* have a death wish, but if you get hurt, it's my job on the line. My career. So I'm taking this assignment very seriously. Things will go much more smoothly if you do, too."

"You think I have a death wish or something? That I don't care about my safety?" He got even closer, until he felt the heat pouring off her body. Until he inhaled her sweet orange scent. Until he wanted to bury his hands in her hair, see if it was as soft as it looked.

Then he saw the pity lurking in the blue depths of her eyes.

Damn it all to hell. Mia was an attractive, interesting woman. The first woman who'd ignited even a spark of interest since the debacle with Gemma. The last thing he wanted from her was pity.

He *hated* that she felt sorry for him. That she saw him as an object of sympathy. Anger at Gemma, anger he'd pushed down for the past year and a half, flared up like a brush fire.

"You think I'm crushed that Gemma dumped me?" He moved close enough to bump her, surprising her into stumbling backward. "That I don't care if I live or die? Here's a news flash for you. When Gemma pulled that…when she walked out on me, it was the best day of my life. So I don't need your pity. And I damn well don't have a death wish."

She stared at him steadily. "You don't want to die? Then act like it. Don't pretend this is a big joke. Pay attention and do what I tell you to do."

"I think I've been pretty damn cooperative with your ninja routine. I've stayed behind you. Let you get out of the car first. Went along when you crowded me into the wall when your buddy got off the elevator. Have I complained about any of that?"

"No. Not in the," she glanced at her watch, "four hours I've been on the job." She put her hand on his chest and tried to shove him backward. But he was prepared this time. He braced himself. Held her gaze as he manacled her wrist.

"Maybe, instead of pushing me around, you could try, oh, I don't know, *talking* to me. I'm capable of grasping simple instructions."

"I know you are, Finn." Her voice had softened. She extracted her hand from his grasp, and her soft, delicate skin slid against his like silk. "I don't think you realize how this could go down. A stalker isn't going to look like a crazed person. He or she will look normal. Like anyone else on the street. And bad things happen in a split second. Knives. Guns. Acid. Two hands on your back, shoving you in front of a bus.

"I may not have time to talk. I have to react. Stop the threat. So when you think I'm pushing you around, I'm really talking in shorthand. 'Stop.' 'Stay behind me.' 'Get down.' Sorry if I'm hurting your delicate feelings.

"I don't really care what you think of me. You can dislike me. Resent me. Be angry at me for disrupting your life. I don't give a damn. Let me do my job for the three weeks that you're here, and we're good. Once you're done filming, I can go back to my job. Take the…" She clamped her mouth shut. "Get back into my routine."

Take what? But he was too focused on his pissed-off-ness to ask. "And what if this nut job follows me back to California?" He hadn't meant to say that. The words had just slipped out of his mouth.

"Not my business," she said. "You're my business while you're in Chicago. Once you leave, you're on your own."

"Fine. I'm glad we know where we both stand."

"Me, too." Mia tugged down her jacket and smoothed down her pants. "Let's check the set decoration staff."

Finn's breath sawed in and out. He was jacked up. Wanted to go another round or two with Mia. But she looked unruffled. Serene. As though their argument had rolled off her back like water off a duck.

"You always this good at hiding your feelings?" he asked.

She glanced at him as she started down the hallway. "I know how to keep my private life separate from my job."

"And your feelings are part of your private life?" Again, the words had somehow fallen out of his mouth without conscious thought.

"Damn straight they are." She pointed to a door half-way down the hall. "That's the set decoration office."

"How the hell do you know that?"

"There's a chart on the floor where your meeting was held. I had plenty of time to study it."

She shoved her hand through her hair, disturbing the dark waves. It looked as if she'd done that more than once already this morning.

She was so damn composed. So self-contained. What would it take to agitate her?

The memory of the touch of her hand, sliding through his, made his skin tingle. The scent of her dark mass of hair flowed around him like a drug. Images of her with far less clothing, in a much more private setting, scrolled through his head. He could think of a lot of ways he'd like to agitate her.

He hadn't expected this reaction to Mia. Since Gemma, he'd been a monk. The thought of getting involved with a woman again made him cringe. The day he'd walked out of their house, he'd sworn he wouldn't be that vulnerable ever again.

And here he was, thinking about getting naked with his bodyguard.

Great timing, genius.

He closed his eyes, took a deep breath, and heard the click of a door opening. His eyes flew open, and he saw Mia stepping into one of the offices. He followed her and closed the door.

Reaching behind her, she tugged on his arm until he was beside the door instead of in front of it. As she let him go, a woman walked around the corner in front of him. "Can I help you?" she asked.

Her eyes scrolled to Finn, behind Mia. "Mr. O'Rourke. What can I do for you?"

Show time.

He stepped up beside Mia and threw his arm over her shoulder. The momentary tensing of her muscles wouldn't be visible to the woman standing in front of them, but he felt a stab of satisfaction. She'd felt the undercurrent pulsing beneath their little disagreement, too.

Then she leaned into him. "I'm looking for Ginny," Mia said in that high-pitched, breathless, grating voice. "She works in this department."

The woman's gaze lingered on Finn's arm around Mia's shoulder, then she shifted to Finn's face. "What's her last name?"

"I have no idea," he said coolly. "I think Mia was asking the questions."

The woman flushed and she turned to Mia. "Sorry. What was Ginny's last name?"

"She didn't get a chance to tell me," Mia said. "She was so nice to me when I was waiting for Finn to finish his meeting. I wanted to thank her."

The woman tilted her head. "There are two Ginnys in our department. Ginny Gaugher is here this morning. It must have been her. But she's not in the office right now. She's somewhere else in the building."

"That's too bad," Mia said, pouting a little. "But will you tell her thank you for me?"

"I can do that. Your name was…?"

"Mia." Mia's giggle made Finn want to laugh. Damn, she *was* good. "She'll remember me."

"Okay, Mia. I'll tell her." The woman's face softened. "It was kind of you to stop by."

"Thank you, Ms…" Mia peered at the name badge hanging from a lanyard. "Ms. Laine. I appreciate it."

"You're more than welcome." Ms. Laine's eyes lingered on Finn's arm over Mia's shoulder. "Glad I could help."

"Me, too," Mia said with a bright smile.

Finn opened the door for her and stood to the side as she exited. As soon as the door was closed behind them, she dropped the simpering smirk. "Where do you need to go now?"

"I have a meeting with the wardrobe people next. They want to check the fit of my costume one last time before we start shooting." He shook his head. "They've checked about twenty times already. But, hey, I might have put on ten pounds in the last week. You never know."

"Been eating too much? Drinking too much beer?" she asked, raising one eyebrow.

He began to bristle at her judgmental tone, then he saw the twinkle in her eyes. "Yeah, I've been pigging out," he said, deadpan. "I like being a diva, you know? Making everyone scurry around at the last minute to fix things I've screwed up."

Her gaze moved slowly down his body, lingering at his waist, then back up. Instinct made him suck in a breath. He didn't miss the tiny flicker of amusement that came and went in her gaze.

"Okay. They're letting your costume out. How about after that?"

"Smart ass." He liked that she went toe to toe with him. Liked that she teased him, too. "Script writers are next. That one shouldn't take long. They made a few last minute changes I need to okay."

"You get to do that?" she said, turning to study him. "Okay script changes?"

"Yeah." He shoved his hands into his pockets. "My agent put it in my contract. Because of the recent, ah, situation, I needed to have some control over my lines." He looked away from Mia and stared at the door to the writer's room down the hall. "I want this part. Badly. And I want to be taken seriously. Last thing I want is to have the writers playing with the Gemma crap. Throwing in lines to make the audience smirk about it. It was hard enough to get this part. I don't want lines that will hurt my career more than it's already been damaged."

"You've had a hard time getting parts because of your…thing with Gemma Radley?"

"Yes." He didn't want to discuss it. "So wardrobe first, then the script writers. It'll take about fifteen minutes to make sure the costumes still fit. And less than that to go over my lines and make sure they haven't been changed."

"You've already got your lines memorized?"

"Yeah." He smiled at the surprise in her voice. "You know what you're supposed to do on this job, don't you? You know, how to protect me?"

"Of course. That's my job."

"Well, this is *my* job. And I come prepared."

"Glad to know I'm working with a pro. It'll make my job easier," she said.

He glanced at her again as they walked down the hall. He might not want her here, but once he'd regained control of his temper, he'd realized she was right. She had a job to do, and her job was protecting him. Needling his godfather Doug by getting in Mia's way was only going to hurt Mia.

So he'd do his best to cooperate. And if his fascination with Mia Donovan was growing by leaps and bounds, he'd learn to control it.

Which shouldn't be a problem, since he'd learned a lot about control since he and Gemma had ended. The vindictive Gemma had manipulated their break-up to give her career a huge boost. And tried to crush his beneath the heel of her stiletto boots. But she'd taught him two important lessons.

The first was 'be in control'.

The second was 'don't trust your lover.'

Both of them were burned into his brain.

CHAPTER FIVE

Mia leaned against the wall and tried to figure out what Finn was saying behind the closed door. It should have been easy enough – he'd been yelling for the past ten minutes.

But the walls in the old building – she'd found a plaque describing the place as a former candy factory – were too thick to hear clearly. She could identify Finn's voice, though.

Really? Through those thick walls? After only a few hours with him?

It was part of her job. Nothing more.

He was in with the screenwriters. Half an hour had passed, and, if she had to guess, the script people had made changes he didn't like.

His voice stopped suddenly. No sounds leaked out of the room. She could feel the weight of the silence, even through the walls. She leaned closer to the door, as if that would make it easier to hear through the thick wood.

The moments stretched longer. Tighter. She curled her fingers around the door knob.

Finn had insisted he knew the screenwriters. That he'd

met with them a number of times in the past months. That if one of them was the stalker, they'd had a lot of opportunities to confront him already. But if the quiet in that room continued for another ten seconds, she'd go in and check on him.

Without warning, the door opened and she was yanked forward. As she stumbled, Finn caught her elbow. "Let's go," he barked. "We're done here."

Mia tugged her arm away from Finn's grasp and stepped away from him. She glanced in the room and saw two men and a woman seated at a table. One of the men, a guy with a shaved head and a goatee, grabbed a pen off the table and hurled it across the room. The woman at the table glanced at the pen thrower.

"Are you finished?" she asked calmly. "Or is there something else you want to throw around? Besides your weight?"

"Shut it, Hildy." The guy glared at the woman, and she stared back at him.

"You lost the lines," Hildy said, folding her hands on the table in front of her. "He," she pointed at Finn, "has veto power. Get over it, Andrew." She jerked her head at Finn. "You won, O'Rourke. Now get lost."

"Happy to. And if you try to sneak those lines back into the script overnight, or give them to someone else, I'll call you out in front of Sean, in front of his AD's, in front of the rest of the cast. We clear?"

"As crystal," Hildy said.

"Those were good lines, O'Rourke." Andrew puffed up his chest. "You're destroying that scene by taking them out."

"Maybe so. Maybe not. But they're gone. My contract says I can cut your stupid-ass lines, Owens. And I just did."

Owens opened his mouth to say something, and Hildy waved Finn away. "Get out of our room, Pretty Boy." She shot a look at Mia. "And take your *friend* with you."

"Fuck you, Hildy." Finn slammed the door so hard that

it rattled in its frame. Then he leaned against the wall, closed his eyes and exhaled.

Mia catalogued the red flares on his cheeks and the way his chest rose and fell too fast. His throat rippled once, then again. It didn't take a genius to put together the tell-tale signs of anger. "Bad meeting?" she murmured.

"You have no idea." He opened his eyes and pushed away from the wall. "Hildy was mostly interested in busting everyone's balls. Owens wanted to add some soulfully crappy lines to give the film deep symbolism and make it 'matter'." He swiped quotes in the air. "And Teddy? He'd added some lines that were snide references to the Gemma situation. But he didn't care that I cut them. All he was thinking about was getting out of the meeting so he could snort some blow in the john."

"Wow. Sounds like fun," she said. She glanced at him as she began to walk, pleased when he stayed beside her.

"It was a real laugh riot." His face darkened. "Until Hildy gave me that parting shot."

"Which parting shot was that?"

"You heard her." He scowled down at her. "*Pretty Boy*."

"Really? *That's* what upset you? 'Pretty Boy O'Rourke' is the favorite phrase of every tabloid on the planet. You must be used to it."

"I can ignore the tabloids. When a co-worker does it? Or someone like Hildy, who's posturing instead of listening to what I have to say? It's a declaration of war."

"Why would Hildy want to go to war with you?" Mia slowed down and grabbed Finn's wrist to keep him beside her.

He took another deep breath and matched his strides to hers. "Because I rejected some of *her* line changes, too. Writers are a pain in the ass. Always think every word they write is a perfect gold nugget. God forbid you change one word in a sentence. Which is why my agent put that clause in the contract."

"You must have ESP or something," she said, trying to

lighten the mood.

His shoulders finally relaxed a little. "Nope. I've been in enough films to know how it works. This one is too important to screw up."

"Too important? I thought it was a summer thriller. Good guys, bad guys, chase scenes."

"It is." He stopped and looked down at her. "It's important to *me*. For my career. It was exactly the role I've been waiting for. Which is why I'm not going to let those three clowns screw it up."

"You were very eloquent in your farewell." She bit her lip to hide her smile.

He scowled. "Hildy deserved it."

"So why does the phrase 'Pretty Boy' make you so angry?"

"Because it's saying I got where I am because of my looks and nothing else." His lips tightened. "*Pretty Boy* makes me sound like a no-talent idiot who can only stand around and look pretty."

"You're right. It's ugly and demeaning. Patronizing." She rested her hand on his arm. In solidarity, she realized. "Welcome to a woman's world," she said gently.

He stared at her for a long moment. Apology, and a piercing focus, lingered in his gaze. "Believe me, I know that," he finally said. "I want to shove a bar of soap in my mouth for every thoughtless, dismissive word I ever said to a woman." The anger leached from his expression and he half-smiled. "On the positive side, I've discovered I'm trainable."

"Good to know," she said, resuming walking down the hall. "I'll probably call you a lot of things during the next three weeks, but I promise those words will never pass my lips. Unless you completely cross the line and make me absolutely crazy. Then all bets are off."

"Is that your way of telling me you have a temper?"

"It is." She bit her lip to hide a tiny grin. "And you'd be smart not to test it."

"Now I'm scared."

She heard the hint of a smile in his voice. Thank goodness. She nudged him with her elbow. "You should be."

Maybe she'd teased him out of his foul mood. That's what she'd been going for.

Not because his words had plucked at her heart strings or anything. And what the hell were heart strings, anyway?

No, there was nothing personal about it. If he was all pissed off, he'd be harder to deal with. More stubborn. Less inclined to cooperate.

Teasing him out of his funk would make it easier to do her job.

"So I don't push your buttons and you don't call me Pretty Boy?" There was definitely a hint of humor in his voice.

She glanced up at him. The red had disappeared from his face and instead of a clenched jaw, he was smiling. "Deal," she said.

"You're on." He whipped his phone out of his pocket and stabbed at a key. Moments later, he said, "Pete? We're ready to go. How close are you?"

Finn listened for a moment, then said, "See you then." He turned into the entranceway and stared through the glass door. "He's three minutes away."

"Okay. Then let's wait in the hall." She curled her hand around his upper arm and hauled him away from the large pane of glass that was the front door. Back around the corner, so they were out of sight of anyone passing on the street.

"You touch me a lot," he said.

His voice had deepened. His low tones evoked thoughts of a five o'clock shadow scraping over sensitive skin. The rasp of calloused fingers catching on strands of hair.

She dropped his arm like it was on fire. He raised his other hand, letting his fingers drift over the spot where she'd gripped him. Then he caught her gaze. "Are you always this touchy-feely?"

She was, but he didn't need to know that. "I'm your girlfriend, remember? Can't keep my hands off you." She swallowed the saliva that had pooled in her mouth and forced herself to smirk up at him. "What was it you said? 'Sell the premise, sell the bit?'"

"You're doing a damn good job selling the premise," he muttered.

"Guess I'll rock it in those extras scenes, then," she shot back.

His mouth twitched as he stared down at her. "I predict you'll draw every eye on the set. If you ever get tired of being a cop, you could find acting work."

She had to suppress the shiver of distaste. Pretending to be someone she wasn't? Putting up a façade, letting other people dictate what she could and couldn't do? "No, thanks. I'm a cop. Period." A detective, she reminded herself, if she could keep Finn safe for three weeks.

Before he could reply, two short blasts from a car horn came from in front of the building. "That's Pete," he said. "Let's go."

The sidewalk in front of the studio was deserted, although people turned into the building across the street. A woman exited, holding a cup of coffee, followed by another woman holding coffee. A coffee shop. Good to know there was one close by.

She hurried Finn to the car, watched him slide across the seat, and followed him inside. As Pete pulled away from the curb, he started raising the thick plastic divider between front and rear seats.

Mia leaned forward. "Hold it a moment, Pete. I need your phone number."

"I was kind of surprised you didn't ask for it earlier," he said.

"Yeah. My mistake. I guess my subconscious wasn't too concerned that you'd hurt Finn."

"Shows what your subconscious knows." He jerked his

head in Finn's direction. "I kick his ass regularly. Until he's begging for mercy."

She rested her arm on the divider and glanced at Finn, who was scowling at both of them. "My guess?" she said, biting her lip to keep from smiling. "He asks for it regularly."

"You got that right," the driver said. Pete extended a fist, which she bumped. He turned a corner and waved her back from the divider. "I'm putting up the screen. I don't want to listen to him whine about his meetings."

"Wait," Mia said. "Phone number first."

He rattled it off, she typed it in and read it back to him and hit 'save.' "Thanks, Pete."

As she slid backwards on the seat, the divider rose silently in front of them. The tiny pop of suction when it sealed made the back seat feel like a small cocoon of privacy. No one could see into the car back here. Pete could see them, but she guessed he kept his eyes on the road.

In this tiny, secret world, separated from the real one by smoky glass and sound-proof windows, so many things could happen. Silly things. Crazy things.

She glanced at Finn out of the corner of her eye, remembering the solid feel of his chest. The strength in his hands. The clean, masculine scent that swirled in the air around him.

Sexy things could happen back here.

Feeling heat flush over her skin, Mia pulled the notebook out of her blazer pocket and scribbled some nonsense on a blank page. She used that ruse with suspects when she was trying to unsettle them.

This time, she was trying to settle herself down.

Finn sat beside her, watching the jerky movements of her pen. Did he suspect that the thought of being alone with him in the back of his car was…bothering her? Or did he only see the business-like image she was trying so hard to project?

She'd never know, so she'd kept her head down and

wrote until she was sure she'd wrapped the remnants of her composure around herself. Then, taking a deep breath, she tapped the notebook back into its pocket.

"What's next?" she asked.

"I don't have any meetings for the rest of the day." He stretched his legs out and leaned against the door, watching her. "Let's go to the Art Institute. I've heard it's a world-class museum. I might not have time to see it once filming starts."

"You want to go to the Art Institute?" Her voice rose, and she stared at him, her stomach twisting. So many things could go wrong in a public place. Crowds of people. Finn staring at paintings, not paying attention. Impossible to notice if someone was following them. "It'll be crowded, because it always is. People are going to recognize you. It will be a disaster."

"Nah, it won't. I'll wear my disguise, the one I wore yesterday. It'll be fun." He grinned, as if he were planning a prank. *Or an escape.*

She hated to be the killjoy. The party pooper. And he was right. He was going to be busy for three straight weeks. So why not let him have some fun today?

Because someone was stalking him. It wouldn't be much fun if he ended up getting hurt.

But his stalker couldn't possibly know he'd go to the Art Institute. "All right," she said reluctantly. "I want to say no. I'd rather you went back to your suite. But what the hell. Let's give it a try."

"Thank you," he said quietly. "I promise to behave myself."

She wasn't the only one who was trapped by this assignment, she realized. He was equally imprisoned. He couldn't go anywhere by himself. He had a stranger living with him, constantly telling him what to do, scrutinizing his every move.

She'd feel suffocated. Like she was caught in a cobweb and couldn't tear herself free of its sticky threads. After a few days, she'd be foaming at the mouth with the need to get away.

"Have Pete swing by the hotel. He can go to your room and grab your disguise. Tell him to put it in a bag so no one can see what he's carrying. You can change in the car."

His whole face lit up. "I think I'm in love."

"I think you're out of your mind," she muttered.

***

Two hours later, they still hadn't been spotted. His baggy khakis, ridiculous plaid shirt and scuffed running shoes made him look like a suburban father. The ball cap he'd pulled low over his forehead hid the upper half of his face. And the big, black-framed glasses gave him an owlish look. Even Mia was forced to admit his disguise was a good one.

He'd moved smoothly from one painting to the next, not lingering too long in front of any of them. Until they got to Edward Hopper's 'Nighthawks.' He stared at it for a long time. Mia glanced around, saw a few people smiling at his absorption with the painting, and she grabbed his hand. Tugged him toward the next room.

"Hey," he said. "I wasn't done looking at that."

"Yes, you were," she said grimly. "You're drawing a crowd." And, based on the excited hum of the voices behind them, she was afraid someone in the group had recognized him.

He glanced over his shoulder one last time before he turned into the next room. "I like that painting. The idea of being invisible. I was looking forward to seeing it."

"And you just did. Time to move on."

"Haven't you ever thought about being invisible?" he asked.

"I mostly am," she said. When she was in uniform, she was a cop. That was all. And when she wasn't? She drew her share of attention, but it was easy to ignore.

"I'm never invisible. And sometimes, it would be nice. Like those people in 'Nighthawks.' No one caring who you are or what you're doing. Able to sit anywhere you like."

"You say that now," she said lightly. "But you wouldn't have gone into acting if you didn't want to be noticed. You'd probably wither up and die without attention."

One corner of his mouth quirked up. "Yeah, probably. Eventually. But once in a while, anonymity would be a gift."

"I don't think you can have it both ways," she said.

"Then maybe I'll have to get an invisibility cloak. Like in the Harry Potter books."

"You read them?"

"Of course I did. They were great books. Well-written." He narrowed his eyes. "Why do you sound so shocked?"

She lifted one shoulder. "Hard to imagine you reading a book, I guess."

They'd moved back into the flow of traffic, but he stopped dead. Several people shot them dirty looks as they eased past them. One studied them as he passed. Mia moved closer to Finn. "Officer Donovan, are you implying that I'm a lightweight? That I don't *read*? I'm horrified."

"Stop it. People are watching."

"Let them. All they'll see is a sloppy guy with thick glasses and a ball cap on his head."

"Sooner or later, someone's going to recognize you," she whispered through clenched teeth. She suspected someone already had. "Especially if everyone's looking at you because you're blocking their way."

"People see what they expect to see," he retorted. "Right now, they see a nerdy guy having a fight with his girlfriend. That's all. Why would they think that guy is Finn O'Rourke?"

"Because you are far more beautiful than the usual nerdy guy who wanders around the art museum. Believe me, they'll look twice."

Instead of arguing further, Finn grabbed her hand, intertwined their fingers and started moving again. "You think I'm beautiful, huh?" He grinned down at her. "Nice to know, Officer. And just for the record? You're not so bad yourself."

CHAPTER SIX

Finn watched Mia sputter, red-faced. His grin widened, and he turned his head so she wouldn't see his smile.

He'd flustered her. Finally.

He'd been tossing out little innuendos all morning. Crossing the line for a moment, then stepping back. She'd been so cool. So unflappable. So in control, that he couldn't help himself. He wanted a glimpse of the real woman hiding behind that façade.

The unruffled way she'd deflected his every effort had made him try even harder.

And him? *He'd* been flustered since the moment he opened the door and found her on the other side. She'd walked into his room like she owned it, and her poise and confidence had intrigued him immediately. So had her lack of reaction to him.

Most women were a little star struck when they met him. A little rattled. And yeah, it made him a jerk to notice that, but it was true.

Since she'd walked into his hotel suite, he'd been trying to figure out what made her tick. And her apparent immunity to his charm had only sharpened the challenge.

He'd been determined to crack her self-control.

Sometime during the day, trying to get a rise out of her had turned into awareness. Then attraction.

At some point, he'd found himself leaning close to her, savoring her scent, focusing too much on the touch of her hands on his skin. When he realized what he was doing, it had taken all his acting skills to pretend to be unaffected. To hide his interest, he'd yanked her chain even harder.

Now, walking down the high-ceilinged corridors of the Art Institute, she was as unsure, as awkward, as he'd felt all day. He intended to milk every moment of it.

Maybe she wasn't as immune to him as she pretended to be.

"So," he said, gripping her hand more tightly. "Beautiful, huh?"

Her shoulders snapped back. She took a deep breath. And when she glanced at him, her eyes were unreadable again. "Fishing for compliments, O'Rourke?" She snorted. "You see yourself in the mirror every day. You know what you look like. That's all I was saying."

"And here I thought it was personal. That *you* thought I was beautiful."

"Of course I think you're attractive. A woman would have to be blind not to notice how you look." Her eyes were as cool as her voice when she glanced at him. "But beauty isn't everything. Other stuff is more important to me."

"Such as?"

She didn't hesitate. "A sense of humor. Honesty. Integrity. They're all more important than good genes." She glanced at him again. "So is honor."

It felt as if she'd punched him in the gut. "Are you implying I lack those qualities?" His voice went flat. He'd thought Mia might be different from the millions of people who'd already judged him.

"Not at all," she answered, no hesitation in her voice. "I don't know you well enough to speculate." She glanced at him out of the corner of her eye and slid her hand away from his. "But I'm betting I will by the end of the next three weeks."

"You think so?" He glanced at her again. "You think you'll know everything about me by the time this job's over?"

"Of course not. No one ever knows everything about another person, even when they've been in an intimate relationship for years." She slowed her pace and studied him for a long moment. "I'm living with you for the next three weeks. Twenty-four seven. Nowhere you can go to escape me. Nowhere I can hide from you. So, yeah. I'm guessing we'll know each other pretty well by then. The important stuff, anyway."

Finn grabbed for her hand again, trying not to think of all the ways he'd like to get better acquainted in the coming weeks. "I guess we'll find out, won't we?"

She tried to pull her hand away, but he tightened his grip. "Don't forget: selling the premise here, Officer," he said, no longer teasing. "So you need to look smitten."

He looked down the long corridor and his mouth tightened. "There's an official-looking woman coming toward us. Staring at me. And not in a good way."

Without looking for the woman, Mia's face softened into the silly, giggly girl she'd been at the studio. "How close?" she asked. The fingers of her right hand fluttered around the bottom of her jacket, as if she was trying to straighten it. He already knew better than that.

"Ten feet."

"Right." He felt her draw in a deep breath. The woman was five feet away now.

She turned into him, so that her right arm was in front of her body. "Oh, baby," she said in a high, breathless voice. "When you're so close to me, it's hard for me to walk straight. Are you trying to sweep me off my feet?"

He bit his lip to keep from laughing out loud. Instead, he bent his head closer to hers. "Of course I am," he breathed into her ear. "Is it working?"

Her sudden, tiny gasp had him tightening his grip on her hand. He moved closer, until his hip was bumping hers.

"Definitely," she murmured. Her low voice rippled over his skin like a caress and made him shiver. "That woman is buying us, hook, line and sinker."

He was an idiot. Mia was playing her role. Nothing more. But she'd worked him up. So as the woman got closer, he bent and nibbled on Mia's ear. "Good. Here's more for her to look at."

He trailed his mouth down her throat, lingering at her collarbone. He'd meant for it to be quick. Marking his territory and nothing more. But the taste of her skin was intoxicating. Sweet. Complex.

Addictive.

She shivered beneath his mouth, tightening her fingers around his. Then eased away from him as the woman moved into their space.

"Excuse me," the woman said. Her low voice was barely above a whisper, and her gaze darted from him to Mia and back again. "I'm Jennifer Barkley, with museum security. Are you...are you Finn O'Rourke?"

"Why do you think so?" he asked calmly. People approached him constantly, asking the same thing. He'd found if he answered with another question, it rattled them. Usually made them back off.

"Because there was a tweet at #ArtInstituteChicago. Someone said they saw you here." Her glance touched on Mia. "With a...friend. I'd like to get you out of here before we have a scene we can't control."

"Damn it," he said lightly, cursing much more viciously in his head. "I guess no one's safe from Twitter these days."

"We monitor that hashtag pretty closely," Jennifer said. "It's good to have a heads-up before potentially disruptive events get out of hand."

"Never considered myself a potentially disruptive event," he said lightly. "But I understand you don't want a scene at the museum. Hard to keep all these paintings safe."

"Yes. Exactly." The woman exhaled. "If you and your friend would come with me, I'll take you to a room where you can wait while we arrange transport for you."

"You mean a getaway car, don't you?" Finn said, forcing himself to smile. "I already have one. Lead the way and I'll call our driver."

Finn heard whispers behind him as they followed the navy-blue-suited woman to a door in the corner of one of the galleries. He didn't turn around, but Mia craned her head to look behind them. She huddled closer, making it look as if she was uneasy. The soft weight of her against his side, the scent of her skin, had him pulling her closer.

She'd shoved her right hand into the pocket of her pants. Beneath her jacket. So it would be close to her gun, he realized.

"Here we go," Barkley said, opening the door. They stepped into what looked like a break room. Two round tables with chairs filled most of the space, with a coffee maker sitting on the counter that lined one wall. There was also a plug-in kettle. For making tea, he assumed. A refrigerator sat in the corner at the end of the counter.

A couple of magazines littered the table. One of them, Finn saw, had *Dark Avenger* on the cover. So a national news magazine was letting the whole world know they were filming in Chicago.

"We appreciate your quick action, Ms. Barkley," he said, smiling at her. "I'll call my driver and have him pick us up."

"Thank you," she said quietly. "The Monroe Street door is the closest one." She swallowed once, but kept her gaze on him. "I hate to cut short your visit, especially since you went to the trouble to…to try to hide your identity. But with that tweet out there, people will be looking for you. It would be uncomfortable for you and a security issue for us."

"I understand." He glanced down at Mia. "I know you're disappointed, honey, but we'll come back another time."

"It's okay, baby," Mia said in that high, breathless voice as her gaze scanned the room. "We saw a lot of art today."

God, how did she *do* that? Sound like an airhead while she took in every detail of the room and the woman standing in front of them.

He pulled his phone out of his pocket and punched a number. "We're ready to go," he said to Pete. "Monroe Street door. The one across from Millenium Park."

"You got it, boss. Be there in five."

"See you then."

Finn slid the phone into his pocket. "He'll be here in five minutes."

Jennifer Barkley twisted her hands together. "Thank you for being so understanding, Mr. O'Rourke. I appreciate it." She studied him for a moment, then smiled. "And for the record? I wouldn't have recognized you. Nice job on the disguise."

"Thanks," he said easily. "Now if you can tell us how to get to the exit?"

"Follow me."

***

Sitting in the back of the car, waiting for Pete to find a break in traffic so he could pull away from the curb, Finn slumped against the seat. Waves of people flowed past on the sidewalk, going wherever they wanted to go. More people sauntered through the park across the street, winding through the gardens and rows of trees. Couples strolled down the paths, holding hands, and parents chased their children over the grass in the pavilion area.

On a beautiful, sunny day, with an intriguing park spread out in front of him and a fascinating woman on the seat beside him, he wanted to be free, too. He wanted to be just another face in a crowd.

He'd chosen this life. Chosen to be an actor, a person who was always on stage, even in his private life. Most of the time, he loved his job. Loved disappearing into a character, bringing him to life on the screen.

But there were days when he hated living under a microscope.

Today was one of them.

He wished he could pull Mia out of the car and wander through the park with her. Hold her hand, even if it was only pretend, and watch her face as she studied the crowds. Looking for an anomaly, for someone watching them.

Hell, he'd gladly exchange the risk of a confrontation with a crazy stalker for the pleasure of that park on this warm, sunny day.

Instead, they'd spend the rest of this gorgeous day inside. It would be a long frigging day, hanging around the suite at the Drake, watching the beautiful weather through a window.

Mia moved on the seat next to him, and he tore his gaze away from the inviting park to glance over at her as the car slipped smoothly into the stream of traffic.

She was studying him, and her eyes looked sad. For him? "Sorry we had to cut the visit short," Mia said quietly. "I was having fun, and it looked as if you were, too."

"Yeah, I was. It's been years since I was there. Before they added that new contemporary wing." He slumped on the seat. "What gave me away? How did someone spot me?"

"My guess? The way you walk."

"Really?"

She shrugged. "It's easy to disguise your appearance, and you did a good job with that. A little harder to disguise your voice, but you're an actor. You'd know how to do that, too. But your walk? Your gait? Pretty hard to change, especially when you're not thinking about it. And if someone recognized your gait, they would have seen through the rest of your disguise."

"So you're saying I should pull a Chester from Gunsmoke. Limp from now on?"

"Of course not." She smiled. A genuine one, because her eyes smiled, too. "That would draw attention." She shrugged. "I don't have a solution."

"Some girlfriend you are. Not telling me what to do."

Her smile morphed into a laugh. "Oh, I can do that. Not sure you'd like it, though."

The car turned onto Michigan Avenue, then stopped again in traffic. They were right in front of what looked like a fountain. Two pillars stood on either end of a cement surface. Little kids splashed in the inch or so of water that streamed over the pavement. A handful of adults, too. The pillars displayed faces that changed every few seconds. A bunch of older kids stood next to the pillars. Tensed, as if they were waiting.

"What is that?" he asked. "And where does the water come from?"

"Just watch," Mia said, leaning around him to look.

Suddenly, the mouths on the faces opened and water poured out of them. Even in the car, he heard the kids squealing.

That looked like fun. He'd like to splash in that water, too. Slog around and get his feet wet.

He watched until the pillars were out of sight, then turned around again. Mia touched his hand. "You want to check out this park, don't you?"

"Yeah. It wasn't here last time I was in Chicago. But I know we can't. Security issues, blah blah blah."

She shifted on the seat so she faced him. "I'm not trying to keep you a prisoner," she said. She lifted one hand, then let it fall into her lap. Had she intended to touch him again? Comfort him?

"I know. It's your job. I get it."

Mia glanced past his shoulder as the park disappeared behind them. Then her gaze snapped back to him. "Did Pete tell anyone where we were going?"

"Nope. That's part of our deal. He doesn't tell anyone. Not even my mother, if she calls. Until he's dropped me off at home. Then I don't care who he tells."

She bit her lip as she studied him. "This is probably a mistake," she said slowly. "But it's your last free day for three weeks. You want to check out the park?"

He shot up in his seat and reached for her hand without thinking. "Are you serious?"

"Yeah, I am." She squeezed his fingers, then gently eased her hand away. "We're not going to eat at the restaurant or sit around in one place, but we can wander through the park. Grab a hot dog from a cart. Check out the garden."

He leaned back to get a better look at her. "What happened to the woman who walked around the studio with her hand on her gun?"

A faint blush stained her cheeks. "A lot of people knew you were going to be there. A determined stalker could have found out fairly easily. So I needed to be ready for anything. But going to the Art Institute was last minute. No one knew in advance."

She shrugged. "We took a chance and someone spotted you. I'm actually kind of surprised it took as long as it did. There weren't huge crowds. People had more time to see everyone around them. And we weren't constantly moving."

Her mouth curled into a tiny grin. "Besides, all the people who saw the tweet will be looking for you there. So we can take a chance on the park. As long as Pete stays close." She nodded her head at him and her smile widened. "Our getaway driver."

"Hell, yes. Let's do it." He rapped on the window that divided them from Pete. When it lowered, he leaned forward. "Hey, Pete, we're going to take a walk through the park. Can you drop us off somewhere? Then stick close, in case we're busted?"

Peter rolled to a stop at a red light, then glanced over his shoulder. "You okay with that, Mia?"

"Yeah. I'm willing to give it a try."

Finn scowled. They were talking around him like they were the adults and he was the reckless kid. "It was *her* idea, Pete. So don't start with the 'Finn is so irresponsible' shit."

Pete raised his eyebrows. "You telling me *Mia*, the woman with the gun, is the irresponsible one? And you're not nervous about that?"

"Just drop us off at the park, Pete," he sighed. "Keep the editorial comments to yourself."

Mia leaned forward. "If I think there's a problem, we'll call." She patted Finn's leg absently. All his muscles clenched. All the way to hallelujah and back. "It's sweet of you to worry, Pete, but I think we'll be fine."

Sweet of him to worry? Finn stared at the side of Pete's head and saw a tell-tale flush on his cheek. "Are you worried about me, old man?"

"Only about losing my paycheck if someone blows you away."

Finn tapped Pete's shoulder as the car rolled to a stop at the curb. "I'll call my attorney and put you in my will," he told his friend. He already had, but Pete didn't need to know that.

"Smart ass," Pete muttered. "We're blocking traffic. Get out of the car before people start gawking."

His good humor restored by getting the last word with Pete, Finn stepped out of the car and held his hand for Mia. She scowled at him, but he wasn't about to let her exit the car into traffic.

Ignoring his hand, she stepped onto the sidewalk and slammed the door a little too hard. Pete pulled away immediately. "What did I tell you about getting out of the car first?"

"Come on, Mia. Don't you think it would look odd if you got out into traffic instead of following me onto the sidewalk?"

She stared at him for a long moment, then exhaled. "Yeah, you're right. Sorry. I was having second thoughts about agreeing to this."

"Don't." He grabbed her hand and dragged her toward the main area of the park. It was kind of pathetic that he felt like a kid who'd been given the keys to Disneyland. But he got to walk around in a park on a gorgeous day with a beautiful, intriguing woman. No one knew they were here. What could go wrong?

CHAPTER SEVEN

The sun beat down on Mia's back, making her uncomfortably warm in the dark jacket. She pushed up the sleeves, told herself they wouldn't be here for long.

They shouldn't be here at all. She shouldn't have given in to the wistful, slightly sad expression on Finn's face as they drove past Millenium Park. But, like a sap, she'd suggested they stop. So she'd make the best of it.

Millenium Park was crowded for a week-day, but it usually was during the spring and summer. On the positive side, there were so many people that no one looked at them twice. They were just another couple, strolling through the park on a late lunch break.

Finn's ridiculous disguise was working. If 'adorable geek' was what he'd been going for, he'd hit it out of the park. Very few people would look at those baggy, shapeless khakis and think 'movie star'.

"Have you ever seen the Bean?" she asked, nodding at the curving, reflective sculpture that resembled a coffee bean.

"Nope." He studied the sleek, smooth shape of the Bean. "It's pretty cool."

They wandered around it and through it, laughing at the distorted images of themselves in the mirror-like surface. Chicago's skyline was reflected in the background. He pulled out his phone and took a selfie of them, the skyline behind them, and she stuck her tongue out at the last moment.

"Now we have to do it again, Officer," he murmured into her ear. He was close enough that she could smell the soap he'd used this morning. Close enough to feel the heat prickling from his skin. His breath stirred the fine hairs on her nape, and an electric shock buzzed through her veins.

He slid his arm around her waist and pulled her tight against his side. "You look kind of dazed. Is the heat bothering you?"

"You could say that," she muttered.

He slid his hand up and down her arm, and she felt his touch through the heavy fabric. "Shouldn't have worn a dark jacket."

She managed to gather her wits enough to snark, "This from the guy who looks as if his mother dressed him."

She felt him smile. "Exactly what I was going for." She heard the click of the camera on his phone. "Got a good one," he announced. "You look all soft and cuddly."

She detached herself from his side and reached for his phone. "Give me that," she ordered. "I am *not* soft and cuddly. Ever." She was a cop, for God's sake.

Instead of handing her the phone, he tapped it into his pocket. "Nope. Not letting you delete that." He grabbed her hand and tugged her away from the Bean. "I saw a hot dog cart behind this thing. I'm starving."

An hour later, they were lingering in the garden plots. They should be calling Pete for a pick-up, but the weather was perfect. One of those rare, late spring days when the humidity was low, the wind was soft, and the air was perfumed with the scent of flowering trees.

She'd been watching carefully as they wandered along the paths through the flower garden. A number of people had glanced at them, then dismissed them as just another couple enjoying the park.

A few women had frowned, as if somewhere in their brain, they'd recognized Finn but couldn't place him. No one had stopped them, although one woman stared longer than the others. But when Mia had glanced over her shoulder, that woman had turned away, as well.

Her fingers and Finn's had been entwined since they'd finished their hot dogs. Her palms were sweaty, and so were his, but neither of them released their grip.

It was good cover, she told herself. No one would be looking for Finn O'Rourke as part of a couple. People who followed celebrity news knew who was dating, who had recently broken up, and who'd been single for a while. Finn was firmly in the single category.

According to all reports, he hadn't been mentioned with a woman since his break-up with Gemma.

Not that she'd sat for hours in front of her computer, googling Finn O'Rourke. But some research had been necessary. To get a sense of who he was.

They exited the last row of garden paths, and as they turned the corner, she caught a glimpse of a woman behind them. It was the woman who'd watched them for a little too long.

She tugged on Finn's hand. They'd been in the park for more than an hour. "I think it's time we called Pete and got out of here," she said.

"Not yet. It's too nice to sit in a hotel room all afternoon."

He was right. It would be a waste of a perfect day to spend it inside. But she didn't have a choice. "The last woman who stared at you?" she said in a low voice. "I think she's following us. We need to go."

He nodded. To his credit, he didn't glance over his shoulder. "Okay. It's been great. But I get it. I'll call Pete."

As he fumbled his phone out of his pocket, they turned toward the Pritzker Pavilion, the park's concert venue, and she caught another glimpse of the woman. Walking in the opposite direction.

Mia let her shoulders relax as they continued to walk. "Ten minutes?" he said. "Okay. We'll head that way."

"There's a huge line at the cashier in the parking garage," he told Mia.

"I think that'll be okay. She went the other way."

As they got closer to the pavilion, classical music suddenly poured from the speakers suspended above the lawn. They turned at the same time to look.

"Oh, my God," Finn said, studying the pavilion. "Frank Gehry designed this, didn't he?"

"Yeah." Mia stared at him, surprised. "You recognize it?"

"No. But it looks like his work."

She studied him, intrigued by the peek behind the shallow celebrity front the rest of the world saw. "You know architecture?"

"That was going to be my fallback career. I gave myself five years to make a living at acting. If I didn't? Architecture school."

"Wow. Hidden depths."

"Yep." His gaze swept down her body, then back up. "I'd like to see yours, too."

"Ass." She rolled her eyes as she elbowed him.

Finn grinned. "There's an orchestra playing in there. Let's go listen."

"Probably the Chicago Symphony." Mia began walking, letting Finn tug her along. He'd been staring at the stage, his whole face smiling. "They practice there in the afternoon sometimes. Before a performance."

"Let's walk past them," he said, herding her toward the stage.

It was on the way to their meeting place with Pete. Kind of, anyway. "Yeah. Okay."

A minute later, they were standing next to the wall on the left side of the stage. People were scattered in the seats in front of the orchestra, enjoying the impromptu concert. As they listened, Mia let her gaze wander over the crowd. She froze when she spotted the woman who'd followed them earlier. She had a camera in her hand, a camera-carrying friend beside her, and they were heading right for Mia and Finn.

"I think we've been made," she said quietly. "Two women, on our right, heading toward us."

He glanced at them without moving his head. "I see them."

"Through that door." Mia nodded toward the door closer to the stage, holding a sign for the restrooms. She tried to remember the floorplan, but it had been a few years since she'd been to the park. "I'm pretty sure there's another way out."

Finn wrapped his arm around her shoulders, and they walked a little too fast toward the doors. Once inside, they hurried down a small ramp and found themselves in a corridor with the restrooms and a set of ascending stairs.

"Those stairs lead to the park next to the pavilion," she said, recognizing where they were. "Go up."

They ran up the steps and burst into the sunlight again. Mia blinked, letting her eyes adjust to the brightness. The path that led to their pick-up spot was straight ahead. But she didn't want to take it. If the women had followed them, she and Finn would be out in the open. Vulnerable.

The women were probably just fans, judging by the way they were clutching cameras. But two people squealing, holding cameras, were a magnet for other curious people. Better to avoid that scene if possible.

"Behind the Pavilion," she said, pointing toward their right.

As they hurried around the curved back of the Pavilion, they passed a couple on a blanket, making out. A little further on, another couple was pressed against the metal of the band shell, mouths clinging and hands roaming.

"Looks like we've found Lover's Lane," Finn muttered.

"Who knew?" she whispered back.

The couple against the metal broke their kiss and stared at her and Finn. She continued along the curve of the building, then pulled him against the side. "Pretend like you're kissing me," she said. "So they stop watching us and get back to what they were doing."

Finn eased her against the cool metal of the pavilion, then bent his head closer. His eyes were the clear, rich green of moss in a sun-dappled forest. Sunlight glinted off his honey-colored hair, making the lighter streaks stand out. His scent swirled around her, something that smelled of the ocean, mixed with the clean, musky sweat of a warm day.

"Should I actually kiss you?" he murmured into her ear. "Like I mean it? Or do you want me to nibble at your neck and your ear? Play with you, get you worked up a little, before moving on to the main event?"

The metal against her back must not be as cool as she'd thought, because heat swept over her. "Whatever's going to make that other couple stop watching us."

"So I shouldn't bring my A game, then." He bent closer, his breath tickling her ear. She held her breath. But his lips barely touched her.

"Why...why not your A game?" God! She wasn't sure if his mouth even touched her neck and she was having trouble stringing her words together.

"'Cause then they'd watch. Looking for tips, you know? From a master."

She wanted to shove him away, but found her hands tangled in his shirt instead. "You are such a jerk. An arrogant, conceited a...ass." She inhaled on a gasp as he tugged on her earlobe.

"Relax, Mia," he murmured, his mouth too close to her neck. "Not doing my best work here. Nothing to get all," he sucked gently at a tendon in her neck, "excited about."

She was *trembling*. From barely more than the brush of his lips. He'd broken down her defenses with only his breath on her neck and his low, intoxicating words. She'd surrendered to him with nothing more than a whimper.

Time to bring *her* A game.

Letting go of his shirt, she slid her arms around his waist. Played with the waistband of his ridiculous khakis. His loose belt left plenty of room to slide one finger beneath the fabric of his pants.

He stilled, his mouth unmoving on her neck. Ignoring the urge to tell him to *do that again*, she slid the rest of her hand beneath his waistband. Then her other hand.

Maybe she'd been too quick to dismiss these baggy pants.

His shorts were silky soft beneath her fingertips. She slid her hands lower and cupped his muscular ass. The ass she'd noticed this morning, nicely displayed by his jeans. Squeezing gently, she pressed herself closer.

Smiled against his skin. She'd managed to shut him up. He wasn't being so cocky now.

Except in the good way. She pressed closer, humming into his neck. The pressure of him, right where she needed it, sent dark pulses of arousal shooting through her veins and strummed every nerve. The only sounds he made were tiny gasps when her hands drifted lower on his rear.

Then he came to life. "Okay," he growled into her ear. "*A* game it is."

He slid his hands up her back, interrupting her 'getting to know you' visit with his ass. Then, fisting one hand in her hair, he tipped her head back and closed his mouth over hers.

He wasn't gentle, or tender, or sweet. He sucked on her lower lip until she opened with a gasp, then swept his tongue over the sensitive inside surface. He tasted tart and lemony, with the sweetness buried deep, like the lemonade they'd had earlier. His tongue stroked hers lazily, but his hips rocked against hers in a matching rhythm. One of them moaned. It might have been her.

As he kissed her, his hand shifted from her hair to her back, pressing her tight against him. His other hand drifted lower, learning the curves of her rear. Dancing too close to dangerous ground. She felt his smile when her tiny murmur of need escaped into his mouth. Vibrated between them.

"You like games, Mia?" His voice was dark with desire, and he closed his teeth around her lower lip and tugged. "I like games myself." He slid his hand beneath her jacket and tugged hard on her shirt. Pulled the tails out of her pants.

She jerked when his warm hand slid over her bare back. His fingertips were slightly callused, and their rasp against her skin had her swallowing another moan.

She surged into him, needing to be closer. She grabbed his shirt again, sending the buttons flying so she could feel his bare skin against hers.

He shuddered against her, then eased his mouth away from hers. Brought his hands around and grabbed her hands, moved them away from his shirt. Pressed tiny kisses down her neck, sucked gently on her collarbones, dipped his tongue into the hollow between them.

Then rested his forehead against hers. "Wow," he whispered.

What the hell had she done? She'd let herself get lost in that...that distraction. Let herself think it was real. Lost all sense of her surroundings. Ten stalkers could have been closing in on them, and she wouldn't have known.

She pushed him away, hard. As he stumbled backward, she tucked her shirt back into her pants. Adjusted her jacket. Put a hand to her mouth.

To wipe away his taste?

Or to hold it closer?

She closed her eyes and shook her head to clear it.

"Good distraction," she managed to say. "Looks like it worked. I don't see those two women."

Finn smoothed down the lapels of her jacket, spread his hand over her abdomen for a long moment. Then he took her hand and twined their fingers together.

The fine tremor of his hand twitched against hers, and she tightened her grip on him. At least she wasn't the only one whose hands were shaking.

"What are we going to do about this, Mia?" he murmured.

"Do about what?" She needed a moment to get her brain working again.

"This polite, rational discussion we just had. Jesus, Mia, what do you think?"

"It wasn't real. It was a ruse. A way to hide from the women following us."

"Not real? Really?" He spun her around to face him. "I didn't think you were a coward, Mia Donovan. Yeah, whatever it was that exploded between us surprised the hell out of me, too. But that…that kiss was as real as it gets."

"We'll talk about this later." When she had time to settle herself down. Think up a reasonable explanation. "Right now, we need to find Pete and get out of here."

"You're right. This isn't the place to have this discussion." He surged forward, hurrying past the couple on the blanket at the end of the pavilion and towing her along behind him.

When they burst out from the space at the back of the pavilion, some of the blood had returned to her brain. She yanked on his arm, muttering, "Slow down. Running like that, everyone's going to look at us."

He eased into a trot, then slowed to a walk. Mia couldn't look at him. She searched the street for Pete's car, finding it idling at the curb. The car behind Pete's, stopped because the traffic had hemmed him in, laid on his horn. Pete's car didn't budge.

Mia wasn't even scanning the crowd. All she wanted was the relative safety of the car. She began walking faster, and Finn wrapped his arm around her shoulders.

"Slow down," he said, his voice softer than she'd expected it to be. "It's not the end of the world. So we made out a little. We had a good reason."

She could allow herself to believe that, but the truth was, that 'good reason' had been smoldering between them all morning. The explosion when they'd finally come together had blown reason to bits.

When they reached the car, she yanked open the door and practically pushed Finn inside. Then she got in behind him, slammed the door and told Pete, "Move."

Pete glanced over the seat at them and, without saying a word, raised the partition between them.

Leaving Mia alone with Finn in that little bubble of privacy.

Day one of this assignment. Her professionalism shot to hell.

It was going to be a long three weeks.

CHAPTER EIGHT

The heavy thud of the car door slamming vibrated through the car and echoed the hard thump of his heart against his ribs. What the hell had just happened?

His body still coiled tight with arousal, Finn tried to steady himself, flexing his fingers as he sat behind Pete. At the other end of the bench seat, Mia stared at her lap, her hands gripping her knees. Her deep, ragged breaths filled the silence in the idling car. She was fighting to regain control, as well.

He shouldn't have looked at her. Should have clamped his hands over his ears to stop the sound of her rapid breathing.

Knowing she was struggling, too, was *so* not helping.

He could slide over to her, cup her face in his hands and continue the kiss that had been interrupted. His body was screaming at him to do just that. And, guessing by the way she huddled in the corner of the car, eyes closed, back rigidly straight, her body was telling her the same thing.

Not here.

Not in the car, in front of Pete. When they only had a short drive to get to the hotel. He wanted far more time than that with Mia.

So he ran through yesterday's baseball box scores in his head. Called up an image of his seventh-grade science teacher, the one with the mole on the side of her nose and bad breath. Imagined his mother's reaction if she found out he wanted to sleep with his bodyguard.

No. That wouldn't help. His mother would adore Mia. Mia was sexy, smart and wouldn't take Finn's shit.

Even better, she wasn't from Hollywood. Had no ties to show business. His mother would be cheering him on.

He shifted on the seat, closing his eyes. He had to get out of this car and walk into the hotel. Soon. He needed to be in control by then.

He called up that final scene with Gemma. Pictured what he'd seen. The words they'd thrown at each other. The secret, shameful relief he'd felt.

He took another, steadier breath. Yeah. Thinking about Gemma? A mental cold shower. Worked a lot faster than a real one.

Pete finally pulled away from the curb, and in moments, Millenium Park disappeared behind them. Thank God. He loved Frank Gehry's work, but he didn't need to see that bandshell again today. The sight of it would set off a stream of memories of what they'd done against the steel back of the damned Pritzker Pavilion.

Set off more than memories.

Mia cleared her throat from the other side of the car. "What are your plans for the rest of the day?" Her voice sounded a little lower than normal. A little throaty. She hadn't looked at him.

A picture of her, eyes closed, pressed against the smooth steel of the bandshell, hidden from the crowds, flashed in front of him. The memories he'd been trying to suppress rose to the surface. Refused to go away.

The dark, spicy taste of her, kissing him as desperately as he'd been kissing her, lingered in his mouth.

The feel of her hands, slipping inside the waistband of

his pants, made him curl his fingers into his palms.

His 'think about anything but Mia' program wasn't working.

"No plans." He wanted to fall with her onto that huge bed in his room. Spend the rest of the day and all night making love with her. "I'll probably go over my script. There will be phone calls. Nothing exciting."

"Okay. Day's been pretty ex…" She sucked in a breath and her face turned red.

Too late. He had no trouble filling in the blanks.

He cleared his throat. "Yeah. Boring rest of the day," he said.

"Good. Boring is good." She took a deep breath, let it out slowly. "I'll have some questions for you. We can talk whenever it's convenient."

"Okay. Yeah. Um, after we get back in the room. We'll talk then."

"Great." She didn't look at him. Instead, she pulled out her notebook and began making notes. Was she actually capable of thinking rationally right now? Or was she doing a masterful acting job?

"What are you writing, Officer?"

Her throat rippled once. Then again. "Making a list of questions I need to ask you," she said without looking up.

"About what happened at the park today?"

Her hand froze, and her knuckles turned white around the pen. "No." She lifted her head and finally looked at him. "I know exactly what happened at the park today. We saw the Bean. Ate a hot dog. Drank some lemonade. Walked through the gardens. Had to hide from a couple of fans who'd spotted you. Typical bodyguard stuff."

"'Hiding from my fans'? That's what you're going with? You were just doing your job?" He narrowed his eyes. Her voice had gotten steadier as she went through the list. Until the last one. Then it had wobbled a little.

Which was good. She was trying hard to hide it, but Mia was as rattled as he was. As off-balance.

He wanted her to stay that way. He was pretty sure it had been as real for Mia as it was for him. But after Gemma, he didn't trust his instincts.

If she was off-balance, maybe he could surprise some honest answers out of her.

The car stopped with a tiny jerk. They were back at the loading dock at the hotel. They'd left only that morning, but Finn's universe had tilted in the past eight hours.

Before Finn could right himself, Pete had opened Mia's door, then come around and opened Finn's. "I'm not sure if we'll need the car later today, Pete. I'll let you know."

"You got it, boss."

Pete closed the car doors, then backed the car out and disappeared around the corner.

Leaving Finn and Mia alone.

He turned and walked toward Mia, who held the heavy hotel door open. They kept at least a foot between them, enough that no body parts could accidentally touch. Like a pair of boxers after the gong sounded, they went to opposite corners when they stepped into the elevator.

Mia squared her shoulders as the elevator approached their floor, then stepped out quickly when the doors opened. Following her, Finn saw that the hall was empty. Of course it was. Tourists would be outside, enjoying the city. Business people would be at work.

He slid the key card into its slot and opened the door, letting Mia enter first. She walked from room to room, checking the closets, the bathrooms, under the furniture. As she knelt beside the couch, the black fabric of her pants clung to her ass, reminding him again how it had felt beneath his hands.

He began to reach for her again, then snatched his hands away and headed for the minibar. "You want a drink?"

"Iced tea would be great," she said, crouching near a chair and peering beneath it. She headed into her bedroom, emerging a few moments later without her jacket. Still wearing her gun.

His gaze slid away from it to focus on the white button-down shirt she wore. It was snug on her slim body, as if it had been tailored for her. It cupped her breasts and revealed the hint of a darker bra through the fabric.

What would that bra look like? Black? Navy blue? Lace? Satin? A combination of both?

His hand shook slightly as he held out the can of iced tea. She took it gingerly, making sure their fingers didn't touch. Then she sat on the couch and pulled out her notebook.

"Mind if I ask you some questions?" she said.

"Not at all." He sat at the other end of the couch. "As long as I can ask you some first."

She glanced at him out of the corner of her eye, then straightened and swung around to face him. She had guts, he'd give her that. She had to know what he wanted to talk about. Instead of avoiding it, though, she was willing to tackle it head-on. "Shoot."

"What happened behind that pavilion today?"

A pink flush crept up her neck and onto her face, and her fingers closed tightly around the notebook. But she didn't look away. "We were trying to avoid a scene that would have drawn attention and led to an even bigger scene." Her voice was calm, but her right knee jiggled. "We did what we had to do to blend in with everyone else."

"That's it?" he asked, incredulous. "You're going to call that kiss part of your job and move on?"

"What do you want me to say, Finn?" She leaned closer, the pink turning to darker red slashes on her cheekbones. "That I forgot my job? That I wasn't paying attention to what was going on around us? That I didn't see anyone but you?" She inhaled sharply, as if she hadn't intended to say that last part.

"Do you want me to admit I screwed up? Because I did. It won't happen again. But if you want to call your godfather and ask for another bodyguard, I understand."

"You think I want someone else? That I'm pissed off

because we made out at the park?" He stared at her in disbelief. She had to know how much he'd wanted her. And all signs pointed to her wanting him just as much.

"*I* would be," she retorted. The color began to fade from her cheeks, a testament to her control. And a challenge to make her lose it all over again. "I have a job. A job I wasn't doing. Losing my focus could have gotten you hurt."

"I'm not pissed off," he said, setting his cola on the end table and sliding closer. "I wasn't hurt. I'm…" Still turned on was what he was. "It's easier to show you than tell you," he said, reaching for her.

"Stop!" She jumped off the couch and retreated to a chair across from him. "That's not happening. Ever again. End of discussion."

"Really? You're never going to touch me again?" He leaned into the couch, anticipation unfurling inside him. He liked games. A lot.

"Nope." She tapped her finger on her notebook. "Unless it's because I'm protecting you from someone."

"I guess we'll see, won't we?"

"I guess we will." She held his gaze for a long moment, just long enough to let him know she'd accepted his challenge. She thought she could win, if her tiny smirk and the determination in her eyes was any indication.

He intended to win, too.

Game on.

***

"So you don't see any of your fan mail?" she asked, frowning, fifteen minutes later.

"Nope. My publicist or the studio sends out canned responses. 'Thank you for your interest in Finn O'Rourke. You can see him in his next movie, *Dark Vengeance*, in the summer of next year. Finn appreciates all his fan mail, and asked me to thank you personally.' Blah, blah, blah."

"What about letters that are disturbing? Or

threatening?"

He shrugged. "I have no idea. No one's ever mentioned nasty fan mail."

She closed her notebook with a snap. "Really? Your," she twirled her hand, as if looking for the correct word, "*handlers* don't tell you about stuff like that?"

"I don't have 'handlers'." The word evoked idiot actors who got into trouble constantly and needed a team to bail them out and do damage control. "I have a publicist, a manager, and an agent. And I pay them to deal with that stuff."

"You need to get in touch with your people and find out. The letter your stalker sent indicated that she'd written to you before. I'd like to know what she had to say."

"Okay. I'll call Angie. My publicist," he added at her questioning look.

Two minutes later, Angie was on the phone with him. "Crank mail, Finn? We've got boxes full of it."

Finn glanced at Mia and pressed speaker. "Threatening stuff?"

Angie inhaled slowly. "Mostly people telling you they'd love to help you get over that bitch Gemma. Lots of them say they'll marry you. Take your mind off your troubles."

Mia was scribbling furiously. She held up her notebook, and Finn squinted at it. Then nodded. "Do you think you could have one of your interns look through it for anything with a Chicago return address or postmark?"

"Yeah, I could do that," she finally said. "Might take awhile. You have lots of that kind of mail. Less since the Gemma thing, though."

"Start with whatever we have after Gemma. Get it together today and express it to me in Chicago."

"Why?" A hint of unease filled Angie's voice. "Is something going on?"

"Nothing serious. I just need to see any letters we got lately."

"Okay, Finn. I'll get them to you."

"You're the best, Angie."

"You got that right. I'll get those off to you today."

"Thanks, Ange. Knew I could count on you." He pressed the 'off' button on his phone and slid it into his pocket. "What's next?"

"I have a few more…" 'Shake It Off' jingled in her pocket.

He raised his eyebrows. "The tough cop uses a Taylor Swift ring tone? Really?"

"Shut up," she muttered, pulling the phone out of her pocket. "Hold on," she said as she glanced at the screen. "I need to take this."

Mia stood up and turned her back. "Hey, Bren," she said softly. "What's up?" She paused, then said, "I wish I could, but I'm working tonight. Sorry. Yeah, I'll miss you, too. Talk to you later." She was about to push the 'off' button, then spoke into the phone again. "Bren? You still there? Could you do me a huge favor? Go to my place and get the bag that's sitting inside the front door. Bring it to the Drake hotel and leave it at the desk with my name." Another pause. "I'll tell you later. Yeah, I love you, too."

Finn sat stiffly on the couch, trying to swallow around the cold lump that had formed in his throat. Was Mia talking to her boyfriend? Telling him she loved him after the way she'd kissed Finn that afternoon?

"Sorry," she said as she sat down on the chair. "When one of my brothers calls, I always take it." Her jaw tightened a little. "They're all cops. Bad stuff can happen."

Finn slumped against the couch, relieved. Immediately uneasy at the depth of his relief. "That was your *brother?*"

Mia frowned. "Who did you think it was?" She stared at him for a long moment, clearly replaying the phone call in her mind, and her eyes widened. "You thought it was my *boyfriend?*"

"You told him you loved him." What sister told a brother that she loved him?

"Do you have any siblings?"

"A brother and a sister."

"Don't you tell them you love them when you talk to them on the phone?"

"No. It's kind of an assumed thing."

"I always tell them I love them. My mom, too. You never know what…"

She closed her mouth, but Finn had no trouble filling in the blanks. "You never know what might happen to a cop."

"Yes," she said quietly. Then her eyebrows pulled together. "Wait a minute. You thought I had a *boyfriend?* After the way I kissed you this afternoon?" Her eyes turned into blue flames as she stared at him. "You think I'm a *cheater?*"

"I didn't say that." Finn watched, fascinated as her expression changed from confused to incensed. Skipped from there to arousal, although she managed to blank her expression almost instantly.

Too late. He'd noticed.

"You implied it," Mia fumed. "I don't cheat. Ever. A guy che…" She pressed her lips together. "If I had a boyfriend, I wouldn't have kissed you. Even if it was pretend. A ruse." Red flared in her cheeks, and her eyes burned through him. "But I guess cheaters always think everyone else is cheating, too."

Her barb caught in his chest and twisted, burying itself deep. He managed to keep his voice even when he said, "I think it's reasonable to assume a woman is talking to her boyfriend when she tells someone she loves him."

"No boyfriend."

He leaned a little closer. Noticed she didn't back away. "If you don't have a boyfriend, you're free to kiss me. So tell me, Mia. What was that kiss, exactly? Pretend or real?"

CHAPTER NINE

Mia took a deep breath. Let it shudder out. He wanted the truth. Acting or genuine…spark.

She didn't cheat, and she didn't lie, either. Except in the course of her job. Lying to suspects and dirt bags was expected. Encouraged.

Finn was her job, but he was neither a suspect nor a dirt bag.

So, the truth.

Mia squared her shoulders and studied his expression. Hurt lingered below the surface. Because she'd called him a cheater?

The truth shouldn't hurt. So maybe he *hadn't* cheated on Gemma. Maybe there was more to the story than Gemma's version.

Finn had never spoken publicly about it. Never addressed Gemma's accusations. His silence had let everyone assume he'd been the one in the wrong.

Suddenly, she was desperate to know the real story.

She refused to think about her reasons.

"I'll make you a deal," she said.

"What kind of deal?" He watched her, his eyes

narrowed. Clearly wondering what she was up to.

"I'll tell you the truth. If you do the same thing."

His shoulders relaxed. "Happy to. I'll tell you exactly what you did to me." His eyes darkened as he leaned toward her. "I won't hold back."

"Not what I meant. I know what I did to you." She let her gaze drift below his waist. Linger there. "Men can't hide...some things."

His eyes darkened. His muscles tensed, as if he was preparing to stand up. Reach for her. As she watched, he took a deep breath and steadied himself. Leaned against the back of the couch. "If not that, then what truth do you want from me?"

"I want to know exactly what happened between you and Gemma. Not the story that Gemma told. I want your side. The truth."

He stilled as soon as she said 'Gemma'. Silence hung between them for a long moment. She didn't move. Neither did he.

Finally he said, "Why do you think Gemma's story isn't the truth?"

Now that she'd re-framed the situation, she wondered why no one else had noticed the discrepancies. She held up one hand and began ticking off her fingers.

"First, it sounded as if she'd barely gotten her stuff out of your house before she ran to every reporter in Los Angeles. Telling them what happened. Making herself out as a saint and you as the scum of the earth. That's not what a devastated woman does.

"Second." Mia touched another finger. "Her career skyrocketed immediately afterward. When she recorded all those songs about being wronged. About how she'd walked in on you cheating on her. Being destroyed by it.

"Third." One more finger. "She got together with her drummer awfully fast. Especially for someone who was 'insanely in love' with another guy.

"Fourth." She hesitated, not sure if she should tell Finn

she'd never liked Gemma Radley. That she'd always found her a little sleazy. A little too opportunistic. How Mia had noticed she'd used Finn's name on Twitter all the time – not talking about how crazy she was about him, or promoting his movies. Just reminding people that he was her boyfriend. Her inspiration, she'd called him.

"Fourth?" Finn asked.

She curled her fingers into her palm. She wouldn't share number four with Finn. It would reveal too much about Mia. About how she used to have a secret crush on him. How disillusioned she'd been when Finn was exposed as a cheater.

About how she'd wondered about herself, being drawn to men who cheated.

Yeah. She'd stick with one, two and three. "Don't need the fourth one. The first three are enough."

"Your evidence is thin. All speculation and no facts." He crossed his legs and settled in, a tiny smile flirting with his mouth as if he thought he had the upper hand. "You're a cop," he said. "You should know the difference between conjecture and facts."

"Sometimes you have to look at motive to get to the truth."

"And what would Gemma's motive be for lying about what happened?"

Mia tilted her head. "You're a smart guy, Finn. All you have to do is look at how her career's taken off since…whatever happened."

His little smile disappeared. "I didn't realize you read the tabloids, Officer. Because your facts are as baseless as theirs are."

Just like when a suspect slipped, she pounced. "So you admit that what everyone said is wrong."

"Not at all. I don't talk about that day. With anyone. The only people who know the truth are the ones who were in that room. And that's the way it's going to stay."

Which meant she'd gotten too close to the truth.

Otherwise, he'd simply tell her the story that everyone in the civilized world could recite by now, then demand her truth. The truth of what she'd felt that afternoon.

Although maybe he didn't need her to tell him. Maybe he'd seen the truth in the way she'd clutched him. The way she'd kissed him.

Heat crept into her face. The way she'd practically ripped his shirt off behind the Pritzker Pavilion.

"So we're good?" she asked, swallowing around the words.

"We're peachy keen." He stood up and walked to the window. Stared down at the Oak Street Beach beneath them.

Mia moved closer and peered out the window. The beach wasn't full, not like in the middle of summer, but there were a fair number of people sitting on colorful towels and beach chairs. The water was still cold and there were few swimmers, but several groups were playing beach volleyball.

"It's the 'see and be seen' beach," Mia offered, trying to change the subject. "Where all the beautiful people go."

"Why did you ask me about Gemma?" he asked in a low voice.

Because she hadn't wanted to answer his question. Because she'd always wondered what had really happened with his ex. "Seemed like a fair trade."

"I don't need to trade. I know what our kiss did to you this afternoon."

"Then why did you ask?"

"I wanted to hear you say it."

"Say what?" Her heart thudded against her chest.

"That you were as into it as I was."

"What difference would it make if I was? I'm supposed to be protecting you. And I can't do that if I'm…if I'm…"

"Fucking me? Are those the words you're searching for?"

"Yes." She was determined to keep her cool. And she

regretted asking him about Gemma. Teasing, fun, easy-to-be-with Finn had disappeared, replaced by this stranger with hard eyes and harder words.

"You don't want to know about Gemma, do you? That's old news. What do you really want from me, Mia?"

She stared at him, puzzled. "What are you talking about?"

"All that elaborate set-up. Asking me a question every reporter on the face of the earth has asked. A question you knew I wouldn't answer." He held her gaze, his eyes as cold as Lake Michigan. "So you must have a hidden agenda. Everyone wants something. A favor. A friend who has a screenplay. A relative who wants to be an actor. There's always a request."

She tilted her head, studying his closed-off expression. His flat gaze. "First of all, I wouldn't take advantage of my job as your bodyguard and try to get something for myself out of it." *Like Gemma did*, she wanted to add. But she took a deep breath instead.

"I asked about Gemma because I didn't want to talk about what happened at the park. You already knew I wasn't faking anything, but you wanted to make me say it. Reveal myself. So I asked you something equally revealing. That's it.

"I don't want a damn thing from you, Finn." She thought about Brendan's book, making the rounds of Hollywood studios. It had never occurred to her to ask for Finn's help with that. "Except to keep you safe for three weeks, wave goodbye when you leave for Hollywood, and get back to my real job."

"You expect me to believe that?"

"I don't care if you believe it or not. It's the truth." She studied him for a moment. "If everyone in your world has an agenda, I'm sorry for you. That's an unpleasant way to live. All I want from you is to do my job and keep you safe. Nothing else."

Her conscience pinged, making her look away from him.

She did have an agenda – passing that detective's exam. But Finn couldn't influence that outcome. It was all on her.

She turned and headed for the smaller bedroom, the one she assumed was hers. "I'll let you study your script. Don't answer the door. Let me know if you want to leave the suite. Behave."

She walked into the sumptuous room and closed the door part way. She'd have a little privacy, and so would he. Both of them could regroup. Settle down. Try to forget what had happened at the park.

Or at least, in her case, put it behind her. Chalk it up as a mistake, and move on.

Grabbing the pad of paper the hotel left on the desk in the room, she threw herself into the leather chair beside the window, pulled out her pen and began listing all the things she needed to do. Starting with examining the letters Finn's publicist was sending.

Fifteen minutes later, she'd itemized a few things, but she'd spend most of her time doodling on the paper.

Instead of trying to organize what she needed to do, she'd been thinking about the heated words she and Finn had exchanged.

He'd been out of line, but so had she. She shouldn't have asked him what happened with Gemma. It was none of her business. Worse, it had no bearing on her job.

Finn knocked on her door. She froze for a moment, then clicked the pen closed. "Come in."

He pushed the door open but didn't enter. Sunlight from the other room haloed around him, making his hair glow golden and highlighting the breadth of his shoulders. "I need to apologize," he said.

"I owe you one, too," she said, standing up. "I shouldn't have asked you about Gemma. It's none of my business. It doesn't have anything to do with my job. I was wrong, and I'm sorry."

His composed expression softened. "I'm sorry, too. That kiss…it was incredible, and I didn't want to stop. I was pretty sure you didn't, either. And when we got back up here, I was still thinking with the little head. It pissed me off that you were so cool and collected about it. I'm sorry I pushed."

He shoved his hand through his hair, and the waves stood up, catching the light. "Gemma…I don't talk about her. Ever. For a lot of reasons."

"I was out of line. So can we let it go and move on?"

"Yeah. I hope so."

"Great." Mia took a deep breath and reached behind her for the pad of paper. "I have some questions I need to ask you. Can we go into the other room?"

"Yeah." His gaze strayed to the bed, then snapped back to hers. "Good idea."

She followed him into the living area and sat in one of the chairs. He sat on the couch across from her. There were at least a couple of feet between them, but she was certain she felt the heat radiating off his body.

Shifting her knees to the side so they were farther away from him, she cleared her throat and glanced at the paper. "First thing. I need a list of everyone here in Chicago who's going to be working at the studio."

He frowned. "I can get that, but it's going to be a lot of people."

"That's okay. I want to check through some databases and see if any of them have records for stalking or similar behaviors.

"Second, I'll need a list of new hires at the hotel. Anyone who started after you settled on this as the place you'd stay."

"That wasn't my decision." His shoulders relaxed and he finally sat back into the couch. "The studio picks the hotel and negotiates the deal."

"Any idea how long ago it was?"

He quirked one eyebrow. "A couple of months? Maybe three? I know there were a lot of discussions about which hotel sent the best message. The old money elegance of this place? The flashy, over the top tackiness of that new place along the river? Something in between?"

"Why?" she asked, puzzled.

"Hollywood is all smoke and mirrors. Image is everything. This is an indie project, so they picked the Drake. Elegance. Class. Reflects onto the project. Gives it more heft."

"Spending that much effort on which hotel to stay at sounds stupid. But whatever. I need that list of new hires."

"I'll see what I can do."

"You'll do better than that." She narrowed her eyes at him. "You're a big star with a lot of power. Use it. If I was stalking someone, I'd find out where he was staying and get a job there. I need to screen any new hires."

"Let me make some calls."

Finn stood up, pulled out his phone and punched in a number. "Hey, Mike, it's Finn. I need the name of everyone who's working at the studio. And whether they're from L.A. or local. How fast can you get it to me?"

He listened for a long moment, then clenched his jaw. A muscle in his face twitched. "You think I'm being a prima donna? You're the one who arranged this bodyguard for me, asshole. Part of her job is checking out the people around me. She needs it tonight.

"And after you do that, get a list of new hires at the hotel. Beginning when we made the reservations for the cast and the staff."

He listened for a long moment. "Fine. I'll tell Officer Donovan that her services are no longer needed. I'll let the police Superintendent here in Chicago know, too. Let him know who's responsible."

Mia stood up and reached for the phone. She wasn't going to let some suit leave Finn unprotected and vulnerable.

Finn spotted her moments before she grabbed the phone out of his hand. He shook his head violently and spun around to keep her away from the phone. Her hand landed on his back, palm flat against him, and she jerked away.

His shirt was warm from the sun, his back firm beneath her fingers. Hard with muscle and bone. Too familiar.

Memories from earlier unspooled in her head. The way he'd shivered when her fingers crept beneath the waistband of his ridiculous pants. The way his muscles had tensed when she touched him.

The way he'd touched her.

She walked toward the window, staring at the people on the beach below her. Finn said something to the guy on the phone, but she didn't hear him through the blood roaring in her ears.

"Hey," Finn said.

She glanced over her shoulder. He was so close that the gold flecks in his green eyes glittered like specks of sunlight.

She turned and stepped back from him. "You're really going to let him fire m… your bodyguard? You know that's a stupid thing to do." She wasn't going to make it personal.

He shrugged one shoulder. "A note and a wedding ring are weird. A little disturbing. But they aren't really threats." He studied her for a beat too long. "I suspect you'd rather be doing real police work. This is your out."

"This *is* real police work, and I don't want an out." The thought of leaving him unprotected was unacceptable. "And besides, you know your godfather would just send someone else. Who'd want the same lists I want."

One side of his mouth curled up. "Glad to know you don't want to leave." He studied her for a long moment, his eyes hooded. "I don't want you to go, either. If my bodyguard has to pose as my girlfriend, it's good there's some…chemistry between us. Makes it more believable."

"Yeah." She cleared her throat, trying not to think about that chemistry. "Besides, people have already seen us together. Awkward to have a different 'girlfriend' show up."

His mouth curled into a smile. "When you knocked on the door this morning, I got the impression you didn't want to be here."

He'd been right. She'd accepted the job because her captain had implied it would give her a leg up in the interview for a promotion to detective. She hadn't looked forward to babysitting a spoiled, obnoxious actor.

Finn was none of those things. She'd...enjoyed his company. And now she was invested in finding his stalker. It had become a challenge.

"It was really early. I hadn't had any caffeine. So any impressions you got were wrong."

"Good to know, Officer." His eyes twinkled. "I guess your little confession means you didn't hear me refuse to fire you."

Her relief was way out of proportion to the significance of this job. Trying to hide it, she said, "Just don't want another officer to have to replicate all I've done so far."

"Yeah, that would be a shame." He leaned closer. "And some parts of it would be impossible for another officer to duplicate."

"What?" She tried to look puzzled and ignore the buzzing in her chest. "You don't think someone else would have confronted Ginny at the studio?"

He tilted his head to the side, and the Finn she'd met earlier in the day was back. "Not what I meant," he said, shoving his hands into his pockets. "Not sure anyone else would have been able to..." He paused, and her heart beat a little faster.

"Bond with Pete so fast," he finally said, the corners of his eyes crinkling in a grin.

CHAPTER TEN

Wide awake and twitchy at one a.m, Finn slid out of bed in his boxers and tee shirt and wandered out of his bedroom. A fat crescent moon hung over Lake Michigan, the reflection of its pale light gleaming on the dark water, roiling and churning with the endless waves.

Finn watched it for a while, the repetitive ripple of light hypnotizing. The lake was restless tonight, too.

The reason for Finn's restlessness slept in the bedroom on the other side of the living area.

Her door was open.

He told himself to ignore Mia's room as he moved forward, drawn by an invisible cord. He stopped in the doorway.

The moonlight glimmered into her room, too, its milky light splashed on the floor. Mia sprawled on her side in the queen-sized bed, one leg drawn up beneath the other. The blankets were mussed, leaving a spaghetti-strapped shoulder bare.

One of her arms was tucked beneath the pillow. The other was draped across the bed, as if she were reaching for her lover in her sleep.

Not a good picture to have in his head.

He'd watched her that evening as she typed on her computer, frowning at the screen in concentration. Occasionally, she'd scribble something on a pad of paper beside her. Completely absorbed in her work.

So absorbed that she didn't see his gaze return to her, time after time. He'd wished he could see into her head. Learn her process. Know her better.

Finally, around ten, she'd stretched her arms behind her head, outlining the shape of her breasts. And that dark bra she wore.

Banishing the memories, he turned away from Mia's door. The Oriental rug was soft beneath his feet as he padded to the mini-bar and removed a can of V-8 juice. He popped the lid and drank it down, then tossed the can in the trash.

When he wasn't watching Mia work, he'd spent the evening going over his script and his blocking instructions, moving around the room to plant the muscle memory in his brain. Mia had glanced at him once, then returned to her work. She'd been so engrossed in it that she hadn't looked up again.

Earlier that day, she'd been equally engaged in kissing him.

Was she as focused in everything she did?

It would be the height of stupidity to find out.

He was afraid he was stupid enough to try.

Sighing, he returned to his room and climbed into bed. Laid down and stared at the ceiling, going over his lines until he fell into a restive sleep.

***

When Finn walked out of his room the following morning in jeans and a tee shirt, he found Mia already standing in the living area, talking on the phone. When she spotted him, she said, "Gotta go. Love you, too.

"Morning," she said, pocketing her phone. "I ordered room service breakfast – the same thing you had yesterday. I should have asked last night what you wanted, but didn't think of it."

"That's fine." He nodded at her phone. "Let me guess – another brother?" He wasn't going to fall into the trap of over-reacting again.

"Nope."

Trying to ignore a tiny flick of jealousy, he struggled to keep his expression politely interested. He knew he'd failed when her eyes twinkled at him.

"That was my mom. Updating me on my cousin Charlotte and her twin brothers, who are waiting in the wings, so to speak."

"Waiting in the wings?" Finn wrinkled his forehead. "What does that mean?"

"My aunt Helen is pregnant. With twins. Just found out they're both boys." She sighed. "Poor Helen."

"She's not happy about it?"

"No, she's thrilled." Mia's eyes sparkled, and Finn couldn't look away. "But my brothers Connor and Quinn were hell on wheels when they were kids. Now Helen has to wrangle two more Donovan boys."

"Connor and Quinn are twins?" When Mia nodded, Finn shook his head. "Jeez. Do you have a spread sheet to keep track of your family?"

Mia tilted her head, some of the sparkle disappearing from her eyes. "Aren't you close to your family?"

"Of course we're close. I see them at Thanksgiving and Christmas. Sometimes a time or two during the year, as well."

"That's too bad," she said softly. "How far away do they live?"

Completely unnecessary guilt swept over him. "My parents and sister live near San Francisco. My brother lives in New York," he said, feeling as if he needed to apologize for his neglect of his family. "Everyone's busy."

"Yeah, it's tough for all of us to get together, too." She studied him for a long moment. "I'm sure you do the best you can."

He could practically hear her thinking, "Loser." Feel her patting him on the head. Telling him, "You did your best." "You tried really hard." "Trying is what counts."

"Yeah," he said. "We have a great time when we're all together." And didn't that sound pathetic.

A sharp rap on the door announced what he hoped was their breakfast. After sleeping very little last night, he needed coffee. As he headed for the door, Mia stuck her arm out. Stopping him. He froze.

"I get the door," she said.

She dropped her hand and squinted into the peep hole. Watching her, Finn rubbed his chest where her palm had flattened against him.

As she squinted into the peep hole, Mia absently touched her hip. Making sure her gun was there.

It wasn't.

"Hold on," she called. "Be right there."

She dashed into her room, emerging in less than a minute with the gun in place, struggling into a suit jacket. Light gray. Her shirt was black.

He wouldn't be getting a glimpse of her bra today.

He'd been looking forward to that more than he should have been.

Flipping the jacket so it covered her gun, Mia opened the door. The waiter rolled a cart inside, positioned it by the window, then pulled a folded newspaper from beneath his arm. "This was by the door," he said, setting it on the table. "There was a letter on top of it." He nodded at the neatly folded newspaper. "It's inside."

The newspaper flopped open to reveal a plain white envelope. No writing on the front. Mia stilled, staring at it. Tucked her hands behind her back. To keep from reaching for it, he realized.

Turning toward the kid, Finn pulled out his wallet and

handed the waiter a few bills. "Thanks," he said.

"No problem, sir." The guy headed for the door, then hesitated. He glanced over his shoulder. "I really like your movies, Mr. O'Rourke."

"Thank you," Finn said, bracing himself for the eager questions that usually followed that statement. "Does everyone in the hotel know I'm staying here?"

"I don't think so. No one's talking about you. I only know because I delivered your breakfast yesterday, too." His gaze flitted to Mia, studying the newspaper, and back to Finn. "I didn't tell anyone. Won't."

"Thanks." Finn really looked at the kid, studied his earnest expression and polite demeanor. He glanced at the boy's name tag. "Josh. I appreciate that. Can you arrange to deliver our meals whenever you're here?"

The kid's eyes lit up. "I sure can, Mr. O'Rourke." He swallowed. "Or, I guess, *you* can. You have to call hotel services and request me. Then, when I'm on duty, I'll deliver everything to your room."

"Great. I'll do that right now." He smiled at the boy. "See you tomorrow morning."

"Yes, sir!" Grinning, Josh stepped into the hall and pulled the door closed behind him.

As soon as the door was closed, Finn turned to Mia. "What's in the letter?"

She was moving toward her bedroom. "I need gloves before we open it."

She returned moments later, pulling a pair of blue latex gloves onto her hands, a clear plastic bag held between her arm and her body. Snapping the second glove into place, Mia set the bag down and picked up the letter, examining the envelope. Turned it over, then back to the front.

Finally, she walked over to the cart holding their breakfast and picked up a knife. Wiggled it into the end of the envelope, then slit the envelope open.

Mia peered inside for a moment, then dumped a piece of paper into her palm. Newsprint. He couldn't see it clearly, but it had jagged edges, as if it had been torn out of the paper.

Frowning down at it, Mia flipped it over. Froze.

Dread snaking through his gut, Finn moved closer. Stared over her shoulder at a piece of newspaper and saw his face – one of his stock publicity photos. A large X covered the middle of the picture. Whoever had done it had pressed so hard that the pen had torn through the paper.

The caption beneath the picture read, 'Finn O'Rourke, in town to film *Dark Vengeance*, was spotted at the Art Institute yesterday. He seemed to be enjoying the art. But it looked like he was enjoying the company of an unidentified woman even more.'

Beneath the photo, the sender had written, 'I should have known you'd betray me with another whore, just like you betrayed me with Gemma. We are through.'

Finn reached for the picture, but Mia put a hand on his arm. "Don't touch it." The latex gloves felt cold and sterile on his skin, and he wanted to rip the glove off her hand. Feel her skin against his.

She took her hand away and carefully slid the picture back into the envelope. Then put it into the zip-closed plastic bag she'd brought from her room, sealed it and peeled off her gloves. Grabbed a pen and wrote something in the white square at the top of the bag.

Her gaze was serious when she finally looked at him. "She's escalating. This is a threat."

"It's just an X on a picture torn from the newspaper," he said. But a chill had shivered over him when he read the words the stalker had written.

"She's deleting you from her life. And maybe she wants to delete you permanently. She was certain you wanted her. That you'd come to Chicago for her. And now you've disappointed her. You were seen in public with another woman."

He couldn't tear his gaze away from the photo, the visible evidence of a tsunami of anger and hatred directed against him.

Moving closer, she set her palm on his forearm. Gently curled her fingers around him, as if she were trying to comfort him. The imprint of her fingers burned into his skin.

"You have to take this seriously." Mia stared up at him, as serious as he'd seen her. "She might be one of the stalkers who tells herself that if she can't have you, no one can." Mia glanced at the bag holding the letter. "That's my take on what she wrote."

She let him go. Slowly. As if she'd rather be touching him.

"Damn it!" He stared at the plastic bag. The envelope looked ordinary. Common. Nothing special about it.

But the picture inside this envelope was anything but innocuous.

Another realization made him freeze. He grabbed Mia's hand. "Maybe she wants to delete you, too." He gripped her hand more tightly, cursing the unknown woman. His godfather, who'd sent Mia to guard him. The production company, who'd decided to film in Chicago.

She didn't pull away. The talc on her hands from the inside of the gloves made her fingers powdery and slick. Cool. She held his hand tightly, studying his face, and he knew she'd see his panic. Mia was a scary smart woman.

"Maybe she does," she said calmly. "But she's not going to delete either of us. I know how to take care of myself. We need to worry about *you*. Not me."

"Of course I'm worried about you. You didn't ask for this. You're not a public figure."

"I did ask for this, Finn. I agreed to take the job. To protect you." She squeezed his hand. "And I will."

She held his gaze, her eyes confident. Reassuring. As if she thought he was afraid for himself.

"Let me be clear," he said. "I'm worried about *you*, not me."

For a moment, her eyes softened. The woman who'd

kissed him at Millenium Park yesterday gazed back at him. Vulnerable. Open. Yearning.

Then her hand dropped away from his. Her expression changed, as if the shutters came down. Instead of Mia, Officer Donovan studied him. "If that's true, you're either a saint or an idiot. She's not interested in me. It's *you* she wants. *You* she thinks has betrayed her."

She pulled her phone out of her pocket. "Who did you call the last two times you found something outside your door?"

All business. He took a deep breath, let it out slowly. He could be business-like, too. "Doug. My godfather."

"The Superintendent."

"Yes."

"What's his number?" she asked, her finger poised over the keyboard of her phone.

He rattled off the numbers. After dialing, she pushed 'speaker'. The phone rang on the other end, then a woman answered. "Superintendent Walsh's office. This is Mary speaking."

"Hi, Mary," Mia said. "This is Officer Donovan. I'm the officer assigned to his godson's protective detail. There's been another note left at his door, and someone needs to come pick it up. Take it to the lab to be analyzed."

"Hold on a moment, Officer. Let me put you through to the Superintendent."

"That's not necessary," Mia began, but she was too late. Bland Muzak played through the phone. Mia glanced at Finn, then looked away. Sorry she'd called? Sorry she'd put the phone on speaker?

Before he could figure out which, his godfather's voice boomed over the phone. "Officer Donovan. This is Doug Walsh. Mary tells me there's been another letter."

Mia's left foot jittered on the carpet. She ran her hand through her hair once. Then again. Interesting. Take-no-prisoners Officer Donovan was flustered by talking to his godfather. "Yes, sir. It was on the newspaper this morning.

It's threatening. More specific than the previous two contacts. I'm concerned, and called to have someone pick up the letter and take it to the lab."

"Threatening how?"

His godfather's voice dropped an octave. Mia darted a glance at Finn, then took a breath. "There was a snippet about Mr. O'Rourke in the newspaper yesterday. The Sun, I think. I checked the Herald Tribune and didn't see it there. It talked about Mr. O'Rourke being spotted at the Art Institute with an unnamed woman." She cleared her throat. "Me. He wanted to see the museum, and I didn't think there was any reason not to. He, um, wore a disguise."

"Those stupid dad pants and the geek glasses?" the superintendent demanded.

A smile flitted across Mia's face, then disappeared. "Yes, Sir. Exactly."

"Told him that disguise was completely lame. He should have worn a beard. Or a wig. Something that would disguise his face better."

Mia's foot stopped jiggling. "I agree, Sir. And next time, he will."

There was a slight pause. Then Doug said, "Good to hear, Officer. I knew I could count on Talbott to put the right person on this job. Finian is important to a lot of people."

She glanced at him, her eyes crinkling as she mouthed, "*Finian?*"

He narrowed his eyes, but Mia didn't notice as she said, "I know he's important to you and the rest of his family. I'm working on figuring out who this stalker might be."

"What have you done so far?"

"I have a list of the people who are part of the film crew, both the ones from California and the local hires. I've also received a list of new hires at the Drake, going back to when the film studio agreed to a deal with the hotel. I've been checking each of them with the database."

"Find anything yet?"

"Unfortunately, no. But I'll continue tonight."

"Why not today?" His godfather's voice sharpened.

"Because filming starts today," she said. Her voice was calm. Unapologetic. "I need to stay with him at the studio."

"Then send a copy of those lists with the letter. I'll have some of my people work on them."

"With all due respect, sir, it's not a job I'd assign to a civilian. I'd be concerned they wouldn't know what to look for."

His godfather snorted. "My people may be office rats now, but they started out on the street. They know how to run a suspect through a database."

Mia's face turned red. "Of course, sir. Sorry. I didn't mean to imply…"

"You're not sorry," Doug interrupted. "And I don't want you to be. I'm glad you're taking this seriously. Thank you, Officer Donovan."

"Of course I'm taking it seriously." Mia bristled. "It's my job."

There was a pause, then his godfather said, "Tell Finn to behave. Although I suspect you have him on speaker. That's what I would do with a knucklehead like him. Behave yourself, Finn," he said more loudly, and Finn heard the smile in his voice. "Don't give Officer Donovan any reasons to call me again."

"Go to hell, Doug," he said.

Laughing, Chicago's Superintendent of Police disconnected the phone.

At the same time, someone knocked at the door.

CHAPTER ELEVEN

Rattled from both the stalker's letter and her conversation with the superintendent, Mia instinctively reached for her gun as she reached the door. As she glanced into the spy hole, her shoulders relaxed and she let her hand fall from the grip of her Glock.

"Pete," she said as she opened the door. "You're early."

Pete frowned. "What are you talking about? I'm right on time." He tapped his watch. "Eight A.M. On the nose."

"God, Pete," Finn groaned behind her. "We haven't even had coffee yet."

"Not my fault, O'Rourke." His gaze shifted from Finn to Mia. "Should I even ask why you haven't had your coffee?"

A hot flush rushed up Mia's cheeks as memories of her dreams from the night before unspooled through her brain. Which was so unfair.

If she was going to blush like an idiot, she should at least have had more than sexy dreams to justify the heat in her face. To make it worse, Finn clearly knew what she was thinking. His suddenly hot gaze made everything clench inside her.

On her other side, Pete raised one eyebrow. Smirked, as if he could see directly into her brain and knew exactly what she was thinking.

Trying to gather her composure, she walked to the mini bar and grabbed two cardboard cups and plastic tops. "We can drink it in the car." She looked over her shoulder. "You want a cup, Pete?"

"Nah, I got up in time for breakfast." One side of his mouth twitched. "But thanks."

She prepared a cup for herself, then glanced at Finn. "What do you want?"

He stared at her, his hunger clear, and her temperature rose ten degrees. Made her clench again. "Cream. No sugar," he finally said.

He wanted the same as her. *In her coffee*, she added when her brain went to the dangerous place again.

She turned her back so neither man could see her hands shake as she poured the coffee. Snapping on the lids, she shoved them both in Finn's direction. "You carry them." At least she had enough wits about her to remember her job.

The ride down the elevator and the walk through the corridor to the loading dock was uneventful. They saw no one on the way.

Once inside the car, Pete raised the screen between the front and back seat without asking. Finn handed Mia one of the cups. They sipped in silence for a long moment.

Finally, Finn said, "I had a hard time sleeping last night, so I went into the living room. Your door was open." Heat simmered in his gaze. "Was that an invitation?"

She sighed in relief. A question she could answer without any subtext or knowing looks. "Of course it wasn't. If I want you in…" She stopped dead, appalled at what had slipped out of her mouth.

Clearing her throat, she said, "I can't close the door when I'm sleeping. I need to be able to hear if someone tries to get into the suite."

"You double locked the door," he said, leaning back against the seat. One corner of his mouth twitched. "Put on the safety lock. We're on the twelfth floor, so no one's coming in through the window. Are you sure you didn't have other reasons for leaving your door open?"

"Are you sure you didn't take a blow to the head somewhere between last night and this morning?" she shot back. "Because you don't seem to have a very good grasp of reality."

"I wanted to come in," he murmured, easing closer to her. "I thought maybe you wanted me in there, too."

She recognized the lemon ginger scent of his soap as it drifted over her – the French milled bars the hotel provided. Knowing she smelled the same way shouldn't have been sexy. But somehow it was. "Really?" she managed to say. "My open bedroom door is what you want to discuss? Not the escalating threats from your stalker?"

"Nothing we can do about that right now," he said. "And we have some time to kill before Pete drops us off. So let's discuss."

She glanced out the window. The streets were clogged with cars, buses and taxis. Pedestrians hurried across the street, many of them darting in and out of stopped cars in the time-honored Chicago tradition of jaywalking.

No way was she going to talk about her open bedroom door and his interest in being invited in. "I have a better idea. Fill me in on what happens today," she said, turning to face him as she pulled out her notebook. "Start from the moment we walk in the door."

He held her gaze for a long moment, his expression promising that he wouldn't forget. Then he eased away from her. "Before or after we get back to the hotel?"

Mia closed her eyes. Between her dreams and the attraction that felt like a bungee cord stretched more and more tightly between them, it was going to be a long three weeks. Time to nip all this sexy flirting in the bud before that rubber cord snapped and they slammed into each other.

"Cut the crap, O'Rourke. I'm not interested in your delusional fantasies. All I want is to keep you alive."

***

More than ten hours later, Mia leaned against a wall and hoped no one had heard her stomach growl. She'd spent the day moving from one set to the next, and from there to a green screen. Every stop had involved more waiting around than actual filming. Making a movie was unbelievably boring.

Watching the costume designer fuss with Finn that morning had been fun, though, especially when the middle-aged woman had busied herself very close to his crotch. At one point, Mia was sure she'd adjusted his package. Finn had squirmed, his eyes darting to hers, and she'd grinned back at him.

She hadn't seen Finn rattled since she met him.

Other than behind the bandshell, her very unhelpful brain reminded her.

Mia had made a request of the costume woman while Finn had changed his clothes. When his dressing room door opened, she'd taken the bag from the woman, stuffed it in her purse and turned around to smile at him.

They'd gone from there to make-up, where he'd chatted with the make-up artist as if they were old friends. After that, they'd headed for the first set.

From then on, it had been take after take of the first scene. Mia could have recited everyone's lines by the time they finished. Then they'd repeated the whole thing for another scene.

She'd been afraid she'd stand out, but thankfully, that wasn't the case. Equipment crowded the studio – cameras, furniture, microphones, moveable walls, and about a million different pieces of electronic equipment. Thick cables criss-crossed the floor, and X's of blue, red and yellow tape covered the floors. The actors' marks, she realized after a while.

There was so much stuff, so many people milling around, calling out orders, shouting at each other, that Mia, sitting off to the side, was essentially invisible.

Exactly what she wanted.

She studied everyone, but focused on the women. Most stalkers were men, and Finn's could be, too, but her gut told her a woman was behind the notes. The wording was...feminine.

As she shifted her feet, stretching tired muscles, a woman who was one of Finn's co-stars walked over. "Hi," she said. "I'm Jenna Stanton. The woman in the love triangle with Derek and Finn's character. Derek is the hero," she added, as if Mia hadn't been watching the filming all day and didn't recognize superstar Derek Sawyer.

Mia shook the woman's hand, sizing her up. She was a few years older than Mia, but strikingly beautiful with long chestnut hair, hazel eyes and perfect features. A slender but very curvy body, a shape Mia was pretty sure wasn't found in nature.

"Nice to meet you, Jenna. I'm Mia."

"So I hear you're Finn's girlfriend," she said, narrowing her eyes just a fraction.

"I am."

"And you're here because...?" The actor raised one eyebrow.

Mia shrugged one shoulder. "I like to be with Finn." Mia had to stop herself from wincing when she heard the high, squeaky voice of her alter-ego. "Plus I wanted to see what he did all day. It's really interesting."

Mia could read Jenna perfectly – she wanted to roll her eyes. Instead, the other woman said, "It's a lot of standing around and doing nothing. What did you do all day?"

Check out people like you to make sure you don't hurt him. "Oh, I watched Finn. He looks completely different."

"Yeah, the costume and make-up will do that." She scanned Mia's suit and flat shoes. "Where did you meet him? You don't seem like his usual type."

And you think you are, Mia realized, her hackles rising. "He's a friend of a friend." Mia faked a giggle. "It was a blind date. We've been…" She'd almost said inseparable. But girlfriend Mia wouldn't use a word like that. "It was love at first sight."

Jenna stared at her for a long moment, her eyes narrowed and her mouth pursed, as if trying to intimidate Mia into handing over rights to Finn.

Girlfriend Mia disappeared and cop Mia took over. "I don't remember seeing any of your films," she said. "What movies have you been in?" Mia had done her homework and knew Jenna had had minor roles in a few short-lived television series and two tiny, barely distributed indie movies. This was her first major movie.

Jenna's expression tightened. "I've been in several projects." The other woman studied her for a long moment. "Probably none that you've seen. They played in art houses."

"I'll look you up on IMDB." Mia smiled. "Can't wait to watch them."

A muscle clenched in Jenna's jaw. "I need to get back to work. Let me know if you need anything while you're on the set. I'd be happy to help you."

Mia watched Jenna walk away, her hips swaying. *Yeah, I just bet you would.*

She'd ask Finn about Jenna Stanton tonight.

Finally, an hour later, Finn headed toward her, stopping only when the director called his name. They talked for a couple of minutes, Sean slapped his back, and Finn smiled. Nodded.

When he reached her, he grabbed her hand. "Let's go," he said, his voice low and a little hoarse.

He didn't say anything as he almost dragged her toward the dressing rooms. After she checked the small space, she waited in the hall while he changed into his jeans and tee and removed his make-up.

Still silent, they walked out of the studio to Pete's waiting car.

As they slid onto the seat, Finn exhaled. Leaned his head against the back of the seat and closed his eyes. Rapped twice on the privacy glass, and Pete pulled into traffic.

Mia had dozens of questions she wanted to ask, but she kept her mouth shut and leaned against the seat, as well. Finn wanted silence. She knew, because she needed to decompress after a day at work, too.

Finn finally opened his eyes and turned to face her. "I don't want to go back to the hotel right away. I need to unwind. Eat something besides hotel food. Any place you could recommend?"

"There are a lot of restaurants downtown that have great food," she began, trying to think of a place where Finn wouldn't be conspicuous. "But they're places where celebrities go when they're in town. Not sure we want to go to any of them."

"See and be seen joints." He shook his head. "No. Not that. I want someplace real. Someplace I can go and relax. I don't want to worry that some celebrity spotter will see us and we'll end up in the newspaper again."

Mia didn't want that, either. A snippet in the celebrity news columns about Finn being seen with a woman, two days in a row, might push his stalker over the edge. "There's a pub in my neighborhood," she said. "Craft beers on tap, decent food and a booth in the back where it's a little dark and you'd be less conspicuous. Oscar's."

"Sounds perfect." He rapped on the window, and it rolled down. "Pete, we're going to get some food and a beer. Oscar's."

He glanced at Mia, and she leaned forward. "Take Lake Shore Drive north," she told him. "Get off at Belmont. I'll pull up the directions on my phone."

Mia slid it out of her pocket, scrolled through her contacts until she found Oscar's, and hit dial. When the hostess answered, she said, "Hi. Is that booth in the back, in the left hand corner, available?"

"Hold on while I check," the woman said. Moments later she picked up the phone. "Not right now, but the people are about ready for their check. Do you want me to hold it for you?"

"That would be great. Donovan's the name. We're maybe fifteen minutes away."

"See you then."

After ending the call, Mia found Oscar's on the map, waited until it mapped out the route, then handed the phone to Pete. "Violet will tell you where to turn."

"Violet?" Finn asked with a twinkle.

"Don't you name the voice on your phone?" she asked, surprised.

"No. Interesting that you do, though. Especially that the tough cop chose such a whimsical name." He smiled, and some of the tension in his shoulders melted away. "You're full of surprises, Officer Donovan."

Mia shrugged. "Makes routine stuff less boring," she said.

He stared at her for another long moment, as if he wanted to ask something else, but finally said, "Tell me about Oscar's."

"Nothing really to tell. It's just a neighborhood place. My brothers and I all live in the area, and we get together there after work once in a while. That's how I know about that booth in the back." She smiled, remembering a couple of dates when she'd been seated back there.

Finn leaned closer. The green in his eyes had narrowed to a tiny rim around his black pupils. "What have you done in that booth in the corner, Officer?"

Without stopping to think, she said, "Drank a beer or two. Talked to my brothers."

She wanted to slap her hand over her mouth and stuff the words back inside. She was *flirting* with him, for God's sake.

Finn moved again, and he was suddenly close enough

that his breath fanned across her neck and ruffled the hair behind her ear. "You weren't thinking about your brothers. Who were you thinking about?"

His low voice and warm breath made her shiver. His shoulder was almost touching hers, and she resisted the urge to move closer. She should move away, but she resisted that, as well. If she moved, he'd know he'd affected her.

It would put her at a disadvantage.

Right now, she needed every edge she could get. Taking him to Oscar's might not have been her best idea ever. She was too comfortable there. She might forget her job, slip up, say things she shouldn't say.

"Must have been one hot date," Finn murmured into her ear. "If it's taking you this long to censor it for a general audience."

"Don't…don't be ridiculous." Her voice was too breathy. Too bothered. And it wasn't because she was thinking about the flirting and occasional handsy-ness that had happened in that booth.

No, it was because she was thinking about sitting in that secluded, intimate booth with Finn.

Pulling herself together, she said, "Nothing has gone on at Oscar's, except a bunch of cops griping about suspects and cases."

"Looks like an interesting evening ahead."

He didn't move away from her, and their shoulders bumped whenever Pete went around a corner. When they finally reached Oscar's, Mia practically leaped out of the car.

Five minutes later, they were seated in the booth. Finn glanced around. "I like this place."

"Yeah," she said, glad they weren't discussing what had or had not happened back here. She pushed her menu away as she spotted their waitress approaching. "You know what you want?"

When the waitress had scribbled their order, she said, "I'll be right back with your beer and iced tea."

"So what did you think?" Finn asked. "Today was boring

as hell, wasn't it?"

"Yeah, but there were a few exciting moments." Mia studied him in the low light. His skin was a little pale, and the tiny wrinkles around his eyes were more noticeable. "How did it go for you?"

He spun the napkin-wrapped silverware in a circle. "Good, I think," he finally said. "Sean seemed happy." He raised one shoulder. "Kind of early to tell."

"You haven't made a movie since your, um, thing with Gemma. What made you choose this one?"

"Lots of reasons," he said, not looking up at the waitress when she brought their drinks. "So tell me what questions you have for me."

Okay, no personal stuff. She ignored the tiny flare of disappointment and told herself that made things easier.

"Tell me about Jenna Stanton."

Finn grimaced. "You met her?"

"I did. She introduced herself. Wanted to know how we met."

Finn smiled, his face suddenly lighter. "I wish I had been a fly on the wall for that conversation."

"I'm going to do some checking on her. See if she might be our stalker."

"I don't think so." He shook his head. "That would be too subtle for Jenna. She has no problem asking for what she wants."

"And what she wants is you." Mia felt a tiny pang of possessiveness. Only because it was her job to protect Finn. She'd happily extend her job to protecting him from barracuda-like women.

"Bingo. You must be a trained observer."

"Tell me how she's come on to you."

"From the first time the cast got together for a meet and greet, she's been very direct about her interest in me. The more I resisted, the harder she pushed." His silverware spun again. "Now I just ignore her. She's the kind of woman who has to be wanted by every man in her general vicinity. When a guy resists, she's just more determined to bring him to his knees."

Mia pulled out her notebook, scribbling a line about what to look for in Jenna's background. "Okay," she said, tapping the notebook away. "She was the big thing that stood out today. Nothing else suspicious, really." She snickered. "Got a few dirty looks from Ginny in set 'décor', but that wasn't a shocker."

As she finished speaking, a man slid onto the bench seat beside her. Turning to look at him, she fumbled beneath her jacket for her gun. Before she could pull it out, a familiar voice said, "Fancy seeing you here, Mimi. Who's the guy?"

CHAPTER TWELVE

"Brendan! What are you doing here?" Mia swiveled to face him, horror blooming in her chest.

"This is where we're meeting tonight."

"You told me The Pipe and Shamrock!" Out of the corner of her eye she saw Finn lean forward, listening to every word. "You were going to see Cilla's old band."

"Changed our minds. I didn't want to go there without Cilla. So we came here instead." Brendan turned to study Finn on the other side of the table. "You blew us off for a date, huh?"

"Not a date. A business meeting."

Brendan narrowed his gaze at her. "Really? 'Business meeting?' You're in the back booth at Oscar's. So involved in one another that you didn't even see me coming. But it's not a date? Right."

"Brendan, get out of here. I'm not fifteen anymore. What I do is not your business, and I don't need you to intimidate guys for me. I can do that just fine by myself."

"I can vouch for that," Finn threw in.

She stabbed a finger at him, irritation lowering her voice. "You shut up."

Brendan turned to study Finn. "So who is this guy?"

Finn stared right back at Brendan. "The guy Mia's with. Who are you?"

"I'm her…" Brendan narrowed his gaze. "God *damn* it. You're Finn O'Rourke. I heard you were filming a movie in Chicago." He held Finn's gaze as he said to Mia, "What the hell are you doing with this douche bag, Mia?"

"Brendan, keep your voice down." She glanced around to see if anyone had noticed the testosterone cloud swirling through their booth. No one was paying attention.

Yet.

"You get your ass out of this booth right now," she hissed, shoving him so hard that he nearly fell on the floor. "And you keep your mouth shut. You tell no one he's here. Do you understand me?"

"No. I don't. Do you have any idea what this guy did to Gemma Rad…"

"Stop. That's enough." She slapped her hand on her brother's chest. "You are *so* out of line. If I didn't care about making a scene, I'd kick your ass into the next county. Now get out of here and leave us alone. I'll explain later."

Brendan leaned across the table, staring at Finn. Finn crossed his arms and stared back. Mia began to shove Brendan again, but he put his hand on her shoulder. Held her there.

"I'm Brendan. Mia's brother," he said to Finn. "There are three more of us. All cops. Except Mac. He's FBI. I don't care who you are. If you hurt my sister in any way, you'll deal with us."

"Brendan Aloysius Donovan, I am going to *kill* you," Mia fumed. Her temples throbbed as a whirlpool of anger built in her head. She hadn't lost her temper in a while, but a few more minutes of Brendan puffing up his chest at Finn and it was going to slip its leash. "Or maybe I'll tell Cilla what you're doing instead. Let her deal with you."

Ignoring her, Finn raised one eyebrow at Brendan. "Really? Your initials are BAD? As in, to the bone? And

Aloysius? Wow. Your parents must have really hated you."

A muscle in her brother's jaw clenched and released. Clenched again. "Maybe we'll have this discussion now, as soon as Mac, Con and Quinn get here."

"No." Mia edged him toward the end of the bench. This was turning into a disaster. A few people had craned their necks to watch them, and pretty soon everyone in the restaurant would be checking out the drama in the back booth. "What you're going to do, Brendan, is walk out of Oscar's. Wait for them on the sidewalk. Then go somewhere else."

"I don't think so, Mimi."

"Really, *Brenny*? You want to go there?"

She stared at her brother and he stared back. Finally, apparently realizing she wouldn't back down, he splayed his hands on the table. "Okay, Mia. You win." He turned to Finn. "But if you pull a 'Gemma' on my sister…"

Before he could finish, Mia shoved him the rest of the way out of the booth. "You don't know shit about what happened there. So leave it alone, Bren, unless you want to make a complete fool of yourself."

Her brother's gaze turned calculating as he watched her. He glanced at Finn once more, then nodded. "Fair enough. But consider yourself warned, *pretty boy*. You mess with my sister and you mess with all of us."

Brendan turned and strode toward the front of the restaurant. He slammed his hand on the door and shoved his way out. Then he stood to the side and leaned on the window. Watching them.

She glared in his direction, but he didn't move. Apparently a long distance threat lost its effectiveness.

"Well. That was fun," Finn said, his lips twitching. "Nothing like a little drama to liven up a quiet, restful dinner."

She wanted to sink into the floor and disappear. "I apologize for my brother," she said stiffly. "He was raised by wolves. We haven't quite civilized him yet."

"So." Finn slumped a little on the bench, tapping his fingers on the varnished wood table. "Three more of those on the spreadsheet, huh?"

"Yes. And if you're very lucky, you won't meet the rest of them."

"It was kind of sweet, actually," he said, his gaze softening as he studied Mia. "Your brother was trying to protect you." He shrugged one shoulder. "Can't blame him. Everyone else thinks I'm a douche bag. Why would your brother be different?"

"Don't make excuses for him," she said sharply. "He was incredibly rude. Interfering. Disrespectful. To both of us."

"Mia, if I saw my sister with a guy the whole world thought was a lying, cheating bastard, I'd have the same reaction," he said quietly. "Cut him some slack." He studied her for a moment. "Are all your brothers older than you?"

"Yeah, I'm the 'baby'." She swiped her fingers through the air. "They think it's their duty to warn guys away from me." She smiled, finally relaxing a little. "Made for a pretty crappy social life in high school. As you can imagine, I didn't go on many dates."

"Intimidating the hell out of guys is a brother's job." He took a drink of his beer. "I did it plenty of times to my sister. She thanked me once in a while, too."

"Yeah, I thanked my brothers a few times. There were a couple guys…" She shook her head. Water under the bridge. "Anyway, what were we talking about before my brother interrupted us?"

"I kind of lost track." He took another drink and smiled. "I was distracted."

Finn was being an incredibly good sport after being insulted and threatened by her brother. Some of the tension in her shoulders eased. He was a decent man. A nice guy.

Studying him as he drank his beer, she wondered again what had happened with Gemma Radley. She couldn't imagine the guy she'd gotten to know in the last two days cheating on his girlfriend. And even if he had, he wasn't cruel enough to do it in a place where his girlfriend would catch him.

***

Finn watched Mia across the table. She was still simmering, which didn't bother him at all. All that heavy breathing was making the snug black shirt cup her breasts in very interesting ways.

Too bad it wasn't another white shirt. Knowing the color of her bra would be a nice bonus.

She didn't notice him checking her out. In fact, she wasn't paying any attention to him. She was too busy staring toward the front of the restaurant, a scowl on her face. Twenty bucks said her brother was staring right back at her.

"Your brother looks a lot like you," he said.

With a start, Mia jerked her gaze back to him. "What?" Her eyes flicked toward the front door, then back to him. "You think I look like that knucklehead?"

"Spitting image. But him calling me pretty boy?" Finn shook his head. "Pot calling the kettle black. I'll point that out next time I see him," he said, biting the inside of his cheek to contain the grin that wanted to escape.

Mia glanced toward the front door again, then back to Finn. She was clearly still angry at her brother and not really paying attention. It took a moment, but delicate pink washed over her face when she realized that Finn had actually said *she* was pretty.

"You think you're going to see him again?" Mia glowered at him. "Not a chance in hell."

"You want to bet on it? Because I guarantee he'll show up. Probably the rest of your brothers, too." Finn smiled happily, anticipating the fireworks. "They'll all want to protect you from the big, bad wolf."

"Not after I tell them I'm protecting the Big, Bad Wolf from an enraged, stalking Little Red Riding Hood. They all respect the job." She glanced toward the door again. A muscle in her jaw clenched, then she slid into the corner of the booth, pressing up against the wall.

"Why did you move?" he asked, sliding over as well so he was across from her again.

"Because the other three knuckleheads are here now, too. They were all watching me. So it was either slide over so I can't see them, or go outside and deal with them." She sighed and picked up her iced tea. "Making a scene would not be a good idea."

He leaned toward her, fascinated. "So if I didn't care about publicity, you'd go out there and confront them?"

"Absolutely." She took another drink of tea, and her shoulders relaxed a little. "I want to keep you *out* of the spotlight instead of getting you back in the newspaper tomorrow. If there wasn't a stalker, if it was just you and I on a date and my brothers pulled that crap, I'd hand them their asses on a plate."

"You've thought about going on a date with me?" he asked, anticipation rushing through him. He slid his hand across the table, stroked one finger over her arm. Felt her tremble.

"I...not...no." She stared down at his fingers, dancing over her skin. When she lifted her head, her eyes were darker. More dilated. "I was speaking hypothetically."

He wondered whether she had any idea how expressive her face was. How easily he could read her. She liked the idea of a date with him. He slid his fingers over her hand, twined them together. "What did you have in mind for our hypothetical date?"

For a split second, her hand softened. Curved around his, accepting his touch. Then she yanked it away from him.

Didn't matter. He'd gotten the information he wanted. She *had* thought about him as more than her job. In great detail, too, based on the color still staining her cheeks.

"There will be no dates, hypothetical or otherwise."

"'The lady doth protest too much, methinks'," he said

softly.

She stared at him for a long moment, then flopped back against the seat. "You know everyone else puts the 'methinks' first. Only a show-off-y actor would know the exact quote," she muttered.

"And a cop, apparently," he said. "You're an interesting woman, Mia."

She held his gaze. "Still doesn't mean we're going on a date."

"I understand," he said. "You have standards. Anyone seeing you on a date with me would think you'd lowered them about as far as possible." He smiled at the waitress as she set his bison burger and Mia's macaroni and cheese on the table.

"You think reverse psychology will work on me, O'Rourke?" She shook her head and dipped her fork into the dish in front of her, picking out a piece of bacon. "I'm a master of it. Four older brothers, remember?"

Mia ate the bacon, then plunged her fork into the still bubbling bowl and took a bite of the cheesy pasta. She closed her eyes and hummed her pleasure.

Finn swallowed, his fingers closing around his own fork. Then he set it carefully on his plate.

He wasn't interested in dinner anymore. He reached for his phone to call Pete, then clenched his fist on his thigh instead. He wanted to drive back to the hotel. Find a much more private setting. Make Mia purr like that again. Feel it vibrate in her throat when he kissed her.

A tiny smile curved Mia's lips as she ate her macaroni. Had she noticed his reaction, or was she just basking in her victory over her brother? Then she glanced at his plate, and her eyes twinkled. "Don't like the burger, Finn?"

She'd noticed his reaction. "Burger looks great." He took a bite and washed it down with beer. "Tastes great, too. But the company looks better."

He took her hand, turned it over and smoothed his thumb over her wrist. Felt her pulse jump. "And I know she tastes better."

Mia's fork clattered onto her plate as she stared at him. Her hand trembled in his, but she didn't pull away. "That was...that was business," she finally said. Her voice was satisfyingly throaty.

"Really?" he asked, pressing his thumb against her pulse a little harder. It leaped against his skin. "Didn't taste like business. Tasted like...something I want to nibble on again. Soon."

Mia swallowed, and he watched the muscles in her neck ripple. Her eyes darkened as she held his gaze, then she slid her hand away.

"You know that would be a big mistake," she said quietly. "I have to protect you. Harder to do if I'm...distracted."

"I'd think it would be easier," he said. His fingers tingled, and he ached to reach for her hand again. She must have recognized the need in his eyes, because she slid her hand into her lap. "You'd know me better. You'd be able to anticipate my reactions." He leaned closer. "You'd be invested in me."

Her eyes went cool. She picked up her fork and began eating, her jaw working like she was chewing on leather instead of pasta.

Finally, she set her fork down carefully and stared across the table at him. "I'm invested in my *job*. And I don't have to like the people I deal with to do the job right. If you were a murdering rapist instead of an egotistical actor, I'd work just as hard to protect you. I took an oath, and I respect that oath. My personal feelings don't matter."

Oh, God. He'd been teasing. He thought she'd realized it.

"Mia, I'm sorry. I didn't mean to imply that you'd somehow do your job better if we were...closer. I've known you for two days, and I can see how seriously you take your job. I was just being...an ass. Teasing you." He shook his head. "My life is built around a fake reality. I guess I don't remember how to behave in the real world. With real people doing real jobs."

She tilted her head and studied him. Finally she reached across the table and took his hand. Her fingers were cool against his, and softer than anything he'd ever felt. "I knew you were teasing. But you tempted me a little too much. Made me want things I can't have. I had to remind myself of what my priorities needed to be."

She squeezed his hand and let him go. "I didn't mean to make you feel bad." She ate another bite of macaroni and smiled. "And you did rack up a few points for knowing you live in a fake world. I'm guessing a lot of your colleagues don't know that."

As he stared at her bright blue eyes and dazzling smile, real became more and more tempting. And harder to resist. "All teasing aside, I want to know what makes you tick, Mia."

Pink tinged her cheeks as she pushed away the empty bowl that had held her macaroni. "My job. My family. My friends. I'm a simple woman."

"I don't think you're simple at all. I think you're one of the most complicated people I've ever met."

She shook her head. "That's where you'd be wrong. I think I'm different than other women you know. And that's why you're interested." She shrugged as she caught the waitress's eye and scribbled on her hand, signaling for the check. "I'm not famous, I'm not a name in the tabloids, I don't do what you do for a living. That's all it is."

His attraction to Mia had nothing to do with what she did or didn't do. And he wasn't comparing her to other women. In fact, when he looked at her, no other women existed.

The attraction he'd felt from the moment he'd opened his door to her had quickly turned into fascination. He was afraid fascination was morphing into need.

He didn't want to *need* her. He wanted her. A lot. But he wasn't interested in forging emotional connections with

a woman, not even Mia. Not anymore. Not since Gemma.
But all he could think about was Mia.
This was not good.

CHAPTER THIRTEEN

Their waitress slid a black plastic folder on the table, then turned to take another order. Finn checked the total, pulled out his wallet and set some bills inside the folder. Then he closed it, called Pete and began to slide out of the booth.

"Hold it." Mia grabbed his arm, then let go immediately. Head down, she fumbled in her bag, finally pulling out a paper sack. She handed it to him, and his fingers slid against hers when he took it. She stilled for a moment, swallowed, then cleared her throat.

"Put that on before we leave."

He quirked an eyebrow at her. "You want me to wear a bag? Isn't that a little extreme, even for you?"

Mia rolled her eyes, but a grin tugged at her mouth. "In the bag, funny man."

He opened the bag cautiously. Frowned as he peered inside it. "Why are you giving me a dead raccoon?"

"It's a beard, doofus." It looked as if she barely resisted rolling her eyes again. "A disguise. Since your dad pants didn't seem to work yesterday."

At the mention of his previous disguise, he forgot every

reason to keep his distance from Mia. "Those pants worked damn well yesterday." He'd dreamt about her hands, sliding beneath the waistband. Cupping his ass. Squeezing it. Yeah. Every muscle in his body remembered that. "I have very…fond memories of those pants."

Color swept over her face. "Yeah, well, we're trying the beard tonight."

He leaned toward her across the table. "Your hands going to end up tangled in the beard, too? Because that would be fine. As long as your mouth is there with it."

"Shut it," she hissed, just as their waitress picked up the black folder.

Finn smiled up at the harried-looking woman. "Thanks, we're good," he said.

"Thank you," she said with an automatic upturn of her lips. Then she cocked her head and really looked at him.

He immediately turned away. Toward Mia. *Damn it.*

"Don't smile at people," Mia ordered as soon as she'd left. "Your smile is as famous as Paul Newman's blue eyes. I don't want that woman swooning. It'll draw attention."

"You're right." He tried to force a serious expression onto his face. "Don't want her to swoon." He picked up Mia's hand, kissed her palm. "There's only one woman I want swooning over me." He smiled. "And it's not our waitress."

"Put on the damn beard," she said. "There's double-sided tape in the bag." She slid to the edge of the bench and stood up, but he saw her hand trembling as she smoothed her jacket over the gun.

The beard was too thick. Too long. He'd bet money it made him look like someone from that duck-calling-family reality show.

And it itched against his skin.

"Where'd you get this thing?" he muttered as he adjusted his baseball cap and stood up.

"Tell you later."

They walked side by side through the restaurant, and he

was surprised no one in Oscar's gave him a second look. When they reached the front door, he watched Mia step outside and scan the street. Looking for her brothers? His stalker?

He suspected they would all get the same treatment from her tonight.

Pete rolled to a stop beside the cars parked at the curb, and Mia hurried to open the door for Finn. As soon as he was in the car, she slid in after him, pulled the door shut, and the car began moving.

"Nice look for you, buddy," Pete said, grinning into the mirror.

"Shut up, Pete." As Pete raised the partition, Finn peeled the beard off and handed it back to Mia. "I'm guessing we're going to use that again."

"You guessed right," she said, shoving it back into the paper sack.

"I'd rather use *my* disguise," he said.

Mia froze for a long moment, her fingers closing around the bag. The sudden crinkle of paper was loud in the quiet car. Then she shoved the paper sack into her bag.

As Pete turned a corner, Finn moved a little closer to Mia. Thank God for slippery leather seats. Their thighs weren't touching, but Finn had high hopes for the next corner. Trying to distract her, he asked, "That beard is hideous. I figured people would be laughing and pointing at me. But no one gave me a second look when we walked out of the restaurant."

"People around here are used to seeing beards. We're close to a hipster neighborhood."

"You're pretty damn clever," he said. She was so smart it was kind of scary.

"It worked, didn't it?" she smirked at him. "No one recognized you."

"Except your brother," he pointed out.

Damn it. He wanted to snatch the words out of the air between them. Why did he have to remind her? He'd rather keep her thinking about their kiss at the park yesterday.

Because it was sure as hell the only thing he could think about.

She relaxed farther into the seat. Apparently, now that her brothers were safely behind them, she could let it go. "He's a detective. He's trained to notice things. People." She snorted. "He's probably running you through the databases right now. And Mac's going through the federal ones."

He frowned. "They're not going to find anything, but isn't that illegal?"

"It's a gray area. Cops can come up with all kinds of bullshit reasons for running someone's name." She sighed. "I'm sure my brothers have run every guy I've dated through the databases." Her eyes twinkled. "The ones they knew about, anyway."

He edged closer, forgetting about her brothers. "Tell me about the boyfriends you hid from your family."

"Not a chance." She leaned into the corner of the seat, a smile flirting with her mouth. "I don't kiss and tell."

"Good to know." The warm leather and another corner moved him close enough to feel the heat from her body. "I don't, either. If we...recreate that moment behind the bandshell, no one will ever know."

"I'd know," she said, her smile disappearing.

"I hope so." Another turn pressed him into Mia, joining their legs together from hip to knee. "If you didn't, I'd be completely distraught. Would need to hide in my room for days to recover. Which would void my contract with the studio. Ruin my career. Just when I was getting it back on track, too. It would be tragic. Horrifying for my fans."

"You're right. All ten of them would be devastated," she shot back.

She remembered his joke from yesterday morning. And she hadn't even had coffee at that point. His mouth twitching with the effort to hold in a smile, he leaned closer. His mouth was inches from hers. "Do you remember every stupid thing I've said?"

"That would be hard, since you've said so many stupid things." Mia's fierce blue gaze burned into him. Challenged him to step over the line she'd drawn.

He loved challenges. "You don't think I'll kiss you again?"

"No," she managed to say. "Not if you're as smart as I think you are."

Their lips were a fraction of an inch apart. Her breath feathered over his mouth, carrying the scent of her lemony iced tea. The car suddenly bounced, and his lower lip touched hers for the barest of moments.

He didn't miss the tiny catch in her breathing.

Thank God for Chicago potholes.

He eased back until he could see the pulse pounding in her neck. Her pupils, almost entirely black. The too-rapid rise and fall of her chest.

"Are you challenging me, Mia?" he murmured. "Throwing down the gauntlet?" The car slowed, and he glanced out the window and saw the now-familiar loading area of the Drake Hotel. "Please say you are."

The car slowed, and Mia had the door open almost before it stopped completely. She rapped on Pete's window as soon as Finn was out of the car, and watched as it rolled away.

"Let's go," she said, hurrying toward the hotel door.

Was she in a hurry to get inside? To continue their conversation?

Eyeing her stiff, straight back, he was pretty sure that wasn't why she was in a rush.

Maybe she thought he'd ignore the arousal he'd seen in the curve of her body toward him. In the pulse fluttering in her throat. That he'd have forgotten about it by the time they got to the suite.

Not damn likely.

But he walked beside her, careful to stay on her left side, away from her gun hand. Didn't say anything. When they got into the elevator, he stopped himself from crowding her against one of the wood panels and kissing her hard enough to knock off the tiny shades on the wall lamps. He suspected that if he touched her now, while she was hyperalert for trouble, she'd knee him in the balls.

Not the way he wanted this evening to end.

She walked into the suite first, and he stayed next to the door while she checked all the rooms. Then she came back out, double locked the door and lifted the security bolt into place. Exhaled.

They were safe inside the suite. All bets were off

She smiled at him, but it wobbled a little. "Long day. You going to run some lines before you go to bed?"

"Nope. No lines." He reached out for her hand, tangled his fingers with hers. Tugged her closer.

***

Mia's heart thudded hard against her chest as Finn slid his fingers between hers and pressed his mouth to hers. The logical part of her brain told her to back away and avoid the quicksand trembling beneath her feet.

But her body wanted to sink into the quicksand. Lose herself in Finn's mouth and spend hours exploring it.

She would give herself a moment. She'd kiss him, then let him go.

She sucked gently at his lower lip, tasting the spicy sweetness of the peppermint candy he'd grabbed on the way out of Oscar's. His hands were at her waist, and as she slid her tongue along the seam of his mouth, he trembled. Tightened his grip on her, until his fingers dug into her hips.

Without any warning, he spun her around and backed her into the wall. Every curve of her body fit perfectly against the hard muscles of his. Swallowing a moan, she gripped the back of his head and pressed her mouth to his.

His hands slid to her ass, igniting more memories of yesterday's kiss. They drew a needy whimper from her throat, and she sucked at his lower lip, needing to taste him. Explore him.

He touched his tongue to her upper lip, tracing its slippery inner surface as if trying to memorize her taste. Lingered there, humming deep in his throat. As if he wanted to spend the night learning her every flavor and texture.

Finally he touched his tongue to hers. He was delicate and gentle rather than possessive, and his careful touch made her heart tremble. Made everything soften inside her. Except her nipples. They were hard as pebbles.

Finn tasted of the tang of mustard and the creaminess of the cheese from his burger. The hoppiness of the beer he'd drunk overlaid it all.

But beneath all of that, she tasted Finn. The man she'd kissed yesterday. The one who'd starred in all her dreams last night.

The man she'd longed to kiss again. And he tasted as good as she remembered.

Lost in their kiss, she wrapped an ankle around his leg. Moved into him as he slid his leg between hers. She twined her arms around his neck to keep him close.

He made her want to press into his leg, ease the ache that was building. Instead, she slid her hands down his back and pulled his shirt from his jeans. Slid her hands over the hot skin of his back, feeling the twitch of every muscle she touched, the tiny hitch of his breath when she found a particularly good spot.

Still kissing him, she burrowed her hands lower. Tried to slide them beneath the waistband of his jeans. She wanted his hard ass in her palms again.

She managed to get only one finger beneath his jeans.

Rearing back, panting, she said, "Where are the dad pants? Why did we go out tonight without them?"

"No idea." He peeled her jacket down one arm and tugged it off. Began working on the other. "I can lose the jeans." He pressed his mouth to her neck and sucked lightly.

"Say the word. They're gone."

"No." She nuzzled his neck, and the tender skin beneath his ear tasted a little salty. A little sweet. Tracing patterns there with her tongue, she worked to unfasten the button of his fly. "Clothes stay on." She tugged at his ear lobe.

As he worked his way down her neck to the open vee at the top of her shirt, she felt his lips curve against her skin. "Okay," he said. His breath caressed her damp skin, making her shiver. "No clothes come off."

He fumbled with the buttons of her shirt as his mouth drifted lower. As each button opened, he followed it with his mouth. Cool air washed over her skin, and he sucked gently at the curve of her breast exposed by her bra.

"Purple," he sighed against her cleavage. "My new favorite color."

Her fingers were shaking too much to push the button through the stubborn denim. Finally it popped free, and his jeans slid lower on his hips.

The denim gaped as she slid her hands over his silk-covered ass. "Mmmm," she said, smoothing her hands over the hard muscles. "Even better than I remembered."

The cool air curled around her nipples, and she looked down to see the front snap of her bra opened. It hung from her shoulders, exposing her breasts.

"What happened to no clothes come off?" she managed to say as he cupped both breasts in her hands.

"You're still wearing all your clothes." He nudged the dangling cup of her bra with his chin. "Bra's right there." His nose brushed over one nipple, and she felt the shock all the way to her core. *Holy mother of God.*

"Not…not really wearing it."

"Not off," he retorted. "I still see purple."

He slicked his tongue over one nipple, then the other, and her legs gave out. She slid down the wall, but Finn caught her in time. Eased her to the floor, then stretched out beside her. Not touching her, though.

Why wasn't he touching her?

He cleared his throat and she cracked an eye open. "Can you, ah, lose the gun? It's kind of cramping my style."

She managed to lift her head and open both eyes. Her shirt fanned out on either side of her body, and her bra was a vivid splash of purple against the black shirt. Her nipples were hard and tight, still aching from the attention from his tongue.

Her Glock was sitting on her hip. Finn was carefully avoiding it. "Don't like my gun?" she managed to say.

"On general principles," he said, leaning away from it, "I don't like my cock this close to a gun."

"I can take care of your principles," she said, working at her belt with trembling hands. When it was unbuckled, she tugged it off and her holster fell to the floor. Finn carefully picked it up and set it on the table.

"My cock thanks you."

She patted the front of his jeans, let her hand explore the thickness of his erect penis. "You're welcome. Wouldn't want him to be...hesitant."

"No hesitation in him. Trust me. Although you'll probably want to check that for yourself." Finn propped himself on one elbow. "Now where was I?"

"We were discussing clothes." Her breasts were swollen. Tight. Aching for his touch. She grabbed his free hand and put it over her breast. "Or lack thereof."

He squeezed gently, and she had to bite the inside of her mouth to suppress a moan. "I vote for lack thereof," he said as he bent to take one nipple in his mouth.

At the first touch of his mouth, she arched into him. "Oh, God, Finn." She blindly reached for him, and her hand slid over the front of his boxers. Let her fingers dance over his hard length. "I like your ass," she said. "Like this better."

"Feeling is...feeling is mutual," he said.

Her hips were moving, and Finn sat up. His fingers moved over her abdomen, and suddenly he yanked her pants lower. The carpet was cool and rough against her bare legs. Finn pulled one leg off and slipped a hand into her panties, and she forgot all about the carpet.

He kissed her as he caressed her, swallowing the moans she couldn't hold in. "You purred when you ate your dinner," he said into her mouth. "I wanted to hear it again. But this is much better."

The sound of his voice, combined with his touch, sent a climax rocketing through her. She gripped his shirt in both fists as it went on and on. Before he could take his hand away, she shoved his jeans down his legs. "Condom," she gasped. "Please tell me you have one."

"In the other room," he said.

She shoved him away. "Go. Now."

He stood up, then hopped on one leg as he rid himself of his jeans. She watched his fine ass as he scrambled into his bedroom, returning a moment later holding a foil packet.

She snatched it out of his hands and rolled it onto him, then pulled him into the vee of her legs. He eased into her, rocking against her muscles, until he was all the way inside her.

As he stroked, she felt another orgasm building. Wrapping her legs around his waist, she thrust with him until they were both moving raggedly. Her legs trembled and she buried her face in Finn's neck.

As she soared over the edge again, he stilled, groaning. Finally he collapsed beside her, rolling over so she was lying on his chest.

She curled into him as her breathing returned to normal and feeling returned to the rest of her body. Then she kissed his chest and sat up. Her face felt hot, and so did her chest. Whisker burn. She couldn't work up the energy to worry about it. "This wasn't supposed to happen. That's why we left our clothes on."

"News flash, babe." He sat up, too, wrapped an arm around her and pulled her against him. "This has been inevitable since the moment we kissed yesterday. Clothes or no clothes."

"It shouldn't have been." The blood was finally flowing in her brain again, and her rational self was screaming 'what were you thinking?' She shouldn't have kissed him. She'd known what would happen.

The moment they kissed, they'd been heading toward this. She should have kept her distance. "This is wrong on so many levels," she sighed. She stood up, hooked her bra and began to button her shirt.

She was reaching for her pants when she heard footsteps in the hall. Shoving them onto her legs, she slapped her hip, then realized her gun was missing. Damn it!

Someone knocked on the door. She and Finn stared at one another.

"Finn?" a male voice called. "You in there."

"Oh, God," Finn whispered, shoving buttons through the buttonholes in his shirt with shaking hands. "It's Doug. My godfather."

CHAPTER FOURTEEN

H is godfather? The superintendent? "What's he doing here?" she hissed.

"I have no idea." He cleared his throat. "Be right there," he called.

Mia's hands shook as she threaded her belt through the loops on her pants and attached her holster. Then she ran her fingers through her hair, which felt as if someone had taken a blender to it. She tried to calm it, but she knew she looked as if she'd just rolled out of bed.

Finn shoved his shirt tails into his pants, smoothed his hair and glanced at her, his eyes wild. "Okay to open the door?"

Mia took a deep breath, closed her eyes and tried to center herself. Which was hard when her body still vibrated with the aftereffects of the sex she'd had. On the floor. With the superintendent's godson.

She unsnapped the flap of her holster and put her hand on the grip of her gun. Finn saw her and frowned. "It's my godfather."

He reached for the door, and she knocked his hand away. "Look in the peephole, damn it. What did I tell you about that?"

"I recognize his voice."

"Look anyway."

Finn pressed his face against the door. "It's him. He's alone."

"Good. Now you can open the door."

He smoothed his hair once more, which made it look more like bed head. Then he unlocked it and smiled. A muscle jumped in his jaw. "Doug. What are you doing here?"

"Have some news for you." The superintendent walked into the room, scanning the suite with sharp, observant eyes. Mia spotted the empty condom packet on the floor and discreetly nudged it beneath the sofa with her toe.

Mia had seen Doug Walsh a handful of times – when she'd graduated from the academy, at the ceremonies when her brothers were promoted to detective, once or twice on the news. He looked a lot more intimidating standing a few feet away from her.

The superintendent was tall and lean, ramrod straight, his white hair cut short. Cleanly shaven, he wore casual clothes – a pair of jeans and a dark green polo shirt, with boat shoes on his feet. Authority still oozed from every pore.

He finished his study of the suite, and his gaze turned to her. "Officer Donovan? I'm Doug Walsh. Good to meet you," he said, holding out his hand.

Mia swallowed and took his hand. Shook it, then let go. His hand was warm and solid, and his grip was just right – not too tight, not dead-fish-limp. "Good to meet you too, sir."

Doug's gaze narrowed as he studied her. Had she forgotten to tuck in her shirt? Was her hair a rat's nest? Could he see the red whisker burn on her face?

Probably not. Her embarrassed flush would hide that.

"Looks like you've had a…long day, Officer," he said.

"Yes, sir," she answered. "It was Finn's first day of

shooting."

"Have any problems today?" he asked.

"No, sir. Everything went smoothly."

"What are you doing here, Doug?" Finn stepped between his godfather and Mia. "What's wrong?"

The superintendent transferred his attention to his godson. Mia wanted to kiss Finn for distracting him.

No. Not kiss him. Thank him. Yeah. She could do that. But no more kissing.

"We got a partial print off the letter you got this morning," Doug said. He glanced at Mia over Finn's shoulder. "Nice work handling that, Officer."

He stepped to the side so he could see both of them. "We didn't get any matches, but if there's anyone you suspect, try to get a print and we'll see if it matches."

"Yes, sir. I'll do that," Mia said. He'd come here and scared ten years off her life to tell them that? He couldn't have phoned?

As if they shared brainwaves, Finn said, "You could have called, Doug. You didn't have to come all the way over here to tell me that. You're too busy to run errands."

Doug's eyebrows pulled together. "I wanted to see my godson." His gaze flickered to Mia. "Make sure the officer that Talbott sent over was up to the job."

"She tells me I'm an idiot," Finn said. "But other than that, we get along great."

"She sounds like a smart woman," the superintendent said. "She taking good care of you, then?"

Mia sucked in a tiny breath and felt her face heat. But Finn said easily, "The best. Takes her job very seriously. Always ordering me around."

Doug studied Mia for an uncomfortably long moment, then nodded. "I'm counting on you to keep him safe, Officer." His glance shifted from her to Finn and back to her. "Stick close to him until we catch his stalker." He tilted his head. "You going to have a problem with that? Finn behaving himself for you?"

142

"Absolutely, sir. He's been very cooperative." He'd cooperated the hell out of her a few minutes ago. "And of course I'll stick close to him. That's my job."

Finn glanced at her, his eyes twinkling. She wanted to kick him, but contented herself with narrowing her eyes at him. Signaling that he'd pay later.

"Good. Glad to hear it." He looked from her to Finn, his lips twitching. "Marie would love to see you, Finny. Can you come over for dinner one evening?" He glanced at Mia. "With Officer Donovan, of course."

No. God, no. She opened her mouth, but before she could think of what to say, Finn said, "I'd love to, Doug, but I've got a pretty tight schedule. Shooting every day to get my part done." He slapped his godfather on the back. "If I can squeeze it in, I'll give you a call."

"Look forward to hearing from you." Doug reached out and embraced his godson, then held out his hand to Mia again. She swiped hers surreptitiously on her pants before returning his shake.

"Hope to see you again, Officer," he said.

"Yes, sir. Me, too, sir," Mia stuttered.

Doug noticed the flowers on the table. "Nice flowers," he said. "They're starting to wilt, though. Make sure you water them."

Finn snorted. "Yes, sir, Mr. Green Thumb. I'll take care of it."

"Have a good night, you two," his godfather said, his eyes twinkling. Then he opened the door and left.

She and Finn stared at one another, silent, until they heard the ding of the elevator arriving. Finn peered through the peephole for a long moment, then slumped against the door. "Elevator just closed. Doug's inside."

"God!" Mia fell onto the couch and shoved her hands through her hair. "The superintendent almost caught us having sex."

"But he didn't," Finn said, flopping down beside her. "I'm sure he didn't suspect a thing."

She turned to look at him, then groaned. "Oh, yes he did. Your shirt. You buttoned it wrong. He knew."

Finn looked at the mis-matched buttons. "Oops."

"Yeah, big oops. Huge one. Not to mention my hair." Mia combed her fingers through it, wincing at the snarls. "Must look like I just got out of bed."

"Hey, it wasn't that bad," he said.

"Not for you. Except for this shirt." She tugged on his sleeve, aching to twine her fingers with his. She dropped the fabric and curled her fingers into her palm. "I have to say, you're a way better actor than anyone knows. That performance with the superintendent? Oscar-worthy. Except for the shirt, no one would have known we were sprawled in a post-coital haze a few minutes earlier."

"'Post-coital haze?' Where do you come up with this stuff?" He smiled at her, that familiar sparkle back in his eyes. "I like the Oscar-worthy part, though."

"Yeah, figures you'd latch onto that." She kept her eyes on his, drinking in happy, carefree Finn. "Instead of the fact that your godfather knows what we were doing.

"God!" She slumped against the back of the couch and covered her eyes with her arm. "Goodbye, detective's star. I'm going to be busted down to traffic for the rest of my life."

"What are you talking about? What detective's star?"

She couldn't keep her mouth shut, could she? The mistakes just kept on coming tonight. She sighed. "I was studying to take the exam to become a detective when my captain asked if I wanted this job." She glanced at him from beneath her arm. "He said it would look good on my record if I caught the stalker."

"So that's why you're here?" Finn frowned. "To curry favor with my godfather?"

"No!" She shot upright and glared down at Finn. "I'd never met him before tonight. And he doesn't pick the detectives." She paced over to the window and stared at the lake. The moon was behind the clouds tonight, and the water was a smooth sheet of black. Dark. Impenetrable. Just like her future.

"There's a written exam and an interview in front of a committee. And they look at your record." She sighed. "My captain implied that doing a good job protecting you would be a plus for me. That's all."

"So you're riding my ass to a detective's job," Finn said, his eyes twinkling.

"Not anymore, I'm not. Not after the superintendent caught me banging his godson. On the job."

"We weren't *banging*, Mia," Finn said, his expression softening.

"Really? Then I must have been in some alternate reality. Because it sure felt as if I had sex with you. The orgasms were especially vivid."

He grabbed her hand and tugged her down until she was sitting in his lap. "That wasn't just hooking up, Mia. I care about you." He skimmed his fingers along her cheek and down her neck, lingered in the vee of her throat. "And I'm really glad you enjoyed yourself. Because I did, too."

Her heart melted into a gooey mess at his words. "We've known each other for two days," she said, laying her head on his shoulder. "Barely enough time to form an opinion about each other."

"Oh, I've formed an opinion about you." He nuzzled her neck. "I like you, Mia. A lot. You matter to me." He slid his fingers between hers. "Sex with you was more than scratching an itch. Okay? That's all I meant."

She stared at her lap, at her pale hand and his golden one twined together. "Okay."

"Let's go to bed," he said. "It's been a long day. You're probably as tired as I am." He picked up her free hand and pressed a kiss to her palm. "And we can spend the morning in bed," he added, his eyes gleaming. "We're shooting at night tomorrow, so we have the morning free."

Spending the morning in bed with Finn was far too tempting. She closed her eyes and bit her tongue before she could weaken and agree.

It was harder than she expected to untangle her hand from his. But she drew it away, then slid to her feet. "I'll see you in the morning."

"Wait." He caught her hand as she walked away. "You're not going to sleep with me?"

"No, Finn. I'm not. That would be doubling down on my mistake." She couldn't sleep in the same bed with him. It was too intimate. Too personal. If she was going to retain any smidgen of objectivity about Finn O'Rourke, she had to keep some distance between them.

"What if I beg? Promise not to touch you?"

She snorted. "Good one, Finn. I'd deserve to get busted down to traffic if I fell for that line." Truth was, she wasn't sure *she'd* be able to resist touching *him*. "I'll see you in the morning," she said as she headed toward her room.

"If you change your mind, you know where to find me," he called as she stepped into the bedroom.

"Not changing my mind," she said over her shoulder.

She should close the door. Establish some separation between them after what had happened tonight. But she couldn't do it. She had to leave the door open.

If she was honest with herself, she'd admit she *wanted* to leave it open, as well.

Drawing a deep breath, she stepped into the bathroom and got ready for bed. Turned out the lights, then slid between the sheets.

She closed her eyes, but found herself listening to Finn moving around in the other bedroom. When she heard the whisper of fabric as he undressed, she trailed her fingers down her abdomen, remembering the touch of his hands when he'd unbuttoned her shirt.

The running water in his bathroom, the splash of it against his skin, made her imagine licking the droplets off his face. His chest.

She waited for a drawer to open, signaling he was pulling on a tee and a pair of boxers, but the soft click of the drawer never came. The next sound she heard was the rustle of the bedspread being pulled back. The fantasy-inducing sound of skin sliding against the hotel's gazillion-count sheets.

Mia closed her eyes. He was naked between the sheets. A handful of steps away. She shuddered with the memory of his hands on her. Of her hands on him. The way his muscles had trembled. The tiny catches in his breath when they'd kissed. The desperate grip of his hands on her body as they'd had...made love.

She threw the covers back and slid out of bed. Padded to the door, then gripped the door frame to keep herself from going any farther into the darkened suite.

She'd never wanted a man this intensely before. Never ached with the need to cross the room and slide into his bed.

After a long moment, she slid back into bed. Rolled onto her side, her face away from the door. Away from temptation.

She'd never slept with a guy after knowing him less than forty-eight hours, either. She'd never been less than completely objective and impersonal on the job.

All kinds of firsts for her today. And she had almost three more weeks on this job. Three more weeks of living with Finn. Not doing what she so desperately wanted to do again.

Unless she got yanked off the job tomorrow.

She didn't want that to happen. The job she'd been reluctant to take had become important to her.

Or maybe Finn had become important to her.

She stared at the ceiling for a long time before she fell asleep.

***

Finn cracked open one eye and glanced out the window. The sky was just beginning to lighten, pink and purple streaks rising from the eastern horizon. The red numbers on the clock beside his bed read 4:37. He didn't need to be up for hours.

After staring at the window for ten minutes, he threw back the blanket and sat on the edge of his bed. He'd run some lines, practice his blocking for the outdoor scenes they'd shoot tonight. Anything would be better than lying in bed for another five or six hours, thinking about Mia. Wishing she were sleeping beside him.

He shuffled to the door. Mia's room was still dark. She, apparently, was sleeping like a baby.

Sighing, he headed for the bathroom and the huge shower, which had plenty of room for two people. He wondered how Mia felt about shower sex.

Not as if he was likely to find out. She'd made it clear they weren't going to have sex again. He could wear her down. It wouldn't be hard – she'd wanted him as much as he'd wanted her.

She was right. Doug had probably figured out what they'd been doing right before he arrived. Finn didn't want to jeopardize her job.

But if push came to shove? Finn turned on the shower jets and stepped into the hot water. He wouldn't let his godfather fire Mia. She was exactly what Doug said he wanted. Conscientious. Smart. She paid attention to detail and took the threat more seriously than he did.

Judging by the twinkle in Doug's eyes as he'd left tonight, Finn was pretty sure his godfather didn't have any intention of firing her. Which meant Mia would be with him for the whole three weeks he was in Chicago. And if she caught this stalker before then?

They could still spend time together, without the threat hanging over his head. Without her job throwing up barricades. Win-win for both of them.

She was the first woman he'd had sex with since the break-up with Gemma. The first woman he'd been interested in since he'd dumped the rocker. He would never have guessed that woman would be a remarkable Chicago cop.

He'd clearly spent too much time living in the artificial bubble that was Hollywood, because he'd almost forgotten that women like Mia existed. She was real. Genuine. She said exactly what she thought and called him on his bullshit. No one had done that for a very long time.

Mia fascinated him. He wanted to know everything about her, and he wasn't going to waste a minute of the three weeks they had together.

His hand clenched around the bar of soap, then he set it carefully into the holder on the wall of the shower. Mia would want that, too, wouldn't she?

He'd never questioned that before. A smile, an invitation in his gaze, and women had fallen at his feet. Not Mia, though.

The sex had been off the charts great. For her, too, he was pretty sure. He'd never connected with a woman so fast. So completely. But for the first time since he was a kid, he wasn't sure of his reception with a woman.

She'd said it wouldn't happen again, but he'd change her mind. She wanted him already. He just had to convince her to act on it.

Fifteen minutes later, dressed in jeans and a button-down shirt, Finn picked up the phone and called room service for coffee. He'd wait until Mia woke up before he ordered breakfast. After he reminded the operator that he'd requested Josh to deliver everything to his room, he wandered into the living area of the suite.

He forced himself to ignore the open door of Mia's room. Leaning against the wall and watching her sleep would be creepy. Mia would throw something at him if she caught him.

His mouth curled as he imagined the words that would come out of her mouth if she opened her eyes and found him staring at her.

She must have heard him moving around, because she wandered into the living area a few minutes later, wearing one of the hotel's long white robes.

"What are you doing up?" she croaked. "I thought you said we could sleep in this morning."

"Couldn't sleep. Go back to bed."

"Can't do that. You're up, I'm up."

Her eyelids drooped as she stared out at the barely lightening sky. She glanced at him over her shoulder. "It's the butt crack of dawn. I need coffee."

"On its way."

"Thank God." She tried to shove her hand through her hair, but it caught on the snarls. A reel of technicolor images scrolled slowly through Finn's head, vivid pictures of her hair getting tangled the night before. "I'm going to take a shower. Don't open the door."

His hands wanted to run through the silken strands of her hair again. Feel them slide through his fingers. Letting the fantasy go, he cleared his throat. "Not even if it's your coffee?"

She glanced over her shoulder. "No. Not even for coffee. I take fast showers."

"Bet I can show you how to slow down in there. With all that warm water. And soap. Don't forget the soap." The mental picture was so inviting he took two steps toward her.

She narrowed her eyes at him. "Keep it in your pants, O'Roarke. The amount of sleep I got last night? I'm not in the mood."

He beamed at her retreating back. She hadn't slept well last night, either.

He had a solution for that.

CHAPTER FIFTEEN

Finn paced the living area, listening to the rumble of water against the walls of Mia's shower. He closed his eyes, picturing her beneath the rushing stream, water running in rivulets down her back. Her chest. Her face.

Damn it!

He grabbed his phone and scrolled through his emails, trying to erase the images from his brain. He clicked on one whose subject line read URGENT, huffing out a breath as he read the reminder that he had to be at the studio at one pm. Duh. Did they think he was an idiot?

Yeah. They did.

The assistant directors in charge of wrangling the cast members were used to actors who failed to show up on time, were drunk or high when they did show up, or disappeared into thin air when their scene was called. It didn't matter that Finn had never been one of those people. He got the same alerts as everyone else.

A knock at the door interrupted his thoughts, and he walked over and squinted through the peep hole. It was Josh. "Yes?" he called.

"I have your coffee, sir," he said, clearing his throat. "It's

Josh."

"Can you hold on a minute, buddy?" Finn said.

"Uh, sure."

Finn hurried to Mia's door. The water had stopped and the door was partially closed. He knocked once and pushed it open, then froze. Mia stood at the dresser, wearing only a tiny pair of red polka-dot boy shorts and a matching bra.

He must have sucked in a breath, because she spun around. Narrowed her eyes into angry slits. "Get. Out." She didn't even bother to try and cover herself.

He couldn't stop himself from studying every inch of her – the way her breasts plumped over the edge of her bra, the swell of her hips in those tiny shorts, the smooth, supple curves of her legs. Her hair hung in damp waves around her shoulders, and he wanted to slide his fingers through it. "Ah, Josh is here. With your coffee. I was just…coming to get you."

"I'll be right there." She bent over and grabbed the robe off the bed, and the shorts slid up a little on her ass, revealing creamy, pale skin. She threw on the robe, tightening the belt with a vicious yank, then grabbed her gun from her night stand, dropped it in her pocket and pushed past him.

She peered through the peephole, then opened the door and took the coffee from Josh. "Thanks, Josh," she said. None of the anger from a moment ago was visible in her smile. "We appreciate you taking such good care of us."

The boy beamed. "You're welcome, Ma'am."

Finn recovered his wits in time to grab his wallet and press some bills into Josh's hand. "We'll call later for breakfast. See you then," he said, closing the door.

By the time he'd re-locked the door, Mia had poured two cups of coffee and added cream to both of them. She stood in front of the window overlooking the lake, her mug clasped to her chest. The sun was beginning to peek over the horizon, and the brilliant colors of the sky bled over the city.

"Sorry," he said awkwardly, taking a sip of coffee and burning his tongue. "I shouldn't have walked in on you."

"Don't worry about it. I'm not awake enough to get all indignant," she said without turning. She raised the mug, blew gently over the caramel-colored surface and sipped. "What are we doing this morning?"

She'd let her anger go pretty quickly. He frowned. Did that mean she didn't care that he'd walked in on her? That it wasn't important?

That what had happened last night wasn't important?

"I'm going to work on my blocking and my lines," he said after a moment. "We're doing complicated scenes tonight – an action sequence. A chase scene. Lot of stuff to work out."

She turned to face him. "Okay. What time are we leaving?"

"Twelve-thirty. Studio first, to walk through the scenes. Costume fitting, again. Then we'll have a couple of hours to eat while they set up the equipment at the scene."

She leaned against the window sill as she sipped her coffee. The white robe gaped at her chest, revealing a tiny sliver of the red bra. He tried to drag his gaze above her neck, but that hint of red had his complete focus.

"Where are the scenes set?" Mia asked.

He frowned, trying to remember what they were talking about. "Downtown. Beneath some El tracks. Somewhere."

"Okay. So, cars weaving in and out of the posts, tires squealing, lights flashing, loud noises. Standard car chase scene. Who's doing crowd control?"

He shrugged. "They usually hire cops to take care of that."

Frowning, tapping one fingernail on her front tooth, she stared past his shoulder. Finally her gaze snapped to him. "How close am I going to be able to be to you?"

"No idea. I've never had a bodyguard during a shoot." He hesitated, thinking about it. "When I'm actually in front of the camera, you won't be close. But no one else will be, either, except for the cast and crew and the director. When I'm not shooting? I'll be right next to you." Even if she wasn't guarding him, he'd make sure he was close to her.

"Okay," she said, nodding. "I'll make it work."

He wasn't a fan of this business-like, focused-on-her-job Mia. Not when all he could think about was what had happened on the floor in this room last night. They had hours before they needed to be at the studio. He'd already memorized his lines. He wanted to spend the time with Mia, rolling around in the big bed in his room. Without their clothes this time.

He watched, wincing as she drained her still-hot coffee and poured more into the mug. After a tentative sip, she said, "I'm hungry. Let's order breakfast. And more coffee."

"You have a bad caffeine habit, Officer. Sure you don't need some help breaking it?" His chest tightened in anticipation. Other parts of him, too. "A distraction, maybe?"

Her lips curved behind the safety of her mug. "No help necessary. I've accepted my weakness and learned to live with it. But just out of curiosity, what did you have in mind?"

"I was thinking about some non-verbal communication."

"No way," she said immediately. "I hate charades." Her eyes twinkled.

He would remember what a difference a cup of coffee made in Mia's attitude.

"Not exactly what I had in mind," he said, letting his gaze drop to the vee at the neck of her bathrobe.

Her smile faded. "I meant what I said last night."

"And I thought about what you said. It doesn't need to change anything. You'll still do your job like the frighteningly competent woman you are. I'll still get on your nerves like the ass I can be. But when we're back here, in the safety of these rooms, we can both drop our guards.

Explore what this is between us."

She raised one eyebrow. "'Frighteningly competent? Makes me sound like a prison warden."

He leaned against the couch, sipping on his own coffee. "Warden works for me," he said with a little smirk. "Handcuffs? A uniform? I'm in."

She shook her head, but her mouth twitched. "In your dreams, O'Rourke." Her smile disappeared. "I know what this is between us, Finn." She lowered the coffee and watched him with serious eyes. "It's an attraction that's hot enough to melt steel. I want you, too. But you're only here for three weeks. I think we're better off if we keep this professional and both do our jobs."

"We could have a lot of fun in three weeks." His hands tingled with the need to touch her.

"Yeah, we could. But if I get…attached, it would make me less effective as your bodyguard. When emotion gets involved, mistakes happen."

She was right. He sure as hell didn't want a messy entanglement. He and Gemma had shared a lot of emotion, and look how that turned out.

But he wanted Mia. She wanted him. Why not indulge themselves? Once he went back to California, he'd be busy with the film. Mia would be busy with her detective's exam. They had different lives in different cities. It couldn't last, but they'd have great memories. Hoping to change her mind, he asked, "Aren't you already involved?"

"It would be worse if we got closer."

She hadn't denied her involvement. "You're going to be able to ignore this," he gestured between them, "for three more weeks?"

"If I can't ignore it, I'll deal with it," she said, holding his gaze. Her knuckles whitened on the mug.

"God, Mia!" He closed his eyes and tilted his head back, desperate to stop the vivid images scrolling through his brain. "You can't say stuff like that, then expect me to pretend that picture isn't rolling around in my head."

"Then order breakfast. More coffee. We can both settle down, then get to work." She stood up and set the mug of coffee on the table. "I want eggs over hard, bacon, wheat toast and fruit."

He watched her walk toward her room, the robe swaying around her legs. He hadn't gotten where he was by waiting for things to come to him. When he wanted something, he went after it with everything he had.

Right now, he wanted Mia.

***

Mia leaned against the small trailer tucked along a curb on Washington Street, watching the crowds on the sidewalks. The indigo sky was fading rapidly to black, and Finn was inside the trailer, putting on his costume. He'd pointed out that she should be inside with him, to protect him as he changed clothes, and she'd rolled her eyes.

The woman from costumes, the same one who'd fitted him yesterday and given Mia the beard, had poked and prodded, arranged and tucked this afternoon. That costume, along with two others he'd need tonight, hung in the tiny trailer closet.

Behind blue police sawhorses on the sidewalks, people packed Washington Street, completely filling the space between the stores and the barricades. The crowd murmured and shifted like flowing water, everyone craning their necks to get a glimpse of the stars. Derek Sawyer's trailer was parked behind Finn's, and Jenna Stanton's behind Derek's. A larger trailer shared by the actors with smaller parts was on the other side of the street.

Finn's stalker could be in that crowd. It was the first time they'd shot a location scene, so it was the first time the fans could gather and watch. If Mia was a stalker, this is where she'd be. Straining to catch a glimpse of her obsession.

A shiver rippled down her spine as she studied the

crowds. Was the woman right in front of her, watching Finn's trailer?

Studying Mia, her supposed rival? Becoming more and more enraged?

Mia straightened a little more. Maybe she'd be a little clingy with Finn. Affectionate. Push the stalker over the edge. Draw her into showing her hand.

Mia was confident she could take care of herself and Finn both.

She ignored the voice whispering that being more affectionate with Finn was exactly what she wanted, anyway.

Tearing her gaze away from the crowd, she studied the surrounding area. Police officers, some in uniforms and some in plain clothes, wandered down the blocked off street, their eyes scanning the crowd, moving closer from time to time to head off more exuberant fans intent on jumping the barricade. As she watched, Mia wondered if she might have been working here tonight, in uniform, if she hadn't taken the job as Finn's bodyguard.

It was a strange thought. Instead of the last three days spent with Finn, getting to know him, making...having sex with him, she could be patrolling on Washington, oblivious to the man inside the trailer.

Completely unaware of the magic that flared between them when they got too close.

It had happened all day today. Casual touches. Brushing against him in the elevator. A quick glance when they shared an unspoken thought. Each time triggered a tiny explosion beneath her skin, a jolt of electricity singing through her body.

She was pretty sure she'd managed to hide her reactions from Finn, but it was a lot harder to hide them from herself. She wasn't sure how she'd manage for almost three more weeks.

As her gaze swept over the police officers and the crowd on the other side of the street, she froze. Swiveled and looked toward Wabash and the El tracks, where the huge lights were being set up.

Damn it.

Curling her fists into her sides, she watched as her brother Connor strolled down the street. He did a double-take, as if he'd just noticed her.

Scowling as he approached, she grabbed the front of his shirt in her fist and shook. "Trying to pretend you didn't know I'd be here?" She snorted. "Don't give up your day job for acting," she said in a low voice, aware of Finn inside the trailer at her back. "Because you suck at it. What the hell are you doing here, Con?"

"I'm working security for this film shoot," he said, raising his eyebrows. "What are *you* doing here?"

"Don't give me that bullshit." She shook him again. "Detectives don't work these jobs. You came here to spy on me."

"Didn't know you'd be here," he said. The tiny tell of his eyes drifting over her shoulder was proof he'd known. "Kiplinger wanted the night off, said she had something she needed to do." He shrugged. "Who can't use a little extra cash? I volunteered to fill in for her."

"Out of the goodness of your heart, right?" She let go of his shirt and shoved him away. "Get lost, Con. Go do your job. Because if you think you're going to confront Finn, you're mistaken."

Instead of backing away, Con watched her with serious eyes. "What's gotten into you, Mia? Why are you hanging around with that dickhead?"

"First of all, Connor Donovan, what I do is none of your damned business. Yes, you, Mac, Quinn and Bren saved my ass a couple of times when I was in high school. And yes, I appreciated it. But I'm not in high school anymore. I'm capable of taking care of myself. And second, he's not a dickhead. So butt out."

Con frowned. "How did you even meet the guy, anyway?"

"He's my job, asshole," Mia hissed at him. "I'm his

protection detail for the next three weeks. Posing as his girlfriend," she added in a harsh whisper. "And if you tell anyone, I will kill you. He has a stalker, and she's escalating. Captain Talbott asked if I would do it, and I agreed."

"Then why didn't you tell Bren last night?"

"Oh, was I supposed to ask your permission? Run it by you and Mac and Quinn and Bren before I took the job? Do you guys have veto power now?"

Connor sighed. "Mia, we're your brothers. It's our job to look out for you."

"Like hell it is." She shoved her fingers through her hair in frustration. "Look, Con, I love you. I love the other idiots, too. But I'm a big girl. I can take care of myself. This is my job, and I've got it. Okay? So stop this. Get lost."

Mia spotted Jenna Stanton walking down the street. The other woman stared at her, eyes narrowed. Mia smiled and waved at the woman.

"Get out of here, Con. Let me do my job."

Before her brother turned away, the door to the trailer opened and Finn stepped out, dressed in loose, worn jeans and a faded flannel shirt. "Hey, Mia," he said, his gaze flicking between her and Connor. "Problem here?"

"Not at all," she said, infuriated. *She* was supposed to be protecting *him*. Not the other way around.

Connor stepped toward him, holding out his hand. "I'm Connor. Her brother."

Finn sized him up as he shook. "Finn O'Rourke." He glanced at Mia as he let go of Connor's hand. "Another one from the spread sheet accounted for. Maybe we're looking in the wrong places for the stalker."

Mia took a deep breath. Let it out. Felt the tension fall away from her shoulders. "That would be too easy. No, my brothers' only problem is an excess of testosterone."

"Hey, now," Finn said with an easy smile, holding up his hands. "Watch your mouth, Officer. Nothing wrong with testosterone." He glanced at Con. "Have to take your side on this one, Detective."

Finn was so good he was scary. He'd remembered that three of her brothers were detectives. And he'd charmed Connor into a smile. "Thanks, man," Connor said, finally relaxing his stiff posture. "A guy's gotta watch out for his little sister."

"You know it."

Finn and Connor exchanged fist bumps, and Mia stepped between them. "The only woman you need to watch out for is Raine," she said, poking her brother in the chest. "And she could kick your ass with one hand tied behind her back. So I think you're done here. Get back to work, Con."

"On my way." He turned to go, then glanced over his shoulder. "You know dinner is next weekend. If you're his," he lowered his voice, "protection, you're gonna have to bring him. We'll all be looking forward to that."

"In your dreams, Con," she called after him.

"Gonna be more fun than watching the dance Bren did with Cilla," he said, grinning over his shoulder. "I can't wait."

She scowled at her brother's back as he walked away. Just before he turned the corner onto Wabash, Con glanced over her shoulder and winked. She gave him the finger and he laughed as he disappeared from sight.

"Well, that was fun," Finn said.

She turned to face him and found him leaning against the trailer. His eyes twinkled, and a tiny grin flirted with his mouth. "It was. I like seeing your brothers go all caveman on you." His smile gentled. "It's sweet."

"It's a pain in the ass, is what it is."

He shook his head. "No. It's a revelation. Do you know how rare that is in my world?" he said quietly. "To see a guy think of someone other than himself? To watch out for a woman with no ulterior motive other than to protect her?"

She studied him, his eyes too soft, his mouth too tender. "You'd do the same for your sister."

He shrugged one shoulder. "Of course I would. So would most guys. But to do it in front of the guy you're protecting her from? That takes balls. Big ones."

The compliment to her family made her all squishy. A piece of mush, standing in front of him. "Don't say that in front of my brothers," she muttered, her face hot. "They'd hold it over my head for the rest of my life."

"Your family is really close, isn't it?"

"Yes," she said. "We are. We all have each other's back."

"The way a family should be."

"Don't people in your world have families?" she asked.

"Of course. But a lot of them are business arrangements. Not a lot of lasting marriages in Tinsel Town. It's all about the image. What it gets you."

"That's really sad," she murmured. His world was so different than hers. All surface, no depth. It had a different landscape. A different language. Completely alien to her.

"Yeah, it is," he said. A ripple of regret flickered through his eyes for a moment, then it was gone. "I'm going to head over to the set. You ready to go?"

She nodded, her gaze scanning the crowd. Suddenly she froze. Grabbed his arm. "Let's go back into your trailer for a moment," she said in a low voice. "Act like you've forgotten something."

Actor that he was, Finn took two steps forward, then stopped. "Damn it. I forgot to change my shoes." He opened the door and walked inside. Mia followed him and slammed the door shut.

CHAPTER SIXTEEN

Mia peered out the window, watching the crowd on the other side of the street. The woman she'd noticed was in the front, pressed against the blue police barricade. Staring intently at the three trailers.

"What's going on?" Finn asked quietly.

Mia motioned him closer. He crowded against her, his arm brushing her shoulder. She tried to ignore the heat swirling between them, filling the small space with tension. She couldn't afford to be distracted.

"There's a woman across from your trailer and a little bit to the right. Front row. Long dark hair, black skirt, flowery print shirt. Mostly reds, oranges and yellow." She waited, keeping her eyes on the woman. "Do you see her?"

"Yes. She doesn't look familiar."

"You sure? You haven't seen her since you've been in Chicago?"

"I can't swear to it. I'd have to get closer. But no. I don't recognize her."

Mia pushed away from the window. Away from the weight and warmth of Finn's shoulder against her. She refused to let herself dwell on how much she wanted it back.

"Her name is Janise Kiplinger. She's a cop from my district. Patrol, just like me."

"So maybe she's a fan. Not necessarily of me, either," he pointed out. "Derek's trailer and Jenna's are here, too."

"Yeah, I know." Mia glanced out the window again, and Janise was exactly where she'd been a moment before. "She was supposed to work tonight, but she asked Con to take her shift. Said she had something she needed to do."

"That doesn't make her suspicious, Mia," he murmured, setting his hand lightly on her back. "Maybe she thought your brother would tease her if he knew she wanted to hang out here and be a groupie."

Mia shifted into his touch until his fingers were pressing against her lower back. "You're right. Con, and probably every other cop in the station, would be merciless if they knew she was here. But I can't afford to overlook Kiplinger, even though she's a cop."

"You going to grab her? Question her?" Finn's hand was massaging her lower back, digging into her muscles and smoothing over the bumps of her spine.

"God, no." She arched into him. "Not without more solid evidence. I'll get her prints from the database and send them to the superintendent. After stripping her identity, of course. He doesn't need to know I'm checking out a fellow cop. Unless it's a match." She shook her head. "What a nightmare that would be."

Finn drew soothing circles between her shoulder blades. "Good thinking," he murmured. "And good eye, spotting her in that crowd over there."

"I probably wouldn't have noticed her if Con hadn't mentioned her name," she admitted, still watching Janise through the window.

"You'd have seen her." Finn pressed his body into hers, crowding her into the side of the trailer. "You pay attention to everything."

Suddenly realizing his hand was on her hip and edging toward her ass, she twisted away from him. "What are you doing?"

He squeezed her ass once, then stepped back, giving her room. "Damn," he said with a tiny grin. "It's been a long time, but I didn't realize I'd lost my touch. I thought it was pretty obvious."

"Yeah, well, I was preoccupied," she muttered.

He'd had his hand all over her back and it had seemed like the most natural thing in the world. Another moment and she'd have been begging him to continue.

She'd done everything except rub against him to mark him with her scent. Which she should consider, since Jenna was in the next scene with him.

Damn it! He wasn't hers to mark. Wasn't hers for anything, except her job.

Uncurling her hands, she nodded at the door. "We probably need to get going."

"Yeah." He glanced down at her, his gaze lingering on her ass. "Probably."

"Come on, O'Rourke." She tugged him toward the door. "You can fantasize about my ass in those red polka-dot shorts on your own time. You need to get to work."

He reared back. "How did you know what…?"

"Your thoughts were blinking in neon above your head," she said, glad that he had to be on the set. Being all snugged up against him had revved her engine. If they had time to spend in this trailer, she was afraid she'd make another mistake.

"Our mind meld is a scary thing," he said as he flung open the door and stood aside for her to exit.

As soon as he stepped away from the trailer and the fans could see him, several of them began to boo. Shocked, Mia wound her arm through his. The boos intensified.

She began to draw her arm away, but he tightened his arm to hold her against his body. "I don't pay any attention to them, and you shouldn't either," he said quietly.

"But they got louder when I took your arm." She tried harder to pull away, but he wouldn't let her go.

"They're gonna boo no matter what you or I do. Just ignore them." He began walking faster. When they turned the corner, the boos turned to cheers. The pressure on her arm lessened. "Derek's probably just come out," he said, his eyes twinkling. "Let him fend them all off. I'm happy that they hate me."

"Really? Why's that?" She turned to look up at him, leaving her arm wound through his.

"Because I'm the villain in this movie." They approached a huddle of men and women, and Finn slowed. "Puts me in the right frame of mind for my scenes."

"Hey, if you want someone to insult you, I can do that for you," she said, trying to lighten things up.

Finn slowed and looked down at her. "Not you, Mia. I don't want you to hate me. Okay?"

Her heart stuttered and she sucked in a breath. "Okay," she said after a too-long moment. "I won't."

"Good." He leaned down to brush a kiss over her mouth, then straightened. "You can probably stand against the building," he said, nodding toward the Macy's display windows on her left. "The cars are starting on that street down the block," he gestured toward Lake Street, "where the El trains turn onto this street." He glanced at the street sign. "Wabash. The chase will go a few more blocks until the cars crash."

Her fingers tightened on his arm. "You're going to be in a crashing car?"

"No, that will be my stunt double." He grinned. "They're not going to take a chance on damaging my pretty face.

"It'll take a long time. Be terminally boring for you. They'll film with me driving for the shots where you see my face, then the stunt double will take over for the tricky stuff. There'll be a car next to us with a camera, a car behind with one and a guy in the back seat of my car with a camera."

One of the guys in the huddle motioned Finn over. He let her go and kissed her again. "Stay out of the way. I'll find you during breaks."

***

By the time they were done filming, it was two in the morning. Street traffic in the surrounding area had thinned, and most of the fans had drifted away a few hours earlier. Finn had been right. Watching the scene being filmed countless times was stupefyingly boring.

It took a lot of hard work to create an illusion. Something that wasn't real.

Finn had found her during his breaks, standing with her as he gulped a bottle of water, explaining what would happen next. She'd spent the rest of the time studying the crew, the cast members, even the caterers. No one rang any alarms, but she hadn't expected them to.

If the stalker was around, and Mia would bet she was, she wasn't going to stick out. She'd blend into the crowd. But if Mia memorized all the faces she saw, sooner or later, she'd see a pattern. Someone where she wasn't supposed to be. Or more often than she should be there.

The stalker wouldn't stay hidden forever. She had an agenda, and that agenda was punishing Finn for his lack of interest. When she stepped into the light, Mia would be ready for her.

By the time Finn was ready to leave, his make-up removed and clothes changed, she was dead on her feet. Finn looked wiped out, too. She hadn't gotten much sleep last night, and she was pretty sure Finn hadn't, either.

Once in the car, he listed against her as Pete turned corners, and she didn't have the energy to shrug his head off her shoulder. Didn't really want to. Instead, she relaxed against him, his big body warming her in the cool car.

Her eyelids must have closed, because she sat up with a start when the car stopped at the front of the Drake on Walton Street. Before she could ask Pete why, he lowered the partition. "Loading dock's busy, so we have to come in this way. I talked to Carlos, the doorman. He's going to show you a quick way to the elevators."

"Thanks, Pete," she said, sliding toward the curb-side door. "Come on, sleepyhead." She nudged Finn. "We're home."

She reached for the door, but the doorman opened it for her. Held out his hand to help her from the car. "Welcome, ma'am," he said, stepping aside as he waited for Finn to emerge from the car.

His name tag said 'Carlos', and he was about her height. Dark hair, dark eyes and a round, smiling face. "Thank you, Carlos," she said.

As soon as Finn was on his feet, Carlos ushered them toward a door to the left of the Drake entrance. "This is a little quicker," he said. "And usually less busy."

Opening the door, Carlos followed them inside. Small shops, closed for the night, lined the dimly–lit corridor; a florist, a coffee shop, a men's clothing store. A woman's clothing store was down a corridor to the left, and a jewelry store was at the end. To their right were the elevators.

"Have a nice night, Mr. O'Rourke. Ma'am," he said as he held the elevator door open. "Anything you need, you let me know."

Finn and Mia slumped side by side against the wood paneled walls. When the elevator stopped and the doors opened, she barely had enough energy to push herself forward and into the corridor. Finn slung an arm over her shoulders, and she wasn't sure if it was to draw her closer, or to support himself. They stumbled across the carpet together, and Mia opened the door to the suite.

Mia forced herself to pay close attention as she searched all the rooms, but the routine she'd already established made the search go quickly. As soon as she was certain there were no intruders, she threw the double locks, closed her eyes, then focused on Finn.

"What time do we have to be there tomorrow?" she asked.

"Same time," Finn said. "One."

"Okay. I'll see you in the morning," she said, weaving toward her bedroom.

"Yeah," he managed to say as he trudged toward his own room. "Late in the morning."

The next few days were all location shoots. The first night, they finished up in the Loop, then went farther west on Lake Street. It was only a mile or two away, and they were still beneath the El tracks, but it was a different world. Vacant factories, boarded-up shops and empty lots with rusting, junked cars gave the scenes a creepy, sinister vibe.

During one break, she and Finn leaned against a metal grate covering the front of a drug store. The diamond-shaped pattern on the grate was cold against her back and dug into her muscles. She shivered as she drank the bottle of water he'd given her.

"Pretty cool, huh?" he said, motioning to the dead street with his bottle of water. "Perfect setting."

"For what?" she asked.

He tossed the plastic bottle into a recycling bin. "Desolation and despair, babe. What this movie's all about."

"I'm not your babe," she muttered, but it was half-hearted. She leaned against him as they watched the crew scurrying to set up for the next scene, and she had no desire to move away. Going to his shoot every night, watching him work, had created a bond between them. Common knowledge. A shared experience.

All layered over the awareness that simmered between them. Ready to burst into a towering flame at the slightest provocation.

Two teens wearing hoodies hovered in the shadows across the street as she and Finn stood there, waiting for his next scene. Mia assumed they were merely curious about the shoot, like so many other people, but their complete stillness, and the way they clung to the shadows, made her keep an eye on them.

Those two teens summed up her world. Gritty. Real. A place where danger always lurked behind the façade.

Nothing like Finn's world of make-believe and glitz. In his world, the only things behind a dangerous façade were wires and cables and pieces of scenery. His world was insulated. Safe. And so far from real that most people in it had probably forgotten what real was.

She'd been worried about the chase scenes, concerned that Finn might get hurt. Now she watched the one being filmed in front of her and realized he was completely safe. Nothing from the real world touched the people in Finn's version of reality.

The next night they filmed in Lakeview, the neighborhood where she and all her brothers lived. They shot scenes in front of houses, two-flats and apartment buildings, as well as some of the small shops on the busier streets.

She nudged Finn during a break. "I shop at that store," she said, pointing toward Frosting, a cupcake bakery.

"Yeah? They any good?"

"I'll get you one. You can judge for yourself."

As soon as the words were out of her mouth, she realized that would never happen. When she would be free to leave his side to buy him a cupcake, he'd be gone. Back in California.

Instead of being relieved, the thought made her sad.

On the third night, they filmed a scene on the patio of Monk Street restaurant on Southport. Finn interrupted a dinner between Derek and Jenna, the two men fought in the street, then Finn stormed away after threatening both Derek and Jenna's characters.

The fight scene took hours to film. The crew blocked off the surrounding streets, and the carefully choreographed fight scene took dozens of takes to complete. By the time Finn slumped against a building beside her, dripping sweat, her own muscles were sore from the tension of the scene.

"We're about done here," he said as a make-up artist

pressed a towel to his face and neck, blotting up the sweat, then added some splatters of blood around his mouth and nose. The young woman fussed with his hair for a moment, although afterward it didn't look any different to Mia. "One more scene, then we can leave."

As the make-up artist fluttered around Finn like a butterfly, Mia glanced at the muddy spots on the cuffs of her pants. She'd gotten splashed by one of the camera cars zooming past her down the narrow street.

Finn worked hard, and what he did wasn't easy. But it was nothing like her world.

He nudged her shoulder with his, drawing her attention back to him. "You going out of your mind yet?"

"Nope," she said, taking up her usual position against his side. "Watching and cataloging."

"You see anything?"

"Not yet. There aren't as many spectators, but no one looks familiar. Don't think I've seen any of them before."

"We haven't heard from the stalker in a while," he said. "Maybe she's given up."

"That would be nice, but I doubt it." A cool breeze blew by, and Mia shifted closer to Finn. "Stalkers are obsessed with their victims. Most of them can't give up."

He draped an arm over her shoulder, pulling her against him. "You cold, babe?"

"Not anymore."

She told herself she was acting for the audience of cast and crew and spectators. She was supposed to be Finn's girlfriend. Of course she'd stand close. Of course he'd call her babe and put his arm around her.

It didn't feel like acting, though, and that set off all kinds of alarms. Warnings that she might be taking this more seriously than she should.

Only two more weeks. For the last several nights, they'd both been too tired to flirt and tease when they got back to the hotel suite. Mia told herself she was happy about that. Less temptation. Less chance of making another mistake.

During these night shoots, Finn sought her out during his breaks. He was pleasant to his fellow cast members and the crew, chatting them up, but he always headed toward her.

And every night, she huddled close to him.

Sean, the director, motioned Finn over, and he pushed away from the wall with a groan. Let his fingers trail over Mia's shoulders as he let her go. She watched him walk toward the group of people, and they all began talking at once.

She did one more sweep of the area with her eyes, spotting a small clump of fans watching from across the street. She cataloged each one, then went back to a short woman standing in the back of the group. She looked familiar.

Then the whole group turned and headed toward the El stop down the street. The woman didn't glance over her shoulder. She was in front of two other people, so Mia couldn't get a good look at her as she walked away.

Maybe she could get some video footage from security cameras in the area. She made a mental note to ask for them tomorrow morning. And double check with the superintendent's office to see if Kiplinger's fingerprints had been a match for the one they'd found on the envelope.

She spotted Finn walking toward her, on the phone. Calling Pete, she hoped. Finn slid the phone into his pocket as he reached her. "Pete will be here any minute." He took her hands, rubbing them between both of his. "No shooting tomorrow. A day at the studio, rehearsing, going over some changes.

"And Sean's throwing a party tomorrow night. Celebrating the first week of production. No disasters, no huge problems. Everything's going smoothly."

"Yeah? Where's this party?"

"At a club. The Seven Club, I think he said. Have you heard of it?"

"Oh, yeah," she said, raising an eyebrow. "It's

an…interesting place." Her brother Brendan had been shot at the Seven Club last fall, in the process of arresting a drug dealer.

"Interesting, how?" Finn asked.

He was curious about everything. Always wanted details. Descriptions. But she wished he hadn't asked about Seven. "It's a little wild." She swallowed. "A pick up place. The kind where people have sex in the dark corners."

Finn frowned. "You've been there?"

She knew exactly what he was thinking. She squeezed his hand. "On the job. My brother was shot there during a drug arrest."

"Is he okay?" Finn asked immediately.

"Good as new. It was Brendan, the one who interrupted us at Oscar's."

"Okay, then." He rubbed her hands once more, then twined his fingers with hers, as if it was normal. As if they did it all the time.

And they did, she realized. The cover they'd concocted was becoming too real.

The thought of being at the sexy Seven Club with Finn made her want to step closer to him. Instead, she forced herself to focus on her job. "Are they renting the whole place out?"

"Doubt it. This is an indie film. Doesn't have a huge budget. And we have a small number of cast and crew."

"So there are going to be outsiders there during this party."

"I guess so."

She took a deep breath. She didn't like that, but no one had asked her opinion. She'd stick close to Finn. Make sure she had her gun handy.

She closed her eyes. She'd have to go back to her place to get something to wear. Which meant taking Finn to her apartment.

That felt too intimate. Too personal. And the fact that she wanted him to see her place? That felt as if she were standing on a precipice, toes on the edge. Already teetering, one slip away from falling off.

Risking getting shattered on the shiny, glittery rocks below.

CHAPTER SEVENTEEN

Finn glanced at Mia, fidgeting on the seat beside him, as Pete drove them toward her apartment. After Finn's meetings at the studio, they'd driven through a Starbucks, and she clutched the cup with a white-knuckled grip.

The only time he'd seen her nervous was when Doug had knocked on the door when they were sprawled on the floor after making love. Or, as Mia had said, in their 'post-coital haze'. He smiled to himself as he took a sip of his own coffee. He loved her words – her snark and her cleverness. Her honesty.

"Are you worried about taking me to your apartment?" he asked.

She flinched, and two drops of caramel-colored coffee spilled out of the sip hole and trailed down the white paper cup. "Of course I'm not worried. Why would I be?"

"I have no idea. But if you were holding that cup any tighter, you'd punch holes in it."

She glanced down at the coffee and set it carefully in one of the cup holders. Then slid her hands beneath her thighs. So he wouldn't notice them shaking?

"Mia, I'd be nervous if I was taking you to *my* place." He

reached over and pried one of her hands out of hiding, lacing their fingers together. "I'd probably spill the coffee all over myself. Get it on the seat of the car. Burn sensitive bodily parts." He shuddered, making it dramatic to coax a laugh out of her.

She glanced at him, rolled her eyes, but finally relaxed her shoulders. "Okay. Yeah. I'm a little nervous."

"How come?" he asked, fascinated. "What is there to be nervous about?"

"I don't let a lot of people into my house. Most cops don't. We have to keep our real self hidden when we're on the job. And a person's home says a lot about her," she said, playing with his fingers. He was pretty sure she didn't even realize it. "The furniture she chooses. The books on her shelves. The pictures on the wall." She swallowed. "If it's messy or neat."

"So you left the place a mess?"

"No." She scowled. "It's not a mess. But I left in a hurry. Probably didn't pick up all my clothes from the floor. Might have left piles of mail on my dining room table. There could even be a bag of junk food in my living room. Stuff."

"So we're not walking into a place that's ready for an *Architectural Digest* photo shoot?" He squeezed her hand. "I'd worry about you if we were." He edged closer. "You think I'm going to judge you? You should see the way I left my place in California."

"Please," she scoffed. "You have a cleaning service that comes twice a week. And don't lie and say you don't."

How did she know that? "Well, it would have been messy before they came," he muttered.

She glanced at him, then down at their hands. "Seeing a person's home is like seeing them stripped bare. It tells you so much about them." She rubbed one finger over his thumb. He didn't think she realized she was doing that, either. "I'm not sure I'm ready for that."

Why was Mia so reluctant to let him into her space?

Yeah, he got that it revealed a lot about a person. But this was more than that.

Was it because she'd already gotten closer to him than she'd planned? Because she wanted to look good to him?

She didn't have to worry about that. The more time he spent with her, the more he wanted her. And not just physically, although he'd lost a lot of sleep thinking about her in that room on the other side of the suite.

He knew a lot about Officer Donovan – how good she was at her job. How smart she was. How quickly she put things together. But the last few days had left him hungering to know the woman behind her cool, capable exterior. He wanted to know *Mia*.

"I can wait in the car with Pete." He wouldn't like it, but he would do it. He'd been looking forward to seeing her apartment. Probably more than he should have been. Because she was right. It said a lot about who you were. "If that would be more comfortable."

"You know I can't let you do that," she sighed. "You have to come with me."

"You can blindfold me," he said. "Lead me up the stairs and into your apartment. Might be kind of kinky. In fact, if we're going with kinky, you can tie me to your bed. Or use your handcuffs on me! That would be even better."

By the time he finished, she was shaking her head. But she was smiling. "You're a goofball. Although I know that's not news to you."

No one had ever called him a goofball. He'd been called lots of things, but never that. Having Mia say it made him feel…lighter. As if she'd looked past all the hype and publicity and movie-star-ness and saw him. Plain old Finn O'Rourke.

The car slowed, then Pete slotted the car into a narrow spot at the curb. The partition rolled down, and before Pete could say anything, Mia leaned over the front seat.

"Hey, Pete, nice job with the parallel parking. We may have to make you an honorary Chicagoan. My brother Mac would weep if he saw you slide this baby into that tiny spot."

Pete turned and grinned at her. "Glad to see someone appreciates my talents."

Finn shook his head. "You're spoiling him," he told Mia. "Gonna give him a swelled head. He'll expect compliments all the time."

"He should get them," she said as she opened the door. "He deserves them."

Pete reached his fist across the seat, and Mia bumped it with hers. Then she stepped out of the car and waited as he followed her.

They stood in front of a two-flat. It was dark brick, with bay windows on both floors. The street was a mixture of two-flats and single family homes, with a couple of apartment buildings thrown in. Maple trees, just budding out, lined the street.

"Pretty neighborhood," he said as he followed Mia to the front door.

"I like it. It's quiet. A lot of families. When I get home from work, I don't want bros throwing ragers and loud, drunk people on the street late at night."

She opened the door, unlocked the inner one, and stood aside for him to start up the stairs. "Hold on a minute," she said, sliding a key into a mailbox. She stuffed the accumulated mail under her arm, then joined him on the stairs and let the door close behind her.

Her apartment was on the top floor. As he waited for her to open the door, he saw her hand tremble as she inserted the key in the lock. The door opened silently, and she waved him inside.

"Stay next to the door while I check the place," she said.

As she disappeared to the right, he studied her living room. She had a comfortable-looking, battered old leather couch and a worn, threadbare recliner sitting next to it. A small table separated the two, covered with a sprawl of magazines and books. A faded Oriental rug covered the center of the hardwood floor.

The coffee table in front of the couch held the junk food. A bag of Cheetos. His favorite.

Photos lined the mantel over the fireplace, and he took a closer look. Most of them were of her family. Mia and four guys who were clearly her brothers. Mia, her brothers and a woman who looked like an older Mia. A picture of five young kids, the woman and a man. Mia must have been six or seven – she was missing a front tooth. They all stood close, smiling and happy.

"Nice-looking family," he said when he heard her behind him.

"Thanks. You want to have a seat while I get the stuff I'll need for the party tonight?"

"Not really. I'd rather help you pick it out."

"Not going to happen, O'Rourke," she said, but her eyes looked more relaxed. "I won't be long."

Finn gestured at the beat-up recliner. "This safe to sit on?" he asked.

Her gaze softened as it rested on the chair. "Yeah, it is."

"Looks like it's special to you."

Her gaze lingered on it for a long moment, her eyes as gentle as a caress. "It was my dad's. My mom still has hers at the house, but she let me have this one."

She ran her hand gently over one tattered arm, lingered near a worn spot. "My dad used to read to me in this chair. The Harry Potter books. We got to the third one before he died."

"I'm so sorry," Finn murmured, wrapping his arm around her and tugging her against his side. "How old were you?"

"Eight." She leaned against him for a long moment, then straightened. Stepped away. "He was a cop, too. Died in the line of duty. Hit by a drunk driver one night."

"Awful." He couldn't imagine losing his father that way. Growing up without his dad.

"It was." She elbowed him gently. "But I didn't mean to make you all sad."

"Give me a moment and I'll be back to my manly self."

She smiled, but it didn't quite make it to her eyes. "I'll be right back."

He couldn't let her carry this sadness away with her. "I know how you can cheer me up," he said. "Let me help you pick out what you're going to wear tonight." He tilted his head. "I'll need to go through your closet, of course, but I'm seeing tight. Short skirt. Something in…red."

Predictably, she rolled her eyes, but her smile reached her eyes. "Sorry, Finn. I guess you're going to have to be sad."

After she left the room, he edged into the dining room, listening to Mia in her bedroom. Hangers clattered in her closet. Drawers opened, then closed. He could picture her trying to decide, her lower lip caught between her teeth.

It made him want to walk around the corner into her bedroom. Show her how beautiful she was. How her clothes couldn't possibly make her more beautiful.

He retreated to the living room. Headed for the recliner, then swerved toward the couch instead. It seemed wrong, somehow, to sit in her father's recliner. Disrespectful. Only someone who had known and loved the man should sit there.

Instead of sitting on the couch, he wandered around the room. Mia's apartment felt comfortable. Lived-in and welcoming. The pictures on the walls were a hodgepodge of styles and subjects, from landscapes to geometric splashes of color. There was no theme. Nothing tying them together.

Except Mia. Her taste. What gave her joy.

Her books were a mix, too. Thrillers, mysteries, romance novels. History. Biographies. As eclectic as the rest of the room.

Finally, he sank into the couch. Mia's casual, homey apartment was so different from his place in California. A designer had put his house together carefully. Matching furniture. Color-coordinated paint on the walls. Art selected by the designer, all from prominent artists. Cool. Aloof. Meant to impress, rather than to be enjoyed.

In his living room, leather-covered books filled the bookshelves and looked impressive, but he'd never read one of them. He kept the books he actually read on a bookshelf in his bedroom.

Mia's home was real. His was part of some 'movie-star' illusion. A great place for interviews and photo ops. Not so great for actual living.

Mia walked into the room, carrying a garment bag and a small duffel. "All set," she said. "Let's go before you notice the cereal sitting on the kitchen table and the Cheetos in front of the couch."

"Too late," he said, too brightly. "Already ate some of the Cheetos."

She glanced at his fingers and shook her head. "You did not." She pointed at his hands. "No orange fingers."

Even the snacks in Mia's house were real.

***

Mia stepped out of the car in front of the Seven Club, tugging her skirt down. She had her back-up gun in a thigh holster, and her skirt was on the short side.

Not because Finn had asked her to wear a short skirt. It was red, too, but she'd chosen this particular dress because it suited the vibe of the Seven Club.

Plus, it was important for her to dress the way his girlfriend would. And if his girlfriend would wear a tight, short red dress, then that's what she'd wear.

That was the only reason.

Yeah. Right.

Clutching her glittery silver bag tight, she turned and waited for Finn, watching the long line of people snaking down the block. Women dressed like her, in short skirts and low-necked tops. Men in black pants and dress shirts open one button too many. Seven was a popular club. It was always crowded.

Tonight it would be a nightmare.

When Finn stepped out of the car, she maneuvered so that she was between him and the waiting line of clubbers. Then she grabbed his hand and hustled him past the bouncers. They stared at Finn and held the door wide open for them.

Once inside, Mia took a deep breath as she scanned the room. The best option would be one of the booths along the edge of the room. Out of the way, easier to keep an eye on the crowd. She started to steer Finn in that direction, but he grabbed her hand and pulled her close.

"Where are you going?" He leaned close to her ear because of the loud music and thumping bass, and his breath tickled her neck and stirred her hair. "The dance floor is the other way."

Of course he'd want to dance. To be in the area of the club she was least able to control. Her gut told her to stay in the safest area, but Finn grabbed her hand and led her toward the densely packed mass of dancing bodies.

She tugged him back, and he bumped into her chest. He grabbed her hip to steady her, and each of his fingers burned into her. The pressure of his chest against hers, the scent of that damn hotel soap and his aftershave that always reminded her of ocean breezes, made her tremble. Move closer.

The flow of people swirled around them as they stared at each other, frozen in place. Someone bumped her from behind, pushing her harder into Finn's chest. His arm curled around her, tucking her against his body from chest to knees.

His eyes, already dilated from the dim lighting, grew even darker. She knew hers looked the same – aroused. Hungry.

Totally out of line.

She stepped back until they weren't touching. So she could think again. Then she leaned close to his ear. "You want to dance? We'll dance. But not here on the edge of the dance floor. In the middle." Where everyone surrounding them would be dancing, as well. Too busy to notice Finn. "Follow me. And stay close."

He set his hand lightly on her hip as she edged her way through the undulating, gyrating crowd. That was good, she told herself. The music was too loud to communicate verbally. At least she knew he was right behind her.

She was such a liar. She liked the pressure of his hand on her hip. Liked the solid feel of him at her back. And not only because she needed him close to protect him.

One of the dancers spun wildly, crashing into her, and Finn's hand dropped away. She glanced over her shoulder, and he was two steps behind her. He caught her eye and nodded. He'd stay close.

They were almost at the center of the dance floor. It wasn't as crowded as the outer edges, probably because it was farther to the bar. She began to turn toward Finn when a man grabbed her arm and tugged her toward him.

"Mia Donovan. All grown up, too. Looks like my lucky day." The guy smirked and drew her closer. He scanned her body, lingering too long at her chest. "Your asshole brothers with you tonight?" he asked.

His dirty blond hair was gelled into a peak, and his clothes screamed 'bro on the prowl'. Kyle Pinckney. God! Mia tried to shove him away, but Kyle was even stronger than he'd been in high school.

He smiled and bent close, and the sour stink of alcohol wafted across her face. "Looks like that's a no, thank God. We have a lot of catching up to do."

CHAPTER EIGHTEEN

"Pinckney." As she stared at him, memories barreled through her like a freight train. Panic that she hadn't felt in years rushed through her in a frigid blast, freezing her in place.

He'd been her high school's star quarterback. He'd pestered her to go out with him, but she'd refused. That hot, sweaty afternoon, he'd appeared out of nowhere, dragging her into the vacant lot. Now, the smell of rotting vegetation swirled around her, along with the smell of his sweat. The cruel grip of his fingers on her arms dug into her muscles, just like that September day. Afterward, she'd worn long sleeves for weeks.

The sick excitement in his eyes as he smirked at her now was identical to the way he'd looked on that sunny afternoon.

A dance song ended with a crash of cymbals on the club stereo, jerking her back to the present. She tore her arm away from his grasp, standing straighter as she stared him down. But her hands still shook. So did the rest of her. "You're still a complete asshole, Pinckney. Get lost. I'm not interested in catching up with you."

He grabbed her wrist, his fingers tightening painfully on the bones. "Who's going to protect you now, Mia?" he said, his low voice filled with glee. "You're all by yourself."

She twisted to look for Finn behind her, but he'd stopped and was talking to someone. Jenna Stanton.

Kyle yanked her closer. "You with pretty boy? Not so interested in you, is he?" he sneered. "So we have as much time as we need."

Jenna wasn't at the top of Mia's list for Finn's stalker. He'd told her Jenna was far too direct to stalk anyone. But not being close to Finn made Mia twitchy.

Kyle tightened his grip on her. "He's not gonna rescue you, Mia. Looks like he's into blondes. So it's just us."

"I don't need rescuing or protecting," she said, turning back to him as her mind finally cleared. "I'm a police officer. Let me go, or you won't like what happens."

His eyes were glassy and he swayed slightly on his feet. Just drunk enough to be stupid with it. "You're a cop? So what? What're you going to do?" His gaze trailed over her as he tightened his grip even more. "You gonna shoot me, Mia? No place for a gun in that dress."

Mia swung her arm up and twisted, breaking Kyle's hold on her. "Get out of my sight, Pinckney. Lose yourself. Now."

She turned back to find Finn. Jenna had her hand on his arm, keeping him close. Finn was edging away, but Jenna wasn't letting him go.

Shivering, aware of Kyle behind her, Mia began weaving her way through the crowd toward Finn. She'd taken two steps when she was yanked roughly backward. As she stumbled, her silver clutch flew through the air, glittering in the lights, then disappeared into the crush of people.

Kyle jerked her against his chest. His arm was a steel band, holding her there. He began dragging her backward, palming her breast with his other hand. "You think you can take me down, Mia? Stupid. I never thought you were stupid. Don't you know the Kylester always gets what he wants?"

Mia stomped on the arch of his foot with her stiletto heel. At the same time, she cracked her head backwards into Kyle's nose. His arm dropped and he pinwheeled away from her. He shook his head, then his face twisted into a snarl of rage.

The people dancing around her had stopped. One guy tried to grab Kyle, but Mia waved him off. She didn't want anyone to get hurt. "Get the bouncer," she yelled to him. He nodded and began shoving through the crowd.

Kyle reached for her again. Gauging the distance, knowing his height worked in her favor, she waited until he got close enough. "Mia," she heard behind her. Finn. "What the hell?"

Finn tried to push past her, but she held him back. When Kyle lunged for her, she brought her knee up, hitting him squarely in the groin. He dropped to the floor like a stone.

Still holding Finn away, she bent down and murmured into the writhing man's ear, "The Kylester always gets what he wants? Stupid, Kyle. Really stupid."

"Damn it!" Finn pushed her arm away, clenching his fists as he reached for Kyle, twitching on the floor.

"Finn, no," she said, grabbing his arm and hauling him back. "He's not going anywhere. Someone's getting the bouncer. Help me find my purse. My badge and cuffs are in it."

He shook her off. "Not until I make sure he's not getting up off that floor."

"Finn!" She grabbed his arms and brought him close to her. "Please," she said quietly. "Thank you for trying to protect me, but I don't want this to end up in the paper." She leaned in to kiss him, then jerked away, aware that everyone around them was watching. "Later, okay?"

His hands settled on her waist, and he glared over her shoulder. "Fucking Jenna. She grabbed me, or I would have been with you. Kept that garbage," he kicked Kyle's thigh, making the now-retching man curl into a ball, "away from you."

Her heart fluttered like a bird caught in a net. She was supposed to be protecting Finn, and he was ready to take on asshole Kyle Pinckney for her. "People are looking at us. Please find my purse, okay?" She squeezed his arm, let her fingers trail down to his hand, then linked their fingers for a moment. She leaned in closer. "You can help me cuff him," she breathed into his ear.

She was lying. She couldn't cuff Kyle in public – it would ruin her cover. But Finn's eyes lit up and he plowed into the crowd.

Before he returned, a bouncer appeared next to her. "What happened here?" he said.

"He assaulted me," Mia said, rubbing her aching left wrist. "Grabbed me several times, including my boob, then tried to drag me away. Call the cops."

"They're on their way. Can I see some ID, please?" the bouncer asked.

"That POS knocked my purse away. My boyfriend's trying to find it." Her heart quivered at the 'boyfriend.'

Finn appeared at her side, holding her purse. She took it from him, opened it and showed the bouncer her driver's license. She kept the badge and cuffs out of sight.

The bouncer pointed a tiny flashlight at it, then handed it back to her. "Sorry, Ms. Donovan," he said, giving her a card he pulled out of his pocket. "Drinks are on the house tonight."

She slid the card into her bag, where it would stay. "Thanks," she said. "I appreciate the way you've handled this."

"Not a problem." The bouncer's gaze touched on Finn, drifted away, then snapped back. "Is that…?"

Mia put her hand on the bouncer's arm. "Yes. Don't say anything, okay? We're trying not to draw attention."

The bouncer glanced at the crowd now surrounding them and snorted. "Good luck with that."

He turned and hauled Kyle to his feet, then hustled him toward the front door. Mia took Finn's hand and followed. When they reached the entrance, two police officers were waiting. As the bouncer handed Kyle over, Mia stepped up to one of them, a woman she didn't recognize.

Opening her bag, she showed the officer her badge. "You can add assaulting a police officer to the charges," she said, holding the badge as the officer copied the number. "Couldn't happen to a better guy. He was a loser in high school, too."

"We'll take care of him." The woman pulled her cuffs off her belt and snapped them on Kyle's wrists, then tightened them down.

The two officers escorted Kyle out the door. He stumbled between them, a little rivulet of drool shiny on his chin.

As the door closed behind them, Finn turned to her. "Do you want to go home?" he asked.

"I'll stay if you want to," she said. "I know you wanted to dance."

"Not in the mood for dancing anymore," he said, his jaw working. "I'll call Pete."

They were both silent on the way home. She sat closer to Finn than she should have, but ugly memories and the fading adrenaline burn had her shivering. She wanted to crawl into Finn's lap and let his heat surround her, but she retained enough sense to stay where she was.

At a stoplight, Finn leaned forward suddenly and rapped on the partition. When Pete lowered it, Finn said, "Little detour, Pete. Swing by Oscar's. I'm going to order some food to go."

"Got it, boss," Pete said.

Finn half-turned to face her. "You want some of that mac and cheese you had the other night?"

"God, yes," she said fervently. "I'd kill for some Oscar's mac and cheese." Comfort food was exactly what she craved right now. Well, the second thing she craved. She edged closer to Finn, leaning into him as he pulled up Oscar's website and hit the call button.

Thirty minutes later, Pete pulled up to the loading dock and Mia climbed out of the car. Her legs and arms were heavy, still shaking, but she took a deep breath and forced herself to head for the door. Steady and strong. Finn grabbed the bag from Pete and wrapped an arm around her waist, and she leaned against him, soaking in his body heat.

The ground floor lobby near the shops was empty, and so was the elevator. When they stepped inside the suite, Mia slipped out of her heels and removed her gun from her thigh holster. Tightening her grip on it, she walked through the suite, checking everything. Just like she did every time they returned. She had a job to do, and she'd damn well do it.

When the suite was cleared, she turned all the locks on the door, resisting the urge to lean against it. Finn brushed her hair behind her ear, his fingers trailing gently over her cheek. Cupping her face for a moment. "You want to take a shower before we eat?"

Mia looked down at the red dress and nodded. "Yeah. Good idea."

She'd worn the dress for Finn. The way his eyes had darkened when she'd walked out of her room a couple of hours earlier had confirmed she'd made the right choice.

Now she just wanted to strip it off. Toss it into the back of the closet and out of her sight.

"I'll just be a minute," she said over her shoulder, already unzipping the dress.

"Yeah. I remember," he said, his voice low. "Short showers."

As she stood beneath the hot water, she leaned against the wall and allowed the tears to fall. Her tears blurred the bruises Kyle had left on her arms and her wrist, but she knew she'd be wearing long sleeves again. She'd had worse in her career as a cop, but none that had been inflicted by someone she knew.

Sighing, she turned off the shower, splashed cold water

on her face and threw on a pair of pajama pants and a tee. The Cops and Robbers shirt she'd stolen from Brendan was soft against her skin. Cilla had it made for Bren after he told the rest of the family about the blog and the book he was writing, but he refused to wear it in public. So Mia had liberated it from him.

Wrapping the hotel robe around herself, she headed into the other room. Finn was staring out the window at the darkness, but he turned when she emerged from her room. "Ready to eat?"

"Yeah," she sighed.

"How about a glass of wine?" He nodded toward the bottle of cabernet sitting on top of the minibar.

"I shouldn't drink," she said. "I'm working."

Finn ran his hands up and down her arms. "We're locked in here. I'm not opening that door to anyone tonight. Not even Doug. So have a glass of wine if you want one."

It would settle her nerves. Loosen the tension in her neck. But she shook her head. "I'll have a sip of yours," she said.

He opened the bottle, poured himself a glass and handed it to her. She took a drink, savoring the flavor, then handed him the glass. "Thanks."

The mac and cheese was still hot, and the gooey, decadent richness relaxed her as she ate. She finished half the bowl, then pushed it away. "Thank you for thinking of this. It was perfect."

Finn laid his hand over hers. "Good. Makes me glad that it helped." He took his time finishing his own bowl. He didn't ask any questions, but he twined his fingers with hers as he ate.

Finally, when he finished, he poured himself more wine and stood up, pulling her to her feet. He led her to the couch, put the wine down and tugged her into his lap. "Another sip?" he asked, offering the wine.

The dark red wine was rich and fruity and incredibly

smooth. But Mia handed it back to Finn after only one sip. She didn't want her mind muddled tonight.

Finn took a sip himself, set it on the table, then wrapped both arms around her. He didn't ask any questions, didn't push her to talk. He just held her against his chest, wrapped in his arms, his cheek resting against her head.

If Finn had asked questions, pushed her to talk, she wouldn't have said a word. But he was patiently holding her, comforting her, without expecting anything in return.

Turning in his arms so she could rest her cheek against his chest, she said, "I went to high school with Kyle. He was the quarterback of the football team. Thought he was all that. Got pretty much whatever he wanted."

Finn's arms tightened around her. "I wish you hadn't called the police tonight," he said, his fingers smoothing up and down her arm. "I think I know where this is going, and I want to beat the crap out of him."

Mia reached for his hand and twined her fingers with his. "He was a senior when I was a sophomore. He'd been sniffing around me, but I wasn't interested. He was an asshat back then, too. I stayed too late after soccer practice one day, and ended up walking home alone. Kyle caught up with me near a vacant lot in my neighborhood."

Her stomach rolled again at the memories dredged up tonight. No one around. A vacant lot full of tall weeds and junk. Kyle cornering her, edging her farther into the tangle of vegetation covering the lot. Mia, helpless against his strength, knowing what was going to happen in this disgusting vacant lot that smelled of garbage and rot.

"What happened?" Finn's voice was soft as he squeezed her hand, but his hand tightened on hers. Twitched against her fingers.

"My mother got worried when I wasn't home when I was supposed to be. She sent Brendan and Connor and Quinn to find me. They spotted me with Kyle in the empty lot. He'd backed me against the wall. I was trying to get away, but he was so strong." She'd been strong, too, but hadn't been able to budge Kyle, even with the added desperation of terror. She'd known what he had planned.

"They pulled him off me and beat the shit out of him. At one point, he threw a punch at Brendan, slipped on an old potato chip bag, fell and broke his arm." Mia smiled. "His throwing arm.

"He was lying on the ground, swearing at them, yelling that he was going to kill them. Con bent down and said something to him. Kyle shut up immediately. Then the four of us turned and walked away."

"And what did your brother say to him?" Finn asked, leaning closer, anticipation gleaming in his eyes.

Mia felt her shoulders relax. "They wouldn't tell me at first. I had to threaten to tell Mom what had happened. Finally, Con said he'd told Kyle that if he came near me again, if he so much as brushed against me in the hall, the three of them and Mac would hunt him down and cut off his dick."

"Ouch," Finn murmured. "Did it work?"

"Oh, yeah. My brothers went a little wild after our dad died. Con and Quinn had graduated by then, but no one had forgotten them. Everyone knew not to cross the Donovan boys. Kyle never came near me again. If he saw me coming, he went the other way."

Mia sat up and touched Finn's face. "Remember when we talked about brothers protecting their sisters? About the sisters thanking their brothers once in a while?"

Finn brushed a wisp of hair out of her face. "Yeah. I do."

"Kyle Pinckney was the guy I thanked my brothers for. And that's why I'll walk through fire for all four of them."

"I'll make sure to thank your brothers next time I see them."

"You're not going to see them again. Now that they know I'm on the job, their chest-puffing, macho stuff will stop."

"You never know," he said, settling her into the curve of

his arm more thoroughly. She should get off his lap. Sit next to him on the couch. But she was too comfortable.

His scent, the solid feel of his chest, the slow, gentle glide of his hand down her arm, were intoxicating. Addictive.

"I'd offer to turn on the TV for a while, watch something silly with you," he said, his voice a low, soothing murmur in her ear. "Help you unwind. But the remote is too far away and I'm not putting you down to get it. So you're stuck with me for entertainment."

"Hey," she said, raising her head to look at him. "I'm supposed to be taking care of you. Not the other way around."

"You're supposed to be protecting me. Nothing to protect me from right now," he pointed out, pulling her close again.

She tried to slide off and sit beside him, but he curled his arm around her and held her close. "You were shivering." It felt as if he kissed the crown of her head. "I'm trying to keep you warm."

"'Keep me warm?'" She snorted, but let herself sink into his chest. His solid body radiated heat and comfort. "Lame, O'Rourke. Is that the best you can do?"

"Of course not," he said. His mouth was so close to her ear that his breath tickled her neck and stirred her hair. "That was my opener. I'm just getting started."

"Okay, well, get the remote and turn on the TV before I fall asleep here."

His laugh made his chest shake beneath her and his arm tightened around her. "You do have a mouth on you, Officer Donovan," he said, his teeth tugging on her earlobe. "A very nice one. I like it. A lot." His thumb brushed the corner of her mouth. Lingered.

Scooping her into his arms instead of putting her on the couch, he grabbed the remote, then settled her against his chest again. He aimed the remote at the TV, and one of the late night Jimmys appeared. "Will this keep you awake? Or are you going to be snoring on my lap in ten minutes?"

"Do women often fall asleep on you, Finn?" She shifted to look at him, knowing she was playing with fire but too comfortable to care.

His mouth curved as he watched her. "Usually not until they've been thoroughly warmed."

Her whole body tingled at his words, and she shifted into his chest, snuggling closer. "Oh, good," she murmured, inhaling the fresh scent of his shirt and the subtle fragrance of his aftershave. "I was beginning to worry."

"Nothing to worry about," he whispered. "I've got you."

He brushed his cheek over the top of her head, and his whiskers caught in her hair. She wanted to feel them rasp against her fingertips, to tickle her chest as he kissed his way down to her breasts.

'I've got you'.

He did. He had her, and she needed Finn. Needed his help replacing all the horrible memories that had churned to the surface tonight.

They only had two more weeks together. Whatever this was between them would go no farther than the hotel suite. There was no future for Mia Donovan and Finn O'Rourke.

She was tired of fighting this magnetic attraction that burned between them. Tired of being professional and business-like when she wanted him so badly. When they walked out of this room, she'd do her job and do it well.

Tonight, though, she was cold. And she needed Finn to warm her.

Reaching up, she slid her fingers through his hair. Let her palms caress his cheek. Felt the rasp of his whiskers against them.

Then she pressed her hungry mouth to his.

CHAPTER NINETEEN

Mia opened her mouth to him, needing to taste him again. Needing to feel the sweep of his tongue against hers. But instead of deepening the kiss, Finn eased away from her.

"Mia, are you sure about this?" He cupped her cheek, running his thumb along the curve of her jaw. "After we, um, lost control on the floor," he leaned closer, so their noses were almost touching and added in a low, raspy voice, "which was and always will be the hottest thing ever, you've been pretty clear that you didn't intend to do that again. That it would compromise your job. I don't want you to do anything you'll regret tomorrow."

Her heart melted into a mushy mess. He wanted her, too – the hard length of his cock against her thigh didn't lie. Most men wouldn't have asked. They'd simply take what she offered.

"Finn." She nuzzled his neck, nipped at his ear. "To ask me that when I know you want me, too…" She shifted on his lap, smiled into his skin when he surged against her. "You're an amazing man. I know I've been giving you mixed signals. But yes. I want this. Want you." She cupped his face with both hands and brushed her mouth over his. "You gonna make me beg?"

"God, I hope so." He shifted and suddenly she was straddling him, her face close to his. "I want to make you moan. Beg. Forget your own name." He nuzzled her neck. "Scream a few times, too."

Mia's chest was so tight, it felt as if her heart might burst right out of it. She nipped at his lower lip. "Just a few times?"

"Oh, no. More than a few." He ran his tongue over the seam of her lips, smiled against them when he felt her shiver. "Didn't want to sound all braggy, though."

She sucked his lower lip into her mouth, let it go with a tiny pop. "Guess you'll have to prove it's not bragging then, won't you?"

He stood up suddenly from the couch, making her clutch his arms. "I love a challenge," he said, heading toward his bedroom.

Mia wrapped her legs around his waist and held on.

She expected him to drop her onto the bed. Instead, after stripping back the duvet and top sheet, he lowered her onto the crisp sheet, trailing kisses across her neck and nosing beneath her robe. Tugging on the tie, he let the robe fall open. Traced the letters on her tee shirt.

"Cops and Robbers," he murmured. "I remember that game." He grinned up at her. "I was always the robber."

"Mmmm." She began to unbutton his shirt. "I have a thing for bad boys."

"Is that so?" He tunneled beneath her shirt, flattened his palm on her belly. Smiled when she twitched beneath his fingers. "I'll do my best to live up to your fantasies."

"You...," she gasped, "you already are." She slid her hands along his shirt, fumbling for the buttons, but her hands shook so much, she couldn't push the small discs through the tiny holes. Finally, frustrated, she pulled on the two sides and ripped it open. Buttons bounced off the headboard with tiny pings, landed on the bed and glittered in the faint light.

He stared down at her, his eyes dark, hungry pools. "That was so hot. If I put on another shirt, will you do it again?"

She ran her hands over his chest, her fingers pressing into his smooth, hot skin. His muscles jumped beneath her palms, and she sat up to press a kiss to his belly button. "You try to put more clothes on and I'll have to get my cuffs."

"Now I'm scared." He smiled down at her, tugging on the neck of her tee. "We'll save the cuffs for another time." He slipped the hotel robe off her shoulders and pushed the sleeves down her arm. It pooled on the bed behind her, and she sat in front of him in only her tee shirt and worn pajama pants.

She swallowed, glancing down at herself and her ordinary, mundane clothing. "Wish I'd packed something a little sexier than my oldest pajamas and the tee shirt I stole from my brother."

Finn smoothed his hands down the front of her shirt, lingering for a moment to cup the weight of her breasts. "You're the sexiest woman I've ever known," he murmured. "You could be wearing rags and all I'd see is you. Beautiful, sexy, smart-mouthed Mia."

He tugged the shirt over her head and tossed it away, then stared down at her. "Look at you, all strong and sexy and sleek muscles. Wearing ordinary pajamas, not something out of a teen-aged boy's fantasies. Your body is real, your clothes are real. Just like you." He kissed one breast, then the other. "Suddenly, real is all I want."

Mia pulled his shirt off, then reached for the buckle of his belt. He took her hands away from his waist and held them clasped in his. "Not so fast, Mia." He kissed her, their hands twined together, his mouth hot and possessive. When he broke away, she was breathless, her heart thundering in her chest, her blood singing through her veins.

And all he'd done was kiss her.

Before she regained her senses, he'd stripped off her pajama pants. She lay on the bed, naked in front of him, but instead of feeling exposed, she felt wanted. Desired. Cherished.

"I'm glad we can take off our clothes this time," he said, grinning at her. "Now I can look my fill."

Her heart stuttered once, then beat harder. To hide what she was sure was a matching sappy grin on her face, she said, "Hard to see where the screams are going to come from if all you're going to do is look."

"Oh, we'll get to the screaming," he said. Standing, he shucked his pants and socks, leaving them in a heap on the floor. Then he pulled off his dark boxers, and his long, thick cock bobbed against his stomach. "Anyone ever tell you you're not very patient, babe?"

A secret, stupidly romantic part of her quivered at the endearment. So she grabbed his hands and tugged him down on top of her. "I need to feel you against me," she whispered into his ear. "Inside me."

His penis twitched against her stomach, and she squirmed to get it where she needed it. Instead of following her lead, he shook his head as he bent to kiss her. "Oh, we'll get there. Trust me," he murmured against her lips. "I don't want to jitterbug with you, Mia. I want to waltz. Slowly sweep you off your feet. Leave you breathless, your head spinning." He brushed his lips against hers, left her craving more. "We have all night. And I'm not going to rush."

He was as good as his word. By the time his mouth moved away from hers, she was shaking with need. Instead of hurrying, though, he kissed his way down her body, lingering at her breasts until she practically levitated off the bed. Then he moved to her abdomen, trailing kisses down to the insides of her thighs.

His warm breath feathered over her core, making her gasp. Then he pressed his lips to the junction of her thighs and tasted her, sucking gently at her. And he'd been right.

She screamed so hard her throat burned.

Before she could catch her breath, he rolled over and reached for the drawer of his night stand. Pulled out a foil packet, tore it open and sheathed himself. Then, while she was still shaking with her orgasm, he slid into her.

She twined her hands with his and held his gaze as he began to move. Finn kissed her, his mouth hot and possessive. Claiming. She tried to keep her eyes open, but as she began to flutter again, her eyes drifted closed.

Finn nuzzled her neck. "That's right," he whispered. "Let go, Mia. Come for me again."

His words trembled through her, and she came again as he groaned and froze above her. She'd never felt anything this intense. This powerful. It went on and on, and she cried out until she was hoarse. Finally Finn collapsed on top of her, rolling so that she was lying on top of him.

Mia could barely open her eyes. She turned her head, found his lips and murmured, "What was my name again?"

***

Finn flopped onto the bed beside Mia after the third time they made love, exhausted. His muscles were loose and lax, his skin hot. His brain was pretty much completely fried.

Drifting in a haze of hormones and contentment, he curled his arms around her and pulled her close. Trailing lazy fingers down her back, he tried to touch every inch of her skin. He wanted to memorize her. Never let her go.

Alarms blared, and he hastily added, 'until he had to leave Chicago.' He wasn't falling in love with Mia. Wouldn't allow himself to do that. The last time he'd fallen in love, it had damn near destroyed him. He refused to make himself vulnerable like that again.

"Tell me a secret," she murmured. "Something no one else knows about you."

His hands tightened on her for a moment, then loosened

again. "You first. My life is an open book. Not many secrets."

She opened one eye and glanced up at him, her gaze knowing. Understanding. Had she somehow figured out what really happened with Gemma?

Finally she nodded, and it was as if he heard her thoughts. She'd allow him his secret. Wouldn't push him to share it.

"When that thing happened with Kyle in high school, I was terrified for months." She spoke into his chest and wound her finger around a curl of his hair. "Never walked home alone again. Always made sure I was with other people in school. I never felt safe until Kyle went away to college. Even then I was nervous. I didn't stop being afraid until I went away to college, too."

"That's awful," he murmured, curling his arms more tightly around her. Wishing he could have protected her teen-aged self. "Didn't your mom make sure you had therapy?"

"I never told her. Neither did my brothers." She shrugged against his chest. "I wasn't actually hurt. And I pretended everything was fine. If my brothers had known how freaked out I was, they never would have let me out of their sight."

"That's awful, Mia." His heart ached for the terrified child she'd been. For the brothers and mother who hadn't recognized it. He cupped his hand around the back of her head, held her against his heart. "They should have picked up on it."

"My brothers were already way too protective. I had to hide how I felt, or they wouldn't have let me out of the house by myself. I got to be an expert at hiding my fear."

Mia's casual words were betrayed by a tiny quiver in her voice. She was so used to hiding that she probably didn't notice it. "You still are, aren't you?" he murmured.

She rolled to the side and one corner of her mouth turned up. "Not so much. I told you about it, didn't I?"

He wondered how many other people had seen her vulnerable. He'd guess not many. "Yeah, you did." He brushed his mouth over hers. "Thank you."

Mia snuggled into his side, her leg tossed over his, her arms curling around him. Her face was buried in his neck, and the soft puffs of her breaths warmed his skin.

"No one knows what really happened with Gemma," he heard himself say.

He stopped, shocked. He hadn't intended to share that secret with Mia. He hadn't told a soul what really happened that day.

Mia fumbled her hand loose from his and pressed her fingers to his lips. "You don't have to tell me," she murmured. "I've already figured out that it didn't go down the way Gemma said it did. I wasn't angling for you to tell me about it."

She trailed her fingers down his cheek to his neck, then replaced her hand with her mouth. "I was going for something like, 'I eat Oreos in bed.'"

He smiled into her hair. "For the record, no, I don't eat Oreos in bed. Mint Milanos are my guilty pleasure."

"Figures you'd go with the classy, expensive cookies."

She was teasing him, trying to make it easy for him to let the Gemma thing go. He combed his fingers through her tangled hair. Her determination not to press made him more determined to tell her the truth.

"I caught her in bed with her drummer. At our house. She'd known exactly when I was coming home. She planned it so that I caught her."

Mia reared back, frowning. "What the hell?"

"I realized pretty quickly she didn't just plan for me to find her. She planned a career." He sighed, rolled onto his back. "I told her to get out. She started to cry, said she was sorry, blah, blah. I stood in the room and made the two of them get out of my bed, put their clothes on and leave." He shrugged. "All those songs she wrote about how I broke her heart made her popular and rich. It shot her from a second-tier musician into the stratosphere. She became the betrayed woman speaking for betrayed women everywhere."

"And you let her get away with it? Why didn't you tell your side of the story?" Mia demanded.

"That's what you would have done, isn't it?" he murmured.

"Damn straight. No way would I have let someone who cheated on me make me the bad guy."

"It wasn't that simple, Mia." He pulled her back down against him. He didn't mind sharing the story so much when he was holding her. "She was ready, and she got her story out first. First one with the story frames the discussion. Calling her a liar would have only made me look like a whiner. It was a no-win situation.

"And I was glad she was gone. The sex was good, she was charismatic and fun, but I'd begun to realize I'd made a mistake. She was tiring to be around – all drama, all the time. The idea of having a family, of having kids, was appalling to her. So I let it go. Realized I was much happier without her."

"The world thinks you're a jerk."

"The people who matter, the ones who know me, don't think so. None of them liked Gemma. They probably suspect she was lying, but I don't care. She's gone, and I'm happy she is."

Mia slid out of his arms and sat up. Brushed his hair off his forehead, trailed her hand across his cheek. The rasp of his whiskers against her fingers was loud in the quiet room

"You're amazing, Finn," she finally said. She smiled. "Far more forgiving than I'd be. I want to shoot the bitch."

Laughing, he pulled her down next to him again. "Thank God you're on my side. Not sure I'd be able to handle it if you were a Gemma fan."

"Never was a Gemma Radley fan," she said, nuzzling his chest. "Her songs always sounded like whining to me. Even before she became famous for whining about you."

He tightened his hold on Mia. She made him feel lighter. As if he'd shared the burden of Gemma, and now he could let it go. Forget about the woman who'd nearly ruined his career. "You're good for me," he murmured.

"Damn right I am. I'm going to find your stalker and kick her ass."

"Didn't mean it that way," he whispered into her hair.

She stilled beside him. Then she said, "You're good for me, too. We've got a good scream count going. Want to see if we can make it better?"

Once again, she was letting him off the hook. "I'd love to," he said, kissing her again.

***

By the time Finn heard the phone ringing, Mia had already slipped out of bed and run into the living room to grab it. Finn pulled his boxers on and followed her out of the bedroom.

Morning light spilled into the room as Mia said, "Sorry, Mom. I'm going to miss seeing all of you, but I'm working today. And I can't have someone fill in for me. It's a special project."

Finn watched as Mia listened to her mother. Saw her scowl. "They had no right to tell you that." Pause. "Yes, it *is* supposed to be a secret."

So one of her brothers had blabbed to their mom about him. Finn settled against the door frame, wondering how Mia was going to handle it.

She listened for a long time. "Mom," she started to say. Stopped again. Glanced at him. "I'm not going to do that. He doesn't want to come over..." Scowled. "Because I know. That's how."

Finn pushed away from the wall. Bent down, so Mia could see him. Nodded vigorously. "Yes," he mouthed. "I want to."

Mia slapped her hand over the speaker on the phone.

"You don't even know what we're talking about. So how can you say you want to do it?"

Anything that got Mia this worked up was going to be fun. "Guessing," he said.

"Fine, Mom," Mia finally said. "We'll talk about it. But don't count on it. Why would he want to spend time with my brothers? They've already harassed him. Embarrassed him in public. I'll let you know later."

She stabbed at the off icon on her phone, then tossed it onto the table. It slid across the marble surface and fell to the floor. Thank God there was a carpet to cushion it.

"Let me guess," Finn said. "Your mom called to remind you to come over for dinner this afternoon. You told her you couldn't make it. She said you should come anyway. You tried to put your refusal on me. So you want me to say, 'no way. I'm not spending time with your loser brothers.'"

"Exactly." She bent down to pick up the phone. "I'll call her and let her know."

He grabbed her wrist as she began to dial the phone. "That's what you want me to say, Mia. What I actually say is yes. I'd love to meet the rest of your family. What's the plan?"

She stared at him for a long moment. Narrowed her eyes at him.

He smiled at her. "Those glares might have unnerved me a few days ago. Might have made me back down. Not anymore.

"I know your weaknesses, Mia. All the ways to make you shiver. To cry out. I know you're a giant mushball beneath that tough exterior. So, no. I don't want to miss this party. What time do we leave?"

CHAPTER TWENTY

Finn stared out the window of the car as they pulled up to the curb in front of a tidy bungalow on Chicago's south side. It looked like every other bungalow on the street, the only differences being the colors of the bricks and the architectural details, like the design of the stained glass topping the living room windows.

"Nice neighborhood," he said as Pete stopped the car.

"It's home," Mia said as she opened the door and stepped onto the parkway grass. Glancing up and down the street, she said, "You can get out. But go up to the porch so none of the neighbors see you. If they do, this will turn into a circus."

"Nosey neighbors, huh?" he asked as he reached for the door handle.

"Yep. The best kind," Mia said, her expression softening as her gaze lingered on the rows of bungalows. "Everyone on the block knows everyone else's business. Always right there if you need them, though. They're great."

"Huh." Finn glanced up and down the street, saw the kids' bikes abandoned in the front yards, a wagon on the sidewalk a few houses down, the chairs on almost every front porch.

Nothing like his neighborhood. Every house on his street was carefully landscaped. Perfectly manicured. Surrounded by tall fences. A toy left on the driveway or sidewalk would be shockingly out of place.

What would it be like to live in a neighborhood like this? A place where everyone knew you. Where neighbors looked out for one another.

A place where *living* was more important than the image your house projected. A place where everyone looked out for each other's kids.

He wouldn't recognize the people who lived on either side of him.

As he began to step onto the grass beside Mia, he turned to Pete. "I'll call you when we need you."

"No, you won't." Mia pushed Finn back into the car. She'd been very…physical all day. Touching him. Sitting plastered against him in the back seat of the car. Taking his hand and playing with his fingers.

He suspected she didn't realize she was doing it. He wasn't about to point it out, either, because then she might stop.

Leaning over Finn so that her breast pressed against his upper arm, she said, "Pete, you're coming in, too. My mother would be horrified if you didn't."

Pete's gaze shifted from her to Finn and back. "That's not necessary, Mia. I'll be fine."

"It's completely necessary." She squatted next to the car, so her eyes were level with Pete's. "You don't come in, Finn and I aren't going in there, either. Then who's going to eat all that homemade lasagna?" She leaned closer, putting her breasts dangerously close to Finn's mouth. He wanted to bend his head and kiss them, but he restrained himself. Who knew who was watching out a window?

Pete's eyes softened. "I haven't had homemade lasagna since Judy died."

"That settles it. Turn off the engine and get out of the

car."

Pete glanced at Finn again. He shrugged. "I'm just along for the ride, too. If Mia says you're welcome, of course you should join us."

Pete glanced back at Mia. "Thanks," he said softly.

As the three of them walked up the steps, the door opened and an older woman who looked a lot like Mia rushed out the door. "Mia! I'm so glad you came."

She hugged her daughter, pressing her cheek against Mia's, and Finn was impressed. Mia's mother was focused completely on her daughter – she hadn't even glanced at him.

Not that he expected her to. But he was usually the first person noticed in a group, and it was unexpectedly refreshing to be the sidekick. To be Mia's 'date' and not the center of attention.

Mia's mother finally leaned back and studied her daughter. "You look tired. Is this job keeping you too busy?"

Finn's face heated. Mia's lack of sleep had nothing to do with her job.

"Not at all. There have been some late nights, but nothing I can't handle," Mia said calmly. She turned around and looked at Finn, and instead of the discomfort he expected, her eyes twinkled. Like she was getting a kick out of their shared secret.

Was she punishing him for pushing to meet her family?

Probably. It would be a very Mia-like thing to do.

Maybe coming to her mother's wasn't such a great idea.

He tore his gaze away from her laughing face and held out his hand to her mother. "A pleasure to meet you, Mrs. Donovan. You have a remarkable daughter."

She beamed at him. "Thank you, Finn. And call me Rose, please."

"Rose. Thanks for inviting me." He grabbed Pete's elbow and dragged him forward. "This is Pete White. My friend from California. Mia insisted he come, too."

"Of course." Rose held out her hand to Pete. "Nice to meet you, Pete."

Frozen in place, Pete stared at Mia's mother for three heartbeats. Then he shook her hand for a few seconds too long. "You, too, Rose," he murmured.

His hand slid away from hers and swallowed. "Mia looks a lot like you."

"I get that a lot," Rose agreed. "Come on in and meet the rest of the family."

Finn stepped into a welcoming living room with a denim-colored couch and loveseat. A coffee table sat in front of it, and a worn recliner stood in the corner. He recognized it immediately. It was the twin to Mia's. Like Mia's, a table sat between it and the couch, holding a stack of magazines and several books. An oriental rug covered the floor.

The whole bungalow would fit into his living room, but he'd rather sit in this comfortable room than his own designer-arranged space. In here, a guy could be himself. Get comfortable on the couch with a beer and a book. Watch a baseball game on TV.

An arched opening led into a dining room that held a long table. Voices and laughter spilled out of the kitchen behind it.

"Mia's here," Rose called, and a tide of people surged out of the kitchen. They stopped, falling silent, when they saw him next to Mia. Then one of her brothers stepped forward. Finn was pretty sure it was Brendan, the one who'd interrogated him at Oscar's.

"Glad you could come," Brendan said easily, shaking Finn's hand as if he'd never engaged in a stare-down with him at the restaurant. "Con told me you're Mia's job. Should have said something the other night. I wouldn't have given you the stink eye. At least not as much."

"Uh, that was Mia's call." Ouch. Could he sound any more lame?

Brendan slapped him on the back. "Yeah, she scares all

of us sometimes, too." He turned around and pulled a beautiful woman with wavy, caramel-colored hair forward. "This is my fiancée, Cilla."

Cilla studied him for a long moment, then nodded. "Good to meet you, Finn." She finally smiled. "Hope you're not overwhelmed by all us Donovans."

"Trying not to be," he admitted.

Cilla leaned closer. "Greatest family in the world," she said, as if she were imparting a big secret. "The first time is a little intense, though."

He met the rest of the family in a dizzying wave. Con shook his hand and apologized for making a scene near his trailer, then introduced his girlfriend Raine. A guy who looked exactly like Con turned out to be his twin, Quinn, whose girlfriend was Tessa. Mia's oldest brother, Mac, was more reserved than the rest of the family. His fiancée Lizzie was warm and welcoming.

Even Mia's aunt Helen, whose clingy dress outlined a baby bump, her husband Jamie and their daughter Charlotte were there. Helen and Jamie didn't look any older than Mia and her brothers, and Finn shot Mia a questioning look.

"Helen is Mom's much younger sister," she said, taking the dark-haired baby who was reaching for Mia. "How's my Charlotte?" she cooed to the little girl, who patted Mia's cheeks with a huge, drooling smile and babbled at her. The drool landed on Mia's shoulder, but instead of freaking out, she pressed a kiss to Charlotte's wet cheek.

As if baby drool was a fashion statement she was proud to make.

Finn smiled as he pictured Jenna Stanton's shriek of horror if a baby drooled on the shoulder of her designer clothes.

Someone pressed a bottle of beer into his hand, then Mia tugged him into a conversation with Jamie and Helen about the house they'd just bought and were rehabbing. As they talked, Mia played with Charlotte's hand, smoothed the baby's curly hair, and replied to every one of the girl's babbling sentences.

They drifted from one group to the next, and after an hour, Finn felt as if he'd known the Donovans forever. They asked briefly about the film and his role, her brothers talked about the security and the stalker, then they moved on to Charlotte's upcoming birthday and the party they'd planned.

Rose questioned him about his family, and the sympathy in her expression when he said they didn't see each other very often made him squirm.

He wanted to point out that not everyone had a family that lived as close as hers, but he knew it was more than that. Finn had focused on his career, and the choices he'd made had limited his time with his family.

Yeah, they couldn't get together for dinner one Sunday a month, but they could get together more often than they did. He had enough money to make it happen. Seeing his siblings and parents, who lived in different cities and different coasts, took effort and planning he hadn't bothered with.

An effort he vowed to make, starting when he finished shooting this film. Seeing the closeness the Donovans shared, the way they truly enjoyed each other's company, made Finn realize how much he was missing.

Mia nudged him, and he turned to her. "You notice my mom and Pete?" she murmured.

Finn glanced around and saw them in the kitchen. Pete was helping Rose set the steaming lasagna on the counter, pulling the salad dressing out of the refrigerator, checking on the garlic bread.

"This smells so good, Rose," Pete said as he removed the second pan from the oven. "I can't wait to try it."

"I'm so glad you came with Finn and Mia," she said, canting a little toward Pete.

"I didn't exactly come with them," Pete said in a gruff voice. "I'm Finn's driver."

"He brought you from California so you could drive him

around?" She laid her hand on Pete's arm, and the older man gazed down at it, his eyes suddenly a little darker. "He must trust you very much."

"What's going on?" he whispered to Mia.

"What do you think is going on?" she asked, elbowing him in the side. "He looked as if he'd been struck by lightning when you introduced him to my mom. Do I need to ask his intentions?"

Finn watched his friend, who'd been grieving for his wife since Finn met him, talking and laughing with Rose Donovan. "Maybe you do," he said slowly.

"I was joking, Finn," she said, leaning against him for a brief moment as she took a sip of iced tea. Even here with her family, she wouldn't drink. She was still on the job. "They're both adults. I think it's kind of sweet."

She eased away from him, and he missed the weight of her body against his. "I doubt he's going to break Mom's heart in the two weeks you'll be here."

Two weeks. He had fourteen days left with Mia.

When he'd heard about the Chicago shoot, he'd shrugged it off as part of the job. He hadn't looked forward to living in a hotel for three weeks, but it wouldn't be forever.

Now, in two weeks, he and Pete would go back to California. He'd move on with his life and career. Mia would stay in Chicago and go back to her normal life, as well.

She'd meet someone else. Fall in love with him. Make a life, probably very much like the life her brothers and mother had. Centered around her job. Her family.

Her husband.

Finn ignored the tiny burn of regret. Of loss. He'd make an effort to get closer to his own family. They couldn't have dinner together once a month, but they'd damn well get together more often than Christmas and Thanksgiving.

Mia wouldn't be part of it, though.

She'd be with that damned *husband.*

He reached for her hand, and after a moment, she twined her fingers with his. Squeezed once, then let him go.

She'd disappear from his life after this shoot, but he'd spend every second of the next fourteen days with her. And after he went home to California?

He'd miss her. A lot. After only a week, it was hard to imagine his life without Mia. His world would center on work. Publicity commitments. Parties with important people he was obligated to attend

Was that the life he wanted?

***

Mia glanced at Finn as the car sped toward the Loop. He'd thoroughly charmed her family tonight. He'd laughed and joked with her brothers, patiently answered questions about movie-making, and teased her future sisters-in-law until the tough women who loved her brothers were giggling.

He'd even let her mom draw him aside for what looked like a serious talk.

As they were leaving, her mother had told Finn she hoped to see him at the next family dinner. Finn, sounding sincere, had said he hoped so, too.

At the next family dinner, he'd be back in California. Already gone for two weeks.

Two weeks would go by in the blink of an eye. But she'd savor every second of them.

Tick tock.

She slid closer until they were pressed together from their thighs to their shoulders. "You were great with my family," she said, taking his hand and pressing their palms together. "Thank you."

He looked at her, his expression puzzled. "You're thanking me? For what?"

She shrugged as she studied their joined hands. "For answering all their questions. For flirting with Tessa and

Lizzie and Raine and Cilla." She smiled, although it was forced. "For letting my mother interrogate you."

"She didn't interrogate me," he said immediately.

"I don't believe you," she said, frowning as she studied him. "I know my mother."

"Okay, she did. But not about you."

"No?" Mia was shocked. She'd brought guys home in the past, and her mother's and brothers' questions and hovering always embarrassed the hell out of her. "About what, then?"

Finn touched the thick plastic window between the front and back seat. Checking to make sure it was closed? "She wanted to know about Pete. If he was married, or engaged or dating anyone."

She let his hand go and gripped his leg as she swiveled to face him. "No way."

"Sorry. That's what she was asking about." He trailed his finger down her cheek, down her neck, lingered at her pulse. She shivered. "You thought she was asking about my intentions toward you?" he asked, his eyes crinkling into a grin.

"No. I'm just shocked because my mother hasn't dated at all since my dad died. At least not that I know of."

"So they didn't ask about my intentions because they assumed our relationship was professional. Right?"

"Yeah. Right." She barely resisted rolling her eyes. "Because none of them noticed we were touching each other all evening. Even Charlotte could tell we were more than business acquaintances."

"That must mean they approved of me." His voice was as smug as his smile.

"Nope. Just means they didn't have to ask. They already know your intentions."

His smile disappeared. "What do you mean?"

"You told them you only had two weeks of shooting left in Chicago. You're leaving after the filming's done. So why bother to interrogate you?"

"What if I'm so hard to resist that you fall madly in love with me in the next two weeks?"

Mia snapped her gaze to his face. His eyes were twinkling. Good joke, Finn. Swallowing once, she flopped back on the seat. "My mama didn't raise stupid children."

Silence filled the car, stretched uncomfortably long.

This wasn't the way Mia wanted the evening to end – thinking about the end of things rather than the time they had left. Determined to lighten things up, she asked, "So what did you tell her about Pete?"

"That his wife Judy died about five years ago. That he hasn't dated since, as far as I know. And that he's a great guy. That I've seen a lot of women hit on him, including some pretty well known movie stars, and he never gave any of them a second glance."

"Oh my God. You did *not* say that to my mother." Mia spun in her seat so she was facing Finn.

"How do you know I didn't?" He tilted his head, a smile flirting with his mouth, as if he was fascinated.

"Because she was laughing. If you told her Pete had ignored movie stars but was interested in her, she would have kicked your ass."

"How come?" He frowned at her. The wrinkles in his forehead only made him look sexier.

"Because she'd assume you were lying, of course. Sucking up to her."

"I wasn't lying. It's the truth." He took her hand. "Your mother's a beautiful woman," he said softly. "I imagine you'll look just like her in about thirty years."

"I was right. You are a suck up," she muttered.

"Nope." He curled his arm around her shoulders and tugged her against him. "You're one of the most beautiful women I've ever seen." He nuzzled her hair, pressed a kiss to her neck. "And I can't wait to get back to our room and show you how beautiful you are."

Desire fizzed and bubbled through her, and she leaned against him. This was what she wanted. Not depressing conversations about him leaving in two weeks. She'd much rather think about what was going to happen in the next hour or two. The rest of the night.

When they reached the hotel, she practically dragged Finn through the deserted hall and onto the elevator. She let him go when they reached their floor, unlocking the door and stepping inside.

Stopped before she entered, her eagerness to get inside vanishing. A white envelope lay on the carpet.

CHAPTER TWENTY-ONE

"What?" Finn asked behind her.

"There's an envelope on the floor," she answered, staring down at it. "Looks like the other ones." She turned to him. "I want you to stay in the hall. Keep the door open, but don't come in, okay?"

"Mia..."

"Don't argue, Finn," she said, her voice sharp with fear. "Just stay here."

He nodded, putting his hand on the door to hold it open. Holding her purse tightly, she searched through his room, then hers. Both closets. Both bathrooms.

Finally, when she was sure the suite was empty, she searched in her suitcase for a pair of gloves and an evidence bag as she called, "Come in, Finn. Close and lock the door."

Snapping the gloves on, she picked up the envelope and slid it into the plastic bag. Then she found the letter opener on the desk and slit it open. Eased out several pieces of paper.

The top sheet was ripped out of a newspaper. It was a story about the fight at Seven with Kyle. Finn's name was prominent, as was the description of her. And the fact that they were plastered together all night. Never apart except for the few moments of the fight.

Next was a photo someone had taken of Mia pushing through the crowd to get to the center of the dance floor. Finn's hand was on her hip, his face easily identifiable.

Then another photo. It was taken from the side. Finn's face was clearly visible, hers, less so. They were near the door, on their way out, and Finn's arm was wrapped around her shoulders. She leaned against him, her arm around his waist.

The fourth piece of paper was a note. Same handwriting as the other notes, same hard, angry strokes of the pen. 'You betrayed me. When you left Gemma, I knew you were ready for me. And when you came to Chicago, I knew you were looking for me. It was our time. Then you dumped me for this slut. We're over. You will pay.'

"Oh, God," she murmured, gripping the top of the evidence bag in her fist as she stared at the photos. "Was she there? At Seven?"

"I don't think so." Finn uncurled her fingers from the bag and tugged it out of her hand. He peered at the first picture through the plastic, his finger sliding over first one photo, then the other. "My guess? These are screen shots. Someone at Seven took the photos, then uploaded them to one of the gossip sites. Looks like the stalker printed them out from her computer."

Mia snatched the bag from him and studied the photos more closely. "I think you're right," she finally said. "I see the edges of the computer toolbar at the bottom of one on them."

"So she wasn't there. And she doesn't know the circumstances surrounding those pictures."

"Doesn't matter," she said without looking at him. "She sees a couple." Mia arranged the article and the two pictures in a row, the note beneath them. "You've betrayed her."

"I've put you in harm's way," he said, running his hand up and down her arm. "Maybe I should have a different bodyguard."

"No." Mia dropped the plastic bag onto the table and gripped the front of Finn's shirt. "She's threatening you, not me. I'm just a slut who's taking what I can get. You're the one who's destroying her dreams. You're the one she has to punish. She's coming after you, not me."

"So what do we do?"

"No more public appearances, for starters." She released her grip on his shirt, smoothed the area she'd wrinkled. "I'm sorry, Finn. Unless you're working, you're stuck in this suite until you go home."

"I can live with that, as long as you're here, too."

"Oh, I will be." She jumped up and began to pace, trying to ignore the flutter of her stupid, sappy heart. She needed to focus on her job right now, not Finn's words. "This is a good thing," she said, forcing herself to think about possible strategies. "She's angry. She'll get careless. Make a stupid mistake, and we'll have her."

"And then you'll leave," he murmured.

She didn't want to leave. Not after they caught the stalker. Not even after her two weeks were up. Mia stopped pacing, terrified by the realization.

Her fingers trembling, she reached for Finn's hand. "Is that what you want? For me to leave after we catch this woman?"

"Of course not," he said, tugging her against him. "I want you to stay until I have to leave." His mouth curled slightly and his eyes twinkled. She was pretty sure she'd see those eyes in her dreams after he left. "In fact, you'll have to stay. To make sure there isn't another stalker."

She wound her arms around his neck. "You think we have nut jobs growing on trees in Chicago?"

Finn's smile disappeared. "Not just in Chicago. Famous people attract them like shit attracts flies."

"Two weeks stuck in a hotel room will be tough. You can have people come here, though. We can make that work."

"Who would I want to hang out with? The people I work with for twelve hours every day? No, thanks." He nuzzled her neck. "My calendar is full for the next two weeks, anyway."

Her heart fluttered with both dread and anticipation. "Plans I don't know about?" she said, trying to lighten the atmosphere.

"I think you can probably figure them out." He pressed a kiss to her mouth, took it deeper when she murmured his name against his lips.

"Hmm," she said against his lips. The sound vibrated between them and streaked through the rest of her body. "Your godfather mentioned having dinner with you." She sucked his lower lip into her mouth, let it go with a tiny pop. "That would be fine. Probably nowhere safer than the superintendent's house." She bit gently on his earlobe. "Call Doug and tell him your schedule opened up."

"I can't believe you're joking about this."

"Not a joke. I'm telling you to have dinner with your godparents."

"That's just mean," Finn said, easing her away so he could study her expression. "Why would I want to spend an evening fending off Doug and Marie's nosy questions?"

"Because you love them and they're your godparents. You grew up with their kids. It's nice to catch up."

He studied her as if she was an alien species. "You're serious. You really like all this family stuff, don't you?"

She didn't hesitate. "Absolutely. Family is important." She pinched him lightly in the side. "And when you get a swelled head, Mr. Movie Star, no one can pop your balloon better or faster than your family." She laughed. "My brother Brendan already found that out."

"Brendan? Why would someone have to pop his balloon?"

"He writes an amazing blog that's a legend among cops, and he's almost done with a novel. A thriller. We all read the blog, but Bren didn't tell anyone about his writing, including us, until just recently. We're really proud of him, but when he starts talking about who's in the running to option the manuscript for his thriller, we all gang up on him. Tease him unmercifully."

"Yeah? What's the name of his blog?"

"Cops and Robbers."

"That tee shirt you wore last night."

"Yup."

"Okay. So the Donovans can be counted on to keep me humble. I'll think about Doug and Marie. And for the record, I try not to get caught up in most of the Hollywood hype."

"I know, Finn." She wrapped her arms around him and leaned against the solid muscle of his chest. Breathed in his scent. "I was trying to take your mind off that nasty stuff." She nodded toward the papers on the table. "For someone who's in so many tabloids, you're remarkably down to earth. It's one of your most endearing qualities."

"One of?" He tightened his hold on her. "Tell me more."

"Hmm," she hummed into his neck. "Let me think." She waited three beats, smiling into his skin, then said, "You wear dad pants really well. They make you look endearingly frumpy. Also endearingly pudgy. And you're kind of a dork. I suspect you actually read."

"Wow. You're giving me a swelled head," he said, nuzzling her ear.

"That's why you need to have dinner with Doug and Marie. They'll shrink it right down for you."

"Speaking of Doug, do we have to call him tonight?" Finn asked.

Mia nestled against Finn, wishing she could forget the letter and the pictures and drag him off to his bedroom. Sighed, knowing that would have to wait.

"Yeah, we should. He'll probably want to send someone over tonight to pick the stuff up."

"Can't it wait until the morning?" His pupils had grown,

and his face was taut with tension. Color flared in his cheeks. He was thinking about that bedroom, too.

"No," she said, letting him go and putting some space between them. "Phone him now and get it over with. The sooner he has someone pick that stuff up, the sooner we can discuss," she bumped her hips against his, "the swelling in other parts of your body."

"Calling right now," he said, pulling his phone out of his pocket while keeping his other arm wrapped around her.

***

"God! Finally!" Finn swept Mia into his arms an hour later. He'd barely been able to carry on a coherent conversation with his godfather, who'd come over himself to pick up the note and the pictures. All Finn had been able to think about was Mia and her plans for discussing the swelling in certain parts of his body.

He'd been hard the whole time Doug was here, and he was pretty sure Doug knew it.

He rested his chin on Mia's head. "I thought he'd never leave."

"I wanted to boot him out the door." Mia giggled against his chest. "Might have been a career-ending move, though."

He loved hearing that happy sound bubbling out of her throat. Every time his serious, focused-on-the-job Mia giggled, he counted it as a personal victory.

His Mia?

His for the next two weeks, he clarified hastily. And he wasn't going to waste a second of them.

"You mentioned something about a discussion?" he said into her hair.

"I did?" She subtly moved her hips against his, turning his already-hard dick into steel. "I lost my train of thought when Doug walked in."

"You and me both," he muttered.

"But we can discuss stuff if you want," she said, her voice

all prim and proper. "A book we've both read, maybe?"

"How about something we've both done? Recently, and not nearly enough." He swung her into his arms, grinning at her surprised squeal as he held her tight against his chest.

"Put me down," she said, wriggling in his arms. "If you hurt your back because of me, I'll be directing traffic in the Loop for the rest of my life."

"Okay." He dropped her onto the bed. Mia bounced twice, then sat up, laughing.

"You're not joining me?" she said as she unbuttoned her shirt. She tossed it aside, and the silky red material pooled on the floor. She reached for the front closure of her black, lacy bra, fiddling with it but not opening it. Finn stared at her lace-covered breasts, mesmerized. Unable to do anything but watch her.

She eased open the button on her jeans, agonizingly slowly. He heard each tooth in the zipper click open as she lowered it, slow enough to make him howl with need. He wanted to dive onto the bed and do it himself.

He made himself wait.

Mia's breasts shifted in the lacy bra as she wiggled out of the jeans, emphasizing her cleavage. He fumbled with his own jeans as he watched her lower the dark denim, inch by excruciating inch. A hint of black lace appeared, and he swallowed. Clenched his fist to his chest, as if that could keep his racing heart from jumping out and falling at Mia's feet.

Once she'd toed off her jeans, Mia leaned back on her elbows, letting him look his fill at her sleek, strong body. He couldn't move. Finally, smiling at him, she slid two fingers beneath the lace of her panties. "Looks like I'm gonna have to start by myself."

Shuddering, Finn stripped his pants from his legs, followed by his boxers. His hands and arms got tangled in his shirt as he tried to yank it over his head, leaving him blind as well as trapped. Beneath the light blue fabric, he could hear Mia laughing.

"Come here, babe," she said, grabbing one hand until he tumbled onto the bed. One of her hands slipped beneath the shirt to stroke his abdomen, her nails scratching lightly against his skin. The other undid the buttons. Slowly.

"You like to tease, huh?" he said, tearing at the fabric that tangled his hands and hid his head. "You can dish it out, but can you take it?"

She popped the last button free and pulled the shirt off his shoulders. Now he could see her, but his arms were trapped in the sleeves. She leaned over him, her breasts achingly close to his mouth. He thrashed at the sleeves, finally freeing his arms.

Hands free, he yanked at the bedspread, pulling it down and over Mia, rolling her into it until only her legs were exposed. "Can you take it, babe?" he murmured, sucking on the inside of her thigh. She quivered beneath him, and beneath the bedspread, he heard her breath catch.

He nipped at her thigh again, higher this time, and she keened as she thrashed her arms, finally freeing herself. "You are so evil," she said on a sharp inhalation.

"You had your turn to tease. Now it's my turn." He wanted to rip off those lace panties and slide into her. Feel her hands gripping his and his mouth feasting on hers, drinking in her cries. But he ignored the ache in his groin, the tightness in his balls, as he slid his palms beneath those panties. Eased them down her legs, tossed them on the floor.

"I'm begging, Finn," she said, her voice breathless and hoarse. "Okay? You win. Now. I need you now."

"I like the begging part. Tell me more about that," he said as he moved closer to the junction of her thighs.

"I swear I'll handcuff you to the bed," she groaned.

"Threats, Mia?"

She whimpered and arched off the bed as he slid two fingers inside her. "Yes." Her voice wavered. "Threats. The things I'm going to do to you, Finn O'Rourke…" She gasped as he found her sweet spot and stroked.

She clenched around his fingers and flew apart, her cries filling the room. Finn eased her down, then reached for the drawer next to the bed.

The next moment, she'd flipped him and was sitting on top of him. "I'm clean and on the pill. You clean?"

"Yeah. Insurance checkup before filming began."

"Then we don't need the condoms."

He stilled. "You sure?"

"I trust you, Finn." She touched his cheek, her fingers feather light. "Now I'm going to torture you for a while."

He lost track of time as he bucked beneath her, choking out her name between curses and moans. She kissed him frantically, as if she needed him as much as she needed air. He gripped her hips, holding her in place as they rocked together.

As they climaxed together, she collapsed onto his chest, her fingers fumbling for his. She bit his shoulder and sucked in a breath.

"Finn. Oh, God, Finn," she sobbed.

He held her tightly, reveling in the press of her limp body against his, the sawing of her breath against his neck.

He buried his face in the mass of her hair, drinking in her scent. Memorizing it. No matter how long he lived, he'd never forget the silkiness of her skin against his.

The soft waves of her hair, falling over his face.

The sound of her voice, calling his name.

He wanted to cling to her forever. Never let her go.

The realization terrified him.

Time to lighten this up.

"Still need those cuffs?" he whispered.

She opened her eyes and stared down at him, a shadow flickering in her eyes for a brief moment. Then she slid off him and trailed her fingers over his chest. "Depends."

"On what?" he asked, his heart tight in his chest. He didn't want to feel this with Mia. Couldn't.

She smiled, but her face didn't light up with joy, as it had earlier. "Whether you're going to be a gentleman and behave yourself. If you are, I definitely need the cuffs."

CHAPTER TWENTY-TWO

Mia took a deep breath as she opened the door to the suite. It had been a week since she'd found the most recent envelope, and every day when they returned after Finn finished working, she'd braced herself to find another one.

The contents of the last note hadn't provided any more information than the previous ones – no fingerprints, no saliva on the envelope, no identifying marks on the pictures.

She stared at the floor as she pushed the door open, sighing with relief when all she saw was the rug. "We're good. You know the drill," she said to Finn, weariness heavy on her shoulders as she stepped inside. "Come in, but stay by the door."

"Relax, Mia. There's been nothing since the last note," he said, leaning against the wall. He had to be ten times more exhausted than she was. He'd been filming action scenes all day, take after take, until he was soaked with sweat and out of breath.

He'd had to change his costume at least three times.

"Not going to relax," she answered as she headed for their bedroom.

She froze. *Their* bedroom?

Yeah. She hadn't slept in the other room since the second time she and Finn had made love. Her suits hung in the closet beside Finn's pants and shirts. She had a drawer for her underwear. This was *their* bedroom.

She swallowed as she began to search the room. Finn left in a week. There wasn't a 'their' anything.

After finishing Finn's room, she checked hers. Completely empty.

"Shut the door and lock it," she said, tossing the purse holding her gun onto the table next to the door. "I'm hungry, and you must be famished. You want me to order dinner?"

"Please," Finn said, heading for the bathroom. "Get me a steak and a salad. I'm going to take a shower." He stopped in the doorway and turned to face her. "You want to join me? Could be dangerous, though. The way my arms ache after those fight scenes, no way could I hold you up. I'd slip and fall. Kill both of us."

"Then I'm not joining you," she called, and he disappeared into the room. "Very romantic to die in your arms, but I'd rather it happen while we were having sex when we're ninety-five."

She slapped a hand over her mouth. Oh, God. Had she really said that out loud?

The sudden silence in the other room told her she had. After a long moment, Finn stuck his head out the door. "Only ninety-five?" he said, his voice light. "I was thinking a hundred at least."

He vanished again, and moments later, Mia heard the rumble of water hitting the slate floor in the shower. Thank God Finn was an actor. Able to pretend to make a joke out of her slip of the tongue. Laugh it off.

Her hand shaking, she reached for the room service menu she'd already memorized. Ordered a steak and salad for Finn, halibut and a salad for herself.

"Fifteen minutes, ma'am," the operator said.

"Thanks," she said as she tossed the menu onto the coffee table.

Collapsing onto the couch, she banged her head into the stiff cushion. Why the hell had she made that stupid crack about dying together at ninety-five? She had no excuse, other than exhaustion. Ever since the last note, she'd been hyper-vigilant at the studio. She'd studied every actor, every crew member, every delivery person, every server and busboy from the catering company. She watched constantly, never letting herself relax.

Every day, when they were finished, they'd returned to the suite and fallen into bed. Gotten up to eat, then retreated to the bedroom again.

Sleep was the last thing on their minds.

They never discussed Finn's departure. Unspoken agreement had them packing as much as possible into every moment as the hours and days ticked inexorably away.

She'd thought about it. When she'd woken in the middle of the night, needing a glass of water, she'd study Finn as she gulped it down. He slept sprawled on the bed, arms and legs encroaching onto her side. On clear nights, his naked body was dappled by moonlight. When it was cloudy, the shadows turned his skin into smooth, dark plains, his spine the tiny hills bisecting them.

His hair would be messy, rumpled by her fingers. His hand was usually on her side of the bed, where she'd had to crawl out from under it to get her water. Sometimes his fingers would twitch as she watched, as if recognizing her absence and searching for her, even as he slept.

Yeah, when she was the only one awake in the middle of the night, she thought about how it would be after Finn went back to California.

It wouldn't be good.

She'd fallen in love with him. It was damn stupid of her, but there it was. Like countless foolish women before her, she'd fallen in love with the wrong man.

At least she wasn't fooling herself into thinking that love

would make everything all right. That they could figure out a way to make this work.

Finn was leaving in a week. He couldn't stay in Chicago. She couldn't go to California. It had been an amazing two weeks, but dying in his arms when they were making love at ninety-five? Not happening.

A knock at the door interrupted her pity party, and she pushed herself upright. Smoothed her pants, her hair, then reached for her purse. The Sig inside made it heavy, but she pushed it aside and dug for her wallet. Finn was generous with Josh, and she would be, too. The kid hadn't betrayed their trust. He hadn't told a soul he was their delivery boy.

She held her wallet in her hand as she peered through the peephole. Nothing but the hall. No one stood in front of the door.

She glanced down and saw the food cart, with the silver covers over the plates, but there was no sign of Josh.

Dropping the wallet onto the floor, she tugged her gun out of her purse. "Josh?" she called. "Are you out there?"

Nothing. The hall was silent. No footsteps on the thick carpet, no sound of movement, no ding of an elevator arriving.

She turned to listen for the shower, but it was off. Finn would be throwing on his robe.

Hurrying through the living room, she stuck her head in the door to find Finn, robed and belted, heading for the living room. She put her hand on his chest when he reached for her. "Put some clothes on," she said quietly. "Dinner is here, but not Josh."

Instead of asking her questions, he shrugged out of the robe and reached for a shirt. Mia didn't linger to appreciate his sculpted body, the way she would have any other night. Instead, she headed for the door, her gun gripped in her right hand, and eased it open.

The food cart blocked the exit. Nudging it gently out of the way with her hip, she slipped out of the room and scanned the silent hall.

A bell boy was almost at the staircase. "Josh?" she called. Why hadn't he waited for her to answer the door.

He raised his hand and waved, but didn't turn around.

She watched until he banged open the exit door and disappeared into the stairwell. Her heart racing, she told herself he had another delivery to make. That's why he hurried away.

She tugged the cart into the room, closed and locked the door. Finn emerged from the bedroom, his eyes lighting up at the sight of the food. "Thank God. I hope you got me the biggest steak they have."

"Yep." She set her gun on the table and steered the cart toward their usual window seats. "Biggest salad, too."

Finn lifted the domed covers off the plates, slid into a chair and picked up his fork. "Come on, Mia," he said as he dug into the salad. "Or I'm going to be rude and start without you."

She stared down at the food but didn't see it. Her mind was still reviewing the sight of Josh, disappearing into the stairwell.

Finn scooped up a forkful of salad and raised it to his mouth. The lightbulb in Mia's head lit up as he opened his mouth.

Leaping at him, she knocked the fork out of his hand, sending bits of lettuce and a piece of tomato flying across the table. A blob of salad dressing landed on Finn's robe.

"What the hell?" He stared at Mia, confused.

"Put the covers back on the plates. Don't touch any of it," she said. "Josh didn't deliver it."

"Who did, then?"

"Don't know. But it wasn't Josh. He was almost at the stairwell door when I saw him. I called, but he waved at me. Didn't turn around."

"He probably had somewhere else he had to be," Finn said, but he replaced the covers over the plates of food.

"Go wash your hands," Mia ordered. "Your face, too, if any of the food touched it."

Finn leaned back in his chair. "Are you sure you're not overreacting?"

"No. That wasn't Josh. It was a woman."

"You sure?"

"Yes. She was dressed like a bell boy, but she walked like a woman."

Finn stood up, holding his hands away from his body. He looked down at them, and she realized they were shaking.

"It's fine," she said. "You didn't actually eat anything. If I'm overreacting, you can tease me all you want. But I don't want to take any chances with you." Her job had become far too personal. If Finn was hurt on her watch, or worse, she'd never forgive herself.

He turned to head toward the sink in the wet bar, and she grabbed the back of his robe. Tugged it off his shoulders and tossed it on the floor. "Don't touch that."

He turned to face her wearing nothing but his boxers, and she nudged him toward the sink. "Wash your hands and face before you do anything else."

Her gaze drifted to his ass, hugged by his boxer briefs, as he lathered his hands and his face. Mia closed her eyes. *Focus.*

"I need you to stay in the suite," she said, putting her hand on his chest when he turned back to her. His heart beat rapidly against her fingers. "Call the kitchen and ask if Josh was the one who picked up the cart. If he was, call down to the desk and ask if Josh is back. If he's not, ask them to call you the minute he returns."

She turned to leave, but Finn snagged her wrist. "Where are you going?" His eyes were dark with worry, and he tightened his grip on her, as if he didn't intend to let her go.

She turned to face him, her heart racing as much as his. "To do my job," she said evenly. "To see if anyone's hiding in the stairwell. Hiding in a recessed room door." She was pretty sure the woman was gone, but she needed to check anyway.

Still trembling from the close call, she lifted onto her toes and pressed her mouth against his for a long moment. "Don't touch the cart or anything on it. Lock the door behind me," she murmured. "Don't open it to anyone but me." A million scenarios rushed through her brain. "Or one of my brothers."

"'One of your brothers?'" He grabbed her as she tried to back away. "What does that mean, Mia? Why would one of your brothers show up instead of you?"

"Trying to cover all the bases," she said. She kissed him again, then pried his hands from her shoulders, locked their fingers together. "I'll only be few minutes, okay? You'll be safe in here with the door locked."

"I'm not worried about me. What about you? Are you going to be safe out there?" He stroked his thumbs over the backs of her hands, a rhythmic, steady movement that steadied her racing heart.

"I have a gun," she said, careful not to make a promise she might not be able to keep. "I'm not going to do anything stupid."

"You damn well better not." He tightened his grip on her hands until he was squeezing her bones together. "Stay here," he blurted out. "Call some other cops to check out the hall."

"I can't do that, Finn. If she's out there, she'll be long gone before any other cops show up." She squeezed his hands, pulled him closer and kissed him again. Then she let him go and walked toward the door, grabbing her gun from the table. Still a little shaky, she bumped into the table. The vase holding the bouquet wobbled, making the fading blossoms tremble. She wrenched open the door and closed it behind her without looking back at Finn.

Forcing herself to forget the man waiting for her behind that door, she started down the hall. Her head swiveled from side to side as she checked every possible hiding place, her gun steady in her hand. She looked over her shoulder every few seconds, making sure no one was behind her.

The door to the stairwell opened easily, and she stood on the landing for countless seconds, listening. No footsteps. No sound of breathing. No sense of life in the stairwell.

She repeated everything in the hall on the opposite side of their room. It was empty, as well. Whoever had delivered the cart was gone.

Just as she'd expected.

Knocking softly on their door, she saw a shadow cover the peephole, then Finn swung the door open. She'd barely made it into the room before he crushed her against him, his face buried in her neck. "I don't like your job," he murmured against her skin.

Setting her gun back on the table beside the door, she locked her arms around his waist and lifted to find his mouth. "I know," she murmured against his lips. "I know. But it's okay. No one's out there."

After a long moment, his desperate grip on her eased. He let her mouth go and sucked in a deep breath. "Josh picked up the cart in the kitchen. He's not back at the desk yet. They'll call when he shows up."

Mia glanced at her watch. It had been more than ten minutes since the food cart showed up. Her heart rate spiked as dread coiled in her belly. "Josh should have been back downstairs a while ago. I'm calling my brothers."

"Why not just call the cops?"

"Not sure I want this to go into a police report," she said. "If Josh is just...just using the bathroom, or calling his girlfriend, I don't want to get him into trouble. I also don't want it in writing that you're staying here. If something's happened to Josh, of course we'll call it in."

Without waiting for him to answer, she plucked her phone out of her purse and pressed Brendan's name. When he answered, she said, "Bren. Are you on duty?"

"Just got off. Heading home."

"Can you come over to the Drake? We've got a situation here."

"You need more than me?" he said immediately. "Cilla's on her way home, too. I'll call her and Quinn. Pretty sure Con's still on duty."

Mia exhaled. "That would be great, Bren. We're in room 1216." She hesitated, but anxiety still gripped her. "And Bren? Light it up."

Less than ten minutes later, Brendan knocked on the door. When she opened it, he stepped inside, cataloging everything immediately – the two separate bedrooms. The windows, looking down at the lake. The lack of a balcony.

The sumptuous furniture, the bouquet of flowers on the table, beginning to fade and wilt. Mia made a mental note to get rid of it tomorrow.

"Nice set-up," Brendan said. Only after checking everything did he turn and hug her. Then, one hand draped possessively over Mia's shoulder, Brendan reached for Finn's hand, studying her lover as they exchanged handshakes. "You look like hell, O'Rourke."

"Feel like hell, too," Finn shot back.

"We've got a missing bellboy," Mia told her brother. "You need to stay here with Finn while I look for him."

"Why can't you stay here and let Brendan look for Josh?" Finn said immediately. She saw the worry in his eyes and touched his hand.

"Because I know what Josh looks like. Bren doesn't."

Finn opened his mouth to argue with her, and Mia shook her head, a tiny movement that Brendan didn't notice. "Call Doug and have him pick up the food to have it tested. I'll be back soon," she said.

Before either of the men could answer, she grabbed her gun, slid it into the holster she'd strapped on after she called Brendan, and headed for the elevator.

It dinged before she reached it. When the doors opened, Cilla and Quinn stepped out. "Thank God," she said. "Cilla, Bren is in the room with Finn. Why don't you stay with them?" With any luck, Cilla would be able to calm the testosterone storm Mia was afraid was erupting in the suite.

"Quinn, you come with me."

As they rode the elevator down to the lobby, she explained to her brother what had happened and her concern for Josh. As soon as they stepped into the lobby, she pulled out her badge and approached the concierge. "I need to know how to get to the kitchen," she said.

The woman behind the desk pointed out the way, and she ran down the stairs, Quinn right behind her. The kitchen was noisy and bright, voices shouting and pots and pans clattering against the burners of the stove. Mia grabbed a server who was reaching for a plate on the warming table.

Showing him her badge, she asked, "How do you deliver room service meals?"

Staring at her badge, his eyes huge, he stuttered, "We take the service elevator."

"How do I find it? Quickly."

He dropped the plate onto the table and said, "I'll show you."

CHAPTER TWENTY-THREE

Finn watched the door close quietly behind Mia and had to stop himself from ripping it open again. To beg her to stay here, to let her brother look for Josh. He didn't want Mia walking into a potentially dangerous situation. What if his stalker had hurt Josh? What if she was still around, and she tried to hurt Mia?

He'd never forgive himself if something happened to her because she was trying to protect him.

He turned to Brendan. "Tell her to come back. You go look for Josh."

Brendan's face softened. "Mia knows what she's doing, Finn. She's a great cop. Careful. Meticulous. Smart. She doesn't take any unnecessary risks." He put his hand on the other man's shoulder and squeezed. "She'll be fine."

Finn wanted to snap at him. Ask him how he'd feel if Cilla was the one out there alone, searching for a possibly injured kid.

As if he'd read Finn's mind, Brendan said, "I get it, man. It's worse for a civilian who lov..who's involved with a cop. You're always going to worry. But Mia doesn't take chances. She's not a hot dog who acts before she thinks."

Finn shook off Brendan's hand and turned to stare out the window. Brendan had almost said 'loves a cop.' He'd caught himself, but Finn knew.

He didn't love Mia. He couldn't. What he felt for her was a tangled knot of emotion and regret, sitting on his chest like a stone.

He wished they had more time together. But they lived two thousand miles apart. Had different lives, different goals. He didn't want to walk away from her in another week, but what choice did he have? He had commitments in Los Angeles. A job he had to do.

Mia's home was in Chicago. So was her job. Her family. Her life was in the Midwest.

Wishing things were different didn't make it so.

Someone knocked on the door. Brendan peered out the peephole, then swung the door open. Cilla walked in and wrapped her arms around him. Brendan bent to kiss her. They murmured to each other for a few moments, too softly for Finn to hear. Then, his arm over her shoulder, holding Cilla against him, he drew her into the room and shut the door.

Brendan had clearly forgotten Finn was in the room. Cilla hadn't noticed him yet. All they saw was each other.

Finn watched them, both envious and sad. He'd never looked at Gemma like that.

He snorted to himself. Compared to what Brendan and Cilla clearly felt for each other, he'd been playing in the kiddie pool with Gemma. Brendan and Cilla were swimming in the deepest part of the ocean.

And Gemma? She'd never loved anyone but herself.

"Hey, Finn." Cilla's voice.

He turned and forced a smile. "Hi, Cilla. Thanks for coming over."

She shrugged. "Bren said Mia needed help."

She spoke as if it was a given. That if one of them needed help, everyone showed up without a second thought. Even the girlfriends and fiancees.

That didn't happen in his world.

In his business, everything was calculated. Everything was about the bottom line. What's in it for me? How will this affect my career? Who'll be there who might be helpful?

"I know she appreciates the way you guys dropped everything to come over here," Finn said.

Cilla shrugged again. "She'd do it for us, too. In a heartbeat." She glanced at the table next to the door. The shiny silver domes over the plates suddenly looked like symbols of his life – beautiful to look at, but mostly hot air inside.

"What are we doing with these?" Cilla asked, tapping her fingernail on one of the domes. A low, hollow sound reverberated through the air.

"I'm supposed to call Doug and have him send someone to pick it up and have the food tested."

"And Doug would be…?" Cilla studied him, her expression curious.

Finn swallowed, suddenly uncomfortable throwing Doug's name around. "My godfather. Doug Walsh."

Her eyebrows shot up. "Your godfather's the Superintendant? Is that why you're getting special treatment? Your own personal cop for three weeks?"

"The studio is paying for it," he retorted, but he cringed inside.

Cilla was right. He didn't think twice about the special perks he got. The privileges he took for granted.

"You'd better call him, then," she said, but her expression softened. Had she noticed his embarrassment? "This needs to get to a lab."

He pulled out his phone, explained to Doug what had happened. His godfather assured him he'd send someone right over.

By the time he was off the phone, at least ten minutes had passed since Mia walked out of the room. She wasn't back. He double-checked his phone in case she'd texted him or tried to call while he was on the phone with Doug.

She hadn't.

He hurried to the door and looked out the spy hole. She wasn't in the hall.

"Hey, Finn, sit down," Brendan said, breaking off a conversation with Cilla. "Relax. Quinn is with her. She's fine."

"I'm worried about Josh," he said. It was true – he *was* worried about the kid. He was just more worried about Mia.

Finn continued to pace the room, his phone clutched in his hand. Cilla and Brendan watched him, but no one spoke. The silence in the room was getting more and more uncomfortable.

He glanced at his phone, realized his finger was poised over Mia's contact information. Clenching his teeth, he slipped the phone into his pocket. Mia didn't need him calling her in the middle of what could be a mess.

Brendan was right. Mia was smart. Quick. A good cop. She knew what she was doing.

That didn't stop him from worrying, though.

Finally he forced himself to sit in the seat opposite Brendan and Cilla, plastered together on the couch. "So." He forced his shoulders to relax, his teeth to unclench. "When's the wedding?"

Fifteen minutes later, in the middle of Cilla's description of their wedding plans, someone rapped on the door. Cilla went to check it, then jerked her head toward Finn. "Come here and verify it's who I think it is before I open the door."

Hurrying over to the door, Finn saw his godfather on the other side. Damn it! Doug *would* show up tonight, when everything had turned into a cluster.

"Doug," he said as he opened the door. "You didn't have to come yourself."

His godfather frowned. "You tell me someone needs to pick up your food and have it tested, and you think I'm not going to check it for myself?"

"Mia said it needed to go to a lab. You going to be the delivery guy?" Finn's voice was sharper than it should have been. Doug was the last person he wanted to see tonight.

"Evidence techs are right behind me." He scanned the room, stopped when he saw Brendan and Cilla, who were now standing near the food cart. "Who's this?"

Brendan stepped forward and held out his hand. "Detective Brendan Donovan, sir. And this is Detective Cilla Marini. Mia needed some help."

Doug shook Brendan's hand, then Cilla's. He studied both of the detectives, then asked, "Where *is* Mia? And why did she call the two of you?"

"I'm her brother," Brendan said. "Cilla is my fiancée. Detective Quinn Donovan, another brother, is with Mia right now. They're looking for the bell boy who usually delivers the food to this suite. He's missing."

Doug's eyebrows rose. "So she called in people she knew she could trust." His gaze softened as he studied Brendan and Cilla. "I knew I made a good choice with her." He nodded at the food cart. "Either of you take a look at what's in there?" He turned to Finn when Brendan and Cilla shook their heads. "Did you or Mia look?" He pulled a pair of latex gloves from his pocket.

"Yeah," Finn said, eyeing the silver domes as if they hid weapons of mass destruction. "I took them off, sat down to eat. I was starving. I almost ate some of the salad, but Mia knocked the fork out of my hand. She'd realized the bellboy who delivered the food wasn't Josh.

"Then she covered the food again. Said we needed to wait for the evidence technicians."

Doug snapped the gloves through his hands as he studied the cart. "Yeah," he sighed. "She's right." He glanced at Brendan and Cilla. "Sometimes I miss being on the street."

Brendan shifted closer to Cilla, but neither of them spoke.

Another knock at the door, and Cilla checked the spy hole again before she opened it. A young woman carrying a bag stepped into the room, her badge on a chain around her neck. She nodded at the cart. "That the food that needs to be tested?"

"Yes, it is," Doug said.

The woman glanced at Doug and froze. "Superintendent Walsh," she said. Her gaze shifted behind him to Finn, and her eyes widened.

"We want to keep this low profile, Officer," Doug said. "You need to keep Finn's identity, and what you're doing here tonight, to yourself."

"Yes, sir," she said. Her knuckles whitened on the handle of her rectangular bag. "Okay if I get started?"

"Please."

The woman opened her bag, drew on gloves, then pulled out large plastic bags. She removed one of the domed lids, slid it into the bag, then did the same with the other. The scent of the food filled the room, making his stomach rumble. But the fat from the steak had congealed on the plate, and the sauce on Mia's fish was clotted and oily.

The technician put the food in separate bags, then bagged both plates. She lifted the domes off the smaller salad plates, and studied it for a long moment.

"I think there might be something in the salad," she said, pointing toward pieces of greens torn into tiny bits. They were mixed into what looked like romaine lettuce. The tiny pieces were thicker than normal romaine, with a pebbly texture and finely serrated edges. "I haven't seen this in a salad before."

"Bag it up and test it," Doug said.

"Yes, sir," she said as she prepared four more plastic bags. Moments later, both plates and both salads were bagged

After dusting the cart for fingerprints and finding nothing, she turned to face Doug. "Anything else that needs to be checked, sir?"

Doug turned to Brendan and Cilla. "Well?"

"We don't know, sir," Brendan answered. "Mia called me and asked me to get here fast. She wanted us to stay with

Finn until the techs arrived."

"Finn?" His godfather turned to him. "You think of anything?"

He stared at the now-empty cart, trying to think about what Mia would want. But there'd been nothing unusual since the note a week earlier. "No, I think that's it."

As the evidence technician was leaving, Doug said, "Let me know as soon as you have any results."

She glanced over her shoulder. "I will, sir. I have some ideas that I'll check as soon as I get to the lab."

"Good." He pulled out a card and handed it to her. "This is my answering service. They'll get in touch with me."

She tapped the card into her pocket and nodded. "I'll call you, sir."

Doug followed her out the door. "I'll talk to you later, Finn."

"Have a good night, Doug," Finn sighed.

As soon as the door was closed, Brendan scowled at him. "Thanks for the heads-up that the damned superintendent would show up."

His concern for Mia growing, and in no mood to appease Brendan, Finn scowled right back. "Kiss my ass, Donovan. I had no idea he'd come here to supervise a kid bagging up food and plates."

Cilla slapped her hand on Brendan's chest as he started toward Finn. "Really, you two? You're gonna go all caveman and start throwing punches?" She stared first at Brendan, then at Finn, her eyes narrowed. "You think Mia's gonna appreciate your manliness?"

Brendan looked at the thin line of Cilla's mouth, then exhaled. "Yeah. Sorry, Finn. I got a little carried away."

"You think?" Finn glared at Brendan for a long moment, then stalked over to the door and stared out the spy hole.

"Hey." Cilla walked over to him and laid her hand on his arm. "She's okay. If she wasn't, Quinn would have called."

"Yeah. I know." He threw himself into the nearest chair, hungry, weary and worried. "I just…we had a long day today."

"And you haven't eaten." Cilla turned to Brendan. "Bren, why don't you go get beef sandwiches. I'll stay here with Finn until Mia gets back."

"I could do that." Brendan took a deep breath and squared his shoulders. "I hate waiting around. It'll be good to actually do something."

"Get some for us and Quinn, too," Cilla said.

Brendan smiled. "Will do."

Five minutes after Brendan left, someone knocked on the door. Cilla beat him to the peep hole, and after a glance, she swung the door open. Mia stepped inside.

Finn scrambled from the chair and swept her into his arms, too relieved to think about their audience. "Are you okay? Did you find Josh? Where's Quinn?"

Mia leaned into him for a long moment, her arms tight around his waist. She closed her eyes and exhaled a long, slow breath. As if now that she was back, it was safe to breathe again.

She pushed away and sank onto the couch, and Finn slid in beside her. "What happened?" he asked softly.

Cilla leaned forward from the chair across from them. "Did you find the kid?"

"Yeah." Mia took another deep breath. "He was lying on the floor in a corridor near the freight elevators. Unconscious. Blood beneath his head."

Finn grabbed her hand and held on tight. "Is he going to be okay?"

"The EMT's think so." Mia leaned her head against his shoulder and closed her eyes for a long moment. Her iron grip squeezed his fingers together, but he didn't flinch. He was too glad she was here. "Looks like someone bashed him in the head, dragged his body where it wouldn't be seen right away, then took the cart and delivered it to our room.

"Josh was starting to wake up before they took him to the hospital. Quinn went with them to get Josh's statement when he's completely awake." She sat up and looked around. "Where's Bren?"

"I sent him out to get some beef sandwiches," Cilla said. "I was afraid there'd be bloodshed up here, too."

Mia frowned. "How come?"

Cilla shook her head. "Too much testosterone, too much worrying, too little to do."

Mia looked at Finn and raised one eyebrow. "Really? You and Bren were bumping chests and growling?"

Mia was back. So was her snark. Suddenly lighter, Finn tightened his arm around her shoulders and grinned. "Nope. No chest bumping. It was mostly pawing the ground and snorting."

She shook her head and gave Cilla a thumbs up. "Good thing you sent Bren on a mission," she said.

An hour later, as Brendan and Cilla were getting ready to leave, Mia's phone rang. Finn peered over her shoulder and saw it was from Quinn.

"Hey, Q," Mia said.

"Just left the hospital. Josh has a concussion and they're keeping him tonight, but he'll be fine. He said he was heading for the freight elevator and that's the last thing he remembers."

"Maybe it'll come back eventually," Mia said, but Finn heard the disappointment in her voice.

"Hope so," Quinn said. "I'm heading home. Tessa just got off shift."

"Give her my love," Mia said. "And thanks, Q. I really appreciate the help."

"Any time, Mimi."

After filling everyone in, Cilla and Brendan said goodnight and left. When the door clicked shut behind them, Finn took a deep breath and locked it. Then he pulled Mia to her feet.

"I was worried about you," he said, nuzzling the soft skin

beneath her ear. "Afraid the stalker had gotten to you."

"I know," she murmured into his shoulder. "I should have called, but everything was chaotic until the ambulance finally left. The evidence techs were still working the scene, and I just wanted to get back up here."

"Much rather have you than a phone call." He wanted to hold her close all night. Allow not even a ray of light between them. But he eased away to look down at her face.

"Let's go to bed. Mimi."

Mia elbowed him. "*Mimi?* You really want to go there, *Finian?*"

"No," he said, taking her hand and leading her toward the bedroom. "I just want you."

CHAPTER TWENTY-FOUR

Mia sat next to Finn in one corner of the catering tent outside the studio the next day, picking at a plate of chicken salad and fruit, too jumpy to enjoy her food. Her gaze drifted from one table of actors and crew people to the next, touched on the uniformed catering staff. Was Finn's stalker somewhere close? Watching them eat? Planning her next attack?

Finn's phone rang, making Mia flinch. The chicken salad tasted like rubber as she watched Finn glance at the screen and push the call button.

"Yeah, she's here," he said, glancing at Mia. "I'll put her on."

He handed her the phone, mouthing, "Doug."

Clearing her throat, Mia said, "Sir?"

"I just got a call from the evidence tech," the superintendent said gruffly. "There were foxglove leaves in both the salads. They contain digitalis. Enough to make you really sick if you ate all of it. Maybe even kill you."

Mia inhaled sharply and closed her eyes, remembering how close that salad had come to Finn's mouth. "Wow. Um, okay. Thanks for letting me know. I'll be even more careful."

"You're doing a superb job, Officer." Doug Walsh's voice softened. "You've got good instincts. Finn told me how you knocked that fork away from him before he could eat any of the salad. Thank you for that." The superintendent cleared his throat. "Finn means a great deal to our family."

He means a great deal to me, too. "I won't take any risks with him," she assured Doug.

"I've spoken to my contact at the studio, and I'm going to put two more undercover officers on this assignment. They'll be in the studio and on the location shoots for the duration of the time Finn is in Chicago."

Mia knew it was the smart thing to do. The stalker was escalating. More people would help. But a selfish part of her was possessive about Finn. She wanted to be the one protecting him. She didn't want to hand him off to someone else.

Finn had his head pressed to hers, listening to the phone call. He grabbed her hand at his godfather's words. Apparently, Finn knew her pretty well.

She wasn't sure if that was scary or thrilling.

Clearing her throat, Mia said, "Sir, I…"

"I'm not doubting your work, Mia," he said gently, interrupting her. "There's no one else I want protecting my godson, and I want you to stay close to him. But there's a lot of territory to cover, and I think you need some help. I can't let this woman endanger a high-profile cast member working on a movie in my city. Beyond my personal concerns about Finn, an incident would damage the city's reputation within the film industry. Cause significant economic damage to Chicago, if studios bypassed us because of safety concerns." He hesitated. "Do you understand?"

Mia let her breath out slowly, letting go of her defensiveness. "Yes, sir. It's a good idea," she admitted. Finn's hand stroked her back. Settled her down. She couldn't be everywhere. Other eyes would be helpful. "What about at the hotel?"

"I've put someone in the kitchen. She'll watch your food being prepared. And she'll escort your bellboy to your suite door."

"Thank you, sir. That's reassuring." Finn brushed his lips over her cheek, and she leaned into him.

"I've got the evidence techs going over the security tapes to try and identify the woman who delivered your food last night," Doug said. "Let me know if you need anything else."

"I will, sir."

"One more thing. I understand there was an incident when you and Finn were at the Seven Club."

Mia tensed again. "Yes, sir. But he never got close to Finn. Mr. Pinckney was arrested with a minimum of drama."

"I know that. Since Finn was involved, I got the report from the lab." He cleared his throat. "I wanted to let you know that the DNA came back on the man who assaulted you. It was a match for several rapes that are connected with The Seven Club. All involving rohypnol."

"Oh, my God," Mia breathed.

"Yes," Doug said, his voice vibrating with satisfaction. "Mr. Pinckney was denied bail. With the DNA, he's looking at a long time in prison."

"Thank you for telling me," Mia said, clutching the phone too tightly.

"I thought you should know," the superintendent said gruffly. "Let me talk to Finn again."

Handing Finn the phone, her head still spinning with the news, Mia edged away to give him some privacy with his godfather. Instead of allowing the distance, Finn pulled her tight against him.

"She's a keeper, Finn," Doug said. "Don't screw this up."

Mia froze, but Finn merely brushed his fingers over her side. Her skin prickled, even beneath the shirt she wore.

"No, sir. I wouldn't think of it."

"Good. Tell Mia to keep me posted."

"I will. Thanks, Doug." He pushed the button to disconnect the call.

"Did you hear what he said?" she asked. "About Kyle from The Seven Club?"

"I did." He reached out and took her hand. "I'm glad, Mia. Glad he's off the street. Happy he won't be hurting any other women."

"Yeah," she said, feeling lighter. "Me, too." Then she tightened her grip on his hand. "What was he saying to you?" she demanded, both afraid of the answer and hoping it meant what she thought it meant.

"He thinks you're doing a good job," Finn said easily. "He doesn't want me to get in your way."

Mia studied him. He smiled at her, but it didn't reach his eyes. They were dark green and bleak, as if something precious was vanishing and he knew he wouldn't find it again.

She swallowed once, then nodded. No matter what Doug said, she knew how this story ended. "You finished eating? Ready to get back to work?" she said, gathering up her tray.

"Yeah." He stood up and picked up his own tray. "Long afternoon ahead."

***

When Mia opened the door to the suite, it was early evening. The cast had been dismissed early after a piece of equipment had fallen onto a set. No one had been hurt, but everyone was rattled and Sean decided to call it a day.

Mia had been concerned, but couldn't investigate without blowing her cover. So she'd had Finn call Doug, who'd sent someone over to check everything out. Unless the target had been Finn, and she was pretty sure it hadn't been, since he'd been on the other side of the set, it wasn't her responsibility.

Her responsibility was keeping Finn safe. So she'd hurried him out the door as soon as he'd cleaned off his stage makeup.

Now he held a pizza box they'd picked up on the way home after a silly argument about the merits of Chicago deep dish pizza versus the joys of the thin crust, artisan pizza he liked. Their teasing had been forced, but Mia tried to keep it light. Tried not to let her worries affect the time she spent with Finn.

As Finn set the pizza on the table by the door, she took her gun out of her purse and cleared the suite, room by room. She knew every inch of the suite by heart, but still she checked everywhere. When she was satisfied that the suite was empty, she slid the gun back into her purse and nodded at Finn to close and lock the door.

They didn't need words to communicate anymore – he knew what she wanted before she told him, and she knew what he was thinking before he opened his mouth.

"Grab the pizza," she said, lifting her holster from her hip and setting it on the table. "Let's eat."

As she watched Finn pick up the box, she stilled. "Stop," she ordered, staring at the table.

The vase of flowers that had been there yesterday was gone. She'd left a note for the maid to dump them out. But there was a new arrangement of flowers on the table.

This one looked...odd.

There were yellow carnations and yellow roses. Orange lilies and a white lily with red stripes. A flower that looked like hollyhocks, which she remembered from her grandmother's garden. Lavender. Purple bell-shaped flowers.

Black roses.

It looked like no flower arrangement she'd ever seen. Mismatched. Strange color combinations. And haphazardly put together.

"Bring the pizza over here," she said as she grabbed the

house phone and dialed the front desk. Barely giving the clerk the time to greet her, Mia said, "This is room 1216. Did you deliver flowers to our room today?"

"I'll check that for you," she said. Moments later, the woman said, "No, ma'am. There were no flowers delivered to your room."

"Who delivers things to guest rooms?" she asked. Finn dropped the box on the table and slid his arm around her waist. He was solid against her. Warm. Alive, and she intended to keep him that way. She had to say goodbye to him at the end of the week, but she'd make sure he made it back to Los Angeles.

"All deliveries go to the front desk, and we either have our guests pick them up there, or send a bell boy up to the room if the guest prefers that."

Her stomach churned as she studied the blooms. "What about the florist on the first floor? Do they deliver any flowers guests might order?"

"No, ma'am," the clerk said patiently. "*Everything* gets delivered to the desk, including items purchased from the merchants in our building. Only bellboys are authorized to deliver to rooms."

Finn wrapped both arms around her waist and pulled her back against his chest. Feeling his breath stirring the hair on her nape, his hands splaying across her stomach, she closed her eyes and tried to relax. Think. She could figure this out.

"Who has passkeys that open all the rooms?" Mia asked after a moment.

There was silence on the other end of the line. Then the woman said, "I'm going to connect you to security. Hold, please."

The line clicked, and after a moment, a gruff male voice said, "Security."

"This is room 1216," Mia said. "We have flowers in here that weren't delivered by the hotel. Who has access to the passkeys that open all the rooms?"

The pause was too long. "The maids have keys for the floors they're working," he finally said, his voice tight. "Hotel managers have keys. And the security supervisors on duty all have keys."

"Is that it?"

"Yes, ma'am. And everyone who has a key is logged in and given a key when they punch in, and hands in their key when they punch out."

"Thank you," Mia said. Dread crept up her spine as she disconnected the call. She put her hands over Finn's on her abdomen and twined their fingers. Held him there for a long moment. Then let him go and turned in his arms.

"Someone got into our room today. No one delivered them."

"Okay." He ran soothing hands up and down her back. "Who would have had access?"

Mia blew out a breath. "Only the maid," she said. "Unless it was one of the hotel managers or a security supervisor." She thought for a long moment. "Most likely the maid."

She pressed her forehead against his chest, running through likely scenarios. "Your stalker has a bellboy uniform. She could come up with the flowers, wait for the maid to open your room, then stick her head in the door." She lifted her head, held Finn's gaze. "Ask if it was okay if she left the flowers. Put them on the table, then walk away."

"We need to talk to the maid."

"Not us. We're both staying in here with the doors locked." She was trying to stay calm, but she was seriously freaked out. Someone had walked into their room. Left nothing but flowers, but what about next time? "I'll call my brothers again. Have them talk to the hotel, find the maid, question her."

She pressed a frantic, desperate kiss to his mouth. "I'm not leaving you alone."

"Good," he said against her lips. "Because there's no way I want you wandering around the hotel by yourself."

She didn't bother to point out that she had a gun. That she knew how to use it. She pulled her phone out of her pocket and called Brendan first.

Three hours later, as they waited to hear from Brendan about his talk with the maid, she and Finn sat plastered together on the couch, watching some mindless sports talk show. Neither of them was paying attention to it. Mia struggled to ignore all the questions swirling through her brain and concentrate only on Finn. On building memories that would have to last forever.

The scent of the ocean that seemed to cling to him. The way he slouched into the cushions, his long body lithe and muscular, even when relaxed. The way his fingers tapped endlessly on the arm of the couch.

The way his other hand played with her fingers.

She wanted to remember everything about him. Her memories were all she'd have to keep her warm after he left.

A quick rap at the door had her leaping off the couch. Peering through the glass, she let her shoulders relax and unlocked it. "Bren." She grabbed his hand and drew him inside, carefully locking the door behind him. "What did you find out?"

"I talked to the woman who cleaned your room this morning. She confirmed that a bellboy came in, asked her if it was okay to leave the flowers. She said yes, he put them on the table, and left."

"Will she work with a sketch artist?" Mia asked.

"She's downtown now, but I'm not sure how accurate a sketch would be. She said the guy didn't look her in the eye. His uniform was pretty baggy, too, so she couldn't really say how big he was. I'm guessing the baggy uniform and the fact that she expected a male influenced what she saw." He shrugged. "We'll see how she does. But she did tell me one thing."

Brendan turned on his phone and scrolled to the picture of the flowers Mia had sent him. He tapped the image of the vase. "This vase is from the flower shop in the building.

It's made specifically for them, and it's the one they use for flowers that go to rooms in the Drake."

"So it had to come from the shop in the building."

"Right."

Mia exhaled and glanced at Finn, who'd stepped up beside her and slid his arm around her waist. She leaned into him and asked, "Can you call Doug and tell him we need a picture of this bellboy from the surveillance cameras, as soon as possible?"

"Sure." He stepped away and began to dial his phone. She wanted to move with him – she missed the weight and warmth of his arm. Instead, she turned back to Brendan.

"The sketch artist will send me the picture when he or she is done, right?"

"Absolutely. She has your phone number and your email. She'll text it over and also email it." He hesitated. "I did one more thing, and I hope you're not pissed about it. I sent a picture of the flowers to Cilla."

"Why would I be pissed about that?" Mia asked.

"Because I know you want to keep this as quiet as possible."

"Bren." She grabbed his arms. "Cilla is family. I trust her. Don't worry about it." She squeezed his arms and let him go. "Why did you send it to her?"

"Her mom is into flowers," he said. "She's got this unbelievable garden. I thought she might be able to tell us something about the flowers." He held up his hand. "And before you kick my ass, Cilla won't tell her what it's about. Only that it was for a case."

Finn was next to her, and he reached for Brendan and drew him into a hug. "I'm going to owe your whole family after this case is over."

"Don't worry about the rest of us, man," Brendan said, slapping him on the back as he stepped away from Finn. "Take care of Mia, and we're good."

Mia was sure Brendan didn't see the shadow that crossed Finn's face. His smile was strained, as well. "I've got Mia covered," Finn told her brother.

He did. For another six days, anyway. "Thanks, Bren," Mia said, ignoring the clock ticking in her head. "You're the best. We'll keep you posted."

"I'll have Cilla send you anything she gets from her mom."

"Thanks. Love to Cilla, too." Mia hugged her brother, then watched him walk away.

She followed him to the door and locked it behind him. Then she turned to Finn. "We've done all we can do for now. Let's go to bed."

His eyes darkened and he reached for her hand. "Best idea I've heard all day."

Two hours later, after making love twice with an intensity and tenderness that almost destroyed her, Mia lay awake as Finn slept beside her. Tears seeping into the pillow, she told herself she was a complete idiot.

But even knowing how this would end, she wouldn't change a thing with Finn. He'd go back to his career and life on the west coast.

She'd finish studying for the detective's exam. She'd take the test. Pass it, she hoped. Become a detective.

And miss Finn for the rest of her life.

CHAPTER TWENTY-FIVE

Finn paced the room the next morning, his phone gripped in his hand so he wouldn't miss the vibration of a text from Mia. Twenty different scenarios ran through his head, none of them good.

She'd left him in the room with strict orders to put on the safety lock, latch the door and not open it to anyone but her. She was going to the flower shop, to talk to the manager and show her the security camera photo and the sketch from the police artist.

He stopped at the window, pressed his palm against the pane of glass. It was a beautiful day – not a cloud in the vividly blue sky, waves cresting gently on the beach, a handful of people playing volleyball on the sand.

They were shooting that night, so the call time was four p.m. He wanted to be on that beach with Mia. Watching the wind whip her hair across her face. Looking at her in the tiny red bikini he'd spotted a few days ago when she'd opened her underwear drawer. Smoothing his hand over the impossibly smooth skin of her belly.

Lying on a blanket on that beach, seeing nothing but Mia and her laughing blue eyes.

Instead, she was chasing a stalker who wanted to kill him.

Who wanted to kill Mia, too.

And he was stuck in this room, with only fear to keep him company.

When he heard a soft tap on the door, he hurried over to the peep hole. Mia stood on the other side.

Wrenching the door open, he pulled her into the room and wrapped his arms around her. She pressed her head into his chest, and her sweet orange scent enveloped him. Settled him.

"Hey," she murmured into his neck. "You okay?"

"I was worried about you," he murmured into her hair.

Mia drew away. "I was only in the flower shop."

"What if she was there? What if she came after you with a...a box cutter." Saying it out loud made him feel silly. Ridiculous. Mia was a cop. A good one. She could take care of herself.

"I wish she had," Mia sighed, smoothing his shirt. "We would have had her then." She cupped his face in her hands. "This would be over. I could focus only on you for the next few days."

A few days. All he had left with her. "Did you find anything?"

She blew out a breath and her shoulders slumped. "Yeah. I did. The manager of the flower shop recognized the sketch and the picture from the security camera. She works in the flower shop. The name she gave them is Barb Riddle, but the social security number is fake and so's the name. Some uniforms are checking her address, but that's probably fake, too."

"Did Doug send more copies of the picture?"

"Yeah, he did. We'll get them to the undercover cops he added to your detail and to the security people at the location shoot. It's just a matter of time, Finn. We'll find her."

"Are you sure this is the woman?" he asked, tightening

his arms around her.

"Positive. She added the flowers from both the bouquets to the wholesale order list. Paid the manager for them." She clenched her teeth. "The manager was impressed by her honesty. Went out of her way to tell me Barb was a great employee."

"And the foxglove?" he asked.

"She ordered that and paid for it, too." Mia blew out a breath. "So glad we have an honest would-be murderer."

She drew away from him. "Cilla sent me an email today, too."

She gripped his hands and led him to the couch. "Did you know that flowers have meanings? From the Victorian period. People would pick specific blossoms to send specific messages.

"The original flowers?" she said shifting to face him. "That gorgeous bouquet that was here at first? All the flowers were about true love, devotion, faithfulness, passion and desire, joy and happiness. The flowers she left here yesterday?" Mia held his hands more tightly, as if afraid he might slip away from her.

"The yellow carnations mean disappointment. The orange lilies? Hatred. The heliotrope? Gone to the grave. The yellow roses? Extreme betrayal. You get the idea."

She swallowed. "And the black roses? I've never seen those before. They mean death."

"No one's dead, Mia. No one's going to be, either. Because of you." He didn't think he'd ever seen Mia so unnerved. Trying to comfort her, he drew her into his arms. "You've done a great job, babe, and you'll find her. Catch her, too. Happily ever after."

Not for him. Or for her, either, he suspected. But Mia would be safe. He would be, too. Able to go back to his home in California, to finish this movie. Make others.

Sean had told him the dailies were amazing. Finn's performance was blowing everyone away. When the studio saw them, Sean assured him, there would be talk of awards.

They'd get behind him, promote him for an Oscar nomination.

When he'd gotten this part, he'd thought of nothing but resurrecting his career. Of playing against type. The complicated, nuanced part of the villain Johnny Santorini had been exactly what he was looking for. He could show off his acting chops. Wallow in all the hatred directed against him and pour it into this role.

Now? He only wanted to get through the rest of the filming. Retreat to his place on the beach and lick his wounds.

Try to figure out how to move on without Mia.

"Those roses creeped me out," she muttered into his neck.

"I know," he said, stroking her back. "Me, too. Why would anyone want to grow something as stupid as a black rose, anyway?"

She eased away from him, struggling to smile. To keep it light. "Someone with a sick sense of humor?"

"I promise I'll never, ever send you black roses."

Her smile wobbled as she stood up abruptly. "I'll hold you to that," she said, her voice thick. "I'm going to take a shower before we have to leave."

She disappeared into their room, and moments later he heard the water running in the shower. Planning on joining her, he headed for the bathroom, shedding clothes as he went.

He grabbed the door jamb to stop his forward momentum at the sound he heard above the pounding of the water. Mia was sobbing.

The despairing sounds made his heart ache. He wanted to go in there. Comfort her. Kiss her tears away.

He couldn't.

Instead, he backed away from the door. He'd give her some privacy to regain her composure. His tough, usually-composed Mia wouldn't want Finn to see her crying.

Cowardly bastard, he told himself as he reached the living room. He ached to go into the shower and wrap his arms around her. Because he knew why she was crying.

She was crying because he was leaving. And since he couldn't stay, there was no comfort he could give her. If he tried, he'd just be a hypocritical asshole.

***

Mia sat in a chair close to the wall on Lower Wacker Drive that evening, watching Finn talk to the director about the next take on this scene. It was a chase that sent his car flying across the barriers of Lower Wacker and into the Chicago River. Because Dark Vengeance was an indie film with a smaller budget, nothing would actually go into the water. They'd green-screen everything later, Finn had told her. Back in Hollywood.

Even without the car careening into the river, though, the chase scene made her uneasy. The screeching of tires as the cars rounded the curves, the eerie green lights that illuminated Lower Wacker and bounced off the windshields of the cars, the dank, fishy smell of the river that rose into the night air, all combined to creep her out.

Which was the intended effect of the setting. It was perfect for the film. She hated these location shoots, though, and this one was the worst by far. At the studio, access to the building was controlled by security. No one got in without authorization.

Outside, there were always fans hanging around behind the barriers, waving at the actors, looking for autographs or a handshake. It made her nervous, but it could be managed.

Lower Wacker was far worse. Too many places to hide. Too much darkness. Too many doorways that led into darker tunnels. Too many shadows that could hide anything. Or anyone.

Her neck had been itching all evening. Her skin prickled every time a breeze stirred. Her head felt as if it was on a swivel as she scanned the crowds constantly, looking for

Barb Riddle.

They'd found her image on a few of the security tapes from the hotel. She looked completely ordinary – average height, average weight, average face. A person who would blend into the background or a crowd. Not the kind of face someone would remember. The technicians thought she was blond, but it was hard to be sure because in the photos they'd found, she'd worn either the bellboy's hat with her hair shoved inside, or a knit cap. The security people all had her picture. They were looking for her.

Mia was still jumpy and on edge.

Finn climbed into the car and they filmed the scene again. Noise, exhaust fumes and blue smoke swirled in the eerie light. He stepped out of the car at the end of the scene, Sean gave him a thumbs-up, and Finn hurried over to her.

"Hey," he murmured, drawing her close. His shirt was damp with perspiration and the musky smell of sweat surrounded him. Mia didn't care. She held him tightly against her, the moisture from his sweaty shirt leaching into her jacket.

When he finally pulled away, he was smiling with satisfaction. "We nailed it," he crowed. "Finally."

"You ready for a break?" She ran her fingers through his sweat-damp hair. "I bet you could use some water."

"Yeah," he said, slinging his arm over her shoulder. "Let's go to the catering tent and grab a couple bottles."

Winding their way through the cables and equipment that lined the inner wall of Lower Wacker, they finally rounded a curve and found the catering area set up against the wall. Several tables and sets of chairs were scattered beneath a large canopy, and a table was against the back wall. It held bottles of water and sports drinks, sodas and iced teas, as well as sandwiches and bowls of fruit. A tray of desserts sat at the end of the table. Several employees of the catering company, dressed in white uniforms, refilled the trays of sandwiches and bowls of fruit and replenished the supply of cold drinks.

As they wound their way through the half-filled tables, Mia spotted a woman carrying a tray of empty bottles and cans toward a bin behind the food-laden table. Mia slowed, watching the woman, as something caught her attention.

"Finn," she murmured without taking her eyes off the woman. "Back away. Go find one of the off-duty cops working security."

"Why?" Instead of leaving, like she wanted him to do, he edged closer to her.

"I think Barb is here. Working for the catering company." She nodded her head in the woman's direction. "I need you to leave and find security. Right now."

"Mia, I'm not…"

"Go. Now." She put her hand on his chest and pushed him away. "This is my job. I don't tell you how to film your chase scenes, you don't tell me how to do this. Now get out of here and find a cop!"

She waited until he moved back, then edged through the chairs and tables to get closer. Barb was pulling water bottles from an ice-filled bucket when she spotted Mia. Her eyes narrowed, and her fist compressed one of the bottles. The plastic popped, and water splashed over her uniform and the table in front of her.

Mia walked faster, shoving chairs out of her way as she got closer to the woman. "Stop, please, Barb," she called. "I need to talk to you."

Barb backed away slowly, but she was heading toward a corner. Her head swung from side to side as she looked for an escape route. For the first time tonight, Mia was happy about all the nooks and corners in Lower Wacker. She was backing Barb into a spot where she'd be trapped.

Moving more and more frantically, Barb kept her eyes on Mia as her hands swept the table. Mia pushed her jacket to the side and put her hand on her gun. "Stop, Barb," she called. "I just have some questions."

"You're the one," Barb said, her voice shrill with venom and hatred. "He was looking for me, but you pretended you were me, didn't you? You stole him from me."

Something flashed in front of her, and Mia took her eyes off Barb's face long enough to see the chef's knife in her hand. "I don't want him now," Barb spat out. "He's unfaithful. A betrayer. He cheated on Gemma, then he lied to me. He has to pay." She held the blade in front of her, testing the edge with her finger. Blood began to trickle down the silver blade and onto the black handle.

"Put the knife down, Barb," Mia said, pulling her gun out of the holster and creeping closer. "It's over. You're not going to hurt him. I won't let you."

Barb edged around the table, holding the knife in front of her, still testing the sharpness of the blade. Blood dripped onto the asphalt, black drops in the dim light. There were only a couple of plastic chairs separating her from Mia.

"You won't let me?" she spat. "How are you going to stop me? You think he wants you? He wants me. He's always wanted me. But he's betrayed me too many times. He has to be punished. When a man betrays you, he deserves punishment." She twisted the knife in her hand, still testing the blade. Blood spattered onto a white table, spreading in a dark red pool.

"Stop, Barb. Put the knife down and raise your hands."

The woman kept moving, her gaze slipping past Mia and zeroing in on something behind her. Or someone. Was Finn there?

Of course he was. He wouldn't leave her to face Barb by herself.

Adrenaline shot through her body, fueled by terror at the danger he was in. It sped up her heart beat. Quickened her breath.

Love flooded her as well, for the courageous, stupid man behind her. "Finn!" Mia yelled. "Get out of here! Right now."

Barb kept moving, her gaze fixed on a point behind Mia. *On Finn.* Hatred twisted Barb's expression into a frightening mask, one that reminded Mia of a medieval painting of the lost souls in hell. "Stop! Now!" Mia ordered, raising her gun. She didn't want to shoot the woman. She wanted to take her into custody. Get her the help she needed.

But she'd do what she had to do to protect Finn.

"You think you can tell me what to do?" Barb's gaze flicked over Mia. Dismissed her. She stared over Mia's shoulder. "You betrayed me," she spat out, her voice rising in intensity. "And now you have to die."

Barb lunged to the side, stumbling over a chair, ignoring Mia completely.

"Get back, Finn," Mia yelled as she sidestepped to avoid the knife and reached for Barb.

Shoving the chair into Mia, Barb lunged again. For Finn.

Steadying herself on the chair, Mia edged closer to Barb. The woman transferred her attention to Mia. "Get out of my way," she screamed, twisting the knife back and forth.

When Mia didn't move, she lifted the knife. Mia tightened her finger on the trigger, aiming for Barb's center mass.

Barb drew her arm back. Just before Mia pulled the trigger, a can of soda flew through the air, hitting Barb's shoulder and sending her stumbling backward. The knife skittered across the asphalt with a harsh scraping sound.

The bullet hit the concrete wall and ricocheted away.

The woman screamed as she rushed at Mia, her hands curled into claws. Mia stepped aside and pushed Barb to the ground, then put a knee on the woman's back as she fished her handcuffs from her belt.

Once her hands were secured behind her, Mia pulled Barb to her feet. The woman twisted and writhed, trying to free her hands, screaming unintelligible words at Mia.

Holding onto Barb's arms, Mia glanced over her shoulder and found Finn a step away. "Did you find another cop?" she asked.

"He's coming. I sent Jenna for him. I wasn't about to leave you."

Remembering the knife in Barb's hand, the way she'd lunged at Finn, Mia's blood ran cold. "She could have killed you!" Mia yelled at him. "You put yourself right in front of her. What were you thinking?" He was distracting Barb, Mia realized, a chill racing through her. Protecting her from the woman with the knife.

As she was yelling at Finn, one of the off-duty officers ran over. "She needs to be patted down," Mia said, her arms aching from trying to restrain Barb. "I couldn't do that and control her at the same time."

A crew member materialized. "I've got her," he said. He had to be one of Doug's undercover officers.

He replaced her hands on Barb and held the twisting, writhing woman while the off-duty cop, a young woman, pulled on gloves and patted her down.

Barb had a small stoppered vial in her pocket, and the cop slid it into an evidence bag. Then they hauled the still-screaming woman to a clear area where they could control her more easily as they waited for the squad car the cop had already called.

Mia backed away, the adrenaline burn making her shake, as she re-holstered her gun. The entire cast and crew of the movie had pressed close, watching and murmuring. The massive lamps illuminating the scene turned them into shadows passing in and out of the light.

The scream of approaching sirens settled Mia, made her take a deep breath. "Get back," she called to the actors and crew members. "On the other side of the street. This is a crime scene."

When no one moved, she headed toward the crowd, her hand resting on her gun. "I'm not going to tell you again. Back up. Now." She scanned the crowd, making eye contact with one person after another. Finally, they began to move.

Jenna Stanton was the last one to back up. She stared at Mia, at the gun on her waist. "You're a cop," she finally said, her mouth twisting in a dismissive smirk. "Nothing more than his bodyguard. You've been playing a game all this time." She tossed her hair. "I knew you weren't his type."

Too shaken to play this game, Mia glanced at the woman, then back at the crowd, making sure they were still backing up. "I don't think you are, either, Jenna."

The woman said something else, but Mia didn't bother to listen. She didn't have to play games with Jenna Stanton anymore. Barb was in custody. Mia's role as Finn's bodyguard was over.

By the time the two squad cars rolled to a stop, everyone was on the opposite side except Barb, the two officers holding her arms, Finn and Mia.

Officers jumped out of both cars and hurried over to take charge of Barb. They wrestled her into the back seat of one of the squad cars, then came back to take everyone's statements.

Mia went first, describing what had happened. Pointed out the knife on the ground, the drops of blood from Barb's fingers, the shell casing on the ground from the bullet she'd fired.

After she finished, the undercover cop and the off-duty woman working security stepped up to answer questions, Finn drew Mia to the side and put his hands on her shoulders. "You all right?"

"I'm fine." She drew in a deep, shuddering breath. "You, on the other hand, are in a shit-load of trouble. I told you to back away, but you didn't." She grabbed his shirt and gripped it in her fists. "She wanted to kill you. Do you know how I felt when I saw the man I love five feet away from a woman with a knife?" She shook him hard. "I could have lost you."

He froze for a long moment. Stared at her. She replayed what she'd said to him, and her stomach swooped to her feet. *Shit.* She hadn't meant to say that. Had never meant to tell him she'd fallen in love with him.

They stared at each other for a long moment, neither of them speaking. Then he put his hands over hers on his chest. "I wasn't going to let you face her by yourself. Who do you think threw that can of soda at her?"

"That was you?" Mia asked, frowning.

He tucked a strand of hair behind her ear. "All-state shortstop in high school," he said with a wobbly grin. "Guess I still have it."

They were going to pretend she'd never said it. That was the smart thing to do. But her heart still ached and tears prickled her eyes. Reaction to the adrenaline, she told herself.

"I guess you do, hotshot." She let go of his shirt and elbowed him lightly in the ribs. "Let's go. You're going to have to wait for me to show you how grateful I am for your heroic pitch. You have no idea how much paperwork I have to do."

CHAPTER TWENTY-SIX

As he struggled out of sleep, Finn automatically reached for Mia. When his hand touched nothing but the sheets, he cracked his eyes open. She was on the other side of the bed.

Only half-awake, Finn rolled over and reached for her. When his hand slid off the silky skin of her shoulder, he forced his eyes to focus and found her watching him. Sunlight flooded the room, making her eyes the bright blue of a tropical sea.

"Hey," he murmured, tugging her closer. "What are you doing so far away? And why are you awake? Didn't I tire you out last night?"

A smile softened her mouth but didn't reach her eyes as she reached for his hand. Slipping her fingers through his, she said, "My brain's too noisy to sleep. All kinds of thoughts bumping into each other up there."

From the sad expression on her face a moment ago, they weren't happy thoughts. "Is that so?" he said, wishing he could wipe away her sadness. He wasn't having any success in banishing his own, though. So he needed another strategy. "Think I can distract you?"

"I hope so," she said, moving close enough to press her body against his. "I didn't know you were such a sleepyhead. I was ready to wake you up to have my way with you."

"You can wake me up whenever you want, babe," he said as he ran his tongue along the seam of her mouth. Mia opened to him immediately, her kiss hard and desperate and needy.

The way she clung to him was a reminder of how little time they had left together. Deepening their kiss, he was determined to make every second count.

He was kissing his way down her body when his phone began vibrating, dancing across the table next to the bed. Ignoring it, he swirled his tongue around her navel, enjoying the way her muscles quivered.

Mia put her hand on his head. "It's someone named Angie," she said, scooting away from him. "She called twice while you were sleeping."

Finn flopped onto the bed beside her. "My publicist. Damn it! Why this morning?"

Mia handed him the phone and slid up against the headboard of the bed, pulling the sheet over herself. "Probably something to do with the mess with Barb last night."

Mia had helped him forget all about Barb Riddle. Leaning against the headboard, he pushed the call button. "Angie. This better be damn good."

"I think you'll like it, Finn. Turn on the Star channel. Interesting interview coming up in five minutes."

"About the film?" he asked, reaching for the remote.

"In a way. I'll call you later."

Finn ended the call and tossed the phone onto the table. "Do you mind?" he asked Mia. "I'll make it up to you."

She looped her arm through his and pressed against him from shoulder to hip. "I'm counting on it," she said, nudging him. "Turn on the television."

By the time they found the Star channel, a perky blond

reporter was looking into the camera, her eyes gleaming with excitement. "…Lars Benson, the drummer from Gemma Radley's band. Lars, welcome to the Star Factor."

"Thanks, Tiffany. Good to be here."

Finn's teeth clenched as he stared at the blond man with the California surfer boy good looks. The last time he'd seen Benson, the asshole had been naked in *his* bed with Finn's girlfriend. "Not sure I want to watch this."

"Maybe you should hear what he has to say." Mia snuggled closer. "You can turn it off any time."

"…shocking revelations on Gawker this morning," Tiffany said, her voice breathless. "Thank you for agreeing to come on Star Factor and clarify them for our audience."

Benson's expression turned serious. As if the jerk had something important to say. "I'm ashamed it's taken me so long to come forward," he said somberly. "But after hearing about what happened last night, I felt as if I didn't have a choice."

"The attack on Finn O'Rourke, you mean?"

"Yeah. O'Rourke's gotten nothing but crap from the press and the public for the last year and a half," he said, turning away from the camera to stare at Tiffany. "From the Star channel and everyone else. It's time someone set the record straight."

"And you're going to do that," Tiffany prodded.

"Damn right I am." He stared into the camera again. "Gemma didn't catch O'Rourke in bed with someone. She was in bed with me at his house. O'Rourke walked in on us banging."

Finn sucked in a breath, and Mia slid her hand into his. Wrapped her other hand around his biceps and held him close.

"That's not what Gemma said."

"Of course it isn't," Benson scoffed. "Gemma knew exactly when O'Rourke would get home. She planned it so he'd catch us."

Finn bit back a gasp. The anger he'd locked up in a dark

place for the past year and a half roared out of hiding. He almost missed Tiffany's next words as he struggled to rein in in.

"That's a serious accusation, Lars. Gemma Radley has already issued a statement accusing you of lying. She said you're trying to punish her because she broke up with you. And Finn O'Rourke has never denied Gemma's story."

"Yeah, I don't know what's wrong with that guy. Does he think he's being all gentlemanly or something? What an idiot. Gemma pretty much ruined his career."

"So these accusations are nothing more than 'he said, she said'," Tiffany said with a smirk.

"Nope." Benson reached into his pocket and pulled out his cell phone. "Gemma released a new song last week. A breakup song. When we took it into the studio and I heard it for the first time, I knew what was coming. So when she said we were over, I recorded our conversation. That bitch has been using me, the same way she used O'Rourke. And after what happened in Chicago last night, it's time to come clean."

"Oh, my God," Mia breathed.

Finn tightened his grip on Mia's hand as Lars pressed a button on his phone. "Really?" Benson said, his voice tinny on the recording. "You're dumping me?" There was the sound of movement, as if Benson had leaned forward. To better record the conversation? "At least you didn't set me up like you did to O'Rourke. Am I supposed to be grateful for that?"

There was a too-long silence. "You're more of a bastard that Finn ever was." The distinctive low, growly voice was clearly Gemma's. "I knew you'd have gotten even if I set you up like I did to Finn."

"What I still can't figure is why you bothered going to all that trouble. If you were sick of O'Rourke, you could have just dumped him."

"You were never the sharpest crayon in the box, Lars. Just dumping him wouldn't have done me any good. My career was tanking, and I need a boost. Other musicians have used break-up songs to break out." Gemma's voice was the sulky whine that had always grated on Finn's last nerve. "Finn has always been such an altar boy.

"If I made him out to be the bad guy, I knew I could play the wronged girlfriend and kick up my record sales."

"Wow, Gemma." Lars' voice. "That's really nasty, even for you. Weren't you afraid he'd call you on your bullshit?"

"Finn wouldn't have contradicted me," Gemma said, her cold voice confident. "He's too nice to do that."

Benson pressed the off button on his phone. "There it is. In Gemma's own words."

Finn reached for the remote and turned off the television. For a long moment, he stared at the black screen, beyond stunned. He wasn't sure he'd heard correctly. He had no idea how to react to Benson's revelations.

"That was...that was amazing," Mia said, swiveling to face him. She cupped his face in her hands. "That guy just gave you your career back."

Finn shook his head slowly, focusing on Mia. Staring at him, joy and love in her eyes. *For him.* Mia was real. Genuine. Happy for him, with no hidden agenda, no plans to use this revelation to help herself.

Mia was the only real thing in his life. Even the movie he was filming, the movie that Sean was so sure would be a breakout performance for him, was only an illusion.

Last night, Mia had told him she loved him. She hadn't meant to do it, but she hadn't taken it back.

Finn had ignored her words. Did that make him as bad as Gemma? Was he using Mia, just like Gemma had used him?

His phone rang again before he could think it through. He grabbed it like the lifeline it was, stabbing at the green call button.

"Did you see it, Finn?" his publicist asked, her voice quivering with excitement. "That loser Benson's interview on Star?"

"Yeah, I saw it." He reached for Mia's hand, and she pressed her palm against his as she curled into him. His skin prickled wherever they touched.

"Why the hell didn't you tell me what had really happened with Gemma?" Angie's voice rose until he had to hold the phone away from his ear. "We could have put a stop to that bitch's lies right at the beginning."

"Angie, you know damn well it wouldn't have made any difference if I'd denied it. Gemma got her story out first. It doesn't matter now. I've moved past it and gotten on with my life."

What a liar he was. Mia had told him she loved him, and he'd ignored her. Because of what Gemma had done to him?

Before today, he would have said no. But before today, he wouldn't have imagined that hearing Gemma's lies revealed would shake him to his core.

"You need to get back here, Finn. Everyone and his brother will want to interview you. This is perfect timing. Great publicity for *Dark Vengeance*. You're done filming, aren't you?"

"I have one more day."

"Location or green screen?"

"Not sure," he lied. It was two scenes that needed to be shot in front of a green screen. But if he told her that, Angie would insist he come back to Los Angeles. He didn't want to cut short his time with Mia.

"I have calls coming in. I'll talk to you later," Angie said, hanging up before he could respond.

He dropped the phone onto the bed and turned to Mia. Reached out and pulled her against him. He breathed in her citrusy orange scent and trailed his fingers over her warm, smooth body, trying to absorb as much of her as possible. Fix her in his memory.

God, he was going to miss Mia. He hadn't realized how much until now. They weren't going to have another few days – he'd be leaving today. He'd been in this business long enough to know what came next.

He'd be leaving Mia behind. Which is exactly what they'd agreed to. Casual. Fun. Three weeks and out.

Was that what he wanted?

He rubbed his chest over his heart. It didn't matter. It was what had to be.

He buried his face in her hair, listening to her hair catch on his stubble. He wanted to memorize everything about her – the steady beat of her heart against his chest. The slow in and out of her breathing. The tiny catch in her breath when he skimmed his fingers along her lower back.

Just as he'd expected, Sean called five minutes later. He reached for his phone, holding Mia against him with one hand.

"You're going back to LA today," the director ordered without a greeting. "Angie's already booked your ticket. This is great publicity for the film. We'll finish your scenes on a set out there. I'll call you." Sean disconnected, but it was too late.

Mia had clearly heard Sean, because she edged back and looked at him. Her lower lip quivered, and he pulled her closer for a kiss. "I'm sorry," he said against her mouth. "I'm…I have to go."

Mia slid out of bed without looking at him. "I know," she said softly. "It's your job." She slid her arms into her short silk robe and tied the knot around her waist. "I'm going to take a quick shower, then I'll pack and get out of here."

Please don't. I don't want you to leave. The plea burned on his tongue, aching to get out. He clamped his lips together and held it back. They'd both known this was inevitable. He'd thought they'd have a couple more days, but it was going to be painful whenever they said goodbye.

As he watched her walk out of the room, toward her own shower, he got to his feet, intending to join her. Then he sank down onto the bed again. What the hell was wrong with him? He'd told her he had to leave early. She'd looked devastated.

Only an asshole would think this was the time for playful shower sex.

***

Thirty minutes later, Mia stood at the door, her bag at her feet, her chest tight with pain as she watched Finn talk to his publicist again. He ran his fingers through his still-damp hair as he talked, making it stand up in dark blond spikes.

She wanted to smooth her hand over his head, tame the sexy spikes into his usual waves. Feel his hair flow through her fingers one last time.

Use her hands to tell him everything they were so carefully not saying.

Finn glanced at her as he listened to Angie, then he said, "Got to go, Ange. I'll talk to you later." He ended the call, then turned off his phone and crossed the floor to her.

"You want me to walk you downstairs?" he asked, taking her hands.

God, no. Saying goodbye in the privacy of their room was hard enough. To do it on the street, in front of anyone who happened to be walking by? That would be unbearable.

"No." Swallowing the lump in her throat, she stepped away from her bag and reached for him. "One last kiss, Finn."

Their lips met and clung and Mia's throat swelled with tears. Drawing a deep, shuddering breath, she refused to let them fall as she eased away from Finn.

Instead of letting her go, he cupped her face in his hands. "These have been the most amazing three weeks of my life, Mia." He smoothed his thumbs over her cheeks. "I thought we'd have more time." He swallowed once, then again. "I'm going to call Angie back," he said, his voice thick. "Tell her I'll come home when we originally planned."

Swallowing twice to force back the tears, she put her

fingers over his mouth. "Shh," she murmured when she could speak without sobbing. "You can't do that. And even if you could, it wouldn't change a thing." She pulled his head down and kissed him one last time, her mouth gentle on his.

She pulled away before he could deepen the kiss. "Go, Finn." She tried to smile, but she knew it was shaky. "It's been wonderful."

"I'll be back in Chicago," he said in a rush, pulling her tight against him. "To visit Doug. My agent was talking about another movie that might be filmed here. I'll call you."

"No," she whispered into his neck, her fingers tightening on his back. "I can't be your hookup in Chicago. I *won't* be your fuck buddy." She needed to make a clean break. If he came back to Chicago for a few days or a few weeks, it would rip the scab off her healing wound, and she'd just bleed all over again when he left. "If you come to Chicago to visit Doug, I don't want to know about it."

"You won't see me again? Even if I come back to Chicago?" Pain and temper swirled in his eyes. "Is this because I didn't tell you I loved you, too? Are you punishing me for that?"

She leaned back to look him in the eye. "Of course not. Did I say you had to love me back?" She'd stupidly thought the pain couldn't get worse. She took a step back. Out of reach. She couldn't bear to touch him. "I never planned on telling you how I felt, but it slipped out because I was scared. It wasn't supposed to be a trap. Or a punishment. It was a gift, freely given."

"I don't want to let you go," he whispered.

"I don't want you to go, either," she said, angry in her turn at his tunnel vision. "And you don't have to go. We could have figured something out. Made this work. You didn't even want to try."

"How could we have done that?" he demanded, his face tightening. "My career is in California. Your life is here.

How could we ever make this work?"

"You're right," she said, reaching for her bag. "What's the use of trying to figure out the hard stuff when we both know this couldn't go anywhere. A cop and a movie star? Not going to happen." Reaching for the door, she said, "Goodbye, Finn. Safe trip home."

She tried to smile, but her mouth was too wobbly. "Good luck with your career," she said softly. "I hope this film is everything you hoped for."

Mia blinked hard, holding back her tears by the force of her will as she fumbled the door open. She refused to let Finn's last glimpse of her be tears streaming down her face.

"Mia…"

"Goodbye, Finn." She stepped through the door and pulled it closed behind her, then walked toward the elevator. A tiny part of her hoped the door would open. That Finn wouldn't let her leave.

But the door to their suite stayed firmly closed as she pressed the elevator call button. She stepped inside when it arrived, turned to face the front. The peephole on the door was dark. Was Finn watching her leave? As the doors closed slowly in front of her, Mia lifted her chin and refused to wipe away the tears trickling down her cheeks.

They clogged Mia's throat and blurred her vision as she stepped off the elevator on the ground floor, and she clutched her bag tightly as she fumbled out the door to Walton Street. Carlos the doorman smiled at her, then stopped in his tracks when he actually saw her.

"You want a cab, Mia?" he asked gently.

She nodded, reaching into her purse for a tip, and Carlos put his hand over hers. "Please, Mia," he said as he signaled for a cab. "Don't insult me."

He opened the cab door, helped her inside, then closed the door gently behind her. The cab smelled of acrid cleaning solution and the faint hint of cigarette smoke.

After she gave the driver her address, she turned and looked one last time at the Drake. Then she faced forward, refusing to watch the hotel disappear from sight.

CHAPTER TWENTY-SEVEN

Three months later

Carrying a bag of takeout Chinese food she'd have to reheat, Mia tugged her mail out of the box and tucked it under her arm as she trudged up the stairs to her apartment. As soon as she'd picked up her order from her favorite Chinese restaurant, she'd gotten a call from her training officer.

Her promotion to detective was new enough that she didn't mind the reheated dinners. Didn't mind the long hours. She was still figuring out how to let the job go once she got home, but that would come.

So when O'Reilly had called, she returned to the station eagerly, stashed her food in the break room refrigerator and headed out again with Kevin O'Reilly. Three hours later, she was finally home.

Dropping the mail on the dining room table, she flipped on the lights in the kitchen, put her Kung Pao Chicken on a plate and shoved it into the microwave. Then she got a glass of wine and retrieved her mail.

She liked these nights when she had to work so late. By

the time she fell into bed, she was so exhausted she didn't even dream.

It was harder when she had too much time on her hands. When she got home at a reasonable hour and still semi-alert, memories and regrets weighed heavily on her shoulders. They whispered in her ear, calling up all the painful 'could haves' and 'should haves' that had marked the last few months.

By the time the microwave dinged, she'd tossed three political ads and a coupon booklet from neighborhood stores into her recycling bin. She set two bills aside, then shoved the face-down copies of *Entertainment Weekly* and *People* to the side as she stood up to retrieve her plate.

In a moment of weakness after Finn left, she'd subscribed to the two popular culture bibles. Now, every week, she both looked forward to and dreaded the stories she read about him.

Her hands itched to turn those magazines over. Devour their contents. But she forced herself to eat dinner and clean up first.

Only when those chores were done did she head into the living room with the last of her glass of wine and settle into her father's chair, the magazines on her lap, still face down.

Taking a deep breath, she finally turned the magazines over.

Finn's smiling face stared at her from the cover of *Entertainment Weekly*. The same picture was in a corner of the cover of *People*, next to a teaser for the article about him. According to the headline on ET, he'd been named as the host of one of the countless Hollywood award shows.

Hating herself, wishing she could put the magazines aside and ignore them, she opened *Entertainment Weekly* and gobbled up the story about Finn. It included several pictures, and her fingers lingered on one of them as she turned the page.

Finally she tossed both magazines to the floor, disgusted with herself. Why did she keep tormenting herself like this?

What the hell was wrong with her?

In the past three months, she'd tried so hard to move on with her life and forget about Finn. She'd failed completely, of course. Once a Donovan found his or her one and done, that was it. And getting these magazines once a week, reminding her of what she'd had and lost, was a stupid mistake.

Grabbing her laptop, she went online and canceled both subscriptions. Then she stood up and strode to the window.

She was better than this.

She looked down on the dark, quiet street. Cars lined the curb, lights twinkled from the other buildings, but there wasn't a soul walking down the sidewalk. Where were the bros and their ragers when she needed a distraction? Arresting a bunch of irritating former frat boys would keep her busy and keep Finn out of her head.

No. She slapped her hand on the radiator cover, hard enough to sting her palm. She was done being weak. Done pining for something she couldn't have. Cancelling the subscriptions was a good first step. Relegating Finn to a distant memory would be the next one.

It would take time. But that was okay. She had nothing but time. It stretched ahead of her like a long, dark ribbon.

By God, she was taking control of her life again. She'd put some color back into it. Some joy.

She reached for her phone and texted her Aunt Helen. The best place to find joy right now was with her niece Charlotte.

'Busy tomorrow?' she typed. 'Can I come by and see you and the munchkin?'

She'd kick this lingering sadness to the curb, starting tomorrow.

***

"Finn, welcome to The Star Factor." Beaming, Tiffany set her hand on his arm and squeezed once. She stood just a hair too close to him, and he had to force himself not to step away.

"Thanks, Tiffany," he said, smiling into the camera. This was his third interview since the announcement that he was hosting the Goldies, and the news had come out only yesterday. "Good to be here."

"We've been dying to have you on Star Factor," Tiffany confided. "We're glad you could finally make it."

He worked to keep his smile easy and affable and resisted the urge to roll his eyes. Tiffany and the rest of the Star channel hadn't been so eager to have him on their shows before the mess in Chicago. Angie had tried repeatedly to book him over the past year and a half, with no success. This time, the Star Channel had come to her. "It's good to be here," Finn answered, trying not to clench his teeth.

Tiffany and Star were the grit he needed to endure. That grit helped form the pearl he wanted his career to be. So he'd smile at her and answer her inane questions.

"We were so excited to hear you're going to host the Goldies this year," she gushed. "You must be thrilled."

"I am, Tiffany. It's an honor," he said, meaning it. Sean, the director of *Dark Vengeance*, had lobbied for it, but he hadn't had to push too hard. Everyone in Hollywood had been fawning over him since he got back from Chicago. "I've always thought the Goldies was one of the classiest award shows."

While the camera was on Tiffany as she chattered about the presenters, trying to guess who would be selected, Finn glanced around the studio. A swarm of young women stood off camera, watching him avidly. Some of them were reporters, some were interns and some were the office staff. At least three or four of them would press their 'cards' into his hand after the taping. Most of them would push close, trying to brush against him. One or two would proposition him.

He was the hot commodity in Hollywood right now.

Hosting the Goldies.

He'd thought he wanted this – the fame, the adulation, the interviews on the celebrity television shows.

The offers of parts in all the hot movies.

It wasn't all he'd thought it would be. Irritating interviews with reporters like Tiffany were an almost daily occurrence.

So were the strangers, both men and women, murmuring about the sex acts they'd like to perform on him.

He was beginning to miss the good old days, when people crossed the street to avoid him.

Tiffany tossed him softball questions for another five minutes, then she smiled into the camera. "There he is, folks. Finn O'Rourke. He'll be hosting the Goldies next month. Watch for The Star Channel and yours truly on the red carpet."

When the cameras stopped filming, she leaned close to Finn, ostensibly to help him remove his mic. Instead of unclipping it, she ran her finger over his chest. "How about a drink?" she murmured. "I have some Johnny Walker Blue in my dressing room."

"Wow, Tifffany, that's tempting," he said with a smile. He reached up to detach the mic and her hands closed over his. "But I have an appointment with my agent. A new screenplay they want me to look at."

Tiffany released him and sat back with a tiny pout. "Another time, then, Finn." She adjusted the cuff of his shirt beneath the jacket sleeve, sliding one finger along his wrist, pressing it into his pulse. "I'd love to get to know you better."

You and everyone else in Hollywood.

Forcing a smile, he stood up. "Thanks, Tiffany. Let's see what we can arrange."

Angie would string him up for not taking Tiffany up on her offer. As one of the more influential entertainment reporters in Hollywood, Tiffany was on every actor's list of must-do interviews.

But there was no way he'd be arranging anything with the woman. Especially not an intimate meeting in her dressing room.

As he hurried away, he pulled out his handkerchief and wiped away the hint of her perfume that lingered on his wrist. The come-ons happened almost daily, even from big-shot reporters like Tiffany. He'd lost count of how many times he'd had to fend one off in the past few months. It was awkward and distasteful every time.

The only woman he wanted was Mia. Which was ridiculous. They'd been together less than three weeks. They'd both known it was short term. But he couldn't get her out of his head.

He and Gemma had been together for two years, and he'd been secretly relieved when she'd pulled her little publicity stunt. And Mia was still in his head after only three weeks?

He slid into his car. It was because Mia had been real. She hadn't been interested in him because he was Finn O'Rourke. She'd wanted *Finn*. The ordinary guy, warts and all. It had been refreshing. Intriguing.

He missed real. He needed to find more of it in his life.

No matter how much he missed Mia, he hadn't had a choice about leaving. He'd needed to come home. Everyone had told him so. His career had to come first.

He wondered now – had that really been true?

He slid into his car, deciding to take the long route to Angie's office. He needed to clear his head and adjust his attitude before he saw her. Before he got back on the hamster wheel.

***

Finn stood in the middle of his living room a couple of weeks later, watching his guests milling around or standing in small clusters, eating his food and drinking his booze. Glasses clinked, the scent of food drifted over from the buffet, and the murmur of conversation overlaid it all. He'd nixed a live band for the party, but even without it, the noise volume in the room was deafening.

Angie was in one of the other rooms or out by the pool, basking in his success, button-holing every Important Person she could find. And there were a lot of them here.

The party had been her idea. She'd told him he had to act like an A-lister because now he *was* an A-lister. In order to stay that way, he had to take meetings. Chat up the studio decision makers. Schmooze with everyone in town who mattered.

He should start by throwing a party. All the other A-listers would come.

She'd been right.

Thanks to Lars Benson's revelations, he'd gotten his life back. Gotten more than he'd had before the Gemma fiasco. He should be ecstatic.

He'd been asked to host the Goldies. His career was soaring. Everyone who counted was at his party tonight. His agent Lisa had a stack of screenplays on her desk – every director in town wanted to work with him.

He felt as if there was an invisible wall around him, separating him from all of his networking, chattering colleagues. Isolated in the crowd. Any other cliché he could trot out.

Had he felt this way when he'd been filming in Chicago? No. He'd been happy there. He'd been busy filming. Waiting for his stalker to strike. He hadn't had time to be lonely.

A woman approached him, smiling. She held out her hand when she saw he didn't recognize her.

"Hi, Finn. Hildy Franklin. One of the screenwriters for *Dark Vengeance.*"

"Of course. I remember you," Finn said, smiling as he shook the woman's hand. "How are you doing, Hildy? Working on another project right now?"

"I always have a few irons in the fire." She took a sip

from what looked like a gin and tonic. "I understand you're thinking about putting together a production company."

Where the hell had she heard that? It was something he'd talked about with Angie and a couple of other people. He forced a smile. He should have remembered there was no such thing as a secret in Hollywood.

"Mulling my options, Hildy," he said, taking a gulp of scotch. "Nothing in concrete yet." He studied the woman in front of him. "What's on your mind?"

"Just offering my services if you're serious. I'd love to write a couple of scripts for you. On spec, of course."

"Wow, Hildy, you're way ahead of me." Another screenwriter had approached him tonight, and three actors had gone out of their way to ask about his future projects. Was everyone at his party looking for something from him?

"But if I did start a company, I'd look at a lot of different stuff. You did a great job with *Dark Vengeance*. So of course I'd look at something from you."

"Thanks, Finn." Her fingers gripped the glass more tightly. "How's your girlfriend? Why isn't she here tonight? Did you break up with her?" Hildy had an avid expression on her face, as if she'd like to audition for the role.

Finn let his gaze drift over her shoulder. "Oops, gotta go," he said, squeezing her shoulder. "Sorry, Hildy. I see someone I need to talk to." He gave her the obligatory air kiss and slid past her.

His girlfriend.

If Mia were here, they'd laugh together about the posturing and the scheming.

Swallowing a gulp of scotch, he wandered over to the buffet and took one of the tiny pieces of lasagna. It was bland and rubbery and the spices were all wrong. Nothing like Rose Donovan's lasagna.

This party was nothing like the Donovan family dinner, either. He'd been nervous about going, but everyone had put him at ease. Mia's family was genuine. Interested in him and the movie he was making, but not looking for something from Finn. As far as he could tell, none of the Donovans cared one bit about his fame.

No one in this room knew who he really was. And none of them cared.

Which was only fair, because he didn't really care about any of them. They were work colleagues. Nothing more.

Was there even such a thing as a genuine friendship in Hollywood? Or was everything based on who could do what for whom?

Was anyone in this town real?

A woman caught his eye, and his heart began to race. From the back, she reminded him of Mia – dark wavy hair, slender curvy body, endless legs. He turned toward her, a sunflower to her sun.

He took a step in her direction, then stopped when she turned her head. She looked nothing like his Mia.

His Mia. There was no such woman.

He swallowed the rest of his drink, the scotch burning his throat, and put it on a passing waiter's tray of empties, then headed to the bar for a refill. It was going to be a long night.

***

One week later

The audience in the glitzy theater was rapt, listening to the latest 'it' band. Finn stood offstage, watching them play. The Goldie award show was going well. He'd been smooth. Charming. He'd gotten applause in all the right places. Now there were only a few awards left – the big ones, for Best Television Drama, Best Actor in a drama, Best Actress in one. He'd be happy to call it a night.

Tonight was the culmination of everything he wanted to accomplish in Hollywood. It didn't get any more high-profile than hosting an international award show.

He wasn't fooling himself – it wouldn't last. It never did.

But for now, he was riding the wave of collective guilt that had caused the industry to embrace him. The buzz about a possible Oscar nomination for *Dark Vengeance* didn't hurt, either.

He should be on cloud nine. Lars Benson's admission had changed his life. He had more offers of roles than he could film in ten years. His agent was sorting through those, picking out the ones she liked best.

He'd found a couple of scripts he'd liked, including an amazing one about a Chicago cop, and he'd directed his agent to buy them for his fledgling production company.

He had the success he'd craved, but he had no one to share it with. No one who'd be genuinely thrilled about his accomplishments. No one who'd congratulate him without thinking *she* should have been getting those accolades.

He was surrounded by people, but lonelier than he'd ever been in his life.

The last time he'd been really happy was in Chicago. With Mia. The woman he'd thrown away for this empty life.

Turning away from the stage, he spotted a monitor and forced himself to look at it. He'd given Pete tickets to the award show, and he suddenly wanted to know who Pete had brought as his date.

He wanted to know who had made Pete so happy.

His driver had been different lately. He still exchanged barbs with Finn, still teased him and acted like a tough guy, but he'd been…lighter. More free. Finn had caught him smiling like a goofball as he talked on his phone. Which he seemed to do a lot.

He always hung up before Finn got close. Refused to discuss the person on the other end of the phone. But Pete was a joyous man again. Judy's death had torn him apart, and Finn was genuinely pleased his friend had found someone.

The tickets were for seats fairly close to the front of the theater. So Finn watched the screen, looking for his friend as the camera panned through the crowd.

He spotted Pete a few moments later, his head bent close to a dark-haired woman. They were both smiling as the woman whispered something in Pete's ear.

She pulled away as the band ended the song, and Finn grabbed the monitor stand to steady himself.

Pete's date was Rose Donovan.

On the screen, he couldn't see the gray in her dark, wavy hair. Couldn't see the fine lines on her face. She looked like a slightly older Mia, and Finn's heart lurched.

God, he missed Mia.

If Finn hadn't been such an ass, Mia could have been waiting for him after the show. She could have walked the red carpet with him, whispering in his ear, teasing him about all the reporters jostling each other to talk to him.

Telling him she was proud of him. That she knew he'd do a great job tonight.

He wanted Mia back. Wanted her honesty, her genuineness, her unflinching grasp of reality.

He wanted her love.

If she could ever forgive him for walking away from her.

He should have called her. Flown out to visit her, in spite of what she'd said. So why hadn't he?

Yeah, she'd said she didn't want to see him, but when had a 'no' ever stopped him?

Tomorrow he was going back to Chicago. Going back to Mia. If she'd take him back, they'd figure out together how to make it work.

For the first time in his career, he was calling the shots. He was the golden boy, and he needed to take advantage of that. There was no reason now that he had to live in LA. Producers and directors would come to him, at least until he wasn't the 'it' guy anymore.

It would be a little harder to run his production company from Chicago, but that's what airplanes were for.

It wouldn't hurt him to take a few risks, either. In their time together, Mia had been the one to take all the risks. She'd made love to him when it could have cost her her job.

She'd told him she loved him.

Now it was his turn to take some risks.

The only reason he hadn't realized that earlier? He was the most stupid man alive.

CHAPTER TWENTY-EIGHT

Mia's hand shook so badly that it took three tries to shove her key into the front door of her building. Finally it slid home, and she stepped into the warm foyer of her two-flat. The warm, stale air heightened the smell of blood and death that clung to her clothes and hair. Closing her eyes, she swallowed once to force back the nausea. *Not now.*

She could fall apart when she was locked into her apartment. Not before. No one could see her like this.

Ignoring her mail box, she forced herself to climb the stairs, one foot after the other. Every muscle in her body ached. Every corner of her soul felt soiled. Unclean. Her heart was a tiny, pinched thing in her chest, raw and burning.

As she stepped onto the landing, she saw a long pair of legs sprawled in front of her door at the top of the next flight. Male. Wearing jeans. Expensive sneakers. She couldn't see his face – she'd have to turn the corner for that.

Resting her hand on her gun, she stepped into view and froze. Her hand fell away from the gun. Her breath caught in her throat at the sight of his dark blond hair. The face she'd been unable to banish from her memory.

He looked up from the book he was reading and snapped it shut. "Mia."

"Finn? What are you doing here?" she managed to say. She gripped the railing on the wall, bracing herself against the storm of emotion that swept over her.

"Waiting for you."

"How did you get in?" She stepped onto the next stair.

"The guy who lives below you let me in." Finn's expression relaxed into a smile that was probably supposed to be charming. "He said he was pretty sure I wasn't an axe murderer."

"What do you want?" Her voice was expressionless. Robotic. Which was exactly how she felt.

He studied her, the charm falling away, his expression turning wary. His gaze zeroed in on the smear of blood on her white shirt as he stood. "To talk to you."

She gripped the railing so hard her knuckles whitened as she pulled herself up another stair. "Go away."

"Sorry. I'm not leaving before we talk." He shifted from one foot to the other, but she saw the resolve in his expression. The stony stubbornness in his eyes.

A wave of welcome anger crashed over her. "You're telling me I have to talk to you before you'll leave me alone? I don't think so, O'Rourke." She managed to make it to the top of the stairs, and she clung to her doorknob as she stared him down. "Get out of my building."

She turned to unlock her door. After three unsuccessful tries, Finn took the key gently from her hand, inserted it and opened the door. He cupped her elbow in his hand and steadied her as she wobbled on her feet.

"What happened, Mia?" he asked, his hand tightening on her.

"Nothing. I'm fine. Please leave, Finn." She was so close to breaking down. So close to falling over the edge into complete misery and despair. She didn't want to share that with anyone. Especially not Finn.

"Not going anywhere, Mia. I'm done leaving." His

expression softened, and she could swear she saw real concern there. Caring. "Whatever happened tonight, I want to be here for you. I'm sticking."

The smoldering embers of banked anger flared to life. She spun around to face him. "Really, Finn? You want to be here for me? Then tell me how I'm supposed to handle a six-year-old baby gunned down on her own damn block." Mia slammed the door and tossed her bag onto the floor. "She was riding her bike on the sidewalk. First time without training wheels."

Tears prickled at her eyes and she couldn't hold them back. They trickled out of her eyes in a steady stream. "Her daddy was running beside her, to catch her if she fell. Which she did."

She sucked in a breath that turned into a sob. "It was a drive-by. Two punk bangers gunning for a rival on the front porch of the house she was passing. Her father caught her, just like he told her he would. But he couldn't do a damn thing to save her."

"You can let yourself out," she said as she stepped around him and headed for her bathroom. All the water in the world couldn't wash her clean after today, but she had to try and obliterate the smell that clung to her.

Finn caught her arm and stopped her, but she stared straight ahead. She didn't want him to see her like this. Raw. Devastated. "I'm not going anywhere, Mia. You shouldn't be alone tonight." He slowly circled his arms around her, his hands resting at her hips as if afraid she'd shove him away. When she didn't move, he drew her back against him.

"I've got you," he murmured into her hair, his breath tickling her scalp. "I've got you. Let go, Mia. You're safe with me. Go ahead and fall apart."

Safe was the last word she'd associate with Finn. But she couldn't hold her anguish back any longer. She closed her eyes as an endless stream of tears poured down her face. She lifted her hands to cover her face as she began to sob.

Finn's gentle hands turned her around. Encircled her

and pulled her against him. Closing her eyes, she buried her face in his chest. His shirt smelled of laundry detergent and fabric softener. Ordinary, homey scents. Was this how Layla's clothes had smelled when she put them on this morning?

Gripping his shirt in both fists, she sobbed until her throat was raw and aching. Sobbed until she had drained every tear from her body. All that was left was a black, empty void.

Finally she let him go and stepped away. "Sorry I got your shirt wet," she said, turning her back on him and heading for the bathroom. "Leave your phone number. I'll call you."

She almost made it through the door when Finn caught up with her. He curled his hand around her upper arm, holding her as if she were made of glass. "Get some clean clothes," he murmured. "I'll start your shower."

"I don't need you to start my damn shower," she said, her voice raspy and broken as she pulled away from him. "Get out of here, Finn. Leave me alone. I can't deal with you tonight."

"Won't leave you alone." He stroked his hand down her arm tentatively. "Not tonight."

"What are you going to do?" she said, refusing to look at him. "Kiss it and make it all better? I don't think so. Get out."

Shaking him off, she stepped into the bathroom, locked the door and turned on the shower. She peeled off her clothes, sprayed stain remover on the blood on her shirt and stuffed everything deep in her laundry basket. Then she stepped beneath the scalding hot spray. She shampooed her hair and washed herself twice, but she was certain she'd never be clean again.

Bracing her hands against the wall, she let the hot water beat down on her. Brendan had warned her she'd get a case like this, sooner or later. The kind that destroyed a little bit of your soul. The kind of case that made you look at people differently.

She hadn't wanted to be that cop. Told herself it wouldn't happen to her, that she'd be firm but fair. Her job was to protect and serve. Everyone.

By the time she and O'Reilly had reached the scene, the neighbors on Layla's block had the fifteen-year-old target surrounded. One guy brandished a golf club. A woman held a broken-off tree branch, the end as sharp as ragged teeth.

As the child lay on the sidewalk, cradled in her father's arms, the mob crowded closer, yelling at the kid, ordering him to give up the shooters' names. A brick flew through the air, and the kid flinched away from it.

Mia knew what would come next. Vigilante justice, ugly and indiscriminate and wrong. But she got out of the car too slowly. For a few moments, she wanted to let Layla's neighbors mete out justice for that murdered little girl.

That made her no better than the mob.

She'd compounded that mistake by handling the kid roughly when they got him away from the mob. Shoving him into the back seat so hard that he fell over. She hadn't bothered to help him up, either.

She twisted the handle and turned off the water, then stepped out of the shower. Weariness made her limbs heavy and clumsy, but she managed to towel her hair and dry herself. Then, shivering, she wrapped the towel around herself and headed into her bedroom.

She'd just managed to put on a long tee shirt and yoga pants when she heard her front door open. Close. Footsteps coming toward her.

She'd left her gun in the bathroom.

Swallowing, she stepped into the hall. Finn was heading toward the kitchen, a brown paper bag in his hands.

"Why are you still here?" she asked.

"You need to eat," he said, glancing over his shoulder. "I got you some food. Oscar's mac and cheese."

Her eyes filled. He'd remembered Oscar's.

Remembered how much she liked that dish. The simple kindness made her throat swell.

She followed him into the kitchen, the smells from the bag making her stomach gurgle. It was late in the evening, and she hadn't eaten anything since breakfast. How had Finn known that?

He set two plates on the table, opened the bag and dished up their meals. He'd gotten her favorite version of Oscar's mac and cheese. Her eyes prickled again.

As she slid onto a chair, he opened her refrigerator, pulled out the opened bottle of white wine and held it up. "You want a glass?"

She shook her head. She'd already made one mistake today – being unprofessional. Too rough with a witness. She wouldn't compound that mistake by using alcohol to deaden the pain of the case.

Sliding the bottle back into the refrigerator, Finn sat down across from her and she began to eat. She was expecting him to talk to her. Tell her why he was here and what he wanted. Instead, he ate without saying a word.

She'd forgotten that about Finn, that he could be so restful. Such an oasis of calm in the middle of a storm.

Finally, when her stomach was full, she set her dish in the sink and ran water over it. She'd do the dishes tomorrow. Finn handed her his plate, and she rinsed it, too.

Her head bowed, she stared down at the two plates, at the stubborn spots of cheese sticking to their surfaces. Finn would be just like that. Sticking to her whether she wanted him to or not.

Finally, straightening, she turned to face him. He was leaning against the wall, watching her. "Thank you," she said. "Getting the mac and cheese was very thoughtful. I appreciate it, but I need to go to bed and you need to leave."

He pushed off from the wall. "Are you sure you don't want someone in the apartment tonight? Sleeping on the couch, of course."

Yes, she wanted company. Desperately. She wanted

someone to curl into, someone to hold her. But it couldn't be Finn. She couldn't lean on him, only to have him disappear again in a few days or a few weeks.

"I can't do this, Finn," she said, heading toward her bedroom. "I told you when you left that I wasn't hooking up with you when you were in town, and I meant it." She edged past him, being careful not to touch him. But she couldn't resist inhaling his scent. That familiar combination of sea spray and sunshine made her eyes prickle again.

Suddenly so tired that she swayed on her feet, she nodded toward the living room door. "Do me a favor and turn out the lights before you leave, okay?"

She stumbled into her bedroom and fell onto the bed, barely managing to pull back the quilt and blanket. As she tumbled into sleep, she heard the faint sounds of footsteps in her apartment, then the quiet click of the front door locking.

She was relieved that he'd listened to her and left. But her last conscious thought before sleep claimed her was regret that he hadn't fought harder for her.

She closed one fist around her pillow and squeezed. Why did that surprise her? He hadn't fought for her last time, either.

***

Mia woke up the next morning with sunlight warming her face. She rolled over and stared up at the ceiling, wondering why her mouth was Sahara-dry and her eyes were gritty and sore.

Then the memories swept over her. Layla. The mob in the street. The fifteen-year-old target, smirking and posturing as she'd cuffed him.

The way she'd shoved him into the unmarked.

Blinking, she sat up and swung her legs over the side of the bed, raking her hands through her hair. O'Reilly had watched her hesitation to help the smirking kid for about two seconds, then he'd barked at her. *Get the lead outta your ass, kid. Cuff him. Jesus, Donovan. Am I going to have to hold your hand every time we get a kid?*

Her gruff, crusty training officer hadn't cut her an inch of slack. Which was exactly what she'd needed. She'd been forced to focus on her job and put her emotions aside.

They'd interrogated the kid for hours. When he'd refused to give them names, they'd thrown him into a holding cell. Mia needed to go in this morning to continue the interrogation.

She had to do it with a clear head.

Coffee. She needed a cup desperately. Walking into the kitchen, she grabbed the carafe and took it to the sink to fill. Stopped dead in her tracks.

Two plates sat in the drying rack, along with two forks.

Finn had really been here. He'd done the dishes before he left.

A key turned in her front door, and she swung around in time to see him walk in, carrying two bags and a tray holding two cups of coffee.

Her heart beat a frantic tattoo against her chest as she watched him walk toward her. "Why the hell are you still here?"

CHAPTER TWENTY-NINE

"I told you last night, Mia. I'm not going anywhere. I'm sticking this time."

"What does that even mean?" she asked wrapping her arms around her waist. He was standing in her kitchen, holding coffee and breakfast, as if it was the most natural thing in the world.

Was this real? Or was she still in bed, dreaming?

The aroma of coffee drifted from the cups in Finn's hand. This morning, when she walked into her tiny kitchen, it had been filled with Finn's scent. She assumed she'd been dreaming, but she'd never dreamt *smells* before. Her heart did a slow roll in her chest, then began to thump.

He was real. Finn was standing in her kitchen, looking just as good as the last time she'd seen him, sixteen weeks and three days ago. Not that she'd been counting.

"Let's have breakfast before we talk." He set down the bag on the kitchen table, followed by the tray with two coffees. He pulled one out and handed it to her. "I learned my lesson about you and breakfast. At the bare minimum, you need coffee before a civilized conversation is possible. Coffee *and* food? Even better."

She lifted the cup to her mouth and sipped the hot coffee. He'd remembered exactly how she liked her coffee – two creams, no sugar. And none of the fancy flavored stuff, either.

Her lips curved on the plastic lid as she remembered that conversation. It had ended up as so many of their conversations had – with the two of them rolling around on the bed.

"Sit down, babe." He squeezed her shoulder and guided her into a chair. "I got bagels and salmon. Capers. An avocado." He laid them out on the plates he'd set on the table, got a knife and sliced open the avocado. "I missed your version of a Chicago breakfast while I was gone."

Babe? "What?" she said, ignoring the endearment as she inhaled the familiar scents. "You don't have avocados in California? No smoked salmon?"

He looked up from the avocado, his fingers green, his eyes even greener as he smiled at her. "I could have had them anytime. But they were too bound up in my memories of you. They would have tasted like sawdust without you to share them with me."

Mia blinked hard and lifted the cup to her mouth to hide her reaction. How did he know exactly what to say to make her all teary and emotional?

She finally set the cup down and reached for a bagel, her hand shaking as she picked it up. Jalapeno cheddar. He remembered her favorite, even though they had never had them when he'd been here.

She was pretty sure she'd only mentioned them once, during those two weeks when they couldn't get enough of each other. That time when every tiny bit of information was snatched up and stored in memory banks.

"Thank you," she finally said.

He looked up from the capers. "I haven't forgotten a thing," he said, his eyes darkening.

She hadn't, either.

It didn't mean she would start up with him again,

though, just because he'd showed up at her door. "I meant what I said when you left," she said quietly, her heart pinching as she smeared cream cheese on a bagel half. "I can't do this again, Finn."

He looked up from the avocado, his gaze piercing. "I understand, Mia. I can't do this again, either."

"Then why are you here?"

"I have something to show you." His gaze lingered on her for a beat too long. His expression softened, turning into something that looked a lot like...

Yeah. Not possible. She needed to stop fooling herself.

Time to lighten this up. "Really, Finn? *You have something to show me?* That line was lame thirty years ago." If she didn't go with snark, she'd start crying. Not what she wanted to show Finn.

"How would you know?" he shot back. "You weren't around thirty years ago."

"I didn't have to be. It's in the history books. Under the category of 'stay away from a guy using this line. He's a loser'."

His eyes twinkling, he picked up the paper towel holding the avocado skins and pit and dumped them in the trash. Then he sat down and reached for her hand. "That's the Mia I remember. The coffee is working its magic already."

He rubbed his thumb over her knuckles slowly. Almost absently. In spite of her determination to keep him at arm's length, she wanted to grip his hand and never let go. Every molecule in her body trembled like a leaf in a strong wind.

Tightening his grip on her hand as she tried to extricate it from his, he asked, "How are you doing this morning? Sounded as if you had a hell of a night at work."

She tugged harder, but he wouldn't let her go. Finally, sighing, she slumped back in the chair.

"Last night was beyond awful. Tragic. Unbearably sad. And completely unnecessary."

"Yeah, I got that. How are you handling it?"

He looked as if he really wanted to know. As if he wasn't

just making conversation. She closed her eyes, and the pictures from last night unspooled in an endless loop in her head. "I can still see Layla lying on the sidewalk. One of her barrettes fell out when the paramedics were working on her. It was a tiny yellow plastic flower, covered with Layla's blood."

She sighed and pushed away from the table, her bagel only half eaten. "I'll see that picture for a long, long time."

Mia stared out the back door of her apartment. Two pots of patio tomatoes sat on her porch, bright red fruit hanging from the plants. The basil in the pots next to them needed water.

The cucumbers and eggplants and peas her neighbor planted in the back yard were heavy with vegetables. Here at her home, everything was normal. Just like yesterday.

But something inside her had changed, and she wasn't sure she'd ever be the same woman again.

Finn's arms curled around her waist, pulling her against him. "You have to let it go, Mia. You won't be able to do your job if you can't put it behind you."

"I know that," she said, pressing her forehead against the glass in the door. "I know I can't obsess about every case. This one was…hard."

Before Finn could answer, her phone rang. Easing away from Finn, missing his embrace as soon as his arms dropped away, she grabbed her phone from the table. O'Reilly. Her training officer.

"Donovan," she said as she pushed the button to answer.

"We got them," Kevin said, hard satisfaction in his voice. "Before I took off last night, I took another stab at that scumbag we arrested yesterday. He gave up their names. We rounded them up early this morning and charged them. They're in Cook County jail. No bail. We're searching their cribs right now. They're going down, Donovan. Won't bring back that little girl, but at least her parents will have some closure."

"Thanks, Kevin," Mia said quietly. "I'm glad you called.

I'll be in as soon as I can get there to do the paperwork."

"I've got this, Donovan," he said. "Take the rest of the day – we must have worked fifteen hours yesterday. You can do the paperwork on the next one. I'll see you tomorrow."

"Okay. Thanks. I'll be there."

"See ya then," O'Reilly said, and clicked off.

She stared at the phone for a moment, then set it on the table. "They caught the two guys who shot Layla," she said. "They're in jail."

"Does it help?" he asked, watching her.

"She's still dead," Mia said slowly. "But those two shitheads won't be shooting anyone else. So, yeah. I guess it does. A little, anyway."

"You want to finish your coffee and bagel?" He gestured toward the remains of her breakfast, sitting on the kitchen table.

She was hungry, she realized, drawing in a deep breath and letting it out slowly. "Yeah. I do."

They finished their breakfast in silence, Finn apparently content to sprawl in the other kitchen chair and watch her while she ate. He sipped his coffee slowly, a man with all the time in the world.

She knew that couldn't be true. He must have a million and one obligations back in California. But he was sitting in her kitchen, sipping his coffee, as if there was nowhere else he'd rather be.

Warmth slid through her at the thought, but she ignored it. Shoving the final bite of her bagel into her mouth, she washed it down with the last of her coffee and carried their dishes over to the sink.

Behind her, Finn pushed away from the table. He squeezed her shoulder and said, "Let me clean those up. You get ready to go."

She turned to face him. "Go where?"

"Like I said, I have something to show you."

"I can see just fine right here."

"What I have to show you isn't portable." He tucked a strand of hair behind her ear, his fingers lingering on her cheek. "You have to see for yourself."

She wanted to press her face into his palm, but she narrowed her eyes at him instead. "Where are we going?"

Finn shook his head, but his eyes were smiling. He slid his hand down her arm, fingers caressing her skin, and she shivered in spite of herself. "You're not going to cut me an inch of slack, are you?"

She tilted her head and studied him. "No," she finally said. "I'm not."

He'd already broken her heart once. It would destroy her if she let down her guard and he broke it again.

"Please, Mia." He slid his palms lower and took her hands. "I'm trying to have a moment here. Would you please put your clothes on?" His gaze raked over her loose tee shirt and yoga pants. His eyes darkened and his hands clutched hers more tightly. "Although if you want to go to our appointment like that, in your pajamas and without any underwear, I'm not going to complain."

Her face flamed and she yanked her hands away from him. He had too much power over her. One touch, one heated look, and all her self-preservation instincts flew out the window.

"Fine," she muttered, stepping away from him. "I'll get dressed. I'm wearing jeans, though." She held his gaze, daring him to object.

"Jeans are great," he said, leaning against the wall and folding his arms. "Take your time."

After throwing on jeans and a light sweater for the late September day, she washed her face and brushed her teeth. After she turned off the water, she heard Finn murmuring on his phone. She strained to hear him, but couldn't make out the words. Finally, scowling at herself in the mirror for bothering but unable to stop herself, she put on mascara and lipstick and stepped into her favorite pair of aqua-blue Chucks.

When she stepped into the hall, Finn pushed away from the wall. "You make those jeans look good," he said, his gaze lingering on her legs. "*You* look good, Mia."

"I wasn't dressing for you," she said, but the tiny voice inside her head called her a liar.

"Thank goodness." Finn grinned at her as he opened her front door. "If you had, I'm not sure I could have handled it."

She started down the stairs, Finn right behind her. The back of her neck prickled, and she knew he was staring at her. "Stop staring at my ass," she said without looking back at him.

The rumble of his laughter made her want to clench her legs together. Closing her eyes for a moment, she took a deep breath and exhaled. *She would get through this without making a fool of herself.*

She stepped into the early autumn sunshine and looked around for Pete. Finn grabbed her hand, led her to a silver Camry and opened the door for her.

When he got into the driver's seat and started the car, she raised an eyebrow at him. "Where's Pete?"

"I think you know where Pete is, Mia."

Pete was with her mom.

Why had things been so easy for the older couple and so complicated and hard for her and Finn? Pete had come to Chicago several times since he and Finn left. Her mom had gone to California a few times, too.

Why hadn't she and Finn been able to do that?

Maybe because both of them were too stubborn. And maybe Finn was as scared of this as she was.

Neither of them spoke as they got on Lake Shore Drive. They exited a few minutes later at North Avenue and continued farther south, winding through the Gold Coast neighborhood. Finn finally pulled to the curb on a street filled with old homes. None of them were obnoxiously big or ostentatious, but they were all well-maintained, beautiful houses.

"What are we doing here? Are we visiting someone who lives in one of these places?"

"Not exactly," he said cryptically. He stepped out of the car and came around to open her door, but she was already out, standing on the parkway, studying the row of houses.

"Now what?"

He glanced at his watch. "She should be here in…" He looked up. "Here she is."

An SUV pulled up and a woman with dark blond hair and a friendly face stepped out. "Mr. O'Rourke. How are you doing?"

"Please, Deborah. It's Finn." He took Mia's hand and pulled her next to him. "This is Mia Donovan."

Deborah held out her hand. "Nice to meet you, Ms. Donovan."

"Mia." Mia shook as she studied the woman. Then she looked back at Finn. "Are you going to tell me what's going on?"

Deborah smiled as she started for the sidewalk. "Show, don't tell, Finn?"

"You got it, Deborah."

The woman led them to a three story brownstone and up the stairs. The landscaping was tidy and neat – clearly professionally done. The windows shone and the paint on the woodwork was fresh. Deborah opened a lockbox on the front door, then used the enclosed key to open the door and usher them inside.

"So this is the first one," Finn said, clearing his throat. He was nervous, she realized.

The house had clearly been renovated recently. The kitchen appliances and cabinets were brand new, and the hardwood floors gleamed. The fireplace mantel was tiled, and the living room and dining room held modern furniture.

The house had four bedrooms and three bathrooms. All of them looked like the rest of the house – in perfect condition.

After they'd toured the whole house, Deborah led them

outside. "I'll meet you at the other address," she said.

As soon as she and Finn were in their car, she swiveled to face him. "What was that all about, Finn?"

He took a deep breath. Let it out slowly. "I'm moving to Chicago," he said, staring into her eyes. "I'm going to buy either this house or the next one, but you need to help me decide. I won't make a decision without your input."

"You can't move to Chicago." Mia took a deep breath, a huge flock of butterflies fluttering in her stomach. "Your career is in California."

Finn put the car into gear and pulled away from the curb. "Let's go look at the second house."

A few minutes later, they pulled up in front of another house. This one's garden wasn't professionally done. A lilac bush in the front yard was shading one of the windows. Hostas surrounded it, and coral bells marched across the front of the house. A row of rose bushes lined the sidewalk to the front door.

It was a beautiful, personal garden

Inside, the house was night-and-day different from the first one. It was a beautiful house, but it hadn't been rehabbed. The fireplace was surrounded by marble and had a carved wooden mantel. The floors were hardwood, but they hadn't been refinished.

The crown molding in the first floor rooms looked original, and a room off the living room had been used as a library. Books filled the shelves that lined the space, and a desk and comfortable chair sat in front of a window.

The second and third floors were similar – charming and vintage. They needed some work, but there was a settled, comfortable feel to the house. As if real people lived there. People who loved the house.

"Thanks, Deborah," Finn said as she locked the door behind them. "I'll get back to you later today."

"I look forward to hearing from you," she said. She nodded to Mia. "Nice to meet you, Mia."

Deborah drove off, and Mia studied Finn as he stood on

the sidewalk, his hands jammed into his pockets. Mia refused to allow hope a foothold. Her nerves jumping, her heart quivering, she asked, "What is this about, Finn?"

CHAPTER THIRTY

"Can we go back to your place and talk?" Finn asked, shoving a hand through his hair. One foot jittered on the ground.

He was nervous, she realized. Unsure of himself. It was a version of Finn she'd never seen before.

She wanted to fall into his arms. Agree to anything he wanted. But she couldn't allow herself to let go. To hope. "What do we have to talk about? And why do you care about my opinion of these houses, anyway?" She would *not* think about possible reasons why he wanted it.

He took a deep breath, as if trying to steady himself. "Mia." His eyes narrowed. "I'm not doing this in public."

"Doing what?"

He stared at her for a long moment, a muscle in his jaw twitching. Then he reached behind her and opened the car door. "Get in the damn car."

She watched him walk around the car and slide into the driver's seat. He started the engine without even glancing at her. His hands clenched the steering wheel and he stared out the windshield. Waiting.

She'd only seen the easy-going Finn. The guy who was

always smiling. Apparently, Finn had a temper, too. It would make for some interesting fights...

No. She wasn't going there.

She slid onto the seat and closed the door. The moment she buckled her seat belt, he pulled away from the curb too fast, pressing her into the seat.

Fifteen minutes later, they were back at her apartment. He followed her inside and up the stairs. Once they were in her living room, she crossed her arms and turned to face him. "Talk."

He crossed his arms, as well, a hint of his earlier anger still lingering in his expression. "You really like busting my balls, don't you?"

"No, I don't," she said. Her arms fell away from her chest and she walked over to the window. Sunlight reflected off the roof of his silver car, making it flash beneath the trees. The glare made her eyes prickle, and she pressed her fingertips against the radiator cover as she swallowed.

"It's been sixteen weeks, Finn. Sixteen weeks and four days since I saw you. Not one phone call. No emails. Not even a damn text message. Did you expect me to fall into your arms, grateful that you'd come back?"

He slid his hands around her upper arms, caressing her gently. "I hoped you'd missed me as much as I missed you. I hoped you'd at least listen to me."

Her throat swelled, and she wanted to tell him how much she missed him. Wanted to tell him she'd cried more in the past three months than she had in the past ten years. But the words stuck in her throat. What if this was a decision fueled by guilt? Or worse, an impulse he'd regret in a few months? If he walked away again, she wasn't sure she'd survive.

His fingers tightened on her arms. "I've been a complete ass. I know that. I shouldn't have walked away from you. I didn't want to, but I didn't think I had a choice. I finally realized that I always have choices. Some are just easier than others. And when I left, I made the easy choice."

It had been easy to walk away from her? She blinked several times, fighting to hold back the tears. Walking away from Finn had been the hardest thing she'd ever had to do.

"I've been miserable without you, Mia. I thought about you every day." His hands slid down her arms, making her nerves spark, and he pulled her against him. His chest was warm and solid against her back, and his arms folded across her abdomen, holding her close. Clinging, the way she wanted to cling to him.

Her fingertips dusted the radiator top instead of wrapping around his arms. If she took a chance, welcomed him in, how could she be sure he would stay?

"I have everything I ever wanted in my career, but it means nothing without you." The low rumble of his voice made her shiver. "When I was hosting that stupid award show last weekend, all I could think about was you. How I wished you were there with me. That you would make it fun, instead of a job. I wanted to laugh with you about it afterward."

He brushed his lips against her neck and she swallowed hard. "I stood behind that stage, watching Pete and your mom, and I wanted what they had. I realized my success was nothing but a mirage. A gilded image that didn't really exist. When I reached out to touch it, it slipped through my fingers like a cold mist. I need you to ground me, Mia. I'm not real without you."

Her heart pinched in her chest. Swallowing once, she said, "Says the guy who thought the easy choice was walking away from me."

His hands tightened on her arms, then he turned her to face him. "You're right. That was a cruel thing to say. But I figured out pretty damn quickly that it wasn't the easy choice. It was the expedient choice. The thoughtless choice."

He skimmed his hands up her arms, making her shiver. "You've been the brave one in our relationship, Mia. You're the one who's taken all the risks. I've hidden behind my career and my obligations to avoid facing what you mean to me. To avoid putting myself out there and risking getting hurt. I've been a damn coward, Mia, but no more. I'm done running away."

Mia stared up at him. She saw nothing but sincerity in his expression. Nothing but honesty in his gaze. She wanted to reach out, but the memory of those three agonizing months held her back.

He must have seen the hesitation in her expression. The wariness in her eyes. His hands tightened on hers. "I love you, Mia. I loved you when I walked away from you, I loved you every single day I was gone, and I'll love you every day for the rest of my life."

"Those are just words, Finn," she whispered, studying his expression. "Words are easy."

He cupped her face in his hands. "Please give me a chance to prove that I mean them. That I'm not going to change my mind. I want to marry you, Mia. Have children with you."

He pressed his forehead against hers. "I know you're not ready for that. You don't trust me, and I don't blame you. But I know what I want, and that's not going to change, not matter how long it takes for you to trust me again. I want everything with you." He swiped at the tears she didn't realize were falling. "Including dying with you while we're having sex when we're ninety-five years old."

God. He'd remembered that. Had he remembered every damn thing she'd said?

Her throat thickened with tears she struggled to hold back. "That was a pretty speech, Finn. As pretty as those gilded images on the screen. I think you even mean it." She swallowed, trying to dissolve the lump that made her throat ache. "But how can you move to Chicago? Your job, your career, is in Hollywood. You can't just disappear. If you're living in Chicago, they'll forget all about you."

He shook his head. "I don't want to sound arrogant, but they're not going to forget about me. I'm the It Guy in

Hollywood right now. All the movers and shakers are bending over backward to prove they never believed Gemma. Thanks to that rat bastard Benson's revelations, my agent has been flooded with offers. I have the currency to do what I want. And what I want is to live here in Chicago. With you."

He wiped another tear from her face. "Will being away from Hollywood hurt my career? Possibly. Will I have to be away from Chicago, and you, occasionally? Yes. I will. But I'll always come back to you. I'll do whatever I have to do to make it work, Mia. I promise you."

"I want to believe you, Finn," she whispered. "I do." She wanted to run her fingers over his face, feel the scruff of his whiskers. She wanted to tangle her hands in his hair, let the silky strands slip through her fingers.

She wanted to kiss him and tell him she loved him, too, and that she wanted everything with him. Marriage, children, the whole nine yards. Instead, she said, "What happens if the roles start drying up because you're not around? What happens when the next It Guy shows up? What then, Finn?"

He laced his hands behind her back and drew her against him. "I knew you'd be skeptical, Mia. Knew you'd make me work for it. That's one of the reasons I love you. To you, I'm not Finn O'Rourke. I'm just Finn, and that's exactly how I want it. I want you to call me on my bullshit."

"You haven't answered my question," she pointed out.

He grinned and brushed this thumb across her lips. "First, I don't think I have to worry that the roles will dry up. If I can draw people to the movie theater, I'll get the jobs. But, even if I don't, I'll still be able to work. I've started my own production company, and I'm negotiating to buy the rights to a couple of scripts and a book. All great stories. No one's going to have to hold a bake sale for me, Mia."

"I want to say yes." She fisted her hands in his shirt to keep from wrapping her arms around him. "Want it more than anything. But I guess I'm having a hard time believing that this is real and not an impulse you'll regret later."

He closed his eyes and rested his forehead against hers for a moment. Then he took her hand and led her to the couch. When she sat down, he sat right next to her. Curled his arm around her shoulders and pulled her against him.

"Okay, Mia. I get it. Pretty words won't do it for you. I knew I'd have to prove it." He buried his face in her hair, inhaled deeply, then took her hand. "Which of those houses did you like?"

"They were both beautiful."

"Yeah, they were. But which one could you see yourself living in?"

His hand tightened on hers. Despite herself, she clung to him, too. She wanted this. So, so much. And she was beginning to let herself believe it could happen. "The second one," she said softly. "It needs some work, but it was real. It felt like a place people lived, rather than a showplace that had had all the life rehabbed out of it."

He let out a long breath. "I thought you'd prefer that one."

"Which one did you like better?" she asked.

He kissed her hand, then slid his fingers between hers. "If I'd looked at those houses six months ago, I wouldn't have even considered the second place." He nuzzled her hair. "I would have grabbed the shiny, polished house. The illusion of the perfect place to live.

"But then I met you. Fell in love with you. Now the first house reminds me of my place in California. All carefully coordinated and perfect and sterile. I want the second place. Now I understand the beauty of a place that's been lived in. A house that has nicks in the wood from kids crashing their trucks into it. Pencil marks on the wall to keep track of how those kids have grown.

"That's what I want. A home that's been loved."

She couldn't resist rubbing her fingers over his chin. His cheek. His mouth. "I know you think you want real," she said, leaning back to see his eyes. "But real can be ugly. Real means there'll be tough times. Times when one of us wants to walk away. What happens when you figure out that real isn't always exciting and fun?"

"I don't expect it to be. I expect to work for what I want with you. I expect we'll get angry with each other. We'll fight. Yell and scream. But we'll always work it out, Mia. Because I love you enough to not give up. I love you enough to never walk away again."

He eased away and studied her, his expression uncertain. "Mia, I love you. Will you take a chance on me, even though I've been a jerk? Will you marry me, in spite of the way I hurt you? There's nothing I want more in this life."

She took a deep breath. Then another one. "I want to, Finn. I do. But…"

"I know. You're scared." He inhaled shakily. "I am, too. I'm terrified. What if I screw this up? I don't want to hurt you again."

"I'm more scared of me than I am of you." She exhaled, the confession of her deepest fear making a weight fall from her chest. "I could screw this up, too." She burrowed into him, holding him tight. "You're not the only one with a tough, demanding job. You saw what I was like last night. I was a wreck. That wasn't a one-time thing. I guarantee it'll happen again. I'm a murder cop. I'll see death and violence every day. What happens when you can't deal with that anymore?"

"Then I'll hold you while you cry. We'll make love until you can't think of anything but me. And the next day, we'll both go out and do our jobs again."

"It's not that simple, babe." She smoothed her fingers over his nape, let the soft, silky hair there caress her palm. "All you've seen is the tough side of me. The cop on the job. Those three weeks we were together, you saw the sexy me. Sure of myself. Confident." *In love with you.* "Last night you saw the woman beneath my bravado."

"I loved her as much as I love my kick-ass Mia." He

pulled her onto his lap. "You think I'm not going to get bad news about my job? Have problems with it? We'll hold each other up, babe. Take care of each other. Comfort each other."

He bent his head, brushed his mouth against hers. When she pulled him closer, he sighed into her mouth as he deepened the kiss.

In moments they were ripping each other's clothes off. He swiveled to lean against the arm of the couch while Mia slid naked onto his lap. When she twined her hands with his, he surged to meet her. But before he could take her breast in his mouth, his gaze drifted over her shoulder. Landed on the chair at the end of the couch.

He froze.

Closing his eyes, he slid farther onto the couch cushions, until Mia was all he saw. "I can't do this, Mia. Not here."

She stared down at him, letting his hands go to tangle her fingers in the soft hair on his chest. "What are you talking about?"

"Your father's chair," he groaned. "It's like he's watching us."

Mia giggled, her heart expanding until it filled her chest. Joy sizzled through her veins. "That's going to be a problem."

"What do you mean?" He shifted to sit up, but held her close while he moved.

"How are we going to christen every room in that big new house of ours if you're afraid of my father catching us in the act in the living room?"

His whole face lit up. He pulled her against him and murmured against her lips, "Maybe we can cover him with a blanket."

"He'll still be able to hear us, you know." She rubbed her nose against his.

"We'll have to be quiet, then. Think you can do that?"

"I don't know," she whispered, tugging on his ear lobe. "You make quiet impossible."

"Then I guess we'll have to practice." He lifted her off his lap and stood up, pulling her close. "A lot. We want to make sure we get it right."

"Yeah," she said, taking his hand and tugging him toward the bedroom. "We'd better get started right away."

EPILOGUE

One month later

Finn had just tightened the last bolt attaching the seat to the new toilet in the master bathroom when Mia called up the stairs. "Hey, babe, the movers are here."

"We'll be right down," he called back.

Jamie was already putting the tools back in the red tool box. "Nice job, rookie," Jamie said with a grin, giving him a fist bump. "Your first toilet install."

"It's a great toilet, isn't it?" Finn stood back and beamed with pride.

"Most beautiful toilet ever," Jamie assured him, biting his lip to keep from laughing.

"Yeah, I'm a nerd," Finn said with a grin. "So sue me." Finn grabbed the tool box and headed for the stairs. "Let's go supervise the movers. Earn our beer."

"Right behind you, plumber guy."

Two hours later, Mia stood in the cardboard box-cluttered living room and lifted her bottle of beer to toast her family. "Thank you, everyone," she said. "You guys are the best moving crew in the city."

"You mean the best supervisors, right?" Finn said, wrapping his arm around Mia's shoulders. "All we did was make sure everything was put into the right room."

He twined Mia's free hand with his as he lifted his own bottle and smiled at his fiancée, loving the way her eyes sparkled. The way happiness spilled out of her, making her glow.

All Mia's siblings and their partners, as well as Jamie, Pete and Rose, raised their beers in response. Helen raised a bottle of sparkling water. "Congratulations, both of you," Rose said. Her eyes twinkling, she added, "I expect some grandchildren to fill up this place."

"Don't be greedy, Mom," Mia said with a predictable eye roll. "Finn and I want some time together before we have kids. And besides, don't you think you'll have your hands full with Charlotte and the twins, and Brendan and Cilla's baby?"

Sitting in Mia's dad's chair, Helen rested her hand on her enormous belly. "She's right, Rosie. You told me you always wanted twins. In a couple of weeks, you'll have your chance to experience them, up close and personal." She nodded at Pete. "You, too, Pete." She clapped her hand over her mouth. "Oops."

"Sorry, Rosie," Helen said, biting her lip. "Hope I didn't scare him away."

"Not possible, Helen," Pete said, drawing Rose closer so they were squashed together in a corner of the couch. "I'm going to love being a grandpa." He gazed at Charlotte, who was toddling between one box and the next, pounding a teething ring on top of each box. Finn bit his lip to hide his grin at the sappy expression on his gruff friend's face.

"We're hoping you guys are old hands by the time our baby is born," Cilla said. She picked up Charlotte, settling the toddler on her lap, holding her against Cilla's barely visible baby bump. Charlotte patted her face with drool-covered hands, and Cilla pretended to nibble her fingers.

Finn couldn't remember ever being this happy. After a

predictable amount of grief from her brothers, which had subsided when he admitted he deserved it, he'd melded seamlessly with Mia's family. He'd bickered with her brothers at their monthly dinners, played with Charlotte, teased Pete and Rose. He and Jamie had even done some work on the house before he and Mia moved in. Not only had they not killed each other, but Finn had loved hammering and sweating, and Jamie had become a good friend.

"Have you two picked a date yet?" Rose asked Mia.

"Nope," Mia said, snuggling closer to him. "The rest of us have already talked," she said, waving her beer bottle in a circle that included everyone. "We have Brendan and Cilla's wedding next month. Then you and Pete are first, Mom. We're throwing the party for you. After that, Finn and I will figure out when we're getting married."

"Don't wait too long," Finn said to Pete and Rose. He picked up Mia's hand and kissed her palm. As he folded her hand over his kiss, her ring sparkled in the sunlight that poured in through the stained glass window over the fireplace. A rainbow of light danced across Mia, as bright and shiny as she was. "I can't wait to marry Mia."

"Right back at you, babe," she murmured in his ear.

She leaned back against the loveseat and took another sip of beer, and her smile faded into a puzzled frown. "Where did Brendan go? He was the one who brought the beer."

"He got a phone call," Cilla said. "From his agent. He went outside to talk to her."

"Good news?" Mia asked.

Cilla shrugged. "I have no idea. His agent sent the book to some film studios, and a few of them have been looking at it. Maybe it's about that."

Moments later, Brendan burst through the front door, scowling. Cilla jumped up and wrapped her arms around him. "Hey, Bren," she murmured. "Bad news?"

Brendan tightened his arm around his fiancée and glared

at Finn. "What did you do, you son of a bitch?"

"Besides make Mia late for work the…" He stopped when Mia's elbow jabbed into his ribs, and Brendan continued to glower at him. "Not that, huh?"

He heard Mia snicker as he studied Brendan. Finn's smile fell away as he realized his future brother-in-law was serious. "What's up, Bren?"

"Did you think you had to buy it because of Mia? Was it a family thing? Because I don't want charity, O'Rourke."

Brendan took a breath, and Finn held up his hands. "Stop, Bren. What the hell are you talking about?"

"Like you don't know." Brendan's jaw worked as he stared at Finn.

"I honestly don't. What's going on?"

Brendan studied him for a long moment, then let Cilla go. "How can you not know?"

"Tell me what it is, and I'll tell you how I don't know it."

Mia looped her arm through Finn's and leaned against him. "Tell us all, Bren. This is beginning to sound like a drawing room farce."

Brendan sat down heavily on one of the chairs. "Your studio just optioned my book. For a hell of a lot of money."

"I bought several books recently. What was the title?"

"Sleeping City."

"Oh, my God. That book was yours? It's amazing. It's the first project I'm going to tackle." He jumped up, pulled Brendan to his feet and wrapped him in a hard hug. "My favorite of all the books and screenplays we optioned."

Brendan eased away from him, his gaze suspicious. "How could you not know it was my book? My name was on every page."

"I made my agent get rid of all the names before I read any manuscripts or screenplays," Finn said. "I didn't want to know who'd written them. I wanted to buy them on their own merit, not based on whether they had a reputation in Hollywood.

"Or because they were from my brother-in-law, if I'd

known he was submitting something. Which I didn't."

"You're paying me a chunk of change," Brendan said, as if it was a bad thing.

"Had to," Finn said easily. "My agent is one of the best. She knew there were several other studios seriously interested. While they were trying to figure out how little they could get away with offering to a newbie, I jumped in and bought it. I went big to discourage the rest of them."

"So you seriously didn't know it was my book." Brendan still looked skeptical.

"You want to ask my agent?" Finn pulled out his phone, tapped a contact and handed it to Brendan. "Call her."

Brendan stared at the phone for a long moment, then handed it back to Finn. "I'll take your word."

Finn sat back down and drew Mia closer. "I read a lot of great stories," he said, leaning forward to lock his gaze with Brendan's, willing the guy to believe him. "More than the others, your book spoke to me – its absolute honesty. Your characters were real and had real problems, but they always faced them square on. Your protagonist had so much integrity.

"I think your story will speak to a lot of people. You're a great writer, Brendan." He glanced around the room, watched everyone smile at Brendan. "I'm not just saying that because you're going to be my brother-in-law. I'm saying it because it's true."

Brendan swallowed once. Then again. "I'm still gonna go over that contract with a fine-toothed comb," he said, his voice rough. "Get Helen to read it, too."

"You'd better," Finn said easily. "Because if you don't, I'll kick your ass."

Mia jumped up from the couch and wrapped her arms around her brother. "Congratulations, Bren," she said. "What great news."

As she hugged Brendan, all of her siblings and their spouses crowded around them. The noise level in the room rose as everyone talked at once. They pounded Brendan's back, hugged him, punched him in the arm.

Finn didn't see any jealousy, any envy. They were genuinely happy for Brendan.

Finn spotted Charlotte, standing by one of the boxes, watching the adults, and he swooped over to pick her up. He cuddled her for a moment, inhaling her sweet little-girl smell, baby powder and milk and fresh air. He couldn't wait until he and Mia had a little girl of their own. Or a little boy. "Your Uncle Bren just got some good news," he said, smacking a kiss to the little girl's cheek. "You want to give him a kiss? Tell him congratulations?"

"Ba," she said, pointing to Brendan.

"One more here who wants a kiss," Finn said, pressing through the crowd surrounding Brendan. He passed Bren his niece, watched him cuddle her close, then he looked for Mia.

She was looking at him, too, blinking hard, her expression soft. She edged over to him, slid her arm around his waist. "Soon, babe," she murmured in his ear. "You know I won't be able to resist you for long."

She nuzzled his neck. "When it comes to you, I never could," she whispered against his skin. "I was yours the first time I saw you."

"Maybe not the first time," he teased her. "I was kind of a jerk that morning."

"Yeah, you were," she said, nipping at his ear lobe. "But by the end of the day? I was sold." She twined her arms around his neck. "I'm all yours. Always will be."

* * * * *

If you enjoyed **Protect Me**, pick up the next book in the series – **Save Me**.

ABOUT THE AUTHOR

Two-time Rita finalist Margaret Watson published her first book in June, 1991. Since then, she has written thirty books for Silhouette Intimate Moments and Harlequin SuperRomance, as well as nine titles in the Donovan Family series.

Margaret's books have won or been finalists in many contests, including the Colorado Award of Excellence, Desert Rose Golden Quill, Holt Medallion, and National Reader's Choice.

When she's not writing, Margaret practices veterinary medicine. She lives in the Chicago area with her husband, three daughters and a menagerie of pets.

* * *

Thank you for reading Protect Me. I'm honored you chose one of my books, and I hope you enjoyed it!

- If you would like to receive an email newsletter when my next book is released, sign up at **www.margaretwatson.com**.
- Reviews help other readers find books they'd like to read. Please leave a review of Love Me at your favorite on-line retailer. I welcome all reviews.
- Please recommend Love Me to your friends and on discussion boards.